COPPER PENNIES

CARRIE D. MILLER

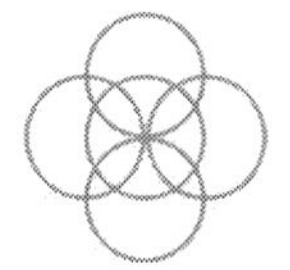

Cover designed by **Lance Buckley Design**.

Ornamental section break design from www.freepik.com.

Published by **FiveFoldPress**

1st edition, July 2019

ISBN: 978-1-947024-07-6

To everyone who has a dream
but thinks they can never achieve it.

PART I

MAGDA

CHAPTER 1

March 1937

Prague, Czechoslovakia

"Mrs. Hlavacova?"

At the older woman's sharp tone, Magda's gloved fingers tightened around the weathered handbag she clutched to her midsection. She dipped her head in reply.

"You are *quite* early."

Vaclav's threat of a beating should Magda be late had put her in motion at sunrise. She'd bargained the wrath of her new employer would be nothing compared to his.

The woman, clad in a plain wool dress nearly the same color as her hair, studied Magda from head to toe, her lips disappearing into a thin line. She stood only an inch or two taller yet was double her width. Magda fought the urge to take a step down.

A blast of icy wind whipped around them, whisking the scarf from Magda's head and taking her breath away. The older woman shivered, retreating.

"Well, you'd better come in."

Magda stepped over the threshold, turning sideways as the woman hadn't moved aside nearly enough. She tucked a wayward lock of her thick black hair back into its bun as the woman continued her inspection. She fidgeted, worry needling her skin. *What will I do if she turns me away? What will Vaclav do?* There was always a chance of rejection wherever Magda sought employment. Her light brown skin and almond-shaped eyes, gifts of her mixed Romani heritage, often brought judgement and ridicule despite her beauty.

"Show me your hands."

Magda lifted her hands, palms up, the handbag dangling on one wrist. Despite her small frame and young age, Magda bore the callouses of years of hard work.

The woman gave a curt nod. "I am Mrs. Tumova, the housekeeper. We may as well get started." She turned and moved toward the back of the house. "Follow me." The housekeeper pulled her right hip higher than the left, each step landing hard on the polished wood floor.

Magda lifted her eyes to take in the spacious room. The foyer of the three-story townhome was lined with rich, dark wood panels and divided into a staircase and hallway at the back. The wall to the left held four leather armchairs facing a door exhibiting an engraved brass plaque. *Doktor Josef Straka.* Beside the door stood an entry table, which held a ledger for patients to sign in and a porcelain vase filled with bright, fresh flowers. Their fragrance mingled with the unmistakable smell of baking bread coming from the kitchen. Magda inhaled deeply, the scents calming her nerves.

The hallway was bare except for a large portrait of a finely dressed older lady in black chiffon and high lace collar. Her face was soft, with the hint of a smile in her eyes. Two electric sconces provided golden light, keeping the shadows in the corridor at bay. Magda loosened the grip on her handbag, a bit more at ease in the warm surroundings despite the housekeeper's ill temper.

Once in the kitchen, Mrs. Tumova stopped abruptly and turned to face Magda, who took an involuntary step back from the woman's rigid form.

"Now, your husband should have told you what this job entails. But since he is a man and they are prone to forget, let me review." She clasped her hands at her waist. Mrs. Tumova's fingers were slightly misshapen and her knuckles enlarged, made white by her clenched hands. Magda did not meet her eyes.

"I am getting old, and you're to help me." She paused, her thin lips pinched, the words clearly the worst she could have said about herself. "You'll do what I cannot: clean mostly, and whatever is needed upstairs or in the cellar as I can no longer manage the stairs. I do the cooking but sometimes will need help with the larger pots. You'll not interact with Doctor Straka until specifically requested."

Magda nodded, her gaze rising enough to rest on the ivory brooch at Mrs. Tumova's banded collar.

The woman let out an exaggerated sigh. "Look at me."

Magda's eyes darted up but couldn't hold the housekeeper's for more than a few seconds.

"I think you may work out well," Mrs. Tumova said. "Most pretty young women, girls"—she snorted—"try to get work here just to catch the eye of a handsome, unmarried doctor. But you…" She was silent for several breaths, making Magda's mouth go dry. "I like the look of you. You keep your head down."

It was a mannerism first beaten into Magda by the nuns at the orphanage, who were free with their scolding and their slaps, and reinforced by her husband's mood swings. Now it had won her a job.

"And your hands seem no stranger to hard work."

Magda swallowed. "I just need to earn, Mrs. Tumova. Sewing and washing no longer bring in what they had." Vaclav had been very clear on that score.

The woman grunted her acknowledgement. "Let's get

started. You can hang your things there." She waved a hand at the row of pegs on the wall by the pantry and turned to the large cookstove. Magda paused and gripped her handbag again. She didn't know how to operate a gas range.

"Get that black pot behind you, top shelf."

As the housekeeper puttered at the stove with her back to Magda, she continued the lecture.

"Doctor Straka comes down at eight and takes breakfast in his study. He takes all his meals in his study. He *lives* in that room." She shook her head. "The patients start coming at ten—I'll see to them—with the last one seen at four. You've no need to address him or his patients. Except on Wednesdays." She stopped her stirring and pushed out a breath. "Wednesday is hell every week, girl."

She half turned to Magda. "He sees the poor then, those who can't pay. Even the Jews and your people, bless him. On those days, you'll need to linger unseen with an eye to the reception area." She flicked a hand toward the front door. "Those people are filthy, and nearly every week someone fouls the floor. You'll need to clean up any mess at once. He may also call for assistance in his study should someone become ill."

Magda grimaced at the idea of cleaning up sick but hid her revulsion. This was a good job for her and paid well; she was lucky to have it.

This opportunity came from one of Vaclav's coworkers, his sister being Mrs. Tumova. Vaclav was adamant she give up her "silly sewing" and take a "real" job. Her earnings had never been enough for him, and he had grown tired of her laziness, something he reminded her of frequently. He'd take every koruna she made, scoffing at the meager amounts. He paid for everything, he told her often, and she should be more grateful he'd taken in someone like her. No other man would have; she'd be a whore on the street, or dead, if it wasn't for him. When Vaclav discovered she'd been withholding a small amount for herself, his lesson ensured she'd never do it again.

Earning here would bring in more than everything else had, and perhaps Vaclav would stop expressing his constant dissatisfaction with her. She would enjoy this time away from their loveless and dingy apartment.

Mrs. Tumova had not exaggerated about Wednesday. When Magda arrived at half past seven, a line of pitiful figures, with faces downcast under tattered hats and scarfs, had formed outside Doctor Straka's home. Each respectfully quiet and careful not to lean against the short iron fence hemming the patch of garden on each side of the front door. Those at the front of the line hung back from the stoop as if they had no right to be there in the first place.

Magda considered herself blessed, for she could easily be standing in that line if it hadn't been for a chance meeting with Vaclav four years ago. Magda had been released from the orphanage when she turned eighteen. They had no work she could do to pay for her keep, nor did they wish her to stay. After seven months, she'd nearly turned to prostitution as a means to survive but decided she'd rather starve to death than do that. Luckily, she'd not needed to do either.

On a busy street one bitterly cold evening, she'd collided with Vaclav, who was in a drunken stupor. He proceeded to cry about his lot: his wife dead, his loneliness growing each day. He wasn't handsome. He was heavyset and rough faced, with bushy brown hair that proceeded down the sides of his face to an unkempt beard, and small brown eyes too close together. But he had a good, steady job at the new automotive plant. She'd taken pity on him and helped the man home, and she'd not left since. They had come to an unspoken agreement—she would be his wife and do all that was needed of one, and he would provide her a home and the protection a husband afforded. It started out agreeable enough, until he began expressing himself with his hands.

Resigned to her fate, she slipped into a melancholy as the months and years crept by. But she had a home and food, and got work when she could at the only skill the nuns had taught her. If she stayed quiet, Vaclav was usually fine, unless his bad day or his gambling losses came home with him.

"Good morning," Magda mumbled as she pushed open the door. The people in line remained silent, arms wrapped tightly around their bodies to fend off the blustering wind.

Yes, I am very lucky.

While Magda scrubbed the lunch dishes, Mrs. Tumova busied herself with kneading dough—bread for tonight's dinner. The older woman had softened over the last two days. Magda assumed she'd proven herself to the housekeeper with her diligent work and lack of outward interest in the doctor.

"I'll make an extra loaf for you to take home," she said, wiping her fingers on her apron. "You look as if you need all the food you can get." Magda had learned this was the level of Mrs. Tumova's humor and smiled at her, muttering a 'thank you.'

"Assistance!" The shout came from the doctor's study, startling Magda. Mrs. Tumova's brows quirked up.

"That's you, girl. Here, take these." She handed Magda a bundle of rags and a bucket, and steered her forward by the shoulders, giving her a little push in the direction of the hallway.

Magda went swiftly down the hall but hesitated at the door to the study. Her stomach fluttered at the thought of meeting the handsome doctor, someone who put aside any bias and gave his services to the poor. The man behind the warm and jovial voice that greeted each patient and boomed through the walls when he laughed, which was often.

But I won't be meeting him. I will do my job and be gone. She nodded to herself.

Magda opened the door, eyes trained on the wood floor, quickly surveying for the mess. Her nose found it first; the sour stench filled the air, and she stopped herself from lifting a hand to her nose. It was beside the doctor's examination table. Not looking at either the doctor or his patient, she set to her task in rapid fashion.

As she scooped up the putrid remnants of someone's meager breakfast, the doctor continued his examination of the patient, who profusely apologized for soiling his lovely floor. Doctor Straka reassured the woman in such a caring tone Magda longed to see his face. She settled for a view of his pant cuffs and shoes, made of the highest-quality wool and leather. But there was a splash of a wet, yellow substance on his shoe—he must not know.

Not wanting to interrupt him or bring attention to herself, her hand shot out from under the table and swiped across the toe of his shoe. His sermon to the patient on the importance of not eating spoiled food, no matter how hungry she was, did not falter. Magda gathered up her things and left the room with all the stealth she could muster.

Once more he'd called for assistance, later in the afternoon when only one patient remained. There'd been an endless stream of them! This time, she cleaned the seat of a chair and a portion of the dark green–papered wall. A man coughed wretchedly, wetness rattling in his chest. Magda stole a glance.

The doctor stood beside the elderly man hunched over on the examination table, with a hand on his back. Doctor Straka was tall and lean, dressed in a plain white doctor's coat over a black suit. She frowned. His back was to her. The doctor's hand rubbed across the old man's thin shoulders. The gesture tugged at Magda's heart.

"I prayed my remedy would have helped you, Mr. Straub." The doctor's words sounded to Magda like genuine remorse, and the deep baritone warmed her cheeks. He removed a handkerchief from his pocket and gave it to Mr. Straub. The old man expelled the bloody contents of his mouth into it. The doctor took the wadded cloth and extended his arm behind him, holding the handkerchief out to Magda without a glance. She took it immediately.

"I can give you something for the pain, but I fear you are past my help now. I am very sorry." Doctor Straka squeezed his shoulder. "God will reunite you with your dear wife fairly soon."

Mr. Straub wiped his watering eyes with an arthritic hand. "You've my thanks, Doctor, for even trying on this ol' sack of bones." He tried to chuckle but coughed instead.

Doctor Straka retrieved an amber bottle from the metal tray stand, dosing out viscous, red liquid into a spoon, and helped the man put it to his lips. In a few seconds, the elderly man took a deep breath, marveling in his ability to do so. His aged, brown eyes shined up at the one person who gave him relief… and respect.

Magda turned to the door, swallowing the lump in her throat. Her eyes flitted to the floor-to-ceiling shelves of books and various medical instruments lining the back wall. A human skull stared back, the large, empty sockets making her cringe. Her gaze was pulled to his desk. More precisely, to a large book atop it.

Her vision narrowed; the sounds behind her vanished. Magda locked her knees to keep from collapsing as the room fell away, piece by piece, until nothing remained but her and the book.

The cover was a sickly gray and uneven; it was puckered and grooved, even along the spine. If it was leather, it was very poor quality. No title or lettering provided clues to its contents. The pages were thick, perhaps vellum, and slightly rippled as if they'd once been wet.

A chill prickled the hairs on the back of her neck, yet she stepped forward, responding to the overwhelming urge to pick it up. She'd never been much of a reader, but her fingers itched for it.

Take it! Take it and run. Magda balked. Not even when she'd lived on the streets, begging for work, had the thought of *stealing* something entered her mind. But now—

A grunt from far away snapped her back. Magda gripped the edge of the desk to remain upright, the sudden vertigo washing away her curiosity, her *need* to have that book. The doctor hadn't noticed her, his attention taken with helping the weak man from the table.

Magda left the room and leaned against the doorframe, inhaling a shaky breath to calm herself.

What was that?

She put a hand to her moist forehead. She'd cleaned up worse messes, and the old man's fate was certainly tragic, but neither would account for Magda's near swoon. It must be from the doctor's manner. Of course. Never had she witnessed such kindness from a man before, or anyone for that matter. She felt honored to be able to help him in his work, no matter how paltry it might be.

"See?" came the condescending tone of Mrs. Tumova, arms across her chest. Magda only nodded, lowering her head, and scurried back to the kitchen to wash her hands.

As Magda pulled the heavy fish poacher from the oven, the doctor's door opened and closed. She expected his steps to continue up the stairwell as he washed and changed before dinner, but instead they proceeded forward.

"Doctor Straka." Mrs. Tumova greeted him as he entered the kitchen. Magda kept her back to them, placing the poacher on the stove top.

"Mrs. Tumova, the salmon smells wonderful." His voice reminded her of rich velvet. She busied herself with the fish.

"That poor old man is done for, I take it."

He sighed. "His fate rests with God now."

"'Tis a shame."

There were several breaths of silence. Magda's cheeks burned, and she wished she was invisible.

"Mrs. Hlavacova, Doctor," the housekeeper said, apparently answering his unspoken question. When Magda didn't turn, Mrs. Tumova cleared her throat. "Magda?"

She pushed the emotion from her face before she turned, another skill learned early at the orphanage, wiping her hands on her apron to keep them busy.

"Doctor Straka." Magda's voice was small as she inclined her head. Her eyes rested on a few drops of blood splattered on his white shirt. He seemed even taller now as he stood beside the housekeeper, his hands clasped behind him. His jet-black hair arced downward along his jawline into a smooth beard, neatly trimmed to a blunt point, and joined with a mustache surrounding full lips. She kept her breathing even and prayed they couldn't hear the rapid thumping of her heart.

"Thank you for your assistance today, Mrs. Hlavacova." The doctor inclined his head, enough to catch her eyes. Magda's breath caught. His eyes were midnight blue—set deep and surrounded by dense, black lashes—and held the smile he kept from his lips. She dropped her gaze, certain he could see into her very soul. Magda's head dipped in reply.

"I look forward to dinner," he said to Mrs. Tumova and withdrew from the room.

Magda turned to continue her work on the fish. She felt the woman's eyes on her back.

"Yes, yes," Mrs. Tumova said, not keeping the laugh from her voice. "You'll do just fine here."

CHAPTER 2

April 1937

MAGDA WAS LATE. SHE HURRIED TO THE KITCHEN, NOT acknowledging Mrs. Tumova's sour expression, and hung her coat and handbag on a peg. She hesitated before removing her scarf, then unwrapped it, knowing she couldn't hide in it all day.

The housekeeper brought her flour-covered hands to her hips. "You'd better have a good reason for being late."

"I'm sorry, Mrs. Tumova." Magda slipped on her apron and went directly to the sink full of dishes, head and shoulders slumped.

The older woman grunted and snatched a hand towel from the counter beside her, the sudden movement making Magda flinch.

"What is it, girl?" She stepped forward, and Magda recoiled on instinct, then silently chided herself for being stupid. She focused on scrubbing the cast-iron skillet. Perhaps if she appeared busy, Mrs. Tumova would return to her own work.

But Mrs. Tumova did not. She paused, then laid a gentle hand atop Magda's hastily moving ones.

"Stop," she said in a softer tone. "Sit." Magda obeyed.

Resting an elbow on the table, she cradled her forehead in

her palm, listening to the housekeeper rattle cups and saucers. Magda's head ached bitterly. She wanted nothing more than to lie down. Mrs. Tumova placed a steaming teacup on the table and eased into the chair across from her. Magda stared at the elegant china reserved solely for distinguished patients and guests, the plum-and-black floral band blurring through her tears. She blinked, and a tear tumbled down her cheek.

Mrs. Tumova cleared her throat. "Look at me."

She raised her face. Mrs. Tumova compressed her thin lips until they were nearly white. She studied the angry cut above Magda's left eyebrow, the blood crusting the length of it, and the red welt around her eye. Magda put the cup to her trembling lips.

Magda was almost finished with her tea before Mrs. Tumova spoke again, her voice tight. "I will ask Doctor Straka to look at that." She left the kitchen before Magda could protest.

"Come in, Mrs. Hlavacova." Doctor Straka gestured to the examination table beside him as he sorted items on the tray stand. Mrs. Tumova guided the young woman in by her shoulders and closed the door upon leaving. Magda wiped her clammy palms on her apron. It was very kind of the doctor to see her before his first patient, but she didn't want to be there. The attention and his ministrations weren't necessary. This was a small thing that would heal just as the others had.

She glanced at his desk for the book, then scanned the room when it wasn't there. Magda hadn't seen it in weeks; she couldn't help but look for it whenever she entered his study.

What use do I have for a book? Magda shook her head at herself, stopping abruptly as the throbbing increased.

Magda sat on the cool leather, hands clasped in her lap. Her mind wandering to escape her predicament, she studied the doctor's lean form as his back was turned. He hadn't donned his white coat yet. His impeccable black suit fit well across his narrow frame; his glossy black hair lay smoothly against his head, trimmed just above the collar.

I wonder if it's as soft as it looks? She blushed at the thought as he turned to face her.

The doctor let out a controlled breath at the sight of her injury, his nostrils flaring slightly. Magda kept her eyes on the top button of his suit jacket.

With his forefinger and thumb, he lifted her chin. Her breath caught at the intimate touch.

But it's not intimate, stupid girl. He's a doctor examining his patient. She focused on the fine stitching of his shirtfront.

Doctor Straka turned her head side to side as he examined the eye, then used two fingers to inspect the angry cut. They were cool against her hot skin, yet Magda winced, and he pulled back.

"Tell me what happened," he said in the same deep, caring voice he used with his patients. Magda exhaled, and her resolve escaped with the breath she'd been holding. She slumped, covering her face with her hands. Doctor Straka rested a hand on her shoulder as she sobbed.

A gentle squeeze brought her back, and she used both hands to wipe her cheeks. "Please forgive me, Doctor."

"There is nothing to forgive, Mrs. Hlavacova." He returned to the tray and soaked a cotton ball with alcohol. "I assume this is your husband's doing."

Magda's eyes fell to her lap.

"I will take your silence as a 'yes.'" The doctor's voice deepened with a hint of sadness, and Magda blinked away fresh tears. He turned back to her. "Now, this will sting, but the good news is you don't need stitches."

Magda closed her eyes as he ministered to her, relieved to hide in the darkness behind them. His face was close to hers, yet not near enough to feel his breath. She listened to his measured breathing, surreptitiously inhaling his scent, picking out the slightly spiced aroma of the beeswax pomade in his hair from the tang of the alcohol. The doctor took care cleaning her wound with slow, gentle strokes. After he finished, Magda heard him rattling items on the tray and grimaced at the whiff of sulfur but kept her eyes closed.

"This ointment does not have a pleasant aroma. I apologize for that. But it is a formula of my own making and quite effective at relieving swelling and pain." As Doctor Straka smoothed the pungent salve on the wound and welt, the pain ceased immediately, replaced by a pleasant cooling sensation. "It also ensures no scarring."

When the doctor stepped back, she opened her eyes to find him gazing at her. Magda's heart leapt. His dark indigo eyes brimmed with compassion, accentuating the tenderness of his smile. His hair, slicked back from his forehead, had a well-defined part on the left, and his graceful beard softened the sharp angles of his cheekbones. She'd never seen a more striking man. Doctor Straka's small smile grew under her momentary ogling. Magda's cheeks flushed, and she pulled her gaze from his.

"I notice you have a scar on your temple." The hard edge to his voice told Magda he no longer smiled. "Does your husband do this often?"

Magda slid from the table, and he stepped back. "Thank you, Doctor. I must get back to work now."

"Nonsense. I am your employer, and I have yet to cause a mess."

Her eyes flitted to his face and caught the playful curve of his mouth. She couldn't help but grin. "They usually aren't *your* messes."

"Quite." His shoulders relaxed. "You haven't answered my question."

Magda frowned, thinking back to his words. "Oh." She stared once again at the button on his jacket. "Only when I deserve it, he says."

Doctor Straka's jaw tightened. "What did he hit you with? This was not done with a hand or a fist."

"A bowl." Vaclav had become angry when the spoonful of porridge was too hot, claiming it burnt his mouth and she'd served it that way on purpose. But Magda didn't say this.

He clicked his tongue, closing the distance between them. Her height brought her to his chest. Magda couldn't retreat; the table stood stationary against her backside. She fought her overwhelming desire to lean against him, to know what it felt like to be held in his arms, enveloped in the compassion radiating from him. Magda remained stock-still with no idea what to do with her hands or where to look. He was quiet for several breaths, not that she could hear them over the blood pounding in her ears.

"Would you like me to speak with him… Magda?"

Her head snapped up; his expression was earnest. "No!" The doctor backed away. "Please, Doctor Straka, that won't be necessary. It would do me more harm than good." She covered her mouth, wishing she hadn't revealed so much.

His brows came together. Magda turned away from his pity, muttering another 'thank you' as she hurriedly left the room.

The following day, not long after the last patient had departed, Magda and Mrs. Tumova were startled by a shattering sound. A mild oath followed, provoking a rare grin from the housekeeper. She sent Magda off with the bucket and bundle of rags before the doctor called for assistance.

Magda halted after opening the door. Clear glass shards littered the floor around the long worktable that stood against the far wall. The waning sunlight glittered within the glass bits, momentarily dazzling her. She wrinkled her nose as the smell of something akin to burnt sugar reached her.

The gray book lay open on the worktable, surrounded by jars and vials of all sizes—some clear, some amber, and each labeled with tiny markings Magda couldn't make out. The doctor closed the book, its stiff spine cracking at the movement. He laid a palm atop its oddly shriveled cover, his long fingers curving protectively around the edge. She felt no desire to pick it up, to *steal* it, this time.

Her eyes traveled from his hand to his face. His expression made Magda take a step back, her skin prickling.

Doctor Straka glared at her, deep grooves creasing his smooth forehead as his face darkened.

Magda blinked and his scowl was gone, replaced by a welcoming smile. The smile and soft gaze coaxed her into the room, yet embarrassment brought heat to her cheeks. Of course, Doctor Straka wouldn't want someone like her staring at his possessions. *I hope he doesn't think me a thief.* She knew well the sordid reputation her gypsy heritage carried with it. *I would never have taken it. Never.*

"My apologies, Mrs. Hlavacova." His voice brought a different kind of heat to her cheeks. "My clumsiness has revealed itself. I hope you brought gloves—the thin glass is quite sharp."

Magda skirted around the opposite side of the exam table. She knelt, picking up each bit of glass gingerly with a rag. Bending over too far made the lump on her eyebrow throb, yet the cut seemed a week old rather than just a day. She wanted to thank him, ask him what was in his miracle ointment, but her courage failed.

She felt his eyes follow her as she moved. Her hands trembled under the weight of his gaze. *He wants to ensure I don't take anything. Stupid girl.*

"I'd like to examine your wound before you go." The kindness in the doctor's voice eased the tautness of her spine.

"Certainly, Doctor."

Magda took longer than necessary to clean up the glass, marshalling her courage. The mere thought of his fingertips on her skin made her pulse increase. She sighed inwardly. He was simply being a doctor to her. It was foolish to think he bore any feelings beyond that. Yet he'd offered to speak to her husband; that must mean something, surely. *Only as a concerned employer, nothing more.*

When she'd finished, Magda exhaled a deep breath and rose, turning to face the doctor. A full smile overtook his mouth, making butterflies dance in her stomach.

Once she was on the examination table, he studied the healing cut and applied a tiny amount of his sulfurous ointment. "Good," he mumbled, nodding. "Very good."

Magda thanked him as she met his gaze. Doctor Straka's dark eyes explored her face with such intensity she clenched her fists to keep from looking away. Men had stared at her before, but their looks had been salacious, or filled with loathing. This man's look warmed her, emboldened her, and roused a desire she'd never felt before.

His gaze came to rest on her parted lips. She held her breath as his hand returned to her face. His fingers trailed along her jaw, sending pleasant ripples across her skin. He bent near. Magda lifted her chin, longing to feel the touch of his lips. She inhaled his warm breath, arching her back slightly to close the gap between them. His palm cupped her cheek, and she leaned into it, letting her worries fall away. He raised his hand to her other cheek, his palms cool against her hot skin.

"You are very beautiful, Magda. You would be a prize to any man." His voice was low, rough, and he swallowed. "Your husband is a fool."

The longing vanished from his face as he seemed to realize the impertinence of his words and the placement of his hands. The doctor straightened and stepped back. "Forgive me."

The rush left her light-headed, disappointment deflating her. Yet Magda stood and snatched the handle of the bucket with sweaty palms.

"I forgive you," tumbled from her lips.

Magda darted from the room. After pulling the door closed, she stopped herself and pushed her forehead against the frame.

The pressure of his palms lingered on her cheeks. Magda inhaled deep breaths through her nose, calming herself before returning to the kitchen.

Magda quickened her pace, not only from the chill but because it was Wednesday. She would see the doctor again! The weekend had seemed unreasonably long, and the days felt as if they purposefully crawled simply to torment her.

It pained Magda to not steal glances at him when he traveled the stairs. She had considered offering to take him his lunch tray, but she couldn't risk giving Mrs. Tumova any reason to suspect that her interest had changed.

The line outside Doctor Straka's home was forming, and she slowed her pace. A little girl, clothed in a coat she'd clearly outgrown several winters ago and a threadbare scarf, lingered at the bottom of the stoop. Magda immediately wanted to give the child her own scarf.

As Magda approached, the little girl fidgeted and lowered her face but not before she had seen the girl's watering eyes and tear-streaked cheeks.

The child's hand shot out from her pocket. Dirt outlined the tiny nails of her fingers, which clutched a bit of torn paper. Eyes still downcast, she waved the paper at Magda, muttering words in a language Magda didn't know.

When Magda didn't take the paper, the girl dropped it, turned, and ran. She continued running despite Magda's call to wait.

"She say that is for doctor," came the broken speech of the woman at the front of the line.

"Oh." Magda retrieved the paper and thanked the woman.

Without unfolding it, Magda presented it to Mrs. Tumova.

"What's this?" Mrs. Tumova took the dirty slip of paper.

"A little girl gave it to me. She said it was for the doctor."

The housekeeper frowned at its contents. "I can't read this. Looks to be Yiddish, I think." She handed it back to Magda. "Doctor Straka is down already." Mrs. Tumova thrust her chin in the direction of his study.

Magda hoped she'd hidden the joy on her face as she turned to leave the kitchen. She stopped at his door to smooth her hair and straighten her coat, to wipe her sweating palms on her sleeves. She knocked lightly on the door.

"Enter."

As Magda did, she halted, unsure whether she should close the door behind her or not. For Mrs. Tumova's sake, she left it open.

"This note was left for you, Doctor."

His eyes flitted to the open door. "Thank you, Mrs. Hlavacova." He took the paper; his gaze made Magda's cheeks flame.

The corners of his mouth turned down as he read the note. "Mr. Straub passed on two nights ago."

Magda's heart ached as she watched the gravity of the loss reflect on the doctor's face. Although he had known the old man's fate, it was obvious that the reality of it came as a blow.

She wanted to go to him, but she hesitated. Who was she to comfort such a man?

The doctor's shoulders slumped, and he leaned against his desk. Magda stepped to him, unable to stop herself. Much to her surprise, he reached out and grasped her hands.

Magda did not shy away but savored the sensations the doctor's strong hands induced. He pulled her closer, until only the distance of their joined hands separated them.

Her name fell whispered from his lips, and she peered into his face. Gone was the sadness that had been there only a second ago. Desire now burned in his eyes.

Magda's knees threatened to give way when he bent toward her. His warm breath caressed her ear, her neck.

"I will call for assistance when the last patient has gone."

Magda was certain her heart had stopped beating. His lips

lingered against her ear but did not touch. Delicious goose bumps tightened her skin. If she turned her head only a little, their lips would meet. Magda's ache grew deeper.

She was reluctant to break away, but she knew she had already stayed too long to deliver a note. He didn't resist when Magda pulled her hands from his. Not meeting his gaze, she nodded and left the room on wobbly legs.

CHAPTER 3

MAGDA GRIPPED THE COLD BRASS DOORKNOB TO THE doctor's study. She had no loyalty to Vaclav; that wasn't what stopped her.

There is no future in this.

She closed her eyes, remembering the thrill of the doctor's touch, the smoldering desire in his eyes, how her name sounded on his lips. Just the memories sent pleasant shivers across her skin. Magda opened the door.

Embarrassment kept her eyes lowered as she closed it, not letting go of the handle. The doctor stood at his worktable, stoppering two vials—one pear shaped, one a narrow tube. The gray book lay on the table beside them. He turned to face her, and her cheeks reddened. With a hand tightening around the doorknob, she shut the door behind her. Part of her wanted to escape from the intensity of his gaze; the other part wanted to escape *into* it.

He held a hand out, extending a lifeline of happiness to her, fleeting though it might be. He offered her a brief refuge from the miserable life she'd made for herself. Magda stepped forward, releasing the brass knob, now warmed through by the heat of her palm.

She crossed the room, still unable to meet his gaze. Yet she took the doctor's hand and held her breath as he bent to kiss her cheek. His lips were hot against her skin, his mustache and beard as soft as Magda imagined. She gasped at the surge of passion enveloping her, and her knees buckled. He caught her around the waist and pulled her to him, his lips crashing into hers.

Magda flung her arms around his neck, her inhibitions burned away. Never had a kiss thrilled her so; Vaclav's had always been sloppy, his fat tongue shoved in her mouth. This man teased her with the tip of his tongue, darting in and out as if asking permission to probe deeper. Magda's fingers weaved into his thick hair, pulling his mouth closer to hers, giving him permission. He groaned as his arms tightened around her back, a hand making its way to her hair, gently releasing her wavy tresses from their pins.

His lips did not leave hers as he lifted her, setting her atop the exam table. His hands moved to cradle her face, his lips pulling back to soft, slow kisses, making Magda ache for deeper ones.

The doctor's lips traveled slowly to her neck. A whimper escaped Magda's throat as he gently grazed her neck with his teeth, his long fingers running through the length of her hair. She'd been a virgin when she married and had only known the rampages of an ox who cared nothing for her needs. The man who caressed her now seemed intent on building *her* passion, his skilled hands and lips doing so effortlessly. He lifted his head to look into her eyes. She held his gaze, reaching up to stroke his beard, elation filling her chest as his eyes closed at her touch. Magda brushed her thumb against his soft lips, and he seized her once more, his desire pouring into her as she inhaled his hot breath.

It took all her strength to put a hand on his chest and push away. He released her reluctantly, then pressed his lips to her forehead. She leaned into them. "I have to go, Doctor."

"Josef," he said against her skin, his arms tightening around her back as if unwilling to let her go.

"Josef," Magda whispered, savoring his name on her lips.

With a sigh, he helped her from the table. She wrapped her arms around him and laid her face against his chest. His heart pounded beneath her ear, or was that hers? *No, it is* ours, *beating as one*. The girlish notion brought a stab of disappointment. Magda knew this wasn't love—how could he possibly love someone like her? Yet such a handsome, successful gentleman *wanted* her, thought her beautiful, worthy of his attentions. Doctor Josef Straka could have any woman, yet he chose *her*. That was enough for Magda.

Her body longed to stay, yearning for more of what he willingly offered, but reality wouldn't allow it.

"He will expect dinner when he gets home." Magda couldn't bring herself to say her husband's name. She grimaced. The mere thought of Vaclav sullied the bliss of their embrace.

Josef pulled away so abruptly, Magda thought she'd offended him. In quick strides, he retrieved one of the vials from his worktable.

"I made this for you." He presented the pear-shaped, red glass bottle to her, his face beaming. She took the vial with questioning brows.

"Two drops will ensure he sleeps through the night. Nothing except the wearing off of the potion will wake him. And"—his hands closed around hers holding the bottle—"it will ensure he does not touch you, either in anger or lust, again."

Magda blinked at the bottle. "Truly?"

"The mixture of herbs will make him more docile, curbing his anger and his… need."

Josef's eyes followed the tear traveling down her cheek. Dizzy from the flood of emotions, Magda clutched his arms, squeezing her eyes closed. Never had someone cared so much for her. He kissed her trembling lips.

A clock somewhere on the bookshelves behind them chimed five. A stab of panic reminded Magda of her duty.

"Two drops only." His voice was low in her ear. "Too much more will stop his breath."

Magda looked up at him with wide eyes, then nodded, slipping the bottle into her apron pocket.

"I will leave the service entrance unlocked—there's a gate to the garden from the alley." The intensity of his hooded gaze riled the fire deep in Magda once more. Yet she shook her head and slipped from the room.

Magda pretended to sort laundry as Vaclav shoveled the sausage-and-potato soup into his mouth, tiny bits of food collecting on his long, wiry beard. Her hand had trembled when she'd used the vial's glass pipette to dispense two drops of the potion.

Josef made this for me to keep me safe. The smile on her face extended down into her heart.

Now she trembled in fright. What if Vaclav tasted the concoction? She could claim it was a new spice. He'd demand to see it then, know what it was called, where she'd gotten it, why she would try something new. The seconds ticked by in silence as she folded the same towel over and over.

She jumped when Vaclav shoved his chair back from the table. Magda held the wicker basket before her, a useless shield if it came to that. He grumbled as he stood, but she couldn't make out the words. He staggered toward the bedroom, and the bed frame screeched under his weight as he fell onto the bed.

Magda set the basket down and tiptoed through the small living room, peering into their bedroom from the doorway. Vaclav lay facedown on the bed. A flash of fear gripped her. Had she accidentally given him more than two drops? A snore erupted, and Magda's spine relaxed.

"Vaclav?" she whispered, then repeated at regular volume. He didn't stir. Back in the kitchen, she slammed a cabinet door and waited, wringing her hands, the rapid shifting of fear and relief making her queasy. The rumbling rhythm of Vaclav's snoring did not falter.

Magda hummed as she gathered ingredients from the pantry for Mrs. Tumova. Vaclav had indeed slept through the night, and no amount of noise nor even a hard shake woke him. She hardly slept, however, as excitement and thoughts of Josef danced in her mind. The potent mixture Josef created *for her* granted much-needed relief from Vaclav and would allow her to go to him, freely and without fear. Magda touched her fingertips to her lips, leaning against the shelves as a wave of desire coursed through her.

The housekeeper returned from the doctor's study with his lunch tray. Magda took the tray with a smile, not acknowledging Mrs. Tumova's upraised brow.

"I hope what's put you in such a fine mood is lasting," the older woman said, her jovial tone taking Magda by surprise.

"As do I," she replied, hoping the reddening of her cheeks didn't give too much away. Magda scraped the remnants of the doctor's lunch into a bucket and began rinsing the dishes.

"The doctor wants to see you."

Magda fumbled a delicate china plate, catching it just before it hit the rim of the sink. She turned to Mrs. Tumova, fear of being discovered draining the color from her face.

"Don't be such a mouse, girl." The housekeeper tsked. "He just wants to give that eye a last look. He's not going to eat you."

Magda's grip on the plate relaxed, and she swallowed, setting it aside.

"Hurry up, now. His next patient comes at one thirty." Mrs. Tumova shooed her from the kitchen.

Josef opened the door when she approached; his look was hungry, making Magda's knees weak. After greeting Mrs. Hlavacova in a doctorly fashion for the housekeeper's benefit, he closed the door behind her and gathered her up. Overwhelmed by his unabashed passion, Magda melted in his arms, her body responding to his mouth against hers, his strong hands gripping her back.

It was several minutes before they parted, both panting for breath but not letting go of one another. Josef buried his face in her neck.

"Come to me tonight," he breathed in her ear, a thumb lightly brushing against the side of her breast. "Let me please you, Magda."

She gasped at the longing in his voice, at his intimate touch, at his desire to give *her* pleasure. "Oh, Josef."

The tip of his tongue traced the curve of her ear, and she moaned, digging her fingers into the shoulders of his suit coat.

"Take me now," she whispered, unashamed.

"I do not want to rush." Josef's hand slid down the curve of her hip. "You tested the potion last night?" She nodded, capturing his lips once more.

His hands slowly traveled to her shoulders. When his mouth left hers, Magda allowed him to gently push her away. Mrs. Tumova's warning about the arrival of the next patient echoed in her mind.

The doctor straightened, readjusting his tie and smoothing his hair back into place. Magda studied his face; the redness of his cheeks faded as he took deep breaths to calm himself. She righted her clothing as well, the corner of her mouth curving at what tonight would hold.

Magda slipped from her apartment, fear that Vaclav would awaken to find her gone twisting in her gut. That knot grew tighter the farther she traveled from the building. She almost turned back.

The cold wind whistled through the quiet street, threatening to snatch the scarf from her head. *No.* She pulled the scarf tighter. *I've never done anything exciting in my life. Even if Vaclav does find out, and he won't, Josef will protect me.* Magda trotted on, emboldened by the sight of the doctor's home in the glow of the streetlamp.

Josef must have seen her coming down the alley from a window, for he stood in the doorway, a tall black silhouette against the dark canvas. A sudden urge to run away halted her steps, accompanied by a jolt of fear colder than the wind whipping around her skirt. Magda staggered backward.

What am I afraid of?

Committing adultery? Vaclav wouldn't find out. Giving herself to a stranger? Josef wasn't a stranger. He cared for her; proof rested in the concoction he'd made and that he'd not ravished her for his own pleasure this afternoon. He could have done so and cast her aside, but he didn't. He wanted to please her; he'd said as much.

Josef took a step down and extended his hand. She trembled, squinting to see his face in the scant light cast by a window in the building behind her.

You're being a mouse again. Magda lifted her chin and took Josef's hand.

He whisked her forward; strong arms behind her back and knees lifted her effortlessly. A giggle tinged with fright escaped her lips, and she covered her mouth.

"Mrs. Tumova does not live in," Josef said huskily, pushing the door closed with a foot. She placed a hand on his cheek and pulled his lips to hers.

In the darkness, her bold sin hidden in the shadows, Magda gave herself wholly and completely to Josef Straka. Feeling safe in his arms, she let herself bask in the pleasures of the flesh, without shame or guilt. The twenty-two years of her life had been harsh and cold, devoid of caring and tenderness. Yet beneath his lips, his hands, his body, she felt bliss and warmth, compassion and desire. Love.

True to his word, Josef did not rush. Magda's bare skin quivered under his attentions, the smoldering fire in her grew hot and wild, crying out to be set free. When he finally granted her request, a devilish smile on his lips, her short nails dug into his shoulders as her back arched from the bed. He covered her gasps with his mouth, plunging into her at last, heightening the ecstasy she'd never experienced before.

Magda rested her head on Josef's shoulder, nestled in the crook of his arm, their legs intertwined. The fireplace crackled with fresh logs, its light playing across their moist skin. Magda was euphoric; her cheeks ached from smiling. Her heartbeat was finally slowing, yet her body tingled, and she curled herself tighter around Josef.

"I have something for you," Josef said, stretching his arm to the nightstand. He flicked open a small wooden box and retrieved a narrow tube. Magda pushed herself up to see, pulling the sheet to her breasts to cover herself. It was the other vial she had seen on Josef's worktable yesterday.

Josef sat up, unashamed at his nakedness, grinning at Magda's modesty. He laid a palm on her cheek.

"At the risk of being indelicate—" He looked away.

"What is it, Josef?" She took his hand from her cheek and held it to her heart, the sheet falling to her lap unnoticed.

He gazed into her eyes, and Magda felt them reach into her soul but did not shy away. She squeezed his hand.

"I made this tonic to ensure we don't have any… consequences from our time together." Josef's brows lifted, his eyes studying her face.

Magda stared at the vial he held, the firelight glinting along the clear glass, yet strangely not reflecting on the dark liquid within. Her forehead crinkled.

Josef sighed. "My dear, we don't want a child to be a result of our union, now, do we?"

Magda's mouth went dry, instantly appalled by what he proposed. In the next breath, unwanted reality wrestled its way back in. This man was not her husband. This was not her bed. This could never be her life. It had been a blessing Magda had never gotten pregnant with Vaclav's child. He wouldn't make a good father.

The gravity of her foolishness crushed the elation of the past few hours. If she were to have his child, the baby's looks would reveal the truth to Vaclav. That would go well for no one. He would throw her out, reveal her shame to the world, and then where would she be? Josef couldn't possibly take her in.

Josef was right. *It was very thoughtful of him to think of this.* She took the vial.

"You only have to drink this once."

Magda removed the cork stopper and drank it quickly. The thin liquid tasted like heavily salted cider. She sucked her cheeks in and eagerly accepted the glass of water in Josef's hand.

He took the empty vial and glass from her, his gentle kiss relieving some of her anxiety. Josef gathered her up in his arms once more, and they lay back.

"How do you know to make such things?" Magda kept her voice small as she let her curiosity win out. Josef was quiet long enough for Magda to regret her impertinence. With a deep inhale, he hugged her to him.

"I learned long ago that modern medicine is sorely lacking in many ways. I felt it necessary to seek different methods."

Magda chewed her lip when he didn't elaborate, biting back words to prompt him to continue. An image of the gray book resting open on his worktable flashed in her mind, followed by the glare Josef had given her when he caught her staring at it.

"You have noticed the book I use."

Embarrassment prickled her skin. "I'm sorry. It's just so

unusual looking…" Shame stole the remainder of her pitiful excuse.

"That it is." He cleared his throat. "When traditional medicine has failed, I've tried witchcraft."

Magda tensed, holding her breath.

"My feeble attempts have resulted in some successes, such as the ointment I used on your cut, and many failures. Mr. Straub, for example." Josef let out a morose sigh, the emotion in it easing Magda's rigid body. She'd seen firsthand how much he cared for his patients, rich or poor. His determination to help them must be great indeed for him to resort to witchcraft.

All Magda knew of magick she'd learned from the nuns who stared at her pointedly when they preached on the evils of it. She was never allowed to forget the blood she carried, even if it was only half, and her people were often unfairly used as examples of the devil's handiwork. Heathens, they were called, with their fortune-telling, cavorting with spirits, spells, and charms. Witchcraft was evil, and nothing good can be made from evil. Or so she'd been taught.

Yet Josef was certainly doing good with his efforts; there was no doubt about that.

Magda pushed up on an elbow to gaze down at Josef. "You took away Mr. Straub's pain. I wouldn't call that a failure."

Josef pulled her atop him, his hungry lips finding hers.

CHAPTER 4

June 1937

Doctor Josef Straka cancelled his patients for the day and the foreseeable future.

He sat at the desk in his study, his voluminous book open before him. He read through the pages of incantations yet again, checking that his memory was perfect. This was a complex and lengthy ritual. Each word, each breathy sound had specific and important meaning. Nothing must be said incorrectly or done out of order.

Josef's eyes ached. He rubbed them as he leaned back in the chair and smiled with satisfaction. Tonight was the night. *At last.* The rewards from tonight would banish the years of planning, the hours of excruciating pain, all done to bring this precious book to life and to fulfill a promise he made long ago.

He wouldn't miss his practice, or any part of his current life. As much as he delighted in the adoration of the pathetic creatures who came through his door, he no longer needed it. Everything was ready.

Then there was the gypsy maid. Dear, sweet Magda. So beautiful, so gullible. Starved for affection and so willing to please. And the silly fool was in love with him. He laughed aloud.

Josef had worried about her in the beginning when she stared at his book with a covetous gleam in her eye. His back had been to her, but his mind's eye showed her standing at his desk, her fingers twitching at her sides. Yet delving deeper proved her innocent: Pure curiosity had driven her and was quickly squelched once he told her what it was. It would've been a shame to send her the way of the curious cat; she'd been a welcome release. Her adoration verged on worship and was most satisfying. Josef hadn't yet decided what to do with Magda; he wouldn't need her after tonight.

He went to the window, pulling aside the sheer curtains to look out at the early evening sky. A dark moon. He closed his eyes. Pride swelled in his chest.

Muraal had chosen him.

Josef had powerful magick in his blood, in his soul. Not the magick of "white" witches who made silly potions for love and luck or to quicken the womb of a barren woman. That magick was nothing. His power came from the limitless shadows. His whole life, he'd kept the blackness inside him hidden from the world of lesser, ignorant fools who couldn't possibly understand such greatness.

Josef had always known he was different, special—and not just in the opinion of his doting mother. When he was very young, he could *feel* the darkness. He could see the shapes stirring in the dead of night. They frightened and tormented him. His mother would stroke his cheek and tell him he was having a nightmare, then hold him tight until he slept. It wasn't until the untimely death of his father that he understood.

The elder Straka had been disciplining his son with a belt, punishment for Josef's temper tantrum. Black anger raged within his five-year-old body until it exploded outward, blasting through his father's head and chest. Everyone believed he died of a ruptured brain tumor, but Josef knew the truth. His power had killed his father.

From that day on, Josef had no fear when the shadows spoke to him. He listened, coming to feel more akin to them than his own kind.

A voice first called to him as an adolescent. He and his cousin had been playing pirates when his cousin snatched the fireplace poker from the embers. Caught up in the excitement, Josef grabbed the glowing point. Searing pain blasted through his hand as a voice of unearthly beauty filled his head. She called his name with a throaty, seductive purr, but as the pain faded, so did the voice. He'd called out again and again, desperate to hear her once more.

Josef had become obsessed with hearing her. His mother believed her only son was going mad. Taking him to the priest proved fruitless for her, but it gave Josef the answer he needed. As Josef shouted at the sour-faced priest, the man struck him across the mouth. The sharp sting brought the voice to him for a brief second, and he realized what he needed to do.

That night, thirteen-year-old Josef put an ice pick to his leg and heard the voice that made the suffering worthwhile. Pain brought her to him. In the throes of agony, Muraal spoke freely. The barrier between worlds and the mundane nature of the human mind made communication all but impossible. Pain altered the brain, opened it, providing her the avenue needed to call to her chosen one.

You are special, Josef Straka. I have waited so very long for one such as you.

I have watched you since you were born; I have seen what you can do, what you hide. There is more power in you than in any other human. Now that you are a man, it is time.

Only you have the power to save me. You are a god among cattle. Free me from my prison and your rewards will be boundless.

Josef *was* a god, able to snuff out a life with a thought.

Suppressing his true nature had been difficult. *All in good time*, Muraal had purred. *There is much to prepare before you can begin.*

Now, at the age of thirty-five, his talents matured and sharpened, and the book finally complete, his plan was in motion. The thirteen men of his coven would assemble once again in his secret chamber, a room in the bowels of the city, unused and forgotten. The coven met often, exploring the wonders of the netherworld, allowing Josef to test his powers, to hone his skills, under the guise of master and teacher to the eager men around him. Tonight's ritual would be very different, and the men he'd collected would finally be used.

These thoughts swam in his head and mingled with Muraal's sultry voice. The idea of finally seeing her fully made his manhood rise. He'd often imagined their first union. When these thoughts took over, he would normally have sought a whore, but Magda would be coming to him soon.

After tonight, the world would be forever changed. His smile curled into a sneer. All of humanity, or what was left, would bow before him.

The vast room, an abandoned pumping junction below the city, was lit only by torches and kerosene lanterns. The harsh lights couldn't penetrate the vaulted ceiling fully, nor reach into the far corners, leaving to wonder what might lurk within the depths of the blackness.

Those gathered paid no notice, too rapt in their chanting and their purpose. The rats had long since scurried away, frightened off by the malevolence radiating from the chamber.

Each man assembled believed he was calling a little-known deity from some forgotten history to bring them power and unimaginable wealth. Josef's ruse worked well with these greedy lower-class men. They were oblivious to the truth: They were pawns, sacrificial lambs as it were, to carry out the deed Josef had promised.

Drenched in sweat, Josef's clothes clung to him under his robe. His throat burned, but he could take no water. An hour had passed since the ritual began, its peak near. The thirteen men before him were as soaked as he, the fattest one more so, to the point Josef feared he might collapse. To keep the men's spirits up, Josef manifested a fiery orb to roil in the air in the center of their circle.

The billowing flames of red and black held the men's attention, their faces gleaming with sweat in its light. The fire pulsed and grew as the men chanted, as Josef's words rose in volume. With each arm gesture, the metal cilice on his leg bit into him with its sharpened prongs. The exquisite pain brought her voice to him. She purred admiration, her exhilaration urging him on. Her freedom was only moments away!

When Josef's words ended, he nodded to the man to his right. *You had better get this right.*

The man couldn't hold Josef's glare. He gulped before beginning his scripted reply.

Every man was required to speak the same words, one by one. Josef had made them practice over and over until the tone and pronunciation was exact.

Spurred on by the irrefutable evidence before him of their magickal workings, the man threw his arms out to each side and his head back, bellowing the words ingrained in his memory.

"Ix u'kih ix'r kurd! Ix u'kih ix'r ryks Zaad!"

With a jolt, his body locked in place, mouth open and eyes bulging. Josef inclined his head to the next man, but by the third man, Josef no longer needed to prod.

Josef hid his smile but twitched his leg just enough for Muraal to sing her praises in his ears again.

Yes, my chosen, yes! You will do this. What no one else could ever do! You are master of these men as you will be of all men.

The thirteenth man tripped over his words in a rush but

recited them again, intentionally avoiding Josef's scowl. When the man's body froze as the rest had—his face to the ceiling, arms cast out from his sides—Josef pulled aside the opening of his robe. From his belt, he withdrew a long dagger of his own design. Its curved blade was edged with finely serrated teeth. The bright metal glinted in the roaring light of the deceptive fireball.

He stepped before the first man, who was short and gaunt, his jugular thumping under ruddy, strained flesh. When Josef raised the blade, the taller fellow beside them tried to speak, his eyes fixed on the dagger. His body jerked at each attempt to move. Now frightened, the man under Josef's blade twitched, also trying to pull away but unable to see what the other man so feared.

Josef's sneered at their feeble attempts. He paused, savoring this moment. Each man writhed under their magickal restraints, under *his* power, fighting against invisible bounds to no avail.

Straka, you arrogant fool! You are not all powerful yet. Continue!

The anger in Muraal's voice stripped him of his hubris. Josef returned to the straining throat before him.

"Ix kih sukar ryks Zaad!"

Josef slid the sharp blade across the man's jugular, releasing his life in a rivulet of blood. Muraal's exuberant cry filled Josef's mind.

He continued to the next unfortunate, who convulsed in his struggles to be free.

"Ix kih sukar ryks Zaad!" The man's blood looked nearly black in the harsh firelight.

As the blood drained from each man, their bodies stayed locked in their stance, with only their wrists going limp as life left them. Each life struck a blow at the Shade, the hardened barrier between this world and the Voll, the prison where Muraal had languished for so long. Once the thirteenth man was sacrificed, the Shade would be penetrated fully, allowing Muraal to tear through, opening the rift further, freeing her and releasing her desperate children.

The seventh man's blood splattered Josef's face. He took no notice and continued. Movement in the corner of his eye drew his attention. *Impossible.*

Muraal shrieked a vile curse as two men broke free from their enchantment and seized Josef.

A third man crashed into them, sending them to the floor.

"You cannot defy me!" Josef shouted before a fist smashed into his jaw.

The larger man wrenched the dagger from Josef's blood-slicked hands. Two others held him down. Josef thrashed in vain as the man plunged the dagger into his belly again and again, the men cursing him, shouting and beating him with their fists. This new pain brought piercing screams from Muraal, demanding he get up, fight back harder.

You must not fail! You must complete the ritual!

The remaining men fell from their entrapment. The dead collapsed, and the ball of fire blinked out. Josef's attackers ran to their living fellows, shouting for them to get away. None gave notice to the bodies splayed on the floor. Josef listened to their racing footsteps in the growing silence of the sewer.

Muraal's rage ebbed with Josef's life. She sighed. The long, low sound soothed him.

Death is not the end, my chosen one. The book can bring you back. Return. Try again. I command you.

CHAPTER 5

Magda lay naked between the soft, white sheets of Doctor Josef Straka's grand bed, drifting in and out of sleep. No embers crackled in the fireplace; no candle flames flickered. He'd left not long ago, and she still tasted him on her lips. She smiled, remembering his hands across her bare skin, his fingers running through her unbound hair, whispering words of love and lust in her ear. She wanted him again right there, but it would be after sunrise before he returned, and she would be gone. Magda hugged his pillow to her breast, inhaling the rich scent of him.

Magda!

She bolted upright. Had someone shouted her name? Several heartbeats passed in silence, and she lay back, pulling the velvet bedcover to her chin.

My love, come to me! I need you!

Magda jumped from the bed, whirling around in search of the specter calling her name. It was Josef's voice, yet not as she'd ever heard him. This voice was full of pain and fear.

Magda, hurry!

Without pausing to wonder how Josef was speaking into her mind, Magda snatched her nightgown and robe from the floor. "Josef, I'm coming!"

Her hand trembling, she lit the bedside lamp and flew from

the room. In the unlit hallway, the urgent voice propelled her to the right, to the always-locked door at the end of the hall. He directed her to the key at the bottom of the vase on the stand beside it. Darkness and musty air engulfed her as Magda went swiftly down the stairs on sure feet, her fear set aside, emboldened by her need to help Josef. The lamplight did little to illuminate her path, seeming to cling to her rather than reach out into the oppressive gloom.

Several turns down old, brick corridors led her to a metal staircase spiraling into an abyss. The only sound apart from her rapid breathing was a fast drip of water somewhere below. She hesitated on the landing. The pain of the rough metal grate pressing her feet through her thin slippers brought the return of rational thought.

"What am I doing? This is madness." Magda grasped the cold iron and looked behind her. Where was she? How far from the house had she gone? Could she find her way back? *Don't be a mouse. Josef needs you!*

She proceeded downward, lifting the lamp high and gripping the support pole in the middle of the protesting metal. The stagnant air was heavy with moisture.

When Magda reached solid ground, she ran, spurred on by Josef's pleading. After traversing what seemed like an unending labyrinth, she reached a metal door. It took two hands to lift the heavy bolt and slide it back, and all her strength to pull the door open.

"Josef! I'm here!"

The door opened into a cavernous room, the wet stone walls lined with torches. The air reeked of a sewer not long abandoned, the acrid stench of kerosene, and… blood.

In the middle of the great room was Josef, lying on his back, in the center of a wide circle of low-burning lanterns. Four posts stood at the quarters of the circle, each topped with a different gruesome animal skull, not completely cleaned of the poor animal's flesh. Five or six other men sprawled on the brick floor.

Magda assumed they were dead, but they didn't concern her. Josef's blood-covered hand reached out; agony distorted his beautiful face.

"Josef!" Magda darted forward and knelt by his side, placing the lamp next to his shoulder to better see. Dark red soaked his chest and belly, and a bloody dagger lay at his feet, the wickedly serrated edge gleaming wet. "Oh, my love! What's happened?" She tried to take him in her arms, but his hands held her at bay.

"Listen." He coughed, choking on his own blood. "You must listen."

"Yes, yes! Please, Josef. Tell me how to help you."

"I am past help, my darling." He smiled at her, his dark eyes welling with tears. "But there is something you can do for me still. You *must* do for me." His face was earnest. "If you love me."

"Of course!" She took his bloodied hand and held it to her heart. Josef struggled to breathe; blood trickled from his mouth. With his free hand, he pointed to something beyond the wavering light of the circle.

"My book. Take it." He swallowed. "Take it. In it you will find the spell to bring me back."

"What? Josef, I don't under—"

"It is a book of powerful magick, Magda. You must take the utmost care."

Magda gripped his hand tighter. "Don't leave me, Josef. Please." Tears streamed down her face.

His smile widened, revealing blood on his teeth. "I will be back. But only if you will do this for me. Magda, promise me."

"Yes, Josef. I promise," she said between sobs.

"Take everything in the black cabinet… in my study." He pulled at his collar, freeing a cord with a small skeleton key dangling at the end. "The money too. *Everything.*"

Magda took the key, nodding at his delusional raving.

"You must do something first before you can read it." He coughed, fighting for each word and breath. "You can only read the words once you have taken a life."

Magda pulled back slightly.

"Be not afraid, my love. You can do this, you are strong." His eyes burned into hers, but she could see their light fading. "You must enjoy taking it, or it will not work."

Magda couldn't be hearing him correctly. He was surely delirious with pain and the fear of death creeping toward him.

"Do this for me. Bring me back. *Promise me,* Magda."

Josef reached out to her face, but his hand fell limp. His chest heaved, and red trickled one last time from his lips. Magda screamed and grabbed his shoulders, begging him to come back to her. She collapsed onto his chest, not caring about the blood staining her nightdress or smearing her face and hair.

She lay there until her body ached from the hard stone floor and her feet were numb from the cold.

The torches sputtered as Magda regarded the only man who had ever helped her, protected her, loved her. She kissed his cold lips, her tears mingling with the blood on his face.

With her lamp in a tight grip, she searched for the book. It lay open, facedown in what Magda hoped was a puddle of water. She picked it up without looking closely and shook the wetness from it.

Hurrying to the door, she prayed she could remember the way back to Josef's bedroom. Magda turned to look upon him once more.

"I promise."

Dawn was breaking as Magda crept into her silent apartment with two bulging bags from Josef's house hooked on each arm. She'd had to move quickly—no time to wrap the many glass jars and vials. She'd felt like a thief taking his things, especially his money, then skulking through the streets in the shadows.

Magda had left a note for Mrs. Tumova, telling her where to find his body. She couldn't just leave him there; Doctor Josef

Straka deserved a proper burial. She balked at what explanation to give. Magda couldn't say how she'd found him, and they wouldn't believe her if she did. Taking his property would be looked upon as stealing and nothing else; the prejudices against her people would brand her complicit regardless. With what she had already done and what she must now do, Magda's only choice was to run.

She hid the bags inside a lower cupboard in the kitchen, a room her husband came into only to eat. She stripped off her bloody clothes and hastily washed her face and arms in the sink, then pulled on a clean dress. Vaclav would be awake in less than half an hour, when the potion wore off.

Now this potion would be her instrument to kill him. Josef's words echoed, *Too much more will stop his breath.* Vaclav must go. No man would ever touch her again. No man except Josef. And she would bring him back, whatever it took.

The porridge was nearly done when Vaclav grumbled awake. He stumbled to the toilet to relieve himself, then pulled on his clothes, grunting and huffing in his morning drowsiness. She dished out the steaming porridge into the ceramic bowl he'd hit her with a month before, cracked along the rim but still usable, emptying the nearly full vial of poison into it. With a shaky hand, she stirred in goat's milk and honey to mask the taste, trying to keep her breathing controlled and her face passive.

You must enjoy taking it, or it will not work. She closed her eyes as she stirred.

Magda recalled several instances of Vaclav's slaps and shoves, listened once again to his frequent curses at her, relived moments of his fucking her, hard and driving, with never a thought to the human being pressed beneath his bulk. Not until Josef did she know the pleasure of a soft caress, that such passion could be spurred within her, and that the bedroom needn't be feared.

She would enjoy his death.

Vaclav sat at the table with a grunt and no greeting to his fair wife. He shoveled the food into his mouth, barely allowing any time to taste it before swallowing. She sat opposite him, surveying his every move. After a moment, he leaned on the table with an elbow as his shoveling slowed. Was the potion taking effect? She couldn't see his eyes with his shaggy head bent over his bowl, and she *wanted* to see them.

"Vaclav?" Her voice was small. She had learned to be quiet with him in the mornings.

He raised his face, his pupils enlarged, mouth slightly slack. His thick brows pinched in a flash of annoyance that was swept away with what seemed to be confusion. The spoon full of food fell from his clutch, splattering his chest. As the color drained from his pockmarked skin, a small smile curved Magda's lips. With no ceremony or struggle, Vaclav fell sideways from his chair to the floor.

Magda stood over him, watching his chest and face. No life appeared in his eyes, but his chest still moved. Vaclav was a horse of a man. *Was that enough poison? It must be!* There was no more. But her worries faded as his rigid body went limp, spittle and porridge spewing from his mouth. With a single twitch, he rolled onto his back as a last strangled breath left his body.

No more of him.

A cry of triumph escaped, and Magda covered her mouth. She smiled beneath her fingertips. She held no remorse for the man on the floor. Magda had done him a kindness with this death; it was silent and quick.

The book!

At the small desk in the corner of the living room, Magda lit every candle and lamp. The building hadn't the luxury of electricity, despite it being in most every other. The landlord wouldn't justify the expense, nor could the tenants afford the rent increase. She pulled the heavy book from Josef's valise. Magda felt no pull toward it, and hadn't since that day she'd seen it on his desk. *Curious.* She'd wanted it so badly—

What's that smell? Had one of Josef's jars broken along the way? Or had a piece of fruit been forgotten and left to rot in the bottom of the bag? Carefully picking through the valise revealed nothing broken. She sniffed the book and recoiled. It was the source of the unpleasant aroma. Combined with its gnarled pallor, the stench rendered the book as repulsive as some of the vomit she'd cleaned up.

Josef had said he dabbled in witchcraft on occasion to help his patients, including herself. She'd witnessed nothing but good come from his magickal attempts, and this was the book he used. But now, as she held the source of his witchcraft in her hands—the cover feeling like cold, hard wax—Magda's instincts pinged alarm.

The ghastly scene of Josef's death returned to her, and she paled. The animal skulls with chunks of flesh and fur still hanging from them, the pools of blood on the floor, the fallen men in robes similar to Josef's. Magda recalled the man closest to Josef, a gaping gash in his neck, and a fearsome knife covered in blood.

She set the book on the desk. Did Josef practice *dark* magick? Was this a ritual gone awry?

Magda rubbed her forehead, pushing away the horrific images and her doubts. Surely, those men had set upon Josef and he tried to defend himself. There was no other explanation. She choked at the monstrous way in which he'd met his end and wiped away hot tears. Magda took solace in having comforted him, that he hadn't died alone in such a horrible place.

Josef said this book could bring him back. Her logical mind scoffed at the impossibility, yet her heart dared to hope.

Magda wiped her sweating palms on her skirt and opened the front cover, her nose wrinkling at a fresh whiff of the book's odor.

"No." She gasped. *I picked up the wrong book!*

Panic gripped her. She couldn't possibly go back down to the sewer to search for another. Magda shouldn't even be taking the time now; she should be packing to leave. The police would surely want to question her after they discovered Josef and the other men. Not showing up for work would only heighten their suspicion.

"No, no, no." Magda wrung her hands. "This *has* to be the right one." It was the same one she'd seen in his study, the same one he said he'd used, the same one she'd wanted to snatch up. Magda flipped through the book. "But I can't read this!"

Bizarre scrawling covered each warped sheet from edge to edge; jumbles of slashes and jagged marks in no apparent order fought for space on the sallow pages.

She inhaled deeply to calm herself and repositioned the lamp to shed more light. Magda ran a hand across the paper, her fingertips traveling along the markings of dark, rust-colored ink. It wasn't vellum after all—something similar but different.

Magda laid a palm flat on the page and closed her eyes.

Josef, I've done what you told me. Please.

She slid her hand away, and continued to stare, almost as if in a trance. Perhaps the markings weren't as illegible as she first thought. She blinked several times and studied a cluster of scratchings. Her jaw unlocked as the marks slowly formed words in a dark corner of her mind. Awkward sentences took shape among the chaos, the meaning of the passage becoming clear like water smoothing of ripples.

"God help me." Magda stood, the chair falling backward. She crossed herself and flipped the book closed. She'd not practiced Catholicism since leaving the orphanage, but at this moment, as dread creeped into her soul, she sought God's protection.

Every instinct in Magda screamed for her to toss the book into the Vltava River, along with the contents of Josef's bags.

"No." She clenched her fists, recalling Josef's warm palm on her cheek, the smile in his piercing eyes, the sound of her name from his velvet voice, casting away the pit in her gut.

If dark magick could return him to her, then so be it.

CHAPTER 6

July 1937

Magda finished with the last shiny, copper coin and placed it in a small wooden chest. Her hands ached from the hours it had taken to etch the required symbols onto the front and back of each of the two hundred coins. The elaborate Bohemian lion on the obverse side of the five stotin was difficult to carve into, even with Josef's sharp boline. She tried not to dwell on the meaning of the vile markings and their effects. It didn't matter; none of it mattered. What mattered was her love coming back to her. She closed the book and rubbed her eyes.

When Magda had found the spell to bring Josef back to this world, she'd stared at the pages in disbelief and cried. Not simply from the absurdity of it but from the loss tearing her heart. Each word, each scratching rather, pushed him further away from her. But there *must* a reason; Josef couldn't possibly be involved in the things this book allowed for, and she would give him the opportunity to explain himself.

She'd never given much thought to magick. It had no place in her life unless it could conjure food or a warm place to sleep. From what she'd read so far, nothing in the book was so charitable. This whole business seemed ludicrous, the spell itself lunacy. Her heart, however, argued with her brain, and her gut reasoned even more differently. It beseeched her to get rid of the abomination, take only Josef's money and start a new life somewhere else.

But she'd already started a new life. It had been nothing to leave Vaclav on the floor of their apartment. Let the landlord find his rotting corpse when the rent went unpaid. Magda rented a room in an old boarding house under a false name. No one would recognize her; she'd never ventured to that part of Prague before, far away from her old neighborhood and Josef's home.

With one of her husband's tools, she teased a floorboard free and concealed the chest underneath.

Magda fell into bed exhausted, yet her mind raced with all she still needed to do and *how* she needed to do it. After her deed tomorrow at Josef's grave, she must wait, and then the search for bodies could begin.

Seven days following Josef's burial, Magda arrived at Vyšehrad Cemetery in the dead of night. The moon hung low in the star-filled sky, providing her with ample light.

The gruesome death of a prominent, charitable doctor had filled the newspapers. Murder, they called it. One or more men had set upon Doctor Straka and the others, killing them in some sort of ritualistic fashion, with no motive as yet determined. It reassured Magda that the police also considered Josef a victim. When they found the man, or men, who killed him, she would put all her doubts aside.

Magda knelt by the mound of earth and held the sob in her chest. It was a small mercy his headstone hadn't been placed yet. Seeing Josef's name and the date of his death would bring a fresh round of grief, and she couldn't afford such a distraction. She must do this and leave quickly; the night keeper came around each hour.

She opened the wooden chest cradled in her lap and poured a handful of his grave dirt over the coins. From her bag, she retrieved a tiny vial and kissed it. She pulled the stopper from the vial and let the droplets of Josef's blood fall onto the dirt within the chest. Josef had left everything necessary for this spell in his cabinet, set aside in its own little wooden box, the same chest she used now for the coins, as if knowing he'd need it someday. Magda put the empty vial in her pocket.

She dug several feet into the mound with her bare hands and laid the chest within. She covered the hole and pulled her things together. Padding through the cemetery, Magda ducked behind each headstone and monument as she went, her imagination hearing every sound as a pursuit from someone unseen.

Magda scanned the newspaper daily, hoping to read that Josef's killers had been caught and to monitor the police's interest in her. The pursuit of the gypsy maid who'd left the note increased after the discovery of her husband dead in their apartment, also fueled by the apparent robbery from the doctor's study, a cabinet emptied in an obvious hurry. The housekeeper adamantly denied Magda Hlavacova's involvement, describing her as a mouse of a woman in both stature and manner, completely incapable of harm or malice. Undeterred, the police speculated that perhaps the maid had colluded with one of the killers to rob the doctor, but things hadn't gone as planned.

As Mrs. Nováková, she hid in her rented room. She went out only when absolutely necessary, a scarf covering all but her eyes. Fear ate at her; if she were caught, she would go to prison, regardless of the lack of evidence. Her heritage made her an easy, and believable, scapegoat.

The interest of the police waned when it was revealed Vaclav had died of a heart attack. After many months, the police investigation reached a standstill with nothing in Josef's home to lead them to his killers, and no witnesses coming forward. The relations of other dead men had been stunned to learn of the death of their loved ones, especially the circumstances, but had no clues to offer.

Magda stayed busy to bide thc slow creeping of time. Thirteen months she must wait. With Josef's money, she'd bought an electric sewing machine, allowing her to get work as a seamstress. She hated to use his money, but she had no choice. She'd taken nothing but a few essentials and clothing from her apartment, leaving behind the tin can where Vaclav kept his money. After a short time, her sewing began to earn enough to sustain her without the help of Josef's money.

When the full moon in August of 1938 arrived, Magda breathed a sigh of relief. It was time to collect the box. She could start the last, and most horrific, part of the spell. Only that task remained before Josef could return.

It had been over a year since the doctor's murder, and it hadn't been mentioned in the papers for months. Magda had no fear as she crept once again into the cemetery under the sliver of moonlight peeking through the cloud-choked sky. She'd not been to his grave since the earlier ritual, and she sprinted as fast as she could while clinging to the narrow shadows. Josef's headstone shone like a beacon atop the low hill.

Magda gazed upon the short obelisk of white granite and let her fingers travel the name etched there.

"Josef."

His name tasted soft on her lips, like his kiss, and she smiled at the polished stone, holding her hands to her heart. The last time Magda had spoken his name aloud, she'd held his bloodied hand to her breast as the life left his eyes. A lump welled in her throat.

Magda broke through the grass-covered ground with a small

spade. She hacked at the compacted earth until she found the chest and wriggled it free. She replaced the dirt and grass as best she could and stole from the cemetery.

The next morning, Magda loaded her possessions into the back of the hired truck for her journey northwest to Okoř.

CHAPTER 7

January 1939

Okoř, Czechoslovakia

The young woman bent over the emaciated corpse. She studied his dirty face with soulful eyes, and didn't flinch as a flea jumped from his hair. Pankrác Prison had not been kind to him, nor should it have been.

With her comforting smile lost on the dead man, she removed the tatters of his prison uniform. Under the gentle eye of Father Kose, she washed the man's filthy body and dressed him in clean clothes donated to the church, although this type of man didn't deserve such care.

Magda hid her true feelings under a veil of compassion and the hymnal tune she hummed as she slowly went about her good work. Father Kose turned away at the sight of the nearly skeletal man, murmuring a prayer to God for his soul.

"What is she doing, Father?" a young nun whispered as she turned to follow the priest, one step behind.

"God's work," the priest said, matching her low tone. He stopped, half turning back to the door of the undercroft, hands clasped behind his back. "Mrs. Nováková came to us some months ago. Distraught, destitute. Begging for the mercy of God. Her husband had committed the gravest sin, you see. He had taken his own life."

The nun's hands flitted to her mouth, covering her gasp before she crossed herself.

"She felt tainted by his sin and sought absolution here. She said God wanted her to care for the most wretched of men, to wash her clean of her husband's sin, as she washes clean the unloved."

Magda's mouth twisted at their whispers.

"But where do they come from, these men?" The nun's voice was barely audible.

"Pankrác has sent their unclaimed dead to us for years," Father Kose said. "They are given the respect in death denied to them in life, no matter their sins. We bury them in the church cemetery although sometimes we do not even know their names. But God knows, and he forgives."

Without another word, the priest turned toward the stone steps, the young nun on his heels.

As their footfalls carried down the long stone corridor, Magda continued her solemn hum, waiting to hear the iron gate at the top of the steps close. The sharp clang of the heavy metal echoed in the oppressive silence of the basement crypt.

She straightened, securing a fallen wave of her thick black hair in her tight bun. She scowled at the despicable man. She'd learned he'd been imprisoned for performing horrific acts on children. He was no different from the others; there seemed to be an endless supply of those she needed.

You deserve this.

Magda drew two dirty copper coins from her apron pocket. Black earth filled the jagged marks scratched into their surfaces. She laid a coin on each of the man's eyes, whispering sibilant sounds in a language that cut her throat. Accustomed to the pain after many months, she ignored the blood in her mouth and did not choke as she'd done so often in the beginning. She secured the coins in place with clean, white gauze as she murmured the phrase once more.

After the small ritual was over, she expelled the blood into a handkerchief. Magda inhaled a deep breath through her nose, no longer noticing the ever-present stench of death and decay lingering in the stagnant air.

She continued with the remainder of her self-imposed duty, bundling the body in fresh, white linen and sewing the edges closed with tight stitches. She gathered his tattered uniform into a basket for the furnace and left. No more bodies would come today.

Once home, Magda stoked the embers in the wood stove, watching the flames slowly come to life. She leaned back in her chair, cradling a small wooden chest in her lap. She fingered the remaining coins inside, pushing them around in the thin layer of earth that still smelled of the grave. His grave.

Only eight more and the spell would be done. The edges of her mouth quirked upward, the muscles in her face not used to smiling.

Soon, my love.

CHAPTER 8

March 1939

MAGDA PAID NO ATTENTION TO THE CRIES AND SHOUTS. She must finish binding the man. The gate at the top of the stairs screeched open and clanged against the stone wall as hurried footsteps shuffled through the corridor. She threw the white linen cloth over the body.

"Mrs. Nováková!" Father Kose appeared in the doorway, one hand on his chest as he wheezed, the other gripping the doorframe for support. "We must go! The Germans will surely come through Okoř on their way to Prague."

Magda hurried her stitches, encasing the man's upper body in the sheet. *No one must see his eyes are covered, no one must remove the coins!*

"Mrs. Nováková!" The priest reached for her arm. She jerked away, both hands clutching the sheet. His eyes implored her, but Magda straightened, lifting her chin.

He withdrew reluctantly, hearing the shouts of his name from the top of the stairs.

"May God protect you and keep you." Father Kose made the sign of the cross and darted from the room.

No, no! I need only four more men!

But there were no more bodies, and the threat of invasion, now a reality, had stopped the dead being brought from the prison. She cried out, angry tears streaming down her cheeks. It had been eight months since she'd begun the binding. It was almost over!

Blinking away tears, she finished stitching the man's shroud. Magda swallowed her frustration, allowing the gravity of what was happening to sink in. She must get home. If she was captured by the Germans, she'd never be able to complete the spell.

Magda threw what she needed into two large, thick cloth bags and spent more time than she should have ensuring she left nothing behind. She stuffed the money into her clothing, dropping much in her haste. She fell to her knees to gather it up.

The streets were in chaos. People screamed and ran, arms filled with whatever possessions they could grab quickly. Soldiers shouted directions to people in the streets, filling trucks with civilians crying for rescue. By the time Magda emerged from her building, the truck out front was full. She begged to be allowed on.

"Leave the bags! There's no room." A middle-aged man shot his free hand out to her. His other hand clutched a crying young girl to his side.

"Hurry!" an older man yelled, bending down to pull her up as the truck lurched forward. "Your things mean nothing, woman!"

"I can't!" Magda cried, chasing after them. "My child is dead. My husband—!" She hugged the bags to her. "These are all I have left of them!"

With a loud curse, the man, still holding his daughter, grabbed the bags from Magda's outstretched arms while the older man pulled her into the truck. He shot her a look amid her sobbing words of gratitude and turned away to take his trembling wife in his arms.

Magda made herself as small as possible, almost suffocating

within the crush of bodies in the bed of the truck. Everyone cried and wailed, cowering in fear as Okoř disappeared behind them. Magda's tears weren't for what they grieved; she'd been so close to finishing. So close to bringing Josef back to her. *I'm so sorry, my love.*

Magda nestled in a darkened corner, feeling more secure with a wall at her back, even a makeshift one. As one of the first people to board the aging cargo ship, she'd had her pick of location. The hold had appeared completely packed with countless crates and barrels, but hidden deep within was a section for human cargo. For the right price, the unscrupulous captain, who blatantly cast a lecherous gaze the length of Magda's form, provided passage from England, where the Germans had set their sights.

It had taken months to get to the safety of London, but it was time to flee once more. Evacuations were underway, with London sending its population to rural areas, but Magda wanted out entirely. As did many other non-British, many *undesirables* —Jews, Romanies, Arabs. Her looks branded her as different, and in the eyes of the Germans, she didn't deserve to breathe air. Who knew how far the Germans would send their planes? And would they invade England just as they had her homeland?

Through official channels, the wait to evacuate to America was years long, if ever. But a new trade developed during wartime, one capitalized upon by men with ships and a bit of empty space. Freedom and safety had a price, and fortunately, Magda could pay with money and not her body.

Their sanctuary was cold and smelled of wood, rusted metal, and fuel oil. Damp hung in the air and filled her lungs. Given the lack of washing facilities for the stowaways, body odors—and worse—would soon be added to the mix. Five buckets, intended to be the toilet for fifty people, sat behind a wall of crates. The journey to Boston would take two weeks, the captain had said—if the good weather held and no U-boats blew them out of the water. Magda shuddered at what awaited her at sea.

People crowded around her, and she extended her short legs to claim a little more space. Magda tucked a bag behind each shoulder, providing a little comfort to lean against. These bags had caused her tremendous trouble, and she was lucky to still have them. She had tossed out everything that wasn't absolutely necessary, which had been mainly her clothing. She made do with only one other skirt and blouse, and a change of undergarments. The paper money she'd sewn into the lining of her skirt, and the small gold bars to her coat, with padding around each so they wouldn't clink against each other when she moved. She *had* to keep the treasures from Josef's cabinet. The spells in the book required so many things she'd never heard of, and she must hold on to all she'd taken. Magda had much more than most, and eyes followed her constantly. She took her bags with her at each trip to the buckets.

The days and nights passed unmarked, with no sky accessible in the depths of the ship. They were not allowed out of their crate-and-barrel enclosure, and it was a labyrinth if one even tried. At the only entrance was a man with a rifle and no signs of compassion on his haggard face.

Each time the guard changed at the entrance, the new man took a head count. This one's eyes lingered on Magda too long for her liking, and she kept her eyes pinned to the open book resting on her upraised knees.

After the meager meal of thin fish soup and stale bread, the bulk of the human cargo settled into sleep. Magda leaned back against her bags and stretched out her legs. Everyone kept to themselves, those alone stayed alone, those with a family member or friend huddled together. Mistrust and fear were rampant, and it felt safer to keep to your own.

When the lights were turned out, the blackness was absolute. No candles were allowed nor even a lamp, due to the possibility of fire. And a flashlight was a luxury they hadn't paid for. If one needed the buckets, the path was a gauntlet of prone bodies and duffels.

Magda paid no attention to the sounds of movement. She had drifted off into a half sleep when a hand clamped down on her mouth. She couldn't see the face of the man lowering his weight atop her; she didn't need to. Who it was didn't matter. She struggled pitifully as he yanked up her skirt. Magda had little strength from months of eating scraps, and no one would come to her aid.

He reeked of sweat and stale cigarettes, his hot breath foul against her face. He grunted, struggling to get his pants down and pry her legs apart with his knees. Magda was tiny under his massive bulk; his weight crushed against her chest, forcing the air from her lungs. She clawed at his face with her free hand. His laugh rumbled in his throat.

Magda's hand frantically sought the pocket of her coat. Her underwear ripped as her fingers curled around the small boning knife.

Passages from the book appeared in her mind's eye; its strange words came to the tip of her tongue. She uttered the words, her lips moving under his calloused, dirty hand, and swallowed the tickle of blood in her throat.

Her body flooded with strength, a hot, electric sensation steeling her muscles and hardening her heart. Magda locked her legs; he would not pry them open further.

She choked out another serpentine phrase, and a deep, green fire blazed along the blade as she plunged it into the man's side. The flames shot into him, locking his body in paralysis. Magda twisted the long, thin knife with her newfound strength. In another instant, a pulse of the same green light overtook him. The hand gripping her mouth vanished; the pressure of his weight was gone in the blink of an eye.

Thin powder and fragments of cloth rained down, getting into her nose and eyes. The man had disintegrated with her words—words from the book.

Magda coughed and sat up, wiping the grit from her face. Those around her still slept, oblivious to what had transpired, or simply ignoring it. She fell back, clutching the knife to her breast.

So the book *could* do good. It saved her, giving her incredible strength and setting the boning knife aflame, flashing away the horrid man. It was a shame she couldn't have bound him to Josef; he was the right sort.

Several minutes passed before her breathing and pulse calmed. Magda slipped the knife back into her pocket. She had to use the toilet. Magda hooked her bags through her arms and tiptoed over her fellow refugees as best she could in the dark.

She made it to the row of buckets when a spasm of pain gripped her spine, sending her to the floor. A cry slipped from her lips, and she clamped both hands over her mouth. Another spike racked her body, causing her limbs to flail wildly, her bags thrown aside. One bag upset a bucket. Putrid liquid splashed everywhere, but she could do nothing to move away from it. Magda writhed in pain on the cold metal floor, praying to God to make it stop.

It was over just as quickly as it came, but it left her prostrate on the floor, fighting to fill her lungs, and nearly vomiting from the stench of urine and feces. Magda rolled away, scrambling up on all fours, and used the crates to pull herself up. Her bladder had emptied with the shock and surprise of the pain. She leaned against the crates and cried.

When the woman called upon him during the attack, he was elated.

He had known that it was only a matter of time before the woman used his power. All he needed to do was wait, and he was well practiced at that.

Mumbling the words from the spell to tether the souls to Straka was not sufficient. His magick must course through her body; she must wield his power for him to be able to penetrate her mundane mind.

It had taken a great deal of strength to reach out to the human without his master detecting it.

His master, *he scoffed. Straka was a tremendous disappointment. Unique among humans, his affinity for darkness coupled with immense natural power made him the ideal candidate. Yet the fool was too enamored with Muraal to be swayed. He had enjoyed witnessing Straka's demise.*

He needed another. His options were limited; the woman would suffice for now. He had only been able to make contact once. As luck and Straka's arrogance would have it, he had not needed to do more.

Unfortunately, the lack of magick in the woman rendered her useless. However, she could be the means to an end. He could not search on his own; his reach was extremely limited in his current form.

He had gambled much to be released into this world. For a time, he seemed to have failed, exchanging one prison for another, one master for another. Yet his cunning had freed him from the Voll, and from the loathsome creature that had subsumed him. That feat alone was gratifying. And with Straka gone, he had opportunities.

Now in her feeble mind, she could be influenced. And he would let her use him for his own amusement, allowing him to feel alive and free if only for a few moments as he bided his time.

He would not allow her to resurrect Straka. She would not remember him at all.

CHAPTER 9

July 1993

Boston, Massachusetts

A high-pitched expletive jolted Magda from her quilting trance. A series of dull thuds followed, and something bumped against the bottom of her apartment door. She stared at the door, blinking until her vision refocused. *Ah, yes. The new people.* A baby's cry pealed out. Magda set aside her bundle of fabric and flexed her aching fingers.

She pushed herself from the armchair with a grunt and waited for the back spasm to pass. She'd sat for too long, hunched over her quilting. Magda frowned at her bony hands, knuckles swollen and red.

A woman's strained yet comforting words were failing to calm the baby. Magda opened the door a crack. A petite young woman crouched on the linoleum, a tandem baby carrier strapped to her torso, gathering groceries fallen from the bottom of a sodden paper sack. The woman's long, straight red hair swung back and forth as she reached for each item. Tiny arms flailed from the front pod, trying to either catch the hair or bat it out of its face, each movement punctuated with an angry wail.

Magda hesitated, preferring to keep to herself as was her habit. But something about the young woman's defeated bearing tugged at Magda. She opened the door a little wider.

"May I help?"

"Oh!" The young woman dropped the armful she'd collected. Her expression fell, giving Magda her answer.

Magda made no outward acknowledgement of the woman's cut, swollen lip and black eye. She was younger than Magda first thought, too young to have two babies clinging to her. *Nineteen, twenty maybe?* Magda placed a hand on the wall for support as she bent to pick up the grapefruit by her door and catch the one aiming to roll down the stairs. The girl stood, clutching the reclaimed armful around her baby, fresh bruises dotting the pale skin of her left arm. To Magda, they resembled fingerprints.

"The bag split," she said, eyelashes glistening wet and freckled cheeks splotched red. She flicked her free hand at the door. "And the damn key is jammed."

Magda crossed the hallway, smiling warmly at the girl, and reached for the key. "These locks are testy. You must be gentle. Lift up just a little, then turn." Magda turned the key with little effort.

Relief melted the young woman's rigid shoulders. "Oh my gosh! Thank you so much!"

Magda opened the door since the girl's arms were otherwise occupied. She thanked Magda again and stepped in, laying her load on a short stack of boxes inside. A glimpse into the apartment revealed a few plastic tubs, a trash bag spilling over with clothes, and an old crib waiting to be reassembled. Not nearly enough boxes for a family move.

The baby snugged into the pod on the young woman's back regarded Magda silently, unlike her twin, who still wailed unmercifully with a handful of her mother's hair in each tiny fist. Magda gazed back at the lovely little girl, tilting her head and making a funny face. The baby's tongue poked out then disappeared, replaced by a saliva-bubble smile.

The woman whipped around, patting the crying baby's back with one hand and extending the other. "Hello, by the way. I'm Vivian Parsons. We just moved in."

"Magda Hlavacova." The woman's slim fingers gave a firm grip, making Magda grimace and pull her hand free quicker than customary.

"I'm so sorry!" Vivian stepped forward, her face stricken.

"Not to worry." Magda clutched her hands together and forced a smile. "Arthritis flare-up. It will pass."

"Are you taking anything for it? I'm going to nursing school. Well, I'm taking a short break because… these two, but I might be able to help. My aunt was a nurse." She took a deep breath, her cheeks flushing pink. "Sorry. I ramble sometimes."

"Quite all right, my dear. And thank you, but no. A cup of tea and a nap should do the trick."

"Well…" Vivian glanced at Magda's hands with a frown. "If you're sure." She turned to pull the key from the lock.

"It sounds like that little one needs a nap." Magda inclined her head at the unhappy baby, a lock of her mother's hair still clutched in a wee fist.

A wave of euphoria struck Magda, and she stumbled backward at the dizzying sensation.

"Ugh, she's been cranky all d— Oh!" Vivian lunged forward, taking hold of Magda's elbow, then slipped an arm around Magda's waist. "I gotcha."

Magda gaped at the baby, now quiet as her large, wet eyes roamed the elderly woman's face. Magda couldn't pull her eyes away. She felt as if she stared intently *at* something but couldn't discern what exactly it was. She saw nothing except a red-faced infant, yet she *felt* she was seeing more. And it made her inexplicably ecstatic.

Vivian was speaking, but Magda barely heard. Something

about diabetes, if she'd had any lunch. A chubby hand released her mother's hair and jutted out, aiming to grasp Magda's nose.

The wave receded as embarrassment burned Magda's cheeks. She stepped free of Vivian's arm.

"I'm sorry. I don't know what came over me." She put a cold palm to her overly warm forehead. "The oddest thing!"

"Are you diabetic? Do you need to eat something?" Vivian's hand hovered under Magda's elbow.

"Not that I know of."

"That's not something you should ignore. Seriously." Vivian's attention turned to her daughter as the baby yawned against her chest, tiny eyelids fluttering closed. She mouthed an exasperated *Finally* to the ceiling.

Magda took the opportunity to escape, giving Vivian a grandmotherly smile as she put a finger to her lips. Vivian grinned and all but tiptoed into her apartment, closing the door quietly.

Her smile vanished. *What was that?* Magda was long past menopause, but she'd never experienced anything even remotely similar during that uncomfortable decade. She couldn't fathom why she had felt jubilation; now, in its wake, she felt uneasy. *And what in the world was I staring at?*

Magda shuffled back to her armchair, her throbbing back welcoming the relief. *Vivian probably thinks I'm a crazy old lady now. Maybe I am.* She tsked. *Poor thing.* The young woman wore her story on her skin. Fleeing from an abusive man—not a husband, for Vivian had no ring on her finger nor even the slightest mark a wedding ring made—with baby twin girls as reward for her suffering. Magda knew well the woman's misery, although thankfully she and Vaclav never had children. She was glad Vivian had gotten away, or seemed to have, anyway. If Magda could help her, she would.

She gazed out the window; her view comprised the roof of the building across the street and a large swath of bright blue sky. *Maybe it* is *time for a doctor's visit.*

A doctor's visit isn't necessary. The book has everything I need, always has.

Her eyes flitted to her witch cabinet, and she nodded to herself. Magda had read through the book many times over the years and knew it offered nothing to alleviate her aches and pains. However, the book was strange. She snorted. *Strange is an understatement.*

With the key on a cord around her neck, Magda unlocked the upper doors of the narrow, antique secretary, its dark red paint chipped and beaten by time. It took both hands to pull the heavy gray book out and set it on the drop-down desk that served as a countertop. She wrinkled her nose; she'd never gotten used to its odor, and it hadn't diminished over time. In fact, the book remained utterly unchanged. Its ugly, wrinkled casing hadn't faded or peeled, or softened in the least; each stiff page still crackled as she turned it; and the words, if one could call the slashes and marks words, were as vibrant today as the first time she'd seen their rusty color.

Magda had once thought the book repugnant. Evil, in fact. It *was* filled with dreadful magick—she had no illusions about that—but its spells and incantations had come to her aid too many times for her to think badly of it. She had recently used its power on a mugger; a few whispered words crippled the young hooligan's hands so he'd never snatch anything again. What she'd been taught years ago by the nuns, that nothing good can be made from evil, had been wrong. *It is your intent that matters.* Not everyone's intent was as pure as Magda's, so the book remained safely locked away.

But there was a price to be paid each time the magick flooded through her. A price she willingly paid.

Magda turned another page slowly, waiting to catch a hint of movement. Witnessing the words *move* was thrilling. Marks on a given page sometimes rearranged themselves to form different words; sentences faded and new ones appeared; the spells and chants morphed, changing ingredients or the actions required, as if it *knew* her need. Both a comforting and unsettling thought—an intelligence within the book. But no, that was fantasy. It was magick, pure and simple.

Under her fingertips, the reddish-brown scratchings quivered, and she drew her hand away. A smile pulled at her lips as Magda read the newly formed passage.

"Oh, my goodness!" Her eyes widened, as did her smile.

Magda selected the bottles and vials for the potion within the deep recesses of the cabinet. Each of the six containers were sealed; the book had never instructed her to use these ingredients.

The doctor from whom she'd acquired the majority of the contents of her witch cabinet had been meticulous, labeling and packaging his herbs and oils with great care. She'd never thrown any of it away; it all seemed important, felt important, and one never knew when something would be needed.

She ground the pungent herbs in her well-worn mortar, mixing the liquids and oils as directed, then scraped the sludge into her small cauldron to boil. The stench wafting from the pot made her eyes water. Lighting several incense cones didn't help, even as she waved the smoky wisps of sandalwood and jasmine directly under her nose. Magda grimaced. *I have to drink this.*

The grit and lumps cooked away, resulting in a smooth liquid, thickening as it cooled. She poured the oily substance into a copper chalice, silently beseeching her stomach to stay quiet. With no ceremony or hesitation, she gulped down the warm oil as fast as the thickness allowed.

If death had a taste, it was this. Yet life swirled within the brownish-black oil. Magda gripped the secretary with aching hands, holding herself upright, clenching her jaw against the overwhelming urge to vomit.

She waited, her fingers throbbing more as she dug her nails into the old wood. Soothing warmth began in her belly, replacing the spasms of rejection, and crept slowly throughout her body. The pleasant heat brought glorious relief from the ailments of her seventy-eight years.

Magda inhaled deeply, filling her newly cleared lungs fully, and marveled at the sensations the elixir brought. She felt the weight of her age lifting away like a tangible thing, as if she were shrugging off a heavy woolen cloak. Magda straightened for the first time in years, the dowager hump on her spine melting away, and flexed her pain-free fingers, where no signs of redness or swelling remained.

Magda walked sure-footed to her bedroom and gazed in the dresser mirror. While her hair remained steel gray, gone were the puffy bags that formed under her eyes when she smiled. Fewer spider veins mapped her many years, and the creases and wrinkles of her skin seemed smoother. She stretched her hands to the ceiling, mentally inspecting her body for pinches and stabs of pain. *Nothing!*

She turned on the radio, its dial never venturing from the "oldies" station, and bowed to her reflection in the mirror, extending her hand as an invitation to dance. She laughed aloud and twirled about, an invisible partner in her arms.

The utter relief and more youthful appearance were worth all the foul oils she would have to drink. The book had never let her down.

He could not contain his exuberance at discovering the sliver of darkness born into the child.

It was not on the scale of Straka, but it did not need to be. It could be cultivated; humans were easily manipulated, their weak minds malleable. It had been nothing to turn the woman away from Straka, to bury her memories and her dreams beneath him in the corner of her mind where he dwelled.

He did not doubt his ability to turn the child's spark into a raging fire. Though he must wait until she matured, it mattered little; time meant nothing.

He had contemplated letting the old woman die, to take his chances with another human. Yet now she must unite him with this suitable candidate. She needed to remain alive and well until his opportunity came. Human lives were short and fragile. Her reliance on him was all-encompassing, and making her turn to him for assistance was effortless.

CHAPTER 10

August 1993

Magda cradled the fussy Avery in her arms as Vivian shook a bottle in each hand. Chloe lay quietly in the bouncer, observing everyone's movement. Magda extended her index finger, spiraling it down to 'get' her nose. Chloe giggled, waving Magda's hand away. This brought fresh cries from Avery. Magda's crossed eyes and clicking noises were not effective distractions.

"You are so great to help me, Magda. I can't thank you enough." Vivian scooped Avery from her arms, and the baby instantly quieted at the sight of the bottle. Avery never fussed when it came to mealtime. Vivian settled into the old but sturdy maroon velour recliner left by the previous tenant. The bruises on her arm had faded to faint blotches, only a small scab remained on her lip, and a light purple shadow under her eye.

"I'm happy to help." Magda lifted Chloe and sat on the only other piece of furniture in the small living room, a sofa relic from the late seventies as green as pea soup—still serviceable if one ignored the reek of mothballs. Chloe regarded Magda, another saliva bubble forming on her lips, then took her attention to the bottle. Magda popped the bubble with the tip, making Chloe smile. She closed her eyes the instant the nipple touched her lips.

"She is such a good baby," Magda murmured.

"Oh, she really is. These two are complete opposites. It's crazy." Vivian let out a contented sigh, enjoying the rare quiet that occurred when Avery had a bottle. "I can't tell you how lucky I feel moving in across from you. You remind me so much of my aunt."

Magda blushed at the unexpected compliment. Vivian sniffled and hugged Avery to her.

"I gather she's passed on?" Magda asked quietly. Vivian had yet to reveal much about her past, and Magda hadn't wanted to pry. A bit of her story had been obvious.

Vivian nodded, her chin quivering. "We both… Aunt Clare and I… had hoped she'd live to see the twins born but… cancer." She gulped back a sob.

"There's no shame in crying."

"I know." Her arms full with Avery and the bottle, she brushed her cheek against her shoulder, wiping away a tear. "I just prefer doing all my crying in the shower." She forced a laugh.

"You said she was a nurse."

"Yep. That's why I want to be one too. Aunt Clare loved helping people, and it made her so happy to make other people feel better." Her eyes glossed once more. "She even set up a trust for me—for my schooling—in her will."

"That was wonderful of her. What did your parents think?"

Vivian shook her head. "No parents. They died when I was little. My aunt was everything." She cleared her throat. "So"—she repositioned Avery in the crook of her arm—"where are you from? There's a little bit of an accent."

Magda accepted the change in topic without hesitation. "Prague."

"Cool! I've heard it's beautiful. I'd love to visit someday."

"It is beautiful. I miss it sometimes."

"Why did you leave?"

"War."

Vivian cocked an eyebrow.

"The second world war brought the Germans to my door—"

"The second world war?" She leaned forward. "How old are you?" She tutted. "Sorry. That was rude. Don't answer that."

Magda dismissed her apology with a soft chuckle. "I was twenty-four when I fled. I spent a brief time in England, but it was not safe for me there either. I came to Boston and have been here ever since."

"Wow, you must be close to eighty!"

Magda grinned at the woman's incredulous expression.

"You don't look it at all. Maybe sixty-five, tops. Well, except for that first day." Vivian's face turned wistful. "I'm sorry. That must have been awful. I can't imagine that. Being forced from your home into a strange place."

"Can't you?"

Vivian gave a weak smile. "I suppose I can."

Magda hadn't meant to turn the conversation back to the unpleasant topic. Vivian sagged into the back of the recliner, repositioning the loudly suckling Avery once more.

"I've got no one to blame but myself, though."

"We don't have to talk about it, Vivian."

"No, it's all right. I can talk about *this.*" She took a deep breath. "I knew Curt was bad for me. Aunt Clare knew it, too, but I didn't listen, obviously." She unlocked her ankles, bringing the heels of her flats down hard on the carpeted floor. "But he was extremely good-looking, like out-of-my-league hot, and he said all the right things, bought me things, blah, blah, blah."

"I can't see any man being 'out of your league.'"

Vivian shrugged a shoulder. "I should've broke up with him when he called me a See-You-Next-Tuesday for the first time."

"A what?"

"See-You-Next-Tuesday. C-U-N-T."

Magda's mouth fell open.

"I know, I know. I'm stupid."

"I am not one to pass judgement." It might comfort Vivian to know some of what Magda had endured, but she waited. This was Vivian's time.

"When I told him I was pregnant, I thought he'd be happy." She kissed Avery's forehead, careful not to dislodge the rapidly emptying bottle. "I couldn't have been more wrong. That's when… things got… physical."

Anger flickered in Magda's gut. "Does he know where you are?"

"No, thank god. I moved from New York, something I said I'd never do. But with nothing to keep me there and him to avoid, leaving felt like the best thing. I was able to transfer my hours to Bay State, and so, here I am."

Magda bit back her questions. Chloe grunted, telling Magda the bottle had strayed from her mouth. She was glad to hear the man was in another state or she'd have to act on her desire to pay him a visit. *Could I do something from such a distance? I wonder—*

"So, what kept you from returning to Prague?"

It was Magda's turn to welcome the change in topic. She took a deep breath, expelling her growing anger in the exhale.

"I was an orphan, and then had a husband much like this Curt of yours." Magda's confession was met with wide eyes. "He died before the war, and thankfully, we had no children."

A flicker of a blurred image in the back of her mind gave her pause. She squinted at the middle distance, trying to recall it. "I'd met another man, but he died also." Her statement surprised her, yet she dismissed it. "There's nothing to return to."

Vivian chewed the inside of her cheek.

Magda inspected what formula remained in Chloe's bottle. "Ancient history. Memories fade."

Both women settled back, Magda closing her eyes.

She hovered at the blissful edge of sleep, soothed by the warmth of Chloe's small body and the faint sound of her suckling. The image returned, resolving into a vague yet tall silhouette of a man. Several seconds passed before she recognized him; it was the doctor for whom she'd once worked as a maid. *What was his name?*

Magda picked through her memories. Why had he given her the book and all those jars of herbs and oils, not to mention his money?

It must have been the threat of the German invasion. Yes, that was why. As a woman, she had a better chance of escape, whereas he might be called to fight, or worse, be captured. A pang of sadness tightened her chest, then fled so quickly she questioned what that feeling had actually been. What did it matter? It was so long ago.

Feet pounding up the stairs jolted Magda from her contemplation. There were only two apartments on this floor. Hairs on her arm rose.

Vivian sprang from the chair with Avery still in her arms, the color draining from her face. "No, no, no," she whispered. "It can't be."

"Vivian!" The angry shout from the hallway made the young woman freeze. A fist beat on the door; the old wood quaked with each blow. "*Vivian!* I know you're in there! PIs are cheap. Open the door. I want my kids!"

Vivian whimpered. The bottle fell from Avery's mouth, and the baby broke into earsplitting cries. She tried quieting the child, holding her tightly against her breast.

"God dammit, woman! You better open this fucking door!"

Vivian shook her head vehemently at Magda, her trembling hand trying to get the bottle back into Avery's mouth. Magda put the ever-quiet Chloe back into the bouncer. As she stepped toward the door, Vivian grabbed her arm with ice-cold fingers and mouthed 'no.' Magda patted her hand.

Magda waited a moment, her mind racing through the pages of the book, searching for a fitting punishment for this unwelcome visitor. Magda took a deep breath; thrusting her chest out and chin up, she stood as tall as her short frame allowed. She muttered words below a whisper, feeling a surge of power through her body. Magda unlatched the door's many locks and grasped the knob.

She opened the door only wide enough for her body to be visible. The man stepped back, his blond eyebrows coming together.

"May I help you?" Magda's voice was friendly, but her eyes were not.

He grunted and placed a large hand on the door, meaning to push his way in. To his evident surprise, the old woman's grip was firm.

"Get out of the way, Grandma. I got no problem going through you." His blue-gray eyes glared at Magda, his strong, square jaw clenching. He was handsome—with thick blond hair and a lean, muscular frame shown off by a blue silk shirt tucked into well-fitting jeans—but he was also a devil.

The magick coursing through Magda's veins revealed the man's true nature. Curt used women, drawing them in with his smiles and money and endless affection. They were toys and trophies, and Vivian was stupid enough to get herself pregnant. His words. And she'd remained pregnant despite several punches to her belly. He wanted the children now; his controlling nature wouldn't allow a woman of his to defy him.

Magda smiled sweetly. "Now, is that any way to speak to an old lady?"

"Fuck you." He put his shoulder into the door, expecting the old woman to fall backward. Neither Magda nor the door moved. A sneer replaced Magda's smile as the man cocked his head, blinking. She reveled in the sensation of invincibility. Her skin tingled as if electricity danced across it, the rush of power steeling her muscles. At this moment, she didn't care about the price she'd pay for using the book's magick.

"All right, you old bitch, you asked for it," Curt snarled, taking a step with upraised hands.

"Het," Magda hissed, the word cutting her throat.

Curt's spine bolted straight and his arms locked to his sides, his protest strangling in his throat. The agony inflicted by that single word bloated his face red, eyes threatening to pop from their sockets. Magda snatched a lock of his perfectly coiffed hair with a hard yank.

"Sukar s'da yi dex. Akree." She clenched her teeth together, drawing out the last word.

His hips twitched as the rest of his body remained rigid. Stifled grunts died in this throat.

"Ix h'het suka." Magda pointed to the stairwell. Curt's body turned in a rapid series of jerks, fighting the force moving him as his legs carried him roughly down the stairs.

She clung to the doorframe, holding herself upright. The invigorating power flashed away, leaving her dizzy—and regretful. Magda leaned her head against the door as she retrieved a handkerchief from her dress pocket and wiped the blood and spittle from her mouth. She closed the door and turned each lock with trembling fingers.

Vivian hadn't moved, and Avery was surprisingly quiet.

"What the hell was *that*?" Vivian's voice was dry. She swallowed and took a half step toward Magda, her face ashen and drenched with sweat. Magda brushed away a few strands of red hair stuck to her cheek and patted it with a motherly smile. Avery's tiny lips formed an *O* at the old woman, her eyes searching. Chloe regarded Magda with a tilt of her head.

Vivian shivered and appeared to return to herself. She sucked in a breath. "He hired a private investigator to find me?" Her eyes filled with tears. "He'll be back."

Magda rubbed Vivian's forearm and gave it a squeeze. "We'll see about that."

Magda sat in the armchair in her quiet apartment, curtains open to allow the moonlight unfettered access to the room. Her nails dug into the cloth padding of the armrests. In her mouth was an old strap of leather, her teeth filling indentations made from years of use. Her body fought the tremors, despite her desperation to relax and let it happen. She'd learned to control her bowels, however, and that was a blessing.

This will pass, she told herself over and over. *Remember the power the book gave you; it was worth this! And you used the magick for good, not ill. It will pass.*

The book gave its dark magick freely and, although the pain was brief, it was no less excruciating. When the last convulsion left her body, Magda took deep inhales until she was herself again.

She thought of Curt. She could use the book to get rid of him; nobody would miss a man like that. *No, that's too easy.* Magda's lip curled. *The curse I put upon his manhood will be a lesson he'll never forget. But there's no time to waste.*

At her witch cabinet, Magda passed over the gray tome, selecting a book of protection spells bound in tattered, red leather.

She scooped a handful of black salt into a small, clear bottle. In the salt, she embedded one brass nail, the tip of which she'd sharpened on a whetting stone, and two dried rose stems with thorns as hard and as sharp as broken glass. Before filling the bottle with more black salt, she placed Curt's hair within, jiggling the bottle until the glossy lock wedged itself among the nail and stems. After beating in a cork stopper with her palm, she dipped the neck of the bottle into a pot of melted black wax scented with black pepper and clove oils. As she turned it upright, the wax bled down the sides, slowing as it cooled.

Magda envisioned her intent for the bottle. *Stay away, Curt Arthur Stiller, father of Avery and Chloe Parsons. You will stay away. So mote it be.*

It was late when Magda tapped Vivian's door with a fingernail, not wishing to wake the little ones. Vivian had said she wouldn't sleep tonight, fearing Curt's return.

"It's Magda."

The door opened enough for Magda to slip through. Vivian secured the locks with quick fingers.

Vivian embraced her and began to sob. Magda returned her firm hug, rubbing her back and murmuring words of comfort.

She let the girl cry; sometimes a good cry was sorely needed.

After a time, Magda gently pulled away. "Shh, shh. Hush now," she said, wiping away the streams of tears from Vivian's puffy, freckled cheeks. "There's no need to worry. Here." She pressed the glass bottle into Vivian's palm.

"What's this?" She turned the object over in her hands.

"It's known as a witch bottle."

Vivian looked up with raised brows.

"Come. Sit." Magda guided her to the recliner. "I am not a witch, there is no magick in me, but I can do certain things. This bottle will keep that man away, I am certain of it. Keep it in your home. On your mantel there would be good."

"I don't believe in that stuff." Vivian's red eyes searched the old woman's sincere face. "But how you got rid of him boggles my mind." She waited, then returned to consider the bottle when Magda didn't explain. "I'll take all the help I can get."

She leaned back, holding it to her chest. "Should I ask what's in it? Hopefully, nothing gross like animal parts or cat pee." Vivian huffed. "Well, actually, I don't care if it does. As long as it works." A corner of her mouth crooked up.

"Ha!" Magda grinned. "Nothing 'gross,' I can assure you. Those things have their uses, but not in this one."

CHAPTER 11

December 1998

DARKER THAN THE MOONLESS NIGHT, A FORMLESS PALL OF black solidified into the silhouette of a tall man. He stood atop a mound of fresh earth. A grave.

He seemed to struggle to retain his shape, as if unseen hands tore at him.

Magda squinted, the image sharpened, and she tightened her strong, youthful arms around the hard gray book held to her chest. *You can't have it.*

The place felt vaguely familiar, like the snippet of an old memory teetering on the edge of being forgotten.

The silhouette lifted his arms from his sides. Fear sent Magda stumbling backward, stopped hard by cold stone. She gasped at the white obelisk towering above her, shimmering with an eerie green aura. Two words were etched deep into its pristine surface.

Josef Straka

As she stared at the name, random images flitted through her mind. Midnight-blue eyes below dark brows, a soft smile surrounded by a glossy smooth mustache and beard. Magda inhaled deeply the scent of spiced beeswax. Her cheek warmed with an unseen touch.

I know you.

Something pulled at her arms, and she looked down. The book was gone.

"No!" She whirled about, desperation stealing her breath. Magda dropped to her knees, scrabbling around in the damp grass for what she *must* get back.

A chill brushed its long fingers across the nape of her neck. Gossamer ribbons trembled in her periphery, and she squeezed her eyes closed, guilt lacing the chill creeping into her bones.

I had to do it. I'm sorry.

Through her closed eyes, she still saw them. Magda clapped her dirt-encrusted hands over her eyes.

"Aan." A chorus of unearthly voices echoed around her, encircling her. Profoundly mournful, hollow. Dead.

Chained. Magda gasped, moving her shaking hands from her face to cover her pounding heart. The chorus repeated the word again and again, each echo a stab of condemnation into her chest.

"You made a promise, Magda."

Magda bolted awake, a scream trapped in her throat, clutching the quilt to her chin. The rich, velvety voice faded slowly, taking the chill with it.

The little giggles and squeals of present opening on Christmas morning drove away Magda's unease. Almost. Twinges of guilt flared as random bits of the dream pushed themselves to the forefront without warning. As she'd lain in bed, she picked through her past, searching for any deed or broken promise that would bring about such regret and shame. Magda's life had been largely uneventful until the war. Although some of her memories were nothing more than jumbles of shapes and colors without sounds or smells, a haze she attributed to old age, Magda couldn't recall any great failure or betrayal of trust.

Beside the fireplace crackling with life, a fragrant rosemary plant decorated with a string of colorful tiny lights and a simple gold star served as the Christmas tree. It was something Vivian's aunt had done, and she wanted to pass along the tradition to her daughters. Avery and Chloe sat on the floor in their pajamas, one on each side of the little tree, inspecting their gifts and guessing their contents.

A scene Norman Rockwell would've painted. Magda held the painting in her mind, forcing all other images away.

Although Vivian hadn't put much stock in the witch bottle, it still sat on the fireplace mantel, dusted and clean, with the girls forbidden to touch it. For months after Curt's appearance, Vivian had left the apartment only when absolutely necessary, her head constantly on a swivel, clinging to the shadows of the buildings as if the half light rendered her invisible. But five years had passed now, and he had never returned.

The five years had flown by for Magda. Until the introduction of these three people, she hadn't realized she'd been living almost a hermit's life, only going out for groceries and fabric or to deliver her quilting commissions. She'd become sullen and tired with no friends, feeling purposeless and drifting through life just for the sake of living. With these two rambunctious redheads and a mother to match, Magda had found joy in everyday life again.

She'd also not needed to take another life-extending potion. Magda wasn't sure if that was due to its potent magick, or if Vivian and her daughters deserved the credit, keeping her moving and making her feel needed… and loved.

Small hands reached for the boxes from their grandmother. Magda grinned at Avery's little huffs of exertion. She'd been caught peeking at the gifts last year, so, this year, Magda secured every inch of seam and fold with invisible tape. Chloe gave in after a few seconds of trying to remove the tape without tearing the bright paper and followed her sister's example of unabashed shredding. Despite the stark differences in personality, the girls appeared identical, from their cheek dimples and slightly pointed chins, to their large hazel eyes and skin liberally adorned with light freckles.

Their knitted sweaters with matching scarves in each girl's favorite color, dark blue for Avery and fuchsia for Chloe, earned Magda neck hugs and cheek kisses. Magda couldn't remember ever feeling so happy.

A shift was developing that he could not comprehend.

Straka was coming to the old woman's thoughts. It had first begun in her dreams, where he had no control. It now seeped into her daily life. He watched, unable to stem the ripples of memory, yet he could still focus her brain elsewhere.

It was the child who was important, and the woman must remain linked with her. He had not needed to steer her too much; her soft heart propelled her into the mother's life. The old woman was the perfect tool.

Yet he was troubled now by this unknown. Vigilance was required.

CHAPTER 12

November 2000

"Did you finish all the chores?" Magda called from her bedroom as the girls entered her apartment.

"Yep!" Chloe said, followed by an exaggerated groan from Avery. Magda laughed to herself. She walked through the kitchen to stand at the threshold to the living room, arms folded across her bosom.

"The vacuuming?" Magda asked. Avery turned away, fixing her gaze on the landscape painting on the opposite wall.

Avery fidgeted under her grandmother's steely gaze. "Yes, Grammy, I vacuumed." She stuffed her hands in the front pockets of her jeans.

"You look guilty," Magda said. Avery's mouth dropped as she finally met Magda's eyes. "Are you sure?"

Avery pulled her hands from her pockets, flinging them in the air. "Yes! I promise! Ask Chloe." The look she gave her sister begged for corroboration. For a fraction of a moment, Chloe pretended not to know what Avery was talking about, but she was never good at deception. She laughed at Avery's annoyed pucker. "Yes, Granny. She did."

Avery harrumphed and slouched onto the sofa.

Chloe presented a white baking dish to Magda. "Here, Granny, all washed and dried. The casserole was yummy, thank you."

"Suck-up," Avery muttered under her breath.

"You ate half of it!" Chloe said.

Magda gave a quick glare at the snickering child on the sofa, then brightened her expression to both girls. "Your mom won't be home until later. She's covering for someone at the hospital."

Avery nodded and lifted her ratty sneakers onto the coffee table, resting her head on the sofa.

"Feet," Magda barked, making the girl snatch them back with a muttered 'sorry.'

"Who wants to help me in the kitchen?" Magda's question was pointless, but she always asked. Only Chloe lent a hand with making meals; Avery only wanted to eat them.

The evening was quiet, with Chloe doing her homework at the kitchen table and Avery watching *The Simpsons* after profusely denying she had any homework. Magda settled into her chair with bags of fabric to sort out the pattern for a new quilt.

Sitting on the floor in front of the television, Avery craned her head back to ogle the bundle of cloth squares in Magda's lap. "Those are really ugly, Grammy."

Magda grimaced at the garish fabric, which contained geometric shapes in every color of the rainbow, then shrugged. "The customer picked these. But I charged her a little more knowing this would give me a headache."

Avery giggled and turned her attention back to Bart Simpson telling someone yet again to eat his shorts.

A yelp came from the stairwell, followed by the shuffle of feet and a thud that rattled Magda's door. A sharp cry brought Magda to her feet, the bundle falling to the carpet.

"Vivian!" She tried to step forward, but the fabric caught around her ankles.

The door burst open, slamming against the wall. Avery

shrieked and scampered to Magda. Chloe ran from the kitchen and huddled behind her grandmother with Avery.

The impossible stood in Magda's doorway. Even in shadow, Magda knew who it was. A meaty hand with Roman numerals tattooed on each finger covered Vivian's mouth. Her face was ghostly white, and one arm imprisoned behind her back. Her free hand gripped the wrist of the man who held her. Curt drove Vivian forward into the bright light of Magda's living room.

"Hello again, Grandma." Curt snorted a laugh, glaring down his crooked nose at Magda. The smell of whiskey and cigarettes followed him into the room. He didn't appear as he had years ago, his good looks marred by bloated cheeks and sagging jowls, dark bags under bloodshot eyes, and many extra pounds.

"It's funny." He jerked his head to fling his greasy locks of blond hair back from his face. "I was at the club a few hours ago watching fake titties bounce and all of a sudden, *bam!* I just had to see my Viv." His voice—coarse and scratchy, no longer melodic bass—sounded as if he'd spent a good portion of the last seven years in smoke-filled clubs. He planted wet lips on Vivian's ear. She cringed as he traced his tongue along its ridge.

Magda's glare darkened. *Something must have happened to the witch bottle.*

"And don't you think for a minute I forgot about you." Curt lowered his inebriated gaze to Magda, mouth curving into a sneer. "I don't know what you did to me, old lady, but I remember everything. Now, anyway."

His eyes darted to the two redheads peeking out from either side of Magda. "Well, well, well. If it ain't my little bitches." Vivian thrust her body backward, pushing back on her tiptoes. He wrenched the arm he had pinned, and she bit back a scream.

Avery's hands made fists in Magda's skirt. Magda reached around and gave her arm a reassuring squeeze.

"You need to leave." Magda's voice was gravel, roughened by the growing power filling her chest. Her call to the book at the instant the door burst open had been silent and automatic.

The man snarled. “Oh, I’ll leave all right.” He shoved Vivian away from him, causing her to stumble. She recovered her feet and turned with an upraised arm, her fingers bent as claws, meaning to rake her short nails across his face. She met the back of his hand on the upswing. The blow sent her crashing against the wall and crumpling to the floor.

Avery screeched and launched herself at Curt. Magda caught her around the waist, grateful for the preternatural strength to hold the wildcat back. Avery kicked and swung her fists at the laughing man. Chloe ran to her mother, asking if she was all right in hushed words. Vivian unfolded, eyelids fluttering, and patted her daughter’s tear-streaked face.

As Curt took a step closer to Magda, she pivoted the struggling Avery to her side, further out of his reach.

“Wow. She may not look like me, but she sure as hell acts like it!” He threw his head back and guffawed at the ceiling. Then he lunged, pushing the old woman into the chair and snatching Avery. He stabbed a finger in the air at Magda as she rose, his expression black.

Vivian pulled herself upright, using the wall to steady herself. “Don’t you dare hurt her, Curt.”

He snorted. “And just what’s your scrawny little ass gonna do?” Curt squeezed Avery’s wrist hard enough to force a cry. Vivian threw herself at him. He cast Avery to the floor, taking hold of both Vivian’s arms, holding her out in front of him as she struggled to get free. His laughter held no mirth. With the roar of a lioness protecting her cubs, Vivian kicked him squarely in the groin.

Curt fell to his knees, clutching his privates, coughing obscenities at her.

Magda and Vivian grabbed the frightened girls and skirted around him, out into the hall.

“That’s our *dad*?” Avery shouted. “You said our dad was dead!”

“No, sweetie, no! That’s not your father.” Vivian pushed

both girls into their apartment. "He's just a nut job. I'll explain later. Lock this door. Do *not* come out. Do you hear me?"

As the last deadbolt clicked, Curt seized Vivian around the neck and waist, a pocketknife under her chin. Vivian froze, eyes locked on Magda.

Magda squared herself before him. "I will tell you this one last time, Curt Arthur Stiller." Her voice no longer matched her withered form. "Leave now, or you will never leave."

Curt stiffened, a momentary flicker of doubt passing across his face as he eyed the old woman's stature. Then his face was stone, and he tightened his grip around Vivian's slender waist. She dug her nails into his forearm; they had no effect.

Magda flexed her aged hands at her side, feeling the power of the book in every bone, every muscle. She gave a nearly imperceptible nod to the frightened woman. Vivian squeezed her eyes closed, then opened them.

Vivian slammed her elbow into Curt's gut and jerked free. He doubled over, the air expelling from his lungs, and dropped the knife. Vivian scrambled to snatch it up.

Magda charged and vaulted onto his back. She grabbed his chin and yanked, twisting it around in one fluid motion. His strangled grunt was replaced by the sickening snap of bone and the tearing of muscle.

With his chin between his shoulder blades, Curt's shocked face gawked at her with dead eyes.

His body collapsed onto the dingy white linoleum, setting Magda on her feet.

She inhaled deeply through her nose, glaring down at the heap with satisfaction. Magda grabbed his ankles and dragged the dead weight into her apartment. Vivian remained locked in place.

"Vivian!"

She bolted to the apartment yet stopped in the doorway.

"Close the door."

Magda went to her witch cabinet and unlocked it, pulling

out the gnarled gray book. "We must get rid of him." She hastily flipped through its pages, then stopped, her fingers running over the markings. She glanced at Vivian, whose eyes were wide and fixed on the dead man.

Vivian swallowed, wrapping her arms around herself. "No cops, then?"

"No police."

Magda muttered as she went over and over the same portion of the page.

"Magda, what are we doing?"

She slammed the book shut and marched to Curt's body. "Getting rid of the body. No one will miss him."

"Okay, wait." Vivian brought her shaking hands to her face. "Just hold on a minute." She pulled her fingers through her hair. "Let's call the police, Magda. This is clearly self-defense. Although how we'll explain that you snapped his neck is beyond me." Then tears sprang to her eyes and her chin quivered, the gravity of what happened settling in. "How are we going to explain this? This was murder!"

"Hush, now, hush." Magda rubbed her hands along Vivian's arms as the trembling woman stared at the body. Tears flowed silently down her cheeks. "Do not cry for him."

"I'm not crying *for* him, exactly." Vivian sniffed and wiped her cheeks with both hands. "I don't know why I'm crying. Shock, maybe. Probably. This is just too much!"

"Listen to me." Magda gripped her shoulders. "If we call the police, you will have to tell them who this man is. The girls will find out."

She blanched. "No. They can't know I lied to them. That this"—she flicked her hand at the floor—"is their father. No."

Magda patted her arm, watching the warring emotions pass across Vivian's face: the frightened young woman, the experienced nurse, the protective mother. Vivian finally nodded, lifting her chest, and shook her hands out as if to rid them of an unpleasant feeling.

"What's your plan?" she asked.

"Stand back." Magda motioned for Vivian to retreat to the kitchen. She knelt beside the body.

"Kyh ix ezus adruk ix'r zeda."

Vivian cried out as green flames erupted from Magda's bony fingers.

"Ezus yeh adruk suka."

She laid her fiery hands onto Curt's back, and the flames leapt from them. The fire quickly traveled the length of the body, growing into thick black flames tinged with luminescent green, like the facets of an emerald held before a candle. It clung to the man's body, not venturing beyond its commanded deed, consuming clothing and flesh and bone.

Within a few breaths, nothing remained of Curt Stiller but a pile of ash.

Magda pushed the wispy gray hairs loosed from her bun away from her face. She rose, then opened the door. "See to the girls. I'll clean this up."

Vivian nodded dumbly, then snapped her jaw closed. She skirted around the long mound as she scurried away.

A minute later, Magda's ancient vacuum roared to life.

Vivian came through the door as the aftereffects of the magick seized Magda's spine. Vivian rushed to her, pulling Magda from the floor and helping her into the chair. With a tremulous hand, Magda fumbled the side table drawer open, retrieving the leather strap, and slipped it into her mouth.

"Is this a seizure? You're having a seizure?" Vivian was calm, and she laid her hands atop Magda's fingers, which were embedded in the armrests. Magda could only nod. She didn't want Vivian to see this. How was she going to explain it? She squeezed her eyes closed, bearing the convulsions as they came, trying to keep the pain from her face.

In the voice of a trained nurse, Vivian instructed her to relax, not to fight. Lightly rubbing Magda's forearms, she urged her to slow her breathing.

Finally her body eased and the pain subsided. Magda opened her eyes, relieved at not seeing the twins. Vivian knelt in front of her with concern in her eyes and a vibrant handprint across the left side of her face.

Magda removed the strap from her mouth and wiped the spittle from it and her lips with a tissue. Vivian took the strap, examining it.

"You've had to use this a lot, I see. And for some time." She regarded Magda. "Why have you never told me? Are you talking any medication?"

To lie about taking medication to a nurse would be foolish. "No. They are manageable." Magda filled her lungs through her nose and held the air for several seconds, releasing it slowly, the fog of her mind going with it.

"You call this manageable?"

"Yes." She nodded. "And they are not as often as you may think."

Vivian presented the leather strap.

"I have a strong jaw."

Vivian pursed her lips. "You need to see a doctor about this. Seriously."

Magda waved her words away. "Where are the girls? What did you tell them?"

Vivian groaned and sat back on her feet. "I told them we threatened to call the police and he left." She put a palm to her forehead. "I told them he was a former patient from when I did a short stint in a psych ward. That he fixated on me. It helped that they look nothing like him."

"That is good." Magda laid her head back against the chair. "Would you please make me a cup of tea, dear?"

"After I do, you're going to explain all that." Vivian's expression conveyed she didn't intend to take 'no' for an answer.

The request for tea gave Magda time to think of what to say. She closed her eyes with a long sigh.

It seemed only seconds later when Vivian touched her shoulder. Magda's hands were steady as she took the delicate teacup. She savored the warmth in her palms, blowing across the top before taking several sips. Vivian sat before her on the floor, studying Magda with stern expectation.

After the fifth sip, Magda set the cup in the saucer on her lap. "The witch bottle is broken, yes?"

"Avery confessed to knocking it off the mantel while she was vacuuming. She said she'd put everything back in it, but I checked. The glass is cracked, and half the black sand is gone." She snorted. "I guess that thing really did work."

"Black *salt*," Magda said. "Combined and sealed, those items kept him away. Once fractured, the spell was broken." She took another sip, aligning her thoughts before continuing.

"You told me back then you weren't a witch. Care to revise that statement?"

"No. I am still no witch. A witch must have magick inside her." Magda could see the annoyance grow on Vivian's face. "I can… access magick. Pull it, so to speak, when in dire need."

"Pull it from where?"

"Who knows where magick comes from? I learned this long ago. I do not use it much. Only if I can see no other way."

The nurse studied her for another moment. "What are these seizures about?"

"That is the price I pay for using magick that is not mine."

Vivian pushed herself up from the floor. She turned, seeing the slight dent in the wall where she'd hit. Her fingertips went to the angry red mark on her cheek, and she winced.

"Do the girls know?" Vivian turned back to Magda.

"No. I would've kept you from knowing as well, but—" She gestured at the floor where Curt's body had been. Neat lines in the aged carpet reflected Magda's recent vacuuming.

"I can't believe you killed him like that," Vivian said in a long exhale. Her eyes grew bulbous once more. The old woman held her gaze without expression. Vivian shook her head. "This is probably the shock talking but… you were like… like a *ninja*. A little old lady ninja!" A snort of laughter shot out, and she covered her mouth. "I'm never going to get that image out of my head."

He derived great pleasure each time the old woman used his power, especially with such ferocity.

In the years since he had touched her mind, he made his power readily available, prodding her to use him at the slightest provocation. She had not always accepted, but when she had, the sensations he experienced were exhilarating.

He would savor the killing of the man for some time to come.

The use of demonfire burned away the remains of the potion in the old woman; its magick was potent but not permanent. In a matter of days, her age fell upon her, and she prepared another potion without his prompting.

His concern heightened after the old woman's body was renewed. The minute essence of Straka lingering within her grew stronger. Her dreams continued to bear the man's image, revealing glimpses of the past he had kept hidden from her.

How was Straka achieving this? He could not reach out from the afterlife; he had no power in his current state, nor could the monster assist him. It had no outlet from the Voll without Straka. The souls shackled to him could not yet be harnessed; the spell was incomplete.

This question continued to plague him as time passed.

Yet human lives were fleeting, and soon the child would be ready. Then he would have no further need of the old woman.

CHAPTER 13

February 2005

"GRANNY!" CAME A CALL FROM THE STAIRWELL. "GRAMMY!" Two pairs of feet slapped the steps as they raced up.

The twins burst through the door. Chloe's bright face beamed, freckled cheeks splotched with exertion. Avery pushed through beside her sister, making sure she was the first one in the room. Chloe ignored her sister's triumphant dance.

"Granny!" Chloe greeted Magda with an outstretched arm, waving a paper in her hand.

"My apartment is not so big!" Magda said, hugging both girls, who held her tightly around the shoulders. At the age of twelve, the twins already stood eye level with her. "This building is not so big."

Chloe pulled away. "I got an A!" She brandished the paper before her.

"Of course you did, *beruško*. Did you expect anything less?"

Chloe hugged her again.

"And what did my other ladybug get?" Magda turned to the girl falling into the armchair.

Dressed in a well-worn T-shirt and baggy shorts, Avery set herself apart from her sister, in her neat blouse and skirt. She yanked the hairband from her ponytail and rubbed her fingers against her scalp with irritation. "B *minus*."

"But that's awesome, you know," Chloe said. "Especially for a subject you hate."

"She's right." Magda detached herself from Chloe and moved to the side of the chair, running her fingernails through Avery's silky straight hair. Avery closed her eyes, savoring her grandmother's nails gently raking through the slight tangles in her hair.

"I hate every subject," Avery said, giving her Grammy a grin. "I'd rather be on the soccer field or at the batting cages. Anything besides sitting *aaaall* day in a classroom."

Magda laughed. "My scholar and my athlete." She turned, heading back to the kitchen. "Your mom has to take another shift tonight—someone called in sick."

"Sleepover!" the two girls cried out in unison.

"Go get your things."

They darted out the door, Avery challenging her sister to see who was fastest.

Upon their return, Avery dumped her blankets and pillows on the floor while Chloe set hers neatly on the sofa, arguing about who got to have television time first.

"Me. I'm almost three minutes older than you, so—" Avery sniffed the air. "Grammy, that smells *so* good." She followed her nose to the kitchen. "What are you making?"

"Český guláš."

"Ew." Avery's face scrunched. "That sounds gross."

"It's not gross." Chloe came up behind her sister, resting her chin on Avery's shoulder. "That's Czech goulash."

"Very good, Chloe." Magda inclined her head to the girl. *"Děkuji."*

Avery shrugged her sister from her shoulder. "Show-off."

"Go, shoo. Do your homework and let me finish this." Magda waved them both from the tiny kitchen. She turned back to the old cast iron pot, slowly stirring the thick, reddish-brown soup with a wooden spoon, inhaling the mouth-watering aromas of paprika and garlic. She ignored a surprised cry from Avery. The two girls sparred constantly. She didn't have to pester Avery about getting her homework done; Chloe would see to that.

Yet now, Magda's instinct flared a doubt. She leaned back, giving her a view of the short hallway. Avery stood, rigid, facing Magda's witch cabinet, something the girls had ignored since Magda told them long ago to leave it be. It looked like nothing special to them anyway. Just an old cabinet and hutch painted decades before they were born. The expression on Avery's face brought Magda to stand beside her.

"What is it, Avery?" Magda's voice was low, but it was too late—Chloe had heard.

"What's in there, Grammy?" Avery continued to stare at it.

"If I wanted you to know, I'd keep it open."

Chloe touched Avery's arm, concern pulling at her eyebrows. "What's wrong, Avery? What is it?"

"It's a book," Avery said with certainty. "A book of blood and skin."

Magda sucked in a breath. *A book of blood and skin.*

She tried to keep her voice calm. "How do you know it's a book?"

Avery took a step and laid her palm on the upper cabinet door. Behind the door, in that exact spot, the gray book rested on its shelf.

"It said my name."

Magda's knees weakened, and she leaned against the door-frame, working hard to keep her face placid. *What is happening?*

"Avery, you're scaring me." Chloe put her hands on her sister, trying to pull her away from the cabinet, but Avery didn't move. She turned her frightened eyes to Magda. "Granny?"

Magda clenched her fingers behind her back. "Tell me."

"When I walked by, something said my name." Avery slid her palm across the door. "It's warm." She slid her hand back to the other side of the cabinet. "The other books are cold."

Chills raced up Magda's arms. *What could this mean? Is there magick in Avery?* Both Magda and Vivian were already concerned Avery's quick temper would eventually go beyond childish schoolyard spats. Having magick in her blood could lend fuel to the fire.

Something else sparked a flicker of fear in her gut. *The book can speak?*

"Chloe, did you hear anything?" Magda asked. They were twins after all.

Chloe shook her head adamantly, still holding on to her sister.

"Do you feel anything?" Magda nodded her head toward the cabinet. Chloe's eyes widened again, but she continued to shake her head.

Avery dropped her hand, seeming to return to herself. "Go on. Don't be a baby."

A momentary look of hurt passed across Chloe's face.

Chloe took a deep breath, puffing out her chest. Despite the determined face, her hand trembled as she placed it on the spot where Avery's had been. Her nostrils flared. She moved her hand tentatively to the right, then back. She pulled her hand away and rubbed the palm with the fingers of her other hand. "It *is* warm, Granny. How can a book be warm?"

Magda gave the twins a flat smile. "Okay, girls, let's sit down." She pointed to the living room, gently pushing Avery, who appeared drained, in the direction of the sofa. Magda needed a minute. She returned to the kitchen, pulled the spoon from the goulash, and tapped it on the side of the pot. *What do I tell them? How much do I say? Should I tell Vivian?* Her breath caught. *A book of blood and skin.*

She'd suspected the words scrawled in a dark rust color were written in blood. But skin? No, it couldn't be. It was the wrong texture and color for animal, or even human, skin. What else was there? And how could it *speak* to Avery?

"Grammy?" Avery called from the living room.

The interruption startled Magda. She let out the breath she'd been holding. "One moment, *berušky*. Just setting this on low." She turned down the burner and wiped her sweaty palms on her apron. Magda took another deep breath, trying to push the anxiety from her face.

She greeted the girls in the living room with a full smile. They sat cross-legged on the floor before her chair. Both twins stared at her eagerly as if she was about to tell them the biggest secret of their young lives. Which she was.

Magda's heart thumped, but she revealed nothing on her face. These girls had become her grandchildren. What could she say to her *berušky*, her ladybugs? The world of magick could be so dark.

She repositioned the lumbar pillow, collecting her thoughts, and settled into the armchair. "It appears you two have magick in your blood."

Avery let out a derisive snort as big eyes blossomed on Chloe. "Seriously, Grammy. Magick? You mean like the Harry Potter wand-waving stuff?"

"No, I do not." Magda met Avery's sarcasm with pinched lips. "I mean the natural, earth magick some people are gifted with."

"What does that actually mean, Granny?" Chloe locked her hands together in her lap, knees bouncing.

Avery rolled her eyes. "You're so gullible. Grammy's just messing with us. There's no such thing as magick." She folded her arms across her chest.

"Do you have another explanation for what you heard, Avery, or felt?" Magda's question was received with a dropping jaw that snapped shut when Avery couldn't think of a retort. Magda let her grandmotherly admonishment melt into a warm smile.

"That means, Chloe, you are different, special. That means you can do things and sense things other people, including me, cannot."

"Like what things?" A hint of sparkle showed now in Chloe's big eyes.

"Like talking books. Shut up." Avery pushed her shoulder into her sister, then mumbled an apology at Magda's *tsk*.

"That book is nothing, it doesn't matter." Magda dismissed the topic with a flick of one hand and scooted forward in the chair, doing her best to convey true excitement. "What does matter is that you two can do magick!"

Her delight was as infectious as she'd hoped. The girls giggled and pressed their shoulders together. "Magick is different for every person. Some can cast wondrous spells, others can move objects with only their minds, or speak to animals—"

"Animals!" Chloe jumped up. "I want to talk to animals!"

Avery joined her. "Me too!"

Perfect.

The girls came to lean against either side of Magda. "Can you teach us to talk to animals?" Chloe asked.

"I cannot." Magda continued to smile as their faces fell. "But there are many books that can." She hugged both around the waist, jostling each as they giggled.

Realization washed over Avery's face and she expelled an exaggerated sigh. "Books?"

"Ha!" Chloe poked a finger at her sister's chest. "Books!"

Avery scowled, then turned to Magda. "Why can't *you* teach us, Grammy?"

Magda indicated for them to sit again, and they did so dutifully, settling in with their knees to their chests and arms wrapped around their knees, staring up at her with glowing faces.

"Unlike you two, I have no magick in my blood." Magda held up a hand to stave off the question on Chloe's open mouth. "Yes, I can do some magick. I can make potions and teas, use stones and runes, but I'm merely using the magick those items innately have. I cannot make things move, or talk to animals, or cast spells requiring the magick to be *within* me. But you two can."

The girls remained quiet. The excitement on their faces morphed into awe as they waited for their grandmother to continue. Magda chose her words, her half truths, carefully. She must sustain their excitement with animals to keep them within the realm of innocent magick. They would be safe there.

"That is why you must learn from books. I have read a great deal and can guide you and explain things." She ignored Avery's pained expression. "There are several bookstores that have everything you'll need to learn the basics of magick and to communicate with animals." Her face lit up with these words, and the girls began to titter with excitement. "This weekend, we'll visit them." She held her hands out, and the girls leapt into their grandmother's arms.

Magda hid the dread growing at this new discovery. Not so much that the girls were magickal, but what the book had done to bring about this revelation. It *spoke*. Why only to Avery? What made her say it was a book of blood and skin?

While the girls fought for sink time in the bathroom, Magda removed the book from the hutch. She must hide it now. Avery's curious nature couldn't be trusted, locked cabinet or no.

Magda tiptoed through the kitchen toward her bedroom, the book clutched to her breast.

"Oh my god, Chloe, you take forever to brush your tee—"

Magda halted and turned her head toward the bathroom, hoping the door didn't open.

"Avery? What is it?" Chloe's mouth sounded very full of toothpaste.

Did Avery sense the book again? Had the book called out to her once more?

"Girls, hurry up and get to bed," she called out in her most grandmotherly tone.

It took the sisters a long time to fall asleep, huddled together in their pillow-and-blanket tent in the living room. They might be burgeoning teenagers, but they still loved to make blanket forts in their grandmother's living room. Magda didn't scold them as she normally would on a school night. She'd told them a wondrous thing, and she wasn't going to object to their girlish chittering and excitement. She lay in bed, listening intently to their whispers, waiting for mention of the book. It was well past midnight when they fell quiet. Magda heard nothing to cause concern in their whispers, and no mention of the book.

Hopefully the sheer joy of communicating with animals would keep their minds from the book. However, it might call to Avery again regardless of where it was hidden.

Magda slid from the bed as gently as she could, attempting to minimize the chorus of squeaking mattress springs. She retrieved the thick tome from the dresser drawer. She felt no warmth from it as the girls had. It was as cold and hard under her fingertips as it had always been. It was all she'd ever known of magick until she came to this country. Here she had found secluded bookshops with secret rooms filled with an astonishing array of different forms of witchcraft. She'd read every volume she could find, relieved at being able to work magick without sacrificing, cursing, or human or animal blood. Magda had only known dark spell-work from the book, yet it had saved her and protected her, so some good lay within it. *It is your intent that matters*, she reminded herself.

After all the years in her possession, she'd heard nothing from it. Magda pushed away the twinge of jealousy. There was no magick in her blood, yet she'd used its power with ease. She didn't need it to speak to her.

Besides, the book didn't belong to her. It belonged to Josef.

What? The dream plaguing Magda came to the forefront;

with it came renewed feelings of guilt and shame. *That was his name, Josef.*

Most of the time, she successfully kept the recollections it forced upon her away. But slowly, over the years, they seemed to grow more… insistent. The part of her battling against the dream—what it was trying to tell her, to show her—was weakening.

I started something for him, for Josef. What was it?

She blinked rapidly as snatches of images raced behind her eyes, too fast for Magda to grasp more than a bit of their meaning.

I made a promise.

Magda put a hand to her forehead, reeling from the wave of emotions, the flood of memories.

"Enough." She straightened, filling her lungs with air. There was no promise. If anything, this was probably the onset of senility. Yes, the book had once been his, but he'd given it to her. And he was long dead, the past with him.

She met her reflection in the dresser mirror. "The book belongs to *you*."

Yet it had called out to Avery. For what purpose? *It said my name.* Her granddaughter's words echoed.

Magda was no fool. The book's power was only beneficial because she used it to be so; it was filled with horrendous things Avery should never learn.

Setting the book on the bed, she extracted her ribbon box from underneath and rummaged through the slips of bright colors until she found what she sought. She dug out the many boxes and bags filling the space and set a tattered old quilt of mostly black hues to the side. Magda stood, taking several deep breaths, banishing her negative thoughts and the pressing notion that she shouldn't do this.

She tied a black satin ribbon around the book crossways.

"You will not speak to my granddaughter, Avery Abigail Parsons, again," Magda said with as much force as she could in whispered words. She tied another ribbon lengthwise and repeated the words.

She wrapped the book in the old quilt and shoved it deep under her bed, filling in around it with what she'd pulled out.

Avery lay awake long after Chloe had fallen asleep. She rubbed the palm of her right hand with her left, remembering the tingling sensation when she'd placed it on the cabinet door. At the moment it happened, she hadn't been afraid. Even the pressure in the air keeping her from walking away hadn't scared her. It was crazy awesome!

But now that Chloe was asleep and Avery's mind wasn't filled with her gabbing, she broke into a cold sweat. She hated that feeling and balled her fists, trying to build up enough anger to push the fear away.

Avery Parsons, the voice had said. Nothing more, except later in the bathroom, something *touched* the edge of her mind. Or at least that's what it felt like. The memory of that strange, deep voice hissing her name made the hairs on her neck rise, despite her clenched fists. She shivered and pulled the covers over her head. Avery couldn't see the cabinet, her view blocked by a sofa cushion and a pink blanket, but it was there. And in the cabinet was a book that said her name.

Bind me if you will, old woman, but I will have the child.

The girl had matured enough for her mind not to cast him off as fantasy; she was on the cusp of adulthood. Her demeanor was ideal: rebellious, insecure, jealous. She may prove a better vessel than Straka could have ever been.

His hopes soared at the brief taste of her energy. The untapped power slumbering within her was strong, ready, yet held within the confines of youthful ignorance. Her sister had power, yes, but it was not the same.

There was time. If he had learned nothing else from the eons trapped in the Voll, writhing inside his tormentor, he had learned patience. It no longer galled him to have no choice but to wait.

What did gall him were the bindings placed onto him by the crone. He could still see the girl through the old woman, but he could no longer sense her energy, no longer touch to her. As a consolation, he kept the memory of her on the surface and savored it.

He would have been able to block the woman from binding him, but for Straka's interference. His influence was getting stronger. This development was troubling, and detrimental to his plan. The cause of this phenomenon remained elusive despite his attention.

CHAPTER 14

March 2005

"Did you get through the rest of those chapters last night, Avery?" Magda asked as she scrambled eggs for the girls. Avery grumbled a 'yes.' Magda stepped away from the stove to peer into the living room.

"By 'those chapters' you mean reading my notes, then yes," Chloe said, pulling her kitten-covered spiral notebook out of her backpack and settling into Magda's chair.

"Why should I read *all* those boring words when you take *such* good notes?" Avery gave her sister doe-eyes, batting her lashes. Chloe snorted and lifted the open notebook before her face to block the view of her sister.

"Are we ready?" Avery turned to Magda, rubbing her palms together. "I'm done slogging through books. It's been a month! I'm ready to try something."

"Breakfast first."

Avery's stomach squelched her half-second protest, and she trotted to the kitchen table with Chloe on her heels.

"You should test us on the basics, Granny," Chloe said as she sat, looking pointedly at her twin. "You know, like the meaning of the pentagram, how to ground yourself, stuff like that."

Avery's middle knuckle rose, readying to make contact with Chloe's upper arm, but fell at her grandmother's pinched lips.

"I think trying out your first spell will be test enough." Magda placed heaping plates in front of each girl, hiding her smirk at Avery's pained expression. "Your mom doesn't get off work until four, so there's plenty of time."

Both girls gobbled their breakfast as Magda sat quietly, sipping her tea, regarding them with grandmotherly admiration. She had told Vivian nothing of their abilities, leaving it up to them to tell their mother if they wished. Magda had expected Chloe to tell Vivian everything the very next day, but she hadn't —an outcome Magda attributed to a little bullying from Avery. Truth be told, Magda was relieved; Vivian's only experience with magick had been that horrible night with Curt, seeing his body consumed in demonfire, and Magda's "seizure" afterward. She'd not relished telling Vivian her daughters were part of that world. But it comforted Magda to know the girls were on a different path. They'd never need to know of the darker side to magick.

Thoughts of the tall man in silhouette crept in with the thoughts of dark magick. Each time she tried to recall his face, his image became a convulsing mass, as if attempting to come into focus but unable to. Magda wondered if deep down she was suppressing the memories on purpose. Perhaps her subconscious had buried some trauma or terrible event that included him. Or she'd broken her word—

"Granny?" Chloe's cool fingertips on her arm pulled Magda from her unpleasant daydream. "Are you okay? Your face is red."

Avery stood beside her, an arm across her shoulders. "And you're really hot."

Magda smiled, waving away their concern. "Oh, I'm fine, *berušky*. I just forgot to eat breakfast."

It was a bright, crisp Sunday morning, a perfect day to be

outside. Although it wasn't technically spring yet, the recent warm weather had coaxed blossoms from the trees and green shoots from the ground. Arnold Arboretum was the perfect place for their special day. It was far bigger than the local parks, so they would have privacy, and it teemed with wildlife.

Chloe didn't like the T. It smelled of things she didn't want to think about and was full of crowds passing germs she didn't want to know about. Magda agreed with her sentiments, usually opting for the bus, but the subway was more direct. Avery made a game out of how many people she could stab with her elbows when they invaded her personal space.

At just after ten, the arboretum was lively with families and older couples eager to take in the unexpected early spring weather. With Magda leading the way, looking surreptitiously around her, the trio broke from the official path and wandered into the depths of the dense trees.

Magda had never been much of a nature lover—too many bugs and not enough places to sit comfortably—but she loved this area of the arboretum dubbed the Conifer Collection. The aromas of pine, spruce, and cedar mingled to create an earthy, pungent perfume that lifted her spirits. She stepped, sure-footed and pain-free, over roots and scrub, still amazed at the lasting effects of the potion. It had been almost five years since she'd last taken it. Yet some nights continued to be plagued with the same dream of Josef Straka. Magda now dismissed them outright, the ramblings of an aging mind. It was a shame the potion wasn't keeping her brain as healthy as her body.

Once they were out of sight of the path, Magda held up a hand. "Now, girls, be quiet as you walk and listen to what is around you."

Chloe nodded solemnly, and Avery pinched her lips with her fingers, pretending to twist them shut.

They picked their way through part of the woods that had been allowed to grow wild. Magda shivered now she was out of the warm sunlight. Tiny patches of snow fought against the oncoming spring, hiding in the crooks of tree roots that never saw the light of day.

Magda spotted the pink ribbon marker she'd placed on a sapling last week during her scouting trip and veered left, searching for its twin. The area she found was a small oval clearing, free of most of the underbrush covering the forest floor.

She gestured the girls forward and opened her collapsible red canvas chair, falling into the low-slung seat with a grunt. Its four legs sank slightly into the damp ground. Good knees or not, the girls would have to pull her out of it.

"So, what are we doing today?" Magda directed the question to Avery as Chloe spread out a blanket for them to sit on.

Avery's eyes bulged, then darted to Chloe. Chloe crossed her arms, waiting for her sister to answer.

"Uh, something with animals."

Magda's eyes narrowed.

"Something with friendly animals."

Her grandmother sighed and turned to Chloe.

"We're going to, um, put our energy out there and see what animals are open to us." Chloe's expression changed from questioning to certain, then she nodded to confirm her response.

"Very good." She indicated for the pair to sit. "Avery, what is a familiar?"

Her mouth popped open and she turned once more to Chloe, who busied herself with smoothing out the blanket before sitting. "It's, uh, an animal who likes you?"

Magda leaned forward. "Did you read *any* of the *Witchcraft for Beginners*?"

"I did!"

"Which part?"

"There was a section about dragons…"

Magda didn't conceal her annoyance. Avery sank to her knees onto the blanket.

"Chloe?"

"A familiar is a witch's companion. The word 'familiar' comes from the Latin *famulus*, meaning attendant." Chloe ignored her sister's snort.

"And why does a witch need a familiar?"

"It can help her, like, boost her spells, even guard and protect her. And sometimes, she can borrow its magick. She could see through its eyes or use whatever traits that animal has."

"Ooo, that sounds cool." Avery stared, rapt, at her sister. Magda pursed her lips at Avery and shook her head.

"Is there more?" Magda asked of Chloe.

"So much!" Chloe's face lit up and she wriggled forward. "There's several types of familiars. The two we've been reading about are physical and astral."

"I didn't understand that astral stuff." Avery scooted around to face her sister.

"It's like, maybe a deceased pet or a mythical creature. A unicorn, maybe—"

"Dragon," Avery said with enthusiasm.

"Okay, dragon. A dragon could be your astral familiar—you could buy a figurine or something if you need a physical object to focus on. You could call on the dragon's strength when you need it or have the figurine with you when you do magick so it can lend its power to yours." Chloe sought confirmation from Magda, who nodded with a small smile.

"That would be really cool if dragons were real," Avery said. "How can you borrow magick from something that isn't real? Now, *snakes* are real." A grin crawled across her lips. "I hope my familiar is a snake."

Chloe shuddered.

"But today"—Magda raised her voice to get their attention—"you're going to see if any physical creature is open to you. Chloe, you go first."

She jumped up, smoothing her pants and tugging at the sleeves of her light pink sweater. She walked to the middle of the clearing and selected a long twig from the ground. Chloe turned in place, using the branch to mark a circle around her, but clumps of grass and weeds made it difficult.

"It doesn't have to be perfect," Magda said in response to Chloe's frown. "Just imagine a full circle, rising around you in a sphere of protective white light, and that is enough."

Chloe closed her eyes, lifting her arms slightly away from her body. She took several deep breaths, exhaling through her nostrils. She peeked out of one eye at Avery, then turned her back to them, rubbing her palms on her pants.

She knelt. With her finger, Chloe drew a sigil in a small patch of soft earth. Avery leaned forward to see, then a hand on her shoulder stopped her from moving closer to get a better look. She caught sight of her grandmother's twisted mouth and settled back onto her feet.

Chloe raised her arms, palms open, on either side of the sigil. A breeze wafted through the clearing, lifting strands of her unbound hair, tickling her neck. She shivered, a little giggle escaping her lips. She turned her face to the trees.

What animal is for me?
Let it be, let me see.
Sacred animal roaming free,
come to me, come to me.

Avery sniggered. The back of Magda's hand smacked Avery lightly on the shoulder. Avery huffed, crossing her arms tight.

Movement in the trees grabbed the trio's attention. Magda smiled proudly at the sight of a squirrel in an old spruce directly in front of Chloe. It scampered down the trunk, its tiny claws crackling along the bark, and stopped halfway, flicking its tail rapidly and eyeing the young girl on the ground.

What animal is for me?
Let it be, let me see.
Are you hiding right before my sight?

My sacred familiar, walk into the light.

It ran around the trunk and came to a stop once more, chittering this time. It moved toward the ground in short spurts filled with chatter, eyes still locked on the girl.

Chloe covered her squeal with both hands.

"Holy crap! You did it!"

The burst of sound sent the little creature scurrying away, leaving a rash of angry barks in its wake.

"Avery!" Chloe threw her arms up.

Avery put on an innocent face and mimicked her sister's arm gesture. "What?"

Chloe stomped back to her place and plopped onto the blanket.

"*Your* turn." Chloe tried on the smug expression Avery wore so often. Avery rose, curling her lip at Chloe.

"Enough," Magda said. "The bad energy between you two will only keep the animals away. Or draw something you don't want. Deep breaths. Push out the negative energy. Fill your body with light."

Chloe did as her grandmother bid, and Avery nodded, turning away with an eye roll.

Avery stood where Chloe had, hands on hips, examining the mark she'd made on the ground and the traces of the circle in the grass. She turned to her sister. "What were those things you were saying?"

"That was an incantation I made up. You can't have it." Chloe screwed up her face into a frown and sat straighter, keeping eye contact with Avery.

Avery turned back and shrugged at the forest. "Here's goes nothing," she mumbled. She shook out her hands, and after several long exhales, her shoulders relaxed. She mimicked Chloe's stance, raising her arms out with palms up.

After no more than a minute, Avery turned to face the

others. "This was stupid, Grammy. Standing here, expecting some animal to stop by and say 'hi.'"

Magda pinched the bridge of her nose. Avery, poised to stomp out of the clearing, flinched when the flapping of wings startled her. She looked up as the other two turned around.

A large hawk sat on a high branch of a tree still trapped in winter's embrace. The bird stared at Avery, its sharp, reddish-brown eyes locked on the girl. Its chest was a brilliant white, stark against the dark band of brown across its belly and the glossy deep auburn feathers on its head and wings. It flexed its talons on the dry wood; the sound gave Magda chills.

Avery opened her mouth to speak as it launched from the branch. She screamed and fell to the ground, covering her head with her arms. The hawk let out a piercing *kree-eee-ar*, circling around to dive once more at the cowering girl. Magda sprang from the chair, much to her surprise, casting her arms high and shouting at the bird. It soared upward, screeching angrily as it did.

Avery uncurled, releasing her head. "Oh my god! What just happened?"

"You tell me," Magda said.

"What are you looking at me like that for? I didn't do anything!" Avery threw up her hands and stomped from the circle, giving her grandmother a wide berth. She continued to the tree line.

"Stop." Magda's tone made Avery halt, but she didn't turn.

Magda swallowed her irritation. "There is something you must understand, my Avery." The softness in her voice made Avery face her. The girl stared at Magda's knees. "Magick is not something you can play at untrained. You cannot 'wing it,' as they say. You must work at it and focus, or"—she pointed in the direction the hawk had flown—"there will be consequences. Ones you will not like." She walked to Avery and took her hands. Avery kept her eyes at their joined fingers. "You risk those around you… and yourself."

Grammy wasn't being fair. It wasn't her fault the hawk dive-bombed her. She'd just done what she'd been told to do.

Magick was too hard. And nothing made sense. Earth, air, fire, and water having magickal powers, seriously? That some imaginary white light would protect her, or a mixture of herbs and oils could bring her good fortune. It was all bull. While she'd felt something in the circle, a light tingling on her skin, that hadn't been magick, that was *wind*.

Except a book had said her name. A book! Its voice was still as clear and sharp as if it had happened earlier in the day rather than a month ago. But Avery convinced herself it had been her imagination, that was all. Besides, she didn't feel anything now when she put her palm to the cabinet door. And she'd stood in front of it several times when her grandmother and sister weren't around, waiting for it to say something. She'd even knocked on the cabinet door once. When she caught herself saying, "Hello? Is there anyone there?" she mentally kicked herself in the butt for being as gullible as Chloe.

CHAPTER 15

June 2005

Magda set her quilting aside as the front door opened. With a bright face, she greeted Chloe, who returned the welcome with downcast gloom. Chloe let her backpack fall to the floor and slumped onto the sofa.

"What's wrong, *beruško*?"

"Avery's in detention." Chloe sighed. "Again."

Magda groaned. "Fighting?"

"Yep."

"Birds?"

"Everywhere."

Chloe recounted the latest episode of Avery's temper. Hugh Hartley, the big boy living a few buildings down, had picked another fight with Avery. He was the neighborhood bully. Taller and much wider than most everyone his age, he seemed to make it his daily mission to see how many kids he could make cry. Recently, he'd begun singling out Avery.

He'd laughed at her new boyish haircut and baggy cargo pants. Hartley taunted her with derogatory names like 'lez-bo' and 'muff diver,' and Avery's face turned scarlet. When Chloe asked what those meant, Magda lied, saying she didn't know.

Avery had warned him last week to leave her alone or else. When he came at her today, she made good on her threat, punching him in the gut with all her might. They were in detention now, and the principal had called both parents.

"He got what was coming to him, that's for sure." Chloe glared at the wall opposite her as if it held the boy's face. "Fat pig. He's always messing with her. Maybe this time he got the message."

"I hope so. Not for his sake, but for Avery's."

The girl's emotions had begun to run amok with the start of her period two months ago. She had been so upset, yelling that she didn't want to grow up, didn't want to 'become a woman.' She'd complained bitterly about how horrible she felt and that so much blood couldn't possibly be normal. Even after her mother's assurances, Avery sulked and whined. Chloe tried to console her by admitting she hadn't gotten her period yet, so Avery had beaten her again. It helped a little, but only for a moment.

"And the birds were all over the place. Hanging out of the ledges and tops of buildings. It was spooky. No squawks, no chirping. Just staring." Chloe's eyes widened as she recalled the scene.

Since the girls' first attempt to call out for a familiar in March, birds gathered around Avery whenever she was angry. Magda had witnessed the chilling phenomenon twice. Dozens of birds, mostly pigeons and crows, roosted around Avery, watching her. When her temper eased, they quietly flew away. When Magda questioned her about it, Avery shrugged and turned away.

"I wish she'd start studying again." Magda sighed.

"No chance." Chloe shook her head. "It was too much work, too much *reading*, and you know how she feels about that. I even offered her my notes. Nothing. But speaking of familiars"—she perked up, covering her huge grin with her fingertips—"I have one now." Chloe gestured to the window behind Magda.

Sitting on the sill was the fattest orange cat Magda had ever seen.

"Oh!" Magda rose and crossed to the window. The cat rubbed its body against the glass.

She opened the old window, allowing the big cat to hop inside. It landed on the floor with a thud and sauntered over to Chloe.

Magda's eyes glittered with awe. The cat sat on Chloe's lap, leaning into her fingers as she scratched its jowl.

"I've named him Garfield."

Magda laughed, closing the window. "Fitting." She returned to her chair and leaned forward, extending a hand for Garfield to sniff. Her eyes turned to Chloe. "Tell me."

Excitement bubbled out of her. "Well, two nights ago, while Avery was showering, I sat on the fire escape and said the little incantation, opening myself up for whatever was going to come. Like you said, I let my energy flow." She grinned sheepishly. "And it worked!"

Garfield's purr was thunderous. He wasn't the typical stray—too fat and well-groomed, although he had no collar. Magda wondered where he lived and if anyone could be missing him. But he came, that was his choice, and he would go back if he wished.

"I'm so proud of you, *beruško*."

Chloe's expression turned melancholy as she stroked the cat's arched back. "Mom says I can't keep him. Avery claims she's allergic, but I know a fake sneeze when I hear it. When she saw him in my lap, she looked upset for a second. Then she started sneezing and coughing." She rolled her eyes. "And the rest of the night, she wouldn't talk to me."

Magda had hoped Avery would grow out of her jealousy toward her sister as she got older and began to find her own strengths. While she excelled at sports, something Chloe failed at miserably, it wasn't enough.

"Why is she like that, Granny?"

Magda plucked at the hem of her blouse. "I never had a sister, so I can't say for certain. You two are so different despite your looks, and as you get older, your talents will show themselves. My guess is that she sees you are better at working magick, and she might resent it."

"She'd be just as good if she'd just try," Chloe said. "Birds are her thing, I'm sure. But she won't listen to me when I say that."

"Then just let her be. She is going through a phase. And you might go through one also. Besides, your mother is right, you can't keep him. He's obviously someone's pet. Looks to me like he's not missed a meal since he was born." She scratched the cat under his chin. "Someone will be missing this one. But he's welcome to come here anytime he likes."

"Oh, thank you, Granny!"

Avery was first through the door; right on her heels was Vivian, face pinched, glaring at the back of her daughter's head.

Avery stopped short and braced her hands on her hips. "What is that cat doing here?" Vivian pushed past Avery, coming to sit beside Chloe on the sofa, and put her hand out for the cat to inspect.

"He's enormous." Vivian chuckled as Garfield sniffed each one of her fingertips.

A forceful exhale brought the attention back to Avery, who proceeded to sneeze. She covered her nose, sneezing repeatedly.

Magda crossed her arms over her breast. "Now, that's enough." Her eyes were hard. "You know you are faking these allergies, and it will stop."

Avery's jaw dropped. Vivian's brows rose at her daughter, who threw her arms in the air. "Mom!"

Vivian shook her head. "You are getting too old for these tantrums, young lady. And after what happened today, you are grounded. Go to your room. Now."

"But, Mom! You know what he called me!" Angry tears sprang to Avery's eyes and she clenched her fists.

Vivian exhaled slowly, bringing calm to her voice. "Yes, Avery, I know. What he said was inexcusable, and I told his parents as much. Even though there's only one week left of school, you are lucky you aren't getting expelled."

Avery's shoulders trembled. With an exasperated shriek, she stormed out, slamming Magda's door behind her. Her feet continued stomping well after she entered their apartment.

Vivian groaned. "I'm going to be getting a visit from the downstairs neighbor. Again." She laid her palm on her forehead. "That girl. What am I going to do with her? She's not even a teenager yet!"

A piercing squawk brought everyone's attention to the window. A pigeon slammed into the glass at full force, leaving behind a long crack in the windowpane. Chloe screamed, making Garfield dart from her lap and disappear into the kitchen.

"What in the world!" Vivian went to the window with Magda at her shoulder. She raised the sash gently, afraid of the glass falling out, and peered down. Splayed out on the fire escape was a pigeon, blood on its beak, its neck in an unnatural twist.

CHAPTER 16

August 2005

Their Saturday afternoon picnic lasted well past the heat of the afternoon. On the edge of the open green, they sat under a large tree, its full-leafed canopy making the perfect umbrella. Magda lounged in her canvas chair, and Vivian lay on a quilt beside her.

"I could so fall asleep right now," Vivian mumbled, eyelids heavy.

Magda hummed in agreement as she watched the twins kick the soccer ball back and forth to each other.

"Magda? Want to lie down? There's plenty of room on the blanket." Vivian propped herself up on an elbow, shielding her eyes from a spear of sunlight coming through the leaves.

"Oh, no," Magda said with a chuckle. "I'd never get back up."

Vivian turned her head to the side, gazing at her daughters. "It's nice to see them playing together. They've been fighting a lot lately." She sighed. "It's been months now, but Avery's not gotten over getting her period. Honestly, I think she uses it as an excuse not to even try to control herself." Vivian returned her eyes to the branches above, which stirred slightly in the soft breeze.

"She is struggling, no doubt about that. Sometimes, Avery seems so… lost."

"I know, and it hurts me to see that. But she won't talk to me about it." Vivian picked at a few loose threads in the quilt.

Magda placed a hand on the top of Vivian's head. She tilted her face up to Magda, and a soft smile replaced her frown.

"Do you ever regret not having a family?"

Magda studied the young woman's face. Vivian had barely aged from when she'd first met her, yet she'd grown so much. "I have one."

"Yes." Vivian beamed and squeezed Magda's arm. "Yes, you do."

"Hey! Give that back!" Avery's unmistakable shout brought Vivian to her feet.

Surrounding the sisters were three teenaged boys, each sporting looks of spiteful glee.

Avery faced the tallest, hands on hips, with all the defiance her thin frame could muster. The boy beside him yanked the baseball cap from Avery's head and put it on, only to discover it was too small. He threw it back at her chest. Avery didn't flinch and let it fall to the ground, not taking her eyes off the sneering bully palming her soccer ball.

"Take it!" said the tall boy with a laugh, chucking it over Avery's head to his friend behind her. The boy caught the ball, and Chloe turned, hoping to snatch it from his hands. He bounced the ball off her face. The three boys guffawed as Chloe fell to the ground with a yelp, hands covering her face.

"Chloe!" Vivian shouted and broke into a sprint. Magda rose from the chair. Running wasn't an option. She marched as quickly as her knees and hips allowed; the potion hadn't taken away *all* of her years. Words from the book sprang to mind. She pushed them aside but kept the phrase close in case the situation couldn't be dealt with another way. Other adults had seen, and two men were walking toward them.

Chloe pulled her hands away, revealing bright blood in her palms, running down her lips. Avery glowered at the snickering boy with the ball. She inhaled deeply through flared nostrils, balling her fists.

From behind Magda came an angry screech and something flew just above her head at great speed, startling her so much she stumbled. A hawk swooped down, angling toward Avery, talons extended.

With another ear-splitting cry, it collided with the boy's face. The bird clawed and shrieked, wings flapping furiously.

The boy dropped the ball, arms flailing, trying to drive the bird away, his screams a higher pitch than any little girl could manage. His friends ran, and he tried to follow, but the hawk stayed with him, catching at the back of the boy's long hair. Everyone stopped to watch, some with their cellphones and cameras out, capturing images of something they'd never seen before.

Magda pulled her eyes from the hawk to Avery, whom everyone ignored. Vivian was on the ground with her arms around Chloe, watching the spectacle with awe.

Avery's face was hard, her head bent down slightly, her eyes never leaving the shrieking boy.

"Avery," Magda said softly, laying a hand on the girl's stiff shoulder. Heat radiated from her.

Her chest heaved. Avery unclenched her fists and let her breath out slowly. With a shrill call, the hawk soared upward and away, disappearing over the tree line. The crying boy bolted, holding bits of torn skin onto his face.

Magda put her arm around Avery's shoulders. "I'm not sorry," Avery said, her eyes clear but still holding their anger. Magda hugged her shoulders.

"Let's not tell your mother," Magda whispered into Avery's ear. She nodded, staring at her sister and mother on the ground.

"It's not broken," Vivian said, inspecting her daughter's face. Chloe held her nose, applying pressure where her mother directed. "Come on, sweetie, let's get you home." Vivian hauled the dazed girl to her feet.

"That hawk was amazing, huh?" Vivian pulled Chloe to her. "Hawk-man to the rescue!" Her bright eyes glittered at Chloe, making the girl smile under her hands.

"I wish I knew who those little bastards were." Vivian glared behind her as they walked back to their picnic. "Their parents would be getting an earful."

Avery remained quiet and put an arm around Chloe, who turned around and hugged her. Magda smiled, certain she had just heard a whispered 'thank you.'

As they packed up, Vivian mouthed to Magda, *Did you do that?*

Magda shook her head. Vivian raised a skeptical eyebrow.

"No, Vivian," Magda whispered. "It wasn't me." Was it time to tell her of her daughters' abilities?

The short walk home was silent. Vivian carried most of their picnic goods so Avery and Chloe could remain arm-in-arm. Magda walked behind. The twins whispered to each other once or twice but were mostly quiet, yet each nodded or shook her head occasionally. Magda had read about certain twins having slight telepathic abilities; since both girls had magick in their blood, it wouldn't have been a surprise. She never questioned them about it. They were sisters, and sisters should have their secrets.

"Come on, Chloe, let's get you washed up," Vivian said, unlocking their apartment door. Only then did the girls separate, with Chloe following her mother.

"Do you want to help me with dinner?" Magda put a hand on Avery's silky hair. Her latest style sported closely shaved sides and back with a messy mop of longer hair on top. Avery's head was warm, her scalp damp. Natural magick coursing through her veins must've been a tremendous feeling indeed. Magda ran her nails lightly through the tresses, arranging them away from the girl's moist forehead.

Avery's eyes were closed as she savored the sensation of Magda's nails. She rubbed the goose bumps on her forearms. "Sure."

Magda pulled items from the refrigerator, waiting for Avery to speak. She slumped in a chair at the kitchen table and began picking at a bit of peeling varnish on the top. Magda handed her the bowl of meat and spices. "Will you roll out the meatballs?"

Avery took the bowl and placed it before her, removing the plastic wrap slowly. She stared at the mound of meat, but her eyes were far away.

Magda sat in the chair opposite her and studied the girl for a moment. Not much daunted the slight yet feisty twelve-year-old, but Avery had been going through a lot in the past few months; puberty and magick could make for a volatile mixture. Yet the incident at the park seemed to have humbled her. She lowered her face to catch Avery's eye.

"Would you like to talk about it?"

"Oh, Grammy." Avery crumpled, and she covered her face with her hands. Tears came instantly.

"Beruško!" Magda got up and moved her chair to sit beside Avery. She bent forward, sobbing hard, while Magda rubbed her back. After a moment, she took several deep breaths and straightened, wiping her face. She met Magda's eyes only for an instant then stared at her fists in her lap.

"I wanted to hurt him *so* bad, Grammy," she whispered, clearly ashamed of saying those words.

"You protected your sister." Magda took the girl's hands. "I don't think I would have done much different."

Avery met her eyes, a measure of relief on her face. Magda put a palm on her hot, red cheek and smiled. "Has this happened before?"

She shook her head. "I don't remember ever being that mad before. But, Grammy—" She swallowed.

"You know you can tell me anything, my Avery."

She swiped at each cheek, taking her gaze to the floor. "When..." She lowered her voice. "When I watched the hawk, what he was doing to that boy... I was glad."

The tiny hairs on the back of Magda's neck rose. Avery looked up, her bottom lip trembling. "I don't want to be bad, Grammy!" She fell into Magda's open arms, sobbing once more.

Magda made shushing sounds and stroked her back. She let Avery cry; sometimes a good cry did wonders. For Avery, it was a rarity. She eventually grew quiet and rested her head against Magda's shoulder.

"That does not make you bad, my Avery." Magda pushed her away gently so she could look into her face. Avery averted her eyes. "Look at me, *beruško*. Don't be ashamed. I am no person to judge. I, too, have had to take... action in my life."

Avery met her grandmother's comforting gaze. "Your sister got into trouble, and you reacted. Not being sorry over that nasty boy doesn't make you bad. If you ask me, he deserved much of what he got."

The corner of Avery's mouth quirked up.

"But now that you know you can do this, you must be careful. Yes?"

"Oh yes, Grammy, yes! I don't want anything to do with magick again. Ever!"

Avery lay awake, staring at the ceiling. She closed her eyes at the memory of the hawk's energy flowing through her. Or had it been the magick? Was there a difference?

Why had the magick worked then when all the other times she'd tried had failed? Avery attempted magick more often than she let on, more than she let her sister or grandmother see. She'd also stolen glances at Chloe's secret stash of magick books, but nothing she read made sense.

When Avery had seen the ball smack Chloe in the face, everything slowed down. The surrounding noises dulled, the sunlight dimmed at the edges of her vision yet stayed bright and clear around her sister. The blood pounding in her ears sounded like a slow drumbeat.

She didn't recall asking for any help for her sister. All she'd known was rage, more than she'd ever felt before, and that was saying something. Then it just happened.

In slow motion, the hawk had flown past her from the side. The beating of its wings had replaced her heartbeat.

Her chest swelled again with the sight of the boy getting what he deserved. Avery huffed and rolled over, pulling the covers under her chin. *Don't enjoy that!*

"Huh? What?" Chloe grumbled. Avery couldn't see her sister across the dark bedroom, but blankets rustled and the headboard creaked as Chloe repositioned herself.

You're still reading those books, aren't you? Avery thought at Chloe. She didn't want to speak aloud. Her mother could hear a mouse fart, and the walls in these apartments were paper thin.

She felt Chloe blush. *No.*

Don't lie. I know you. You can't help yourself.

You woke me up just so you could pick on me? Go back to sleep.

Ugh, don't be a baby. Avery bit her lip. Her tone softened. *I can't sleep.*

Chloe sighed audibly. It took several minutes for her to speak. *You know I'm still reading them— you've been through my notes. I can tell.*

No, I haven't.

Chloe sighed again. Avery was used to that reaction from Chloe. It was hard to find the words; Avery didn't want to ask for help or admit to Chloe that she was starting to believe in this magick business. But after today, after what she did and how she felt, she had to. Part of her was afraid of what she'd done; the other part wanted to do more.

Avery swallowed the remaining lump of pride stuck in her

throat. *Anything in them to tell me what I did today?* If Chloe sighed again, she was going to get jumped.

Chloe rolled onto her back. *I've been thinking about that.*

Avery waited while her sister scanned through all the books she'd memorized. Her impatience grew the longer Chloe thought. *And?*

Honestly, not really. The books Granny got for us are pretty rudimentary, in my opinion. I want to go on my own to get more, but…

Avery's gut reaction was to jab at her sister for not having the guts, but she bit the inside of her cheek instead. Neither of them could risk searching online with their mom tracking everything they did on her computer.

Bummer. If Chloe thought those books were rudimentary, then Avery must really be stupid.

But, Chloe continued, *I think what you did was pure instinct, and maybe a hawk, or some other kind of bird, is your familiar.*

Familiar? Avery didn't keep the sarcasm from her thoughts. *Seriously?*

If you're going to be a jerk, why did you ask me in the first place?

Avery needed to not be a jerk right now. She wasn't a fan of admitting her sister was smarter. Avery took comfort in knowing she could outrun, outfight, and outtalk Chloe anytime, anywhere. She managed a weak *sorry* and felt Chloe smile, knowing how much it annoyed her sister to apologize.

Avery sensed Chloe's brain gathering her next thoughts as she would papers strewn out on a desk.

Every time you've gotten really angry, a flock of birds show up. Watching you. Which is really creepy and really cool at the same time. And today, a bird came to the rescue. My guess why the spells never worked for you is because you don't take it seriously. You think it's all stupid. You don't focus, your thoughts aren't clear or precise.

Chloe paused. Avery knew she was waiting for a remark, but Avery decided to be good.

Today, you saw something that shocked you, made you really mad. You love me, despite the frequent jerk behavior, and you reacted. No other thoughts got in the way, no distractions, no sarcasm, only your intention *to help me was there. Your energy reached out to the hawk, and he came.*

Avery's eyebrows rose as she digested this. Maybe Chloe was on to something. While the hawk thing had happened in slow motion, it was *clear.* But Chloe was wrong about one thing. Avery's mind hadn't been focused on helping her sister; she'd focused on hurting that boy.

A wave of shame washed over Avery. Heat flushed her body. She squeezed her eyes closed.

Don't be ashamed for wanting to hurt him, Chloe thought. There was no way of hiding her intense swing of emotions from Chloe. Avery's heat pushed passed Chloe's defenses, and the flush of embarrassment washed into her.

Avery's eyes filled with tears. She clenched her fists and tightened herself into a ball.

Chloe threw off the covers and rushed to her twin. She wrapped her arms around Avery, feeling her heat and sweat physically now. She held her as Avery fought off the strong desire to cry.

CHAPTER 17

April 2007

Magda, why have you abandoned me?

Josef Straka's voice assaulted her mind as Magda struggled against vomiting the potion.

The soothing warmth the foul elixir brought seemed to carry his voice, as if he traveled along its path through her.

You promised me.

She stumbled backward, stopped by the wall, and slid down it. Magda sat across from the old red secretary, tears of loss and shame streaming down her pale cheeks.

I am waiting.

Images of copper coins, emaciated corpses, and the white mist of writhing souls bombarded her. She cried out, covering her eyes with her arms. The images continued, pushing through the darkness, out of her dream and into the short hallway.

"No! Go away!" Magda flailed her arms, attempting to drive them away. "I won't do it!"

A split second of pain burst through her brain, as if the warring factions collided. Then all went quiet.

Magda woke, stiff from lying on the floor for however long. The sun was still out although the shadows were lower on the wall, and her cabinet was open, the bottles and tools for making the life-extending potion lined up. She got to her feet, using the secretary to steady herself, and quickly put everything away.

She leaned against it. *Why was I on the floor?* It had been many years since she'd last drunk the mixture; perhaps its ghastly taste had overwhelmed her? No, it was something else.

Josef wants me to do something, something I promised to do years ago. I started it but never finished. An image of a skeletal corpse with dirty copper coins on its eyes appeared as a burn when she blinked. *What?* A surge of guilt caught in her chest.

What have I done to feel such guilt? Magda put her hand over her heart. *Did I do something terrible? Is it because I've forgotten the man I loved?*

I loved him?

Magda's cell phone buzzed. The ridiculous, dull black device vibrated on the coffee table. Vivian's concern for her health had pressured Magda into getting the thing. It had been difficult to find a "nonsmart" phone, as Magda called it. All those brightly colored bells and whistles were confusing. Much to the girls' disappointment, Magda hadn't gotten the shiny hot pink model. The chunky flip phone was sufficient to soothe Vivian's concerns.

Only three people called her on it. Except this time.

"Mrs. Hlavacova?" She recognized the all-business voice.

"Mr. Troup." Magda's grip tightened on the small phone. "What has Avery done this time?"

"More of the same, I'm afraid. However, I have to suspend her for two weeks. You'll have to collect her. I was unable to reach Ms. Parsons."

Magda listened with the required grandmotherly concern as the principal recounted Avery's latest offense. The Hartley boy had gone too far, pushing Avery against the lockers. He was bigger than he'd been two years ago when he'd started his taunting, and it was apparent he'd not forgotten the beating she gave him. At the encouragement of his peers, he made his move during lunch.

She watched the video with silent pride. Slight and quick, Avery got in several punches to the face and a kick to the groin before the big boy knew what was happening. It was clearly self-defense, but suspension of both students was required. Hartley was given three weeks and a meeting with a counsellor. It was a good thing Vivian was at a seminar, unable to answer her phone. Magda was certain she'd insist on involving the police.

Something else happened on the video the principal hadn't noticed, or if he had, he'd not commented. As the boy lay writhing on the floor with both hands on his privates, blood burst from his nose. He gripped his head and screamed. Avery loomed over him, fists trembling at her sides. Was that a faint spark across her knuckles? Magda squinted. Or a glitch in the video feed? The blood stopped when teachers broke though the tight ring of teenagers encircling the pair. When Avery's fists opened, the boy released his head and fainted.

Avery had hit him once or twice in the nose. Perhaps the bleeding had been delayed.

"Don't tell me you condone this?" Mr. Troup's horrified expression surprised Magda. The brown birthmark on his pasty forehead seemed to redden.

"Whatever do you mean?"

"You're smiling."

"I am?" Magda released the muscles in her cheeks. She *had* been smiling. Only then did she become aware of the eerie, and deeply inappropriate, jubilation filling her chest. She coughed, covering the lingering curve of her mouth as the sensation passed. Magda was certainly proud of Avery for standing up to the Hartley boy, but the feeling went far beyond pride. And she wasn't nearly as disturbed as she thought she should be that Avery's uncontrolled magick was getting stronger.

"I'm old—that is my face. I have a tic." Magda batted a hand at his dubious stare. "So, tell me, Mr. Troup, how should Avery have responded to this much larger bully?"

"She *should* have gotten a teacher right away." He set his bony elbows on his desk, lacing his equally bony fingers together. "This type of thing won't be tolerated."

"Is that so? It's my understanding this boy takes others' lunch money frequently and picks on smaller children. Why have you not dealt with *that*?"

The principal bristled. "His parents have been spoken to."

"Quite an effective tactic, it appears."

Mr. Troup rose. "Miss Parsons will be permitted to return on the twenty-first." He came around his desk and opened the door for Magda, the muscles in his neck tight. Magda didn't have to look up to meet him square in the eye. Raising his chin, he pulled the door open wider.

Avery sat in a metal folding chair outside the principal's office, not acknowledging the world around her. Magda's touch on her shoulder put her in motion.

The walk home in the cool afternoon sun was silent, aside from ever-present noises of the city. Avery's face remained hard, her jaw locked. Her hands clutched the straps of her backpack, the knuckles on her right hand red.

Magda followed Avery into her bedroom and sat on Chloe's bed as Avery fell onto hers with a groan.

"Will you listen to me now?" Magda said.

"'Bout what?" Avery asked into her pillow.

Magda remained silent long enough for Avery to roll onto her side to face her.

"Since the hawk incident, you've stopped studying, stopped everything that could help you learn to use your magick, to control it. You told me then you didn't want anything to do with magick, but do you see now you cannot ignore what is inside you?"

"I've done pretty good since then."

"You have *not.*"

Avery's mouth popped open.

"I have seen you try to drive Garfield away."

The girl reddened.

"And that last argument with your mother. Coffee mugs don't crack on their own."

Avery rolled onto her back, whipping the pillow over her face.

"What is wrong me with me, Grammy?"

"Nothing, *beruško.*" Magda came to sit beside Avery, who scooted over to make room, her arms still wrapped around the pillow on her face.

"Look at me."

It was several breaths before Avery obeyed.

"You must stop fighting yourself, and fighting the dar—your nature." Magda had started to say 'darkness,' a word she wasn't thinking. The sense of eager joy returned in a rush, leaving her dizzy.

"Are you all right, Grammy?"

"Oh, yes. It's just a little hot in here." She fanned herself, then turned her attention back to her granddaughter. "I know it frightens you, and you aren't alone in that. There are things inside every one of us we'd rather ignore. But you are special, my Avery." She took the girl's right hand, her thumb gently brushing across Avery's swollen knuckles. "You must learn to control your magick."

"But every time I try, I fail! When I don't try, *bam*. My problems are gone."

"Your problems are not gone. Far from it."

"Ugh, please don't give me the same song Mom does." Avery made a face. "*Violence never solves anything*. Blah, blah, blah."

"No, I don't believe as your mother does. Bullies like that

should be dealt with. But you need to *think*." She poked Avery's forehead. "You could really hurt someone."

"Why are we even talking about this? I didn't use magick this time, Grammy. Just my friends Punch-o and Lefty." Avery presented her fists.

Magda's nostrils flared. "I saw what you did."

Avery dropped her hands.

Chloe cleared her throat. She stood in the doorway of their bedroom, a ziplock bag of ice in her hand. "Hi."

Magda patted the foot of Avery's bed. Chloe sat, and Avery took the proffered bag of ice. She laid it across her knuckles with a long 'ah.' The girls exchanged glances, and Chloe nodded.

"You named your fists?" Magda asked with a chuckle. Avery shrugged.

"The entire chess club wants to thank you, by the way," Chloe said. "They get to keep their lunch money for three weeks."

"Ha!" Avery sat up. "Happy to help."

"I heard you gave Hartley an awesome beating. He *sooo* deserved one." Chloe sighed. "But Mom's not happy."

"No surprise there." Avery scooted to the head of the bed to lean against the headboard. She cradled her right hand in the ice pack.

"Oh"—Chloe brightened—"Mallory asked me to let her know if you're okay."

Avery blushed.

Vivian entered Magda's apartment so quietly, Magda hadn't heard her coming. She closed the door, her face ashen—even her freckles seemed lighter against the dark maroon of her scrubs. Vivian had been working the overnight shift for the past month, and it showed, but more so now with the crescents darker under her eyes, the lines around her mouth deeper.

Without a word or a glance to Magda, she walked to the window, the one that had been damaged when the pigeon struck it two years prior. Her fingers traced the glass where the crack had been.

"Vivian, what is it?" Magda put aside her quilting.

She turned to Magda, palm against the glass. Vivian's dry lips parted. "Hugh Hartley is in a coma."

Magda didn't recognize the name immediately. She sank back into the chair as realization dawned. The bully that had picked on Avery last week, the boy Avery had pummeled in response. Pummeled and… something inexplicable.

"His parents brought him in to County early this morning. I was dropping off some charts but detoured over to the ER when I heard all the shouting. Then I saw his name on the board." Her fingers left the glass. "He was raving, grabbing his head and screaming, blood trickling from his nose. I couldn't make out what he was saying, if he was saying anything."

Vivian seemed dazed as she walked to the sofa and sat on the edge of a cushion. "Then he went quiet. And not from the sedative."

Magda kept her thoughts from her face, but the burn of her ears couldn't be hidden.

"That's terrible." She fidgeted with the quilt bundle then set it beside her on the floor, arranging it into a neat pile. "Do they know what's wrong with him? If you're worried that a punch from Avery caused some sort of brain damage, I highly doubt the fist of a small girl could—"

"It's not that." Vivian stared at nothing in the middle distance. "On the video, I thought… I saw something, not really sure what. I would've completely dismissed it if it weren't for some things I've noticed about Avery. And your… abilities."

"Something on the video of the fight?"

A flare of irritation passed across Vivian's face but morphed to doubt and then melted away altogether. She pressed the heel of a palm to her forehead. Vivian dropped her hand and locked eyes with Magda.

"Does Avery have your abilities?"

Magda maintained a neutral expression despite the knot tightening in her gut. She held Vivian's burning stare as the woman's tired, bloodshot eyes probed her face, searching for any sign of confirmation. Magda's brain raced for a response, but nothing came in time.

Vivian nodded, her chest deflating. "Your silence is my answer."

"No, Vivian, no." Magda raised her hands. "Your question just surprised me." She scooted forward. "It was me."

Vivian's back snapped straight. "You?"

"I knew his bullying wouldn't stop, that Mr. Troup would do nothing. And you've met the boy's parents. The apple didn't fall far from the tree."

"Magda!" Vivian stood. "How could you do that? He's just a child!"

"A child who will grow up to be a man of the same character."

"That's no excuse. You had no right! Curt was one thing but —" She squeezed her eyes closed. "Take the spell, or whatever you did, off of him. Now."

"Vivian, sit."

She remained standing.

Magda sighed and pushed back into the chair. "I cannot. Nature must run its course." She hoped what she said was true, not having any idea what Avery had done.

Vivian shook, anger returning the color to her face. "This discussion isn't over." She stomped from the apartment.

Magda paced the living room, waiting for Avery to come, assuming Vivian would still let her. Magda hadn't thought twice about taking the blame for Avery. Vivian simply could not know her daughter had such power, such darkness, inside her.

Darkness.

The word stopped Magda's pacing. The eerie joy she'd felt twice before returned, and she placed a hand on the wall to steady herself. *What is wrong with you, Magda Hlavacova?* Her self-recrimination forced the feeling away. She righted herself as Avery opened the door.

"Boy, Mom's in a *mood.*" She stopped when she saw her grandmother's look.

"I'm sure she's just tired," Magda said a little loudly, and put a finger to her lips. Vivian had the hearing of a bat. Her schedule had her sleeping in the middle of the afternoon, but she might not be asleep yet. Magda beckoned Avery to her bedroom.

Magda closed the door. "What did you do to that boy?"

The accusation immediately made Avery's spine straighten. "What are you talking about?"

"You have beaten up some other boy in the last week?"

"Oh, Hartley? You know what I did. A couple of punches and a kick to the 'nads." Avery fidgeted under Magda's deepening scowl.

"Your mother hasn't told you?"

Avery slid her hands into the front pockets of her shorts; they folded to fists. "Told me what?"

Magda paced to the closet, then back to the bed, all of six steps. "There is no sense in hiding it from you. You'll find out regardless," Magda muttered under her breath, then stood before her granddaughter. "He is in a coma."

The color drained from the girl's face.

"Tell me what you did."

Avery's mouth opened to speak, but only a strangled sound emerged. She shook her head and took a step back.

"Grammy," Avery said, pulling her hands from her pockets. "I..." She retreated another step but was stopped by the door. "I didn't do anything, I swear!"

Magda stopped herself before she let her mood darken. Avery would only respond to anger with anger. She released her negativity in a long exhale, relaxing her rigid shoulders, and took Avery's hands.

"Avery, you stood over him. You did something, I saw it. I must know, *beruško*. We have to fix him."

Under her grandmother's compassionate energy, Avery began to crumble. Her fingers were ice in Magda's hands. "Grammy, I don't know what I did. Honestly." She gulped. "I was so mad! I just wanted him to *hurt*."

Magda's heart sank. "I was hoping you knew. It is so much worse that you do not know."

"What do you mean?"

Magda released Avery's hands to cup her face. The girl placed her hands over her grandmother's. "How can you fix something if you don't know how it's broken?"

"I'm sorry," Avery said, her voice choked.

Magda kissed her forehead and went to the window. She stared out between the gap of the lace curtains at the red brick building across from hers.

How can I fix this?

Two boys ran down the alley, laughing, thumbs and forefingers extended, yelling 'bang bang' with each step.

She searched her memory of the book's contents. It offered nothing helpful but…

Perhaps I could unbind it, just for a few minutes. The words might change to give me something useful. It's never failed me before.

Another boy jumped out from behind a dumpster, cocking the imaginary shotgun poised at his waist. He shot at the oncoming boys with loud booms. Each grabbed their stomach and howled, falling to the pavement with all the melodrama ten-year-old boys could muster.

The boy with the shotgun brandished it above his head, proclaiming himself victorious.

No, I can't risk it reaching out to Avery. Especially now.

A thin stab of pain at the base of her skull made her gasp.

"Grammy?"

But if I'm quick about it—

The boy stood over his two dying enemies and shot each once more.

"No," Magda said through another stab of pain. She staggered from the window, gripping her temples. A flurry of angry cries billowed in her mind.

"Grammy!" Avery caught her at the elbows. "Are you okay?"

From Avery's fingers flowed cooling tingles. Tiny sparks of soothing electricity traveled up Magda's arms into her throbbing head. Whatever rampaged through her brain retreated, taking the pain with it.

Avery helped her to the bed. "I'm getting Mom."

Magda caught her by the wrist, shaking her head. She focused on Avery's face, staring into the young girl's panicked eyes and seeing a blossoming young woman, afraid of what she didn't understand and even more afraid of finding out what it could be. But there was hope.

"You helped me, just then." Magda smiled. Avery's forehead crinkled.

"Your magick," Magda continued, holding her granddaughter's cold hands. "It pushed away my pain."

"Oh, Grammy," Avery said, "that's just your imagination."

Magda sighed, patting Avery's cheek. "I think I know how we can fix this."

CHAPTER 18

WHEN VIVIAN LEFT FOR WORK SHORTLY AFTER MIDNIGHT, Avery crept into Magda's apartment and locked the door behind her. She hesitated in the doorway of her grandmother's bedroom.

"Okaaaay," Avery said in her very teenage way, a wary gaze traveling around the room.

Magda motioned her forward and shut the door, turning the knob's lock. "How is Vivian? Did she say anything to you?"

"Nope. And she's still super pissed."

"Watch your language."

Avery blew out her cheeks. "Anyway, I was the good daughter. I did all the laundry and stuff. Avoiding her seemed best." She did a double-take at the bed. "So, what are you up to, Grammy?"

"Not me. Us."

Three deep blue pillar candles cast the only light. One perched on the shelf above the headboard, and the other two sat atop rustic, wooden candleholders stationed on each side of the footboard. Magda had placed her antique copper oil burner on the floor at the foot of the twin bed. It simmered with a concentrated mix of frankincense, lavender, and sandalwood oils. With both hands, she wafted the heady aroma into the air around

Avery. Magda bade her to inhale deeply. The girl obeyed, coughing on the third breath.

"Why is your oil burner on a cookie sheet?"

"In case your big feet knock it over." Magda mounted the bed and sat.

"That kinda kills the whole magick vibe, you know."

"Enough with your sarcasm. Come. Sit. Face me."

"Makes me really want cookies now," Avery mumbled as she crawled onto the bed. "Why all of this, though?"

They sat cross-legged, facing each other. Magda grunted as she used her hands to pull her legs into place. She wouldn't be able to sit like this for too long.

Magda closed her eyes, resting her hands on her knees, palms up. "We sit within a pyramid—"

"We're sitting on your bed, Gram."

Magda tsked. "Now is the time to use your imagination, Avery. The candles represent the points of a pyramid, and their blue coloring will—" Magda scowled. "Don't give me any more of your looks. You must take this seriously. What you did to that boy is no joke."

Avery flinched. Even within the shadows of the flickering light, her flush was vivid.

Magda softened her tone. "I know this is strange to you. I can see the questions on your face, but you must trust me."

Avery nodded. She shook out her hands, puffing out a breath, and mimicked her grandmother's hand placement. "Let's do this."

"Close your eyes and listen to my voice. Cast out your negative thoughts, your doubts, your fears with every exhale."

Behind closed eyes, Magda listened to Avery's breathing. Each breath grew less exaggerated until they were quiet flows through her nostrils.

"The objects around you will aid you and protect you. While I can do no magick, I can lend you what you do not have, the one thing that is key. Focus. You will travel to where the Hartley boy lies, and you will forgive him."

"What?" Avery said at full volume, her eyes bulging at her grandmother.

"It is my belief that the boy suffers because you are still connected to him. Your anger, your desire for vengeance. If you release that, you will release him."

Magda held up a hand at the protest readying to spew from Avery's lips. "You have a history with this boy. Your anger against him goes back years. *That* is holding you to him. In order for you to break the cycle of anger, you must forgive him."

"There is no effing way on this planet I'll forgive that fat piece of cr—"

"Enough!"

Magda searched her granddaughter's hard face, the tendons in her neck tight, the hollows of her collarbone black in the dim light. "You said you wanted him to hurt. You've done that, but now it has gone far past hurt. He could… you could kill him, Avery."

It was several seconds before Avery's face changed, as if it took time for her to fully register the meaning of Magda's words.

She almost felt guilty for the fear the young girl now radiated, the gravity of her actions finally coming to light. But Avery must learn the reality of uncontrolled magick, of the consequences of her untrained power.

Magda held out her hands. "You've gotten your revenge, my Avery. Now, let him go."

Avery swallowed and placed her fingers into her grandmother's hands.

The touch sparked a rush of giddiness from the depths of Magda's mind. Her own dread at the unpleasant feeling made her want to let go, but Magda found she couldn't release Avery's fingers.

He had not known the potential of human magick until that moment.

The old woman had bound him from speaking to the girl. However, now that their skins touched, each one's mind opened and awaiting their connection, he need not speak at all. He was able to touch *the girl.*

What sensations! Her young mind was chaotic, confused. Her strong heart thumped wildly. Her hot blood raced beneath her tingling skin. He craved more, yet the lack of magick in the crone hindered his movements.

Damn the old woman. She swept past him, reaching for the girl's attention to take her focus to the boy. The presence of Straka emboldened her, gave her the strength to defy him once more. The girl slipped from his faint grasp. He followed.

The girl watched the boy unseen from above. He reveled in the warring emotions within her: triumph at bringing such a person to his current state, curiosity at what more she could do, fear at what she had done, and an unfortunately brief impulse to let him die.

Oh, yes. She is perfect.

The girl's power surprised the old woman but not him. He knew what dwelled within her and eagerly awaited owning it.

The crone's voice droned on about forgiveness and release; the girl had done what she had set out to do, and now it was time to let go. To his delight, the girl wavered. He yearned to fully possess her and coax her toward what she could not fully admit she wanted.

Yet he could not silence the old woman; she disregarded him completely now, her focus on the girl and what this moment meant to her future. If he could push through, touch the girl once more, she would fall to him. But he could not. The black smear of Straka stood against him, flowing thick within the woman's blood. His anger grew. How was he here?

He shrank away as the answer came to him.

Straka had crafted his herbs and oils with magick, using his blood to fortify their properties, to strengthen their inherent power.

Straka's own blood.

It was those herbs and oils the woman used for the potion.

Straka's blood was inside her. Each time the old woman consumed the potent mixture, she took more of Straka into her.

He raged at his own shortsightedness. Straka had not known of him, he was certain of that, yet he had underestimated the man's ingenuity.

Straka was the only one who could release Muraal. Of course, there would have been a plan. Should Straka's life end, his resurrection scheme had already been established. Whomever ingested Straka's blood took his essence into them; his essence would eventually take control and lead the person to do his bidding.

He had been a fool. He had delivered the woman back into Straka's hands.

He must not allow the old woman to take another potion. She must die. Although bound, he would take his chances without her. What more could he lose?

The girl's decision snatched his attention back, and he recoiled at the softening of her heart.

When she uttered the words, "I forgive you," his tenuous hold on her was broken.

CHAPTER 19

Present Day

Magda scowled at the broad stairwell leading to her floor. It taunted her today. When had the stairs become so many?

She put a hand on the wood newel-post, worn shiny from years of use, and pulled herself onto the first stair. Magda gritted her teeth against the shooting pains in her hand and the protests of her hips, each step a sharp reminder of her advanced years. They'd crept up on her slowly; she'd not noticed as time went by. Yet at this moment, she felt them more than ever.

And that elusive annoyance in the back of her mind pestered her more as of late. Much of the time she called it dementia and put it aside, but now, it vied for attention with her aching joints. Magda pondered as she climbed what unfinished business she might have. The itch insisted she'd forgotten to do something—something important.

The pit of guilt in her gut wouldn't go away. She wasn't behind on her quilting orders; she hadn't taken a commission in over a year. Her arthritis wouldn't allow it. All was right with Vivian and the girls, so what was it then?

As Magda rounded the last set of stairs, Vivian bounced out

of her apartment, humming as she locked the door. Her step had been brighter in the last few months than it had been since the twins moved out.

She must have met a man. It was only right. Vivian was still a beauty. She'd kept her silent promise to her daughters she'd told Magda of years ago—no men until they were on their own. As far as Magda knew, she'd kept to it.

She missed her granddaughters. But growing up was inevitable, and Chloe was eager to start college. It seemed only natural that Avery moved out with her, although college was not on her agenda.

"Magda!" Vivian's bright face fell when she locked eyes with the old woman. She ran to her, dropping her hobo bag. She met Magda on the stairs and took an elbow, wrapping her other arm around the elderly woman's thin waist.

"My god, Magda, you look terrible." Vivian bore a considerable amount of Magda's weight, although Magda hadn't meant to lean on her so much.

"Oh, pish." Magda steadied herself against the railing, but Vivian didn't let go. Her 'thank you' was nearly breathless when they reached the top of the stairs.

She stared at Magda with worried eyes, unspoken questions on her lips. They were pointless to ask. 'What's wrong?' and 'what can I do to help?' were questions Vivian had been asking more and more in recent years.

Vivian guided Magda to her door. "You really need to take it easy. You should've told me you needed things from the store. I'd have gone for you."

Magda patted Vivian's hand, still locked painfully around her elbow.

"I'm all right." Magda forced a smile and fumbled for her keys at the bottom of her handbag. Vivian tutted and used her spare to open the door.

She steered Magda to her chair and eased her down.

"Really, Vivian, I'll be fine. I only need to rest a bit." Magda tried her best to hide the pain behind a bright face.

"I know when you lie to me, old lady." Vivian's lips pursed with mock censure, yet there was real admonishment behind her words.

Oh, no, you don't. Magda laughed to herself. Vivian cocked an eyebrow, and Magda made a dismissive motion with her fingers.

"Let me make you some tea. I've got some time before my shift starts." Vivian turned, not waiting for Magda's reply. It was best to let Vivian fuss over her now or there'd be more of it later, and she'd probably recruit the girls as well. Magda didn't want *three* stubborn people telling her what to do. One was plenty.

Magda relaxed and closed her eyes, listening to the clinking and clanking from the kitchen. She had just about nodded off when warm fingertips touched her arm.

Vivian placed the teacup and saucer on the side table and sat in the adjoining chair. Magda inhaled the aroma of fresh peppermint and chamomile, her favorite blend. Vivian studied Magda with the practiced eyes of a nurse. Only now did Magda see the lines at the edges of her eyes and mouth, the two creases between her brows deepening the longer she stared at Magda.

"When was the last time you saw a doctor?"

"You mean I'm not seeing one now?" Magda chuckled but stopped when Vivian's lips thinned.

"Seriously, Magda, I'm worried about you." Vivian picked up the teacup and handed it to her, not releasing it until both of Magda's hands were around the delicate saucer. Magda worked at keeping her hands steady though her arms ached, the discomfort traveling to her neck. Vivian scrutinized each movement as Magda held an 'I'm perfectly fine' expression on her face.

"Have you *ever* been to the doctor?"

"Of course, I have," Magda said, looking at her cup.

"Lying," Vivian said in a sing-song voice. "Look, after the girls leave tonight, I'll have my new, um, friend come by and see

you." Vivian stumbled over the word 'friend,' and a pink tinge rose on her cheeks.

"What is this?" Magda's mouth made a sideways smirk. "Vivian Parsons is *dating*?"

"Oh, stop." She giggled, slapping Magda's leg.

"Tell me." Magda settled back in her chair and took a sip.

Vivian's ears reddened under Magda's lascivious grin. "It's just one of the new doctors," she said, her light tone dispelling the importance of her statement. She laughed again at Magda's ogling.

"All right, subject-changer." Vivian snorted, getting up. "Expect a house call tonight." Vivian folded her arms over her chest. "I'll come over when he's on his way."

Magda nodded. It was pointless to argue.

"And if you're not up to having dinner with me and the girls, they'll totally understand." Vivian waited at the door with her hand on the knob.

"No, no." Magda coughed lightly as she tried to talk and drink at the same time. "I will be there. It's been over a month since I've seen them, they're so busy! I'll take a nap shortly and be right as rain by dinner time."

"Okay. I'm heading to work now. Call me if you need anything, you hear me?"

Magda set the cup and saucer in her lap and brought her hands together before her chest, bowing as a servant would.

Vivian laughed and blew a kiss before closing the door.

Magda drained her tea with a single gulp, hoping the peppermint would quell the sudden nausea. The discomfort in her arms and neck subsided, only to be replaced with tightening in her chest. Pretending in front of Vivian must have really taken it out of her.

Or I'm having a heart attack. She tried to laugh, but the breath wasn't there. Magda closed her eyes, an ineffective attempt to keep the room from spinning. She aimed to sit quietly and wait for it to pass, but she trembled, trying to remember where she'd put her cell phone. If she called out, was Vivian too far away to hear? Did she even have the breath for that?

Light worked its way into Magda's darkness. With it came sunny images of two redheaded babies cooing and gurgling in her arms; the warmth of their little bodies chased away her chills. A young Vivian walked across the stage to accept her degree, the smile on her face as big as the swell of pride in Magda's heart. Giggling Avery and Chloe danced around Magda as they sang her happy birthday, Vivian carrying a homemade cake topped with so many candles it blazed an aura around the scene. The embrace of Vivian's forgiveness after the Hartley boy's recovery was followed by a group hug when Avery introduced her first girlfriend to the family. A four-way pillow fight spawned from packing up the girls' things from their bedroom. Magda held Vivian as she cried in the living room of her empty nest.

The light and images retreated slowly, leaving their happiness in their wake. Magda was ready to die. She felt complete. She'd lived a long life filled with love and laughter, and no regrets.

Except one.

Josef Straka held her hand as they walked underneath trees breaking out of their winter slumber. The small park within the big city was empty, too cold for most, but the heat from Josef's body kept Magda from feeling the nip in the evening air.

The stench of dank sewer filled her nostrils. Josef lay at her feet, his black robe spread like wings beneath him, his torso soaked with blood.

"Do this for me. Bring me back. *Promise me*, Magda." A trembling hand covered in crimson reached toward her face but fell limp.

Magda's eyes flew open. She gasped for breath, each intake painful. She stood before her witch cabinet, one hand on it to keep her up, the other pushing against the pressure in her breast.

Unused and nearly forgotten, the secretary held what she desperately needed. *Where's the key?* A snippet of memory fought its way forward, past the ever-present blur of forgetfulness, and Magda saw herself take the black cord from around her neck and toss it atop the cabinet.

She stretched, groping for the key, turning her face away from the years of dust wafting down.

What do I need in the cabinet? Magda had known a second ago—it was very important—but now it was gone.

Her fingers closed around the cold metal of the key. *The potion!*

The spark of pain in the back of her brain seemed to scream 'no.' Magda pushed her fists into her temples.

Josef gazed down at her, love curving the corners of his mouth.

She fumbled the key into the lock and threw the doors open. She snatched up the bottles and vials and dumped them onto the fold-down counter. Magda struggled to assemble her cauldron, her hands clenched into fists, refusing to obey any further. She bit her lip and cursed.

Magda forced her fingers open as pricks of light stung her vision. She held on to the sliver of memory that lingered, the first time she'd seen Josef's eyes, the midnight blue eyes that peered into her soul.

Waiting for the ingredients to cook and cool seemed an eternity. She couldn't let herself die, she'd made Josef a promise! What it was she couldn't recall, but it didn't matter. Magda had forgotten so much. The guilt she'd carried with her for decades had been the price of her neglect. Or had it been her deeds? She shook her head. *No more.* Magda returned her focus to his eyes.

Magda gulped down the warm oil, for the first time not minding the smell or taste.

Euphoria replaced agony, strength replaced weakness, clarity replaced fog.

Memories of a stranger flooded back to her. Magda didn't recognize the woman bending over a twitching Vaclav as he frothed at the mouth on the floor, or the steady hands of the woman who placed filthy copper coins on the eyes of a dead man, or the lithe, naked beauty shuddering beneath Josef.

But they weren't the memories of a stranger.

"Oh, Josef." Magda sank to her knees at the realization of all the time she'd forgotten him. "I'm so sorry." Sobs held down for decades broke free, his loss renewed as if he'd died only hours ago.

Magda rose without ache or pain and wiped the wetness from her cheeks. The itch in her mind was gone. The vague images of a discarded past were clear now, each memory sharp and crisp, and equally painful. She would admonish herself later; there was no more time to waste. She must get back to Prague. Only four souls left to harness and Josef would come back to her.

Jars lay around her feet, their contents scattered, the syrupy liquids from several vials now mingled with other ingredients on the counter or soaked into the carpet. As Magda scooped up a pile of small black husks and red chalky bits, the realization of what she'd done crept across her skin like ants on a march.

Oh, no.

In her haste to make the potion, the struggle to make her hands obey, she'd made a terrible mess.

"No, no, no."

The elixir was made with precise measures of each ingredient, some a great deal more than others, and some just a minuscule amount. Magda couldn't simply gather it all up in a sandwich bag. Too much of something and not enough of another could kill her! Or worse.

Magda rifled through the other bottles and jars stored in the cubbyholes of the cabinet, scanning the label of each container then knocking it aside, searching for more of what she needed. Magda grew more desperate with each panting breath. She couldn't run to the local herbal shop or new age store to get more. Many of these ingredients had been a mystery from the beginning; she'd only matched the scratching of their names with those in the book. Some of the names were unrecognizable now, their parchment labels faded by time.

It was impossible to put each bit back in its proper container.

Magda squeezed her eyes closed, fighting the urge to throw the jars in her hands to the floor. She set them down as she exhaled a long breath.

She wouldn't be able to create another potion.

CHAPTER 20

"GRANNY!" "GRAM!" EXCLAIMED CHLOE AND AVERY IN unison when Magda entered Vivian's apartment. Their voices and bright faces pushed aside Magda's troubles.

The girls—no, the young *ladies*, she had to keep reminding herself—wrapped her in hugs and dropped exaggerated kisses on her cheeks. They might stand a full head taller than her, but they were still her little ladybugs. Vivian's jaw dropped, but she clamped it shut as her daughters guided Magda to the dining table.

"Wow, you look fantastic, Granny." Chloe hugged her shoulders again. "Day at the spa?" Magda patted her cheek in reply, turning away from Vivian's scrutiny.

But there was no hiding the elixir's effects. Her face was fuller, her eyes brighter, and the bags under them much less prominent. The swelling of her knuckles had vanished, her back was straight, and no limp slowed her walk.

Vivian straightened the forks and knives at each place setting. "Perfect timing," she said, not looking up.

"Mom, dinner smells amazing," Avery said. "Thanks for making meatballs."

"Of course!" Vivian beamed, then turned to Chloe. "And veggie meatballs for you."

"Yum." Chloe sat beside Magda, primly scooting forward and crossing her legs under the table. Avery plopped in the chair on the opposite side, yanking it forward with a hand on the seat between her legs. Magda smiled. The differences between the two had ripened as they'd grown older. Avery's hair remained short—her latest hairstyle was a choppy pixie cut—and she had small piercings on almost every fold and curve of both ears. Chloe's hair remained long, her ears unpierced. She didn't like pain.

"So, how are you and Paul doing?" Vivian's question made Chloe cough. She shook her head, taking a long sip of wine.

"What? You two broke up?" The hurt on Vivian's face was obvious. "You never told me."

"I'm sorry. I meant to tell you, Mom, honest. I've got so much going on." Chloe twirled her fork in the pasta. "Trying to date showed me I just don't have time for that."

"And he *was* kind of needy," offered Avery.

Chloe ignored her sister. "I also had to cut back on volunteering at MSPCA. This semester is killing me."

"Well, I'm glad you cut back." Vivian gave a conciliatory smile. "You've got only two more years until you are officially Doctor Chloe Parsons, DVM. Then, you can give back all you can afford."

"True. I didn't think about it that way."

"Plus," Vivian continued, "I never see you. *Either* of you."

"Here we go." Avery shook her head. "Guilt trip time!"

Magda cleared her throat loudly. "So, Avery, do you miss working at the zoo?"

"Nope."

"Yes, you do," Chloe said.

Avery speared a meatball. "I don't miss not getting paid, but I do miss working with the birds."

"Enough to take some college courses?" Magda asked even though she knew the answer.

"Oh hell no." Avery's exaggerated look of shock made her

grandmother laugh. "Besides, that new administrator is a real bitch. Almost two years interning there counted for nothing with her, only a stupid piece of paper did, which is BS. Even when I showed her how well the birds responded to me, nothing."

It had taken years of persistent needling for Chloe to talk Avery into having anything to do with magick, and a forged internship application to Franklin Park Zoo to get her motivated. Avery nearly throttled her sister when she found out what Chloe had done but then praised her sneaky ingenuity. Avery went, insisting there would be no magick involved whatsoever. She loved it immediately, even though it took months to talk the internship coordinator into reassigning her to the bird exhibit. Avery had been devastated when they let her go, citing the new rules requiring every intern have at least two years of college in some animal- or science-related field.

Avery shrugged. "It doesn't matter. Bill's added more self-defense classes, and I'm his best instructor, so I'm just too busy for it anyway."

Magda recalled a sullen and withdrawn fourteen-year-old Avery. The Hartley boy's recovery hadn't had the effect she thought it would on her. Avery once again gave up anything related to magick. She'd refused to talk to Magda about what she'd experienced during her astral visitation of the boy in the hospital room, and Vivian worried about her shutting down entirely although she never knew the whole truth.

It wasn't until months later that Avery had watched a kick-boxing match on television and proclaimed she wanted to learn how to do that. Both Vivian and Magda saw the merit in it as a means for Avery to release her aggression in a constructive way, and to learn a little discipline. The family-owned gym a short bus ride away had classes for young people, and it turned out to be exactly what Avery needed. She liked the place so much she worked there unofficially each summer as water girl, towel washer, janitor—whatever was needed. She'd gravitated toward self-defense and seemed a natural at showing people how to protect themselves. They hired her as soon as she graduated high school.

Outwardly, Magda smiled and laughed with her daughter and granddaughters as they all caught each other up on their busy lives. She had a true family here—

Magda.

His voice traveled through her blood, the deep tone sending ripples across her skin.

Josef waited. He'd been waiting so long. Her one-way plane ticket was purchased, and she was already packed.

"Magda?"

Her eyes fluttered opened. She was standing. Three confused faces looked up at her.

"I—"

"Are you feeling okay?" Vivian came around the table and put a hand on Magda's forehead. "You're freezing!"

She didn't feel cold, quite the opposite. The warmth the potion imparted as it traveled through her body, relieving her aches and pains, hadn't dissipated this time. And the sound of her name from Josef's lips swirled the warmth anew.

Vivian steered Magda to the sofa and she sat, Vivian wrapping a fleece throw across her shoulders. She asked Avery to make some tea for her grandmother. Chloe sat beside her and took a hand, rubbing Magda's cold fingers between her hands to warm them. They exchanged worried glances.

Magda took a deep breath. "I'm all right." She smiled at Chloe's hand rubbing hers. "It's just… I have something to tell you. All of you."

Vivian's face fell. She sat on the edge of the armchair opposite Magda, hands clamped onto her knees. Avery returned to the living room, leaving the mug of water heating in the microwave. Their faces held the same look of apprehension. Magda had rehearsed what she planned to say before she'd come to dinner, but this would work much better. She didn't want to lie to them, but in truth, Magda had been lying to them for years, decades. What did one more matter?

"Your expressions tell me you already know what I'm going to say." Magda dropped her eyes to the carpet when Vivian's chin quivered.

"Don't say it, Granny," Chloe whispered.

She squeezed Chloe's hand but didn't look up.

"Magda, if you're sick with something, I'm sure there's a treatment—"

"There is no treatment for simple old age," Magda said, raising her face to Vivian. Her heart sank. Avery held her mother's hand, her lips pinched and her free hand a fist. Vivian struggled to maintain a calm exterior.

This is a terrible thing I am doing to them.

"And I want to die in my homeland." Gasps pushed the tears from Magda's eyes. "The last time I saw my country, it was in ruins. I don't want that to be my last memory of it."

It was close to one in the morning when the girls left; they hadn't wanted to, but both had early commitments. The twins promised to visit Magda every day until she left. Magda hugged them tight, feeling pain in her chest that wasn't physical. She cursed herself for doing this, but she must get back to Josef without further delay.

Magda tried to leave with them, cowardly using the girls' departure to shield herself from Vivian's questions. But she offered Magda a cup of tea and tapped the back of the sofa.

"Okay, Magda." Vivian handed her the cup and sat on the ottoman with another glass of wine gripped in her slender fingers. "What is really going on?"

Magda kept her face placid, but her palms were damp under the teacup. She took a sip, keeping her eyes on the floor. "What do you mean?"

"I know when you're lying to me!" Vivian's flash of anger startled Magda. Tears filled Vivian's eyes, and she looked away, taking a large gulp of wine. She closed her eyes as she swallowed, tears spilling over. She wiped them away and turned back to Magda.

"I deserve to know what's going on. You are like a mother to me, you know that. You were at death's door this morning but tonight, you look twenty years younger. And not for the first time—don't think I haven't noticed. Then you announce you're dying and moving back to Prague!" More tears followed the trails the first ones started.

The knot twisted in Magda's belly. She stared at her cup for a long time.

She licked her dry lips. "I have to go back. I made a promise, and I'm running out of time to keep it." Magda closed her eyes as Josef's warmth soothed her.

Vivian drained half her glass. "You have to be over one hundred. How are you staying alive? Is it magick?"

Magda nodded. "I have an elixir to keep me going."

Vivian's brows rose high on her forehead. "That's quite an elixir." She leaned forward, elbows on knees with the glass in her hands. "Can I help you somehow? I don't need to know what this promise is, but can I go with you? Do whatever it is you need done? Magda, please… tell me what I can do."

"Oh, Vivian." Magda bowed her head; the warmth no longer consoled her. If Vivian knew the terrible deeds she'd done or what she still needed to do. Shame flushed her cheeks. "This I must do alone. I have waited too long, you see. The ingredients for the potion are gone. Once they are—"

Vivian sank to the floor by Magda's knees, sobbing openly now, and laid her head on the old woman's lap. Magda stroked her hair, her chest tightening.

"Is there no magick that can keep you here, can keep you from…" Vivian choked on the words.

"No, my daughter. And even if there was, I would still have

to go back." Magda closed her eyes at the sound of Josef's urgent voice. "The promise I made cannot be broken."

He had fought the onslaught of Straka's essence, but the blood's power had been overwhelming. Much of him already polluted her. The latest draught proved impossible to stave off.

Now he floated adrift, no longer able to cling to any part of her. And he seethed.

You chose your words well, old woman, but they were not lies. You will die.

He could not influence her mind, but he was still there, still inside her. And he would burn away the potion from the crone's body before she could complete the spell.

He would not allow her to raise Straka.

CHAPTER 21

Prague

Magda stepped off the train into the blessedly muted lighting of Staroměstská station. The harsh fluorescent lights in the car had given her a headache. She tried to tune out the echoing noises of the crowd around her, including a group of rambunctious young American tourists. They complained loudly, wanting the train to move on so they could take selfies against the "badass" tiles—metallic red and gold dimples—lining the tunnel. The quartet of men and women were about the same age as her granddaughters. Her heart ached at the thought of them and Vivian. She struggled with the yearning to go home. Not to the cramped, dingy apartment she had near Vyšehrad Cemetery, but to the *home* she'd had in Boston, the home filled with warmth and laughter and the people she loved.

Josef had loved her also. His fate rested in her hands. And she'd promised.

Magda shuffled to the escalators. Her trip to Okoř had been fruitless. While the church was still there and the prison was still in operation, they no longer sent their unclaimed dead to the church for burial. There were rules and laws now.

Her shoulders slumped with the weight of her disappointment. She wandered from the station, not caring which direction. She found herself in Old Town Square and uttered a mild oath. It teemed with people. Crowds were gathering around the astronomical clock; its hourly walk of the Twelve Apostles must be any minute. The raucous laughter of tourists and their loud expressions of awe at their surroundings amplified her pounding head. After searching in vain for a quiet place to sit, she opted for the only empty bench under the trees beside the clock tower.

How can I possibly complete the spell? She pulled in a shaky breath, gripping the weathered wood of the bench.

"Ma'am, are you all right?" The high-pitched southern drawl of an American woman standing over her jolted Magda upright. She smiled at the young woman, whose two small boys were clinging to her sides. The husband was strolling up, hands filled with cups.

"Oh, yes, yes." Magda nodded to the woman. "Just too much excitement." She waved a hand at her surroundings.

"I can understand that!" she exclaimed. "It's amazing, isn't it?"

Magda nodded again, praying they didn't strike up a conversation with her. Thankfully, the husband steered his wife and children away, desiring to sit on the steps surrounding the massive bronze monument in the middle of the square. Magda watched the happy family stride away, the boys jumping and laughing around the couple.

She waved away the surge of unwanted emotion. Magda's wrist popped at the motion, and she examined her wrinkled hands, gently rubbing the slight swelling of the joints in her fingers.

It had only been a few weeks since she'd drunk the potion, yet her age was returning. Before, Magda had gone many years without needing another. What was different now? Had the ingredients been too old, lost their potency? Magda feared each ache, each deepening wrinkle. She was running out of time.

I must find a way to access dead bodies! Magda clenched her handbag, her fingers digging into the pleather. *I am so close!*

She could *take* the last lives.

Magda huffed aloud at the revolting idea, scaring the pigeons milling about, and stood. Moving too quickly, she stumbled forward, righting herself with an angry grunt.

She walked with no destination, wishing she could leave behind the part of herself that had those horrible thoughts.

Her mind wrestled with how to gain access to dead men, and the notion of murder kept niggling her. *Murder!* That's what it would be. *I won't do that*, she repeated, *no matter how bad the man is*. But it would be so easy. She knew the precise words needed; some things she hadn't forgotten. *No!*

Magda had no idea how long she wandered. She also had no idea where she was. She searched for the nearest bus stop. When she sat on the hard metal bench, her legs protested the distance she'd gone. Magda stretched her legs out with a wince, leaning forward to rub her knees. *This shouldn't be happening.*

Movement in the corner of her eye got her attention. A leaflet taped to the side of the plexiglass wall flapped in the gentle breeze.

She clicked her tongue and slouched back with a snort, a smile tugging at her mouth. *Brož Funeral Home. Where dignity in death is their last rite.*

It had required quite a long conversation with the funeral home's director before he would allow someone of Magda's years to work there. And Mr. Brož was nearly her age—or rather, the age she told him. When she introduced herself, she was delighted by the gold crucifix tiepin he wore. The tiepin held down a plain brown tie against a worn white short-sleeved shirt molded to his protruding belly. He had an amiable manner, with soft blue eyes edged by deep wrinkles, and pronounced liver spots speckling his forehead and sagging jowls.

Magda used the same story that had gotten her into the Catholic church in Okoř: a husband lost to suicide, a mortal sin in the eyes of God, and her desire do what she could to distance herself from his horrific deed.

After she allowed copious tears to flow, Mr. Brož relented, his heart melting at Magda's tale, understanding the gravity of her husband's sin. But he couldn't pay her—his business was steady yet small—nor could he allow her to tend to the bodies themselves. There were laws, and she had no license or proper training. Yet she could assist with dressing them for viewing and arrange the flowers in the viewing chamber and chapel, and other menial tasks she'd be physically capable of performing.

It was several agonizing weeks before Magda was left alone with a body. She'd kept her movements slow and meticulous, garnering sighs of impatience from the employees, who eventually left her alone to finish her tasks. She was a harmless little old lady after all, and they were busy people.

Magda passed her hand over each dead man's face, muttering words she knew well. The magick revealed their past deeds, flooding the dark canvas behind her closed eyes. None yet had been evil enough in their lives to warrant an eternal damnation in the afterlife. Many times she searched twice, ensuring she'd not missed anything.

A month crawled by before someone with a black soul came into the preparation room. His outward appearance was normal enough, and Magda expected nothing from her trespass into his past. Her palm hovered above his sealed eyes as she whispered the phrase.

She gasped, clutching the metal table to keep herself upright. Both revulsion and joy washed through her as the man's monstrous acts raced in her mind's eye. He would drug women he met in bars and do unspeakable things to them. He was a true Jekyll and Hyde, having kept his alter ego hidden since he was a young man.

The man's viewing was filled with distraught family and friends, making Magda want to shout out his foul deeds to the grieving. He didn't deserve their tears, and she eagerly awaited binding the man to Josef.

That evening, having watched the preparation process, she crept into the prep room, knowing the casket lid would not yet be secured for burial.

The room was dark, and the sharp tang of formaldehyde clung to the still air. She didn't click on the overhead lights, opting instead for a headlamp on her forehead. Magda unlatched the top half of the casket and lifted it. The man's past poured into her psyche once more, and she squeezed her eyes closed, pushing away the memories of what the words had showed her.

Magda placed one of the dirty, etched copper coins on each eyelid.

"Sukar ryks'zu yeh krya Der'zu."

The words rolled off her tongue. She coughed at the blood in her throat, momentarily forgetting the side effect of speaking the wretched words. She repeated the phrase, in case she'd mispronounced anything, and expelled the blood into a handkerchief.

With a great sense of relief, she closed the lid. *Only three more.*

As luck would have it, the next week brought another man of horrendous character: a pimp who beat his women, some of whom were merely girls of fifteen and sixteen, and took most of the money they earned.

The following days passed slowly for Magda. She'd let herself get excited with the recent flow of bad men, and her hopes rose high. It was almost over.

But days turned into weeks, and weeks into a month. Her body ached with each movement, her knuckles so swollen and painful that buttoning up shirts and blouses became excruciating. Mr. Brož watched her with a concerned eye, saying she appeared to be getting older and more frail by the day. Magda insisted she was fine and went about her daily chores without complaint.

She was dying. Her lungs hurt when she took full breaths, her heart thumped irregularly, and the fingers of her left hand gnarled into a fist, making the hand unusable. In her desperation, she dug out the book, still bound with the black ribbons, from her chest of blankets. Already familiar with every passage, she knew there was nothing to help her.

But *perhaps* the words would change as they'd done in the past and give her an answer, or at least some relief.

No. She wouldn't risk it calling out to Avery even this far away. She had exhausted her ways to cheat death. *It is hopeless.*

With a cry of frustration, Magda shoved the book from the desk. The thrust took her off balance, sending her to the floor of her bedroom. A fresh round of pain blasted through her back and hips, freeing the sobs held in her chest.

"Josef!" Magda cried. "I am so close! Please help me!"

She lay on the floor, paralyzed with grief and disappointment, until the streetlights replaced the sun coming through the bedroom window. Josef couldn't help her; there was no one and nothing to help her. She'd come this far, she'd left her family, and she'd failed.

A sharp clap of thunder woke Magda. Rain beat against the window. She rolled onto her back, and every stiff joint revolted. She lay there for several minutes, contemplating how she was going to get up. All her years had caught up with her in two months' time. Magda *felt* one hundred and two now. Gritting her teeth, she pulled herself up using the bed's footboard. The clock read a quarter to five in the morning. There was no point in going to bed; she wouldn't sleep.

Magda changed her clothes slowly. She collected her things for the day and left the apartment, taking each stair one by one, with her good hand gripping the railing.

It wasn't unusual for Magda to be the first one at the funeral home. She rarely got a full night's sleep. Mr. Brož, also an early riser, could be expected at any moment. In the quiet mornings, they sometimes sat in the kitchen with mugs of coffee and reminisced. He'd tell her of the tumultuous times she'd stayed away from, how the country's struggles had taken their toll on his family. She'd let him ramble on, smiling and nodding politely.

Magda opened the door to the prep room and flicked on the light. She grimaced at the sudden brightness. Two caskets lined the far wall of the long room, waiting for their burial today. The much smaller one held the body of a six-year-old girl. Her mother occupied the other, the two having died together in a car accident. Magda stared at the caskets and fingered the coins in her dress pocket. *No.* She turned away and lifted her hand to the light switch. *No, I can't do it.*

Her hand trembled as she held the switch with her throbbing fingers. She inhaled a deep breath, but her lungs refused such an intake. Magda coughed and clutched her chest, leaning against the doorframe as her legs weakened under the strain.

Do this for me. Bring me back. Promise me, Magda. His words were so close, raw and fresh. She could smell his blood, her hands warm with it, the taste still on her lips.

"I promise," she repeated, her words echoing with the voice of the younger Magda.

She limped to the mother's casket. Magda didn't look upon the woman's damaged face, much too damaged for a viewing, as she placed the coins on her eyelids and secured them with a strip of white linen. She muttered the words hurriedly and closed the lid.

Magda stared at the small casket, placing her palm atop it. Hot tears streamed down her face as she gazed upon the little girl.

"I'm sorry," she whispered. Magda had never bound an innocent soul. She had taken solace in choosing to bind only the worst of men. None had deserved a peaceful afterlife in the wake of what they'd done in this one. But this little girl and her mother were different. Bound to Josef, their souls would be denied peace, unable to move on, giving him the power to rise again. Forever tethered to their unseen master, forever trapped in a dark limbo, never to continue their journey.

Sobs racked Magda as she performed the ritual over the little girl. She apologized between each sob. Magda resealed the lid and steadied herself against the small casket. What should have been joy at binding the last soul, marking the end of the long spell and the return of the man she loved, was filled with agony and regret… and shame.

CHAPTER 22

Magda stood at a small side gate to Vyšehrad Cemetery. The newer padlock looked out of place against the weathered iron bars, thick with numerous layers of chipping black paint. It had changed little since she was last there, except the ivy seemed to blanket more of the stone slabs and had been allowed to twine around many long-dead trees, making them green once more.

The gate had been unlocked when she'd come years ago. She certainly couldn't climb over the fence, spike-tipped or not. But though no more was required of her—the spell was complete—she wanted to be as close to his grave as she could. The moon was nearing its zenith.

Any time now.

She gripped a bar with her good hand, staring intently at the white granite headstone of Doktor Josef Straka. The short, thick obelisk facing her glowed eerily in the light of the moon, or Magda's exhausted mind played tricks. His grave stood out in the tight row; it was the only one with a boundary of matching granite in which a manicured carpet of bright green grass grew. The others were topped with slabs of smooth stone or bordered with elaborate fencing.

The night was warm, the air thick, and no breeze cooled the

sweat on Magda's forehead and upper lip. A light fog sat on the ground, clinging to it like a shroud. The shifting of her feet sounded overly loud in the oppressive silence.

Magda's entire body ached, begging her to go home and lie down. This had been the longest day of her long life; the memory of the sweet little girl's dead face, eyes covered with dirty copper coins, refused to leave. She pushed her forehead against the iron bars, trying to push away the haunting image.

She forced her mind to travel back to the day she first came here, as a devastated young woman, the love of her life, short as it had been, torn from her so brutally. So much time had passed, so many unforgivable things she had done since.

Magda's thoughts wandered to Vivian and the girls, and what they would think of her now, standing at the edge of a cemetery in the dead of night, hoping, no, *praying* for her old lover to return from the grave.

Her time before them seemed like another life, she another person entirely. But here Magda was again, stepping back into the shoes of the person she was before. She was grateful that they would never know this side of her.

Magda's eyes darted to the moon again. The book hadn't indicated what would happen. Each minute crawled. Each minute fed the fear eclipsing her dwindling hope—fear the spell hadn't worked, that she'd done something incorrectly, or worse, that it had been pointless nonsense from the start. Magda's heart fought against her brain, and her stomach churned with doubt.

"Please."

A sudden chill made Magda shiver. She released the breath she'd been holding; it turned to frost. The stagnant air shifted; it rustled the hem of her dress and cooled her overheated skin. She welcomed the wash of freshness encircling her aching body, yet the chill was unnatural. Goose bumps rose on her arms, not from the cold but from what this could mean.

Eyes locked on to Josef's grave, Magda tightened her grip on the bar. *Please, please, please.*

Was the mist moving?

The stagnant fog swirled, the white churning in unusual ways. It thickened, engulfing his grave and headstone, reaching into the sky and forming a column. A blast of cold wind rushed around her and she gasped, gripping the bar harder to hold herself upright. The wind had shape; opaque tendrils travelled up the low hill where his grave lay, taking the mist with it as it moved. It whipped around the hill and up the column of fog and then was gone.

Everything was quiet once more. The air was as warm and thick as it had been only a moment ago.

In front of Josef's headstone was the silhouette of a tall man, arms resting at his sides. She clasped her hands to her breast. "Josef?"

The man strode toward her, his long legs moving with confidence over the uneven ground. She took a step back out of reflex. A wind whipped around him, and he was gone. "No!" Magda lunged forward.

"My love." The deep, velvet voice came from her left and she blenched, covering her mouth as she turned.

Standing before her was Josef Straka in the same beautifully tailored black suit she'd always seen him in, the same angelic face, glossy dark hair and beard, the same smile in his midnight blue eyes. Eyes looking at Magda no differently than they had eighty years ago.

"Josef." Her legs collapsed. He caught her, cradling her to his chest. She inhaled his scent. It was not the smell of dirt or the grave but of *him*. She clung to him; he was solid, he was warm, he was *real*. Magda crumpled in Josef's arms, unable to speak.

"Shh, shh, my dear." Josef stroked her hair and kissed the top of her head. He hugged her tight.

When her crying ebbed, Magda wanted to pull away to look upon his face, but shame stopped her. She was old now, so old. He wouldn't feel as he had before, how could he?

"I'm sorry it has been so long, Josef."

"Hush, now. Time is nothing to me." Josef gently pushed her from his chest. Magda turned her withered face away. He hooked a finger under her chin, lifting it to meet his gaze. "Do not be ashamed, my dear Magda. Time has been cruel to you. But you no longer have to suffer."

Her brows drew together.

"You have fulfilled your promise." Josef rested his palm against her wet cheek. "I am very grateful to you, my love. If you choose, you can be young again and walk beside me as I continue my work."

"Be young again?" Magda choked. "You can make me as I was?" Her heart fluttered, and her eyes once again filled with tears.

Josef laughed lightly. "Yes, my love, yes. If that is your wish. But you must ask for it." His smile never left his eyes.

Magda searched his face, her mind swimming with his words. He wanted to continue his work, helping those in need. She felt honored that he would want her beside him.

"I wish to be young again, Josef! I wish to be yours once more."

As he wrapped her in his embrace under the moonlight, Josef whispered words she'd never heard before, but the familiar hissing sounds made her stiffen.

Panic tightened Magda's spine. But these words were none she'd ever read. Josef nuzzled her tighter. He'd never hurt her.

"All will be well, my love. Do not fear."

The cold wind returned and whipped around them. She cried out in fear as a sudden freezing sensation seized her. Still murmuring sibilant words, Josef let go and stepped back.

"Josef!" She reached for him but could not move. Fingertips of icy wind dug into her flesh. His face still held the smile she'd fallen in love with.

The cold pierced her bones, like needles burrowing deep. She struggled to break free but had no strength. Her chest convulsed, and her body thrashed within the confines of the gale holding her fast.

"Josef, please! It hurts!" *Can he hear me*? The rush of wind was deafening, and she could barely see him through it. He didn't move, only continued to gaze at her. Magda tried to scream, terror clutching her old and failing heart. *He's killing me! No, it can't be!* The whirlwind's grip tightened, lifting her from the ground. Her spine bolted straight, her shoulders snapped back, and unbelievable pain forced the air from her lungs.

Josef, please, don't do this! She could no longer see him. *My love, please!*

Magda's release was so sudden she collapsed to the ground, knees crashing onto the uneven cobblestones. She fought for breath, holding her chest with one hand and bracing herself with the other. Blood pounded in her head. She blinked furiously to clear her vision, chest burning as she gulped in deep breaths.

What held her up was the smooth hand of a young woman, without gnarled fingers or blue-black bruises.

CHAPTER 23

MAGDA MARVELED AT HER NAKED SELF IN THE LONG dressing mirror, unable to believe what reflected. The beautiful young woman from her youth, with glowing skin and waves of long black hair, ogled back, her eyes also unable to believe the reality of it. Gone were the scars that had chronicled her unfortunate childhood and marriage, and the palms of her hands showed no signs of a single hard day's labor. She was new.

Josef stood behind her, smiling at her reflection. "As I promised."

She met his gaze in the mirror. Magda could now relive her life with this man, make up for all the years she'd spent without him. They could marry, have children. Her heartbeat quickened. *Children.*

He laid his hands on her shoulders. Chills rippled across Magda's renewed skin. His fingers were warm and soft, and slowly trailed down her arms. He kissed her neck and continued down to her shoulder, his hands cupping her firm breasts. She leaned against him, lightheaded from the rush of passion she'd not experienced in so long.

Josef propped himself on an elbow, gazing at Magda's euphoric face.

"Where is the book, my love?" He brushed strands of hair away from her moist cheek.

She beamed at him. "Here. Let me get it." She rolled away and stood. A burst of dizziness and weak legs made her giggle. Magda knelt, amazed yet again at the absence of stabbing pain in her knees and back, everywhere. She felt glorious, happy, overjoyed. The dreadful deeds she'd done for him, the long years she'd forgotten him were washed away. It had all been worth it. Josef still loved her, and his magick made her young again! She couldn't have dreamt of a better outcome.

Magda pulled the heavy book from under the bed and laid it before him.

Josef pushed up from his elbow with a sharp inhale. His manhood rose from beneath the sheet, and she peered at him. He didn't meet her eyes, his gaze fixed on what lay before him. Josef bolted onto his knees and snatched the book. Magda flinched slightly, then leaned forward to catch his eye, but he paid no notice. She laid her hands atop his as he freed the book from the black satin bindings. He snatched it away, a low growl in his throat.

"Josef!" She stepped back.

He blinked at her several times, as if he'd forgotten she was there. His feral snarl melted into his everyday smile.

"Forgive me, my dear." He gazed at the book he hugged to his chest. "I have waited a long time to be reunited with this."

Magda stiffened. "But it is filled with the most horrific things, Josef."

His head snapped up. Josef's glare made her take another step back. "You've read it?" Then his face softened, and he laughed lightly. "Of course you've read it. I told you to read it. How else could you have brought me back?" Josef glanced at it once more, caressing its cover. "And you're wrong. It's filled with the most wondrous things."

Magda had always denied he indulged in the depraved magick of the book. Not her Josef. He'd helped many patients with it; he used it as she had, turning bad to good, hadn't he? She'd seen it! Yet the expression growing on his face revealed something much different.

She swallowed. "Please tell me why you have it."

Her heart sank as Josef's widening grin took on a sinister curve.

Oh, no, Josef, no.

Magda steadied herself. "Where did it come from?"

"I wrote it."

Magda covered her mouth. "You can't have written it. That book is evil."

"Evil? What has kept you alive all this time? I know you used it not just for the potion. I know you used it to maim, Magda, to *kill.* I know everything the book has done." His eyes narrowed. "You should be more grateful."

She shook her head. *No, it's not possible.* Magda knew everything the book contained. If Josef had written such horrific things…

Magda's legs threatened to give out as she studied the changed face of the man she loved. Gone was the Josef she'd held in her memories, the man she'd sacrificed everything for. A sneer had replaced the ready smile he'd always regarded her with. It looked far too natural on his face.

It had all been a lie.

"Oh, Josef!" She turned away.

He snatched her wrist. "You must see, Magda! Only then can you truly understand." She pulled, but his grip only tightened. Burning pain shot up her arm, and she screamed, desperate to run.

"Suka yeh ris," he hissed.

"No!"

With a flourish of his left hand, the air quivered. The whole room contracted; sections of it broke apart with echoing cracks and pops and fell away, disappearing into the blackness now under Magda's bare feet. She gulped for breath, fear making it difficult to pull air into her lungs.

He released her, and she fell backward but caught herself on something cold and hard.

Magda was no longer in her bedroom. Pitch blackness surrounded her; only her frightened gasps and rapid heartbeat filled her ears. There was no wind, but she was freezing, the cold biting into her bones. She wrapped her arms around her breasts. Magda was still naked.

Something crunched behind her, and she whirled with a shriek. A presence made itself known in the distance. As Magda's eyes adjusted to the scant, red light coming from it, her brain screamed to run, but fear locked her in place.

A giant creature sat high atop a pedestal throne. Its skin was matte black, like hardened lava, and spiderwebbed with red, fiery cracks. Thick horns curved from its forehead to the back of its neck, and its—what were they, wings?—enveloped it like a shroud. Its eyes opened, flashing red, then glowed like fresh embers as it keyed on to a visitor to its realm.

It was the only light in the vast, black world. There were no stars or moon in the heavens, and no sounds save for the creature's movements, like boulders crushing against one another.

The monster rose, and Magda fell to her knees. She couldn't acknowledge the pain of the sharp rocks digging into her skin, her terror crippling her senses. The face of the creature transformed into that of a woman, and a wry smile grew on its… her lips. The grotesque horns rippled under that smile with what Magda could only guess was laughter.

Her enormous wings opened, the sound of sails unfurling, and she stepped from the stone pedestal to the ground. The creature's body continued its transformation. It was now shaped as a voluptuous woman yet without nipples or slit; her skin remained smooth black and veined with thin fractures of liquid fire.

As her wings expanded outward, white shapes poured from

within them, racing toward Magda. They took solid form when they reached the ground. There were hundreds of them, each the same. Hairless skin a sickly shade of white, pulled tightly across a small frame of bones and little muscle, only a slash across their "faces," the slash filled with tiny, sharp teeth. No eyes, no noses, no ears.

And they *screamed.*

Magda cowered on the ground, arms covering her head, her screams drowned out by the tumult. Blood trickled from her ears; laughter filled her head. Deep, throaty laughter. She didn't —couldn't—look up and didn't need to. It came from the demonic creature.

With thoughts pushed into her mind, unwanted and unwelcome, she knew what they were, and what they desired. Another wave of restrained laughter came from the demon.

They were creatures forever in darkness and cold. They were allowed to gather within their sovereign for the meager light and warmth it imparted, yet often thrust out for they were noisy, unruly children.

What they wanted most of all, what they craved more than anything, was to feel heat on their icy skins and walk under the sun. Their master had promised them all the pleasures of Man, and they yearned for them. They watched the world of Man, seeing without eyes, envious of every detail, and they craved it. To walk in the skin of a man, to taste the flesh of beasts, to drink the fire water flowing so freely, to rut with their fellows. All Muraal had promised them. And now they *demanded* it.

They streamed passed her, the force buffeting her. Their stench threatened to choke Magda. But that stench was familiar…

The great demon released Magda's mind, and she tumbled backward. A force pushed at her chest, commanding her to look.

Magda didn't trust her legs as she hauled herself from the ground. She kept her face lowered, afraid of what she would see.

Witness, the monster spat, shoving at Magda's back with greater force. Magda clenched her fists as she raised her eyes.

A mantle of shimmering black rose endlessly before the massive, writhing throng of small white demons. The barrier surrounded their entire world, which felt small to Magda now, constricted and tight, as if she were locked in a closet or prison cell. They jumped and clawed at something they couldn't reach: a thin but long gash appearing in the mantle high above them. They hissed and screamed at the solid surface as they climbed atop each other in vain attempts to get at it.

Magda stared horrified; *her* world lay on the other side. A busy city teeming with people on a bright, sunny day. Was that Wenceslas Square? Magda squinted. She was certain what appeared through the gloomy black haze was the horse and rider monument, standing guard in front of the National Museum. The angels flanking the central tower were unmistakable.

The horde salivated, crying to be one with them, to live in them. They were promised!

But the rip was superficial.

Josef caused this. He is helping her… them!

The creature approached the damaged barrier, growing larger with each step. The fire beneath her matte skin flowed rapidly. Her long fingers, nails like talons, sank into the tear and wrenched it open, making it wider, longer. If the ripping of the mantle made a sound, Magda couldn't hear it, for the horde urged their master on, begging her to allow them through. Their shrieks were deafening.

With an immense roar, the monster rent the breach open. Muraal stepped aside and watched with a triumphant smile as her children poured into the mortal world.

CHAPTER 24

Magda's bedroom snapped back around her. Finding herself back on worn carpet rather than rocky ground did little to comfort her. She lay on the floor in a fetal position, arms wrapped around her knees. Josef stood naked, regarding her with hooded eyes.

"Now you understand."

"I don't understand at all!" Magda scrambled up but fell backward against the wall. Bile swam in her stomach, and she gulped deep breaths to quell the surge.

He laughed as she struggled to rise, using the nightstand as a crutch.

She couldn't look at him. *What have I done?* Magda covered her face. The darkness brought the grotesque shape of that massive demon thing as a bright burn behind her eyes. She immediately dropped her hands.

Josef's face softened. "Muraal is trapped, you see. She and her children wish only for light and warmth… and freedom."

The compassion in his voice was like a blow to Magda's stomach.

"Only! They mean to take over our bodies, Josef! To live *inside* us. How can you help them?"

Josef snorted and cast a dismissive hand. "Humans are

stupid and weak. There are nothing. Is it fair they have all the pleasures of this life and Muraal's children have none?"

Magda could find no words; only a strangled sound left her throat.

"I'd almost succeeded all those years ago," he said, taking the seat at her dressing table. Josef's face darkened, jaw muscles tensing as he gnashed his teeth. "But I was betrayed." Josef's eyes dropped to the floor, shame taking over for a breath, then he graced her with his smile. "I'm fortunate you found the life-extending potion, my dear, and even more fortunate that you are so obedient, so easily swayed."

Magda paled.

"Come now." Josef gave her a look as if he were reprimanding a child. "No, of course, how silly of me. You wouldn't have known." He continued to smile at her but didn't elaborate.

She gulped and took the bait. "Wouldn't have known what, Josef?"

"There is purpose in everything I do, Magda. I picked you initially as a pleasant distraction, but you proved most useful when my situation turned… regrettable. I knew you'd do as I bade—however, I added some insurance to the ingredients in my cabinet. Whatever potion you brewed, it did not matter. You would still be mine."

Magda's eyes widened as clarity dawned. The tainted ingredients explained the resurgence of his memories, the persistent dreams, the feelings of guilt for a promise broken. Then the overwhelming urge to return to Prague, to disregard and *lie* to the people she loved. They'd begun when she'd first drank the potion.

She'd been his pawn. Nothing more.

"And good thing I did, since you appeared to have forgotten me, which is puzzling—but no matter." He rose. "You brought me back, Magda. I cannot thank you enough. Now, I can begin again. There will be no mistakes this time."

Her knees threatened to give way, and Magda put a hand on the nightstand.

It was all a lie. Josef never loved me.

The words repeated in the hollow of Magda's heart. Their echo faded as anger fought its way in.

All she had done, all she had sacrificed, all the souls now cursed for eternity. All for him!

Fury now steeled Magda's muscles. She drew herself straight, her nakedness no longer a concern. She thought of the book. She'd used it before to hurt men, to *kill*, and Josef was still just a man, wasn't he?

"Sukar ryks yi kaaz!" Magda threw the words at him with all her strength. Josef's eyes bulged, and he staggered back, banging against the tall mirror. Magda's upper lip twitched. *It's working!*

She stepped toward him.

"H'zir sukar dree," she hissed, drawing out the last word between clenched teeth.

Josef slumped against the wall, hands gripping the sides of his head. Emboldened by her success, she took another step.

"H'zir sukar—"

Josef's hand shot up and gripped her throat; his long fingers dug into her skin. He stood, his face bent over hers.

"You *dare* use my book against me." His breath was hot on her face, and she whimpered. She pulled at his wrist, but his grip was stone. "The book will not go against its master." He threw her to the floor.

She scrambled forward on all fours. He caught her by the back of her hair and crouched beside her, yanking her head up, forcing her to look into the mirror before them.

"Magda," he said in her ear, as close as a lover but with none of the sentiment. "Your youth belongs to me."

The reflection of the petrified young woman changed. Her radiant youth melted away, revealing the ancient woman she had been only hours ago. Her pains renewed, doubled this time.

He released her, and her forehead smacked the floor. Magda

couldn't push herself upright; the arthritis in her joints wouldn't allow it. Josef tossed the book beside her; it landed with a thud only an inch from her nose. The stench of its skin flooded her nostrils.

Oh! She gasped, recalling the horde of nightmarish white demons racing past her, their stink overwhelming. *It's the skin of one of those horrid creatures!*

"You've taken such good care of it, *my love*." Sarcasm dripped from his words. "I'll leave it in your care once more. Perhaps you can find something in there to restore your youth better than I." He laughed, a deranged laugh that made Magda shudder.

Josef dressed without haste, never taking his eyes off the crumpled old woman until he finished. He inspected himself in the mirror, adjusting his tie and smoothing the front of his suit jacket.

"We'll continue this conversation when I return. I have the sons of traitors to deal with now."

When the front door closed, she allowed herself to breathe. *What have I done?* she repeated, letting the sobs free, each one an uneven mixture of shame and loss. The love she was certain she'd felt from him had been nothing but a lie. He'd *used* her from the start, and then used her love against her.

By raising Josef from the dead, I have let pure evil into this world. And he will release something much, much worse.

The rumble of Muraal's laughter stole Magda's breath.

She couldn't absolve herself by blaming the tainted potion. It had been *her* hands performing those unforgivable deeds—the innocent mother and daughter bound forever!—*her* conniving that brought the monster to the threshold of this world. Perhaps Magda had forgotten him because her subconscious knew better.

Magda had no magick to fight him, and the book was of no use if it wouldn't go against its master. Josef mocked her impotence by leaving it with her.

Muraal and her, its, horde will enter this world and possess the bodies of every man, woman, and child. And it will be my fault.

The faces of Avery and Chloe filled her vision, with Vivian entering to wrap her arms around the beautiful young women.

No! Magda pushed herself up, ignoring the screams of her body. *That won't happen.*

Never in her right mind would she have brought the girls into this. Yet sitting powerless on the floor, racked once more with old age verging on death, the book appearing larger and more sinister than ever before, she could think of nothing else.

Magda relaxed against the bed, trying to slow her racing mind. She huffed as she glanced down, her nakedness rousing her.

"You're right, Josef," she said, using the bed and one arm to help herself up, the other clutching the foul book to her chest. "My youth may belong to you, but my old age belongs to me." She glowered at the empty doorway as if he was standing there. "And so does your *death*."

Magda laid the book on the dresser. She hadn't opened it in so long and dreaded to do so now. *But I've made my bed. Now, I must make it right.*

She hastily flipped through the pages, cringing now, knowing what it was made from. *A book of blood and skin.* Avery had been right.

Oh, Avery. Magda put her hands to her face. *Chloe. Vivian.*

She straightened, jaw set, and returned her attention to what she sought in the book.

Magda mumbled a spell, testing the words on her tongue, running her fingers along the passage of scratches and marks. *Such an ugly book you are.* Magda flipped it closed. *Filled with such ugly things. To think I relied on your aid for so long.* A deep sigh escaped her lips. *But you've always given me what I needed.*

Magda pulled a sheet of paper from the desk drawer and scribbled. She placed the book inside an old hatbox, stuffing newspapers around it. She brought the note to her lips and kissed it, pressing the paper to her face.

"Please forgive me." Magda placed the note atop the newspaper and sealed the box.

She pulled on the clothes she'd worn earlier and crept out the door.

A short time later, she returned with a FedEx slip in her fist. She put a match to it, watching it burn with stony eyes. Now that the adrenaline propelling her march to the nearest shipping drop-off had faded, she collapsed, shaking, into the recliner.

One more thing to do.

She stared at her wrinkled palms through vision warped by old tears and horrific deeds. *The things I've done in my life, what I made happen. Bewitched or not, I deserve this.*

Magda recited the short passage from the book, aloud and with much force, twice.

In each of her palms arose vibrant green flames. They leapt and danced, but only the barest amount of heat bloomed in her hand.

"Josef, I will be free of you, and I will keep my soul with me."

Magda lifted her palms to her eyes.

CHAPTER 25

Josef Straka was no longer restrained by his mortality, his mind no longer fettered by the limitations of the human brain. He could speak to Muraal freely now. He slowed his pace along the dimly lit sidewalk and lifted his face to the mass of clouds hiding the moon behind them.

My lady, Muraal. His mind breathed out slowly, reaching through the Shade to the creature that had given him purpose—and power.

Josef, Muraal purred. Hot desire washed over his body. *Good, my chosen, good. You have returned to the human world.*

He watched her languid form ease back into her stone throne, her long, smooth legs crossed, and her sleek talons gripped the armrests. Heat centered into his manhood, and he steadied himself against the light pole.

It won't be long now, my lady. Josef rested his cheek against the pole. *The sons and grandsons of the men who defied me will be easy to secure. You will be free soon.*

A noise deep in her throat brought him a fresh wave of passion. *I know you will not fail me again.*

The heat of shame replaced his passion, and he straightened. *No, I will not fail you again.*

Josef scoffed at the memory of that arrogant, foolish woman daring to use his book against him. In his annoyance, he had briefly considered dispatching her. But, no, she had her uses. He could keep her old until his passion rose, then make her young long enough to satisfy him. He grinned to himself. Magda had always been quite useful.

When he reached her apartment and found the door locked, he laughed. Josef passed his hand over the doorframe, and its bolts slid back. A dark room greeted him; the scent of burnt flesh filled his nostrils.

Had she tried to burn his book? No matter if she had, it couldn't be burned—or harmed for that matter. *Stupid woman.* He went toward the bedroom and tripped over a lump in his path. At his silent command, light filled the room.

Josef hissed. Magda lay on her side with her back to him. He knelt and grasped her shoulder. She was cold. He rolled her over.

He stood at the gruesome sight. Magda's eyes were burnt to hollow sockets, her withered lips frozen in a mocking grin.

"You think you were clever, putting out your eyes." He glared at the husk of his lover. "I don't need your soul. You gathered plenty for me. I have all the power I need." He stepped over her to the bedroom where he'd left the book. Pity, though. Shackling Magda's soul would have given him great pleasure.

The lamp on the nightstand switched on as he entered the room. It looked the same as when he'd left: rumpled sheets, a toppled stool, the tall mirror askew on the wall. He didn't immediately see the book, and panic shot through him. He darted to the bed and threw off its covers and pillows. He tore open the dresser drawers, tossing out their contents with flicks of his hand.

It was nowhere. He reached out with his senses, searching the apartment. He could not feel its presence.

"What did you do with it?" He ran to Magda and grabbed the sides of her face, his eyes probing her blackened pits. His mind tried searching her last movements, but he saw nothing. He growled and threw her head back to the floor. Not only had she escaped her soul's enslavement to him, but she'd also made it impossible for him to view what she'd seen with her eyes.

"You *bitch*."

He rejoiced.

The old woman's intentions were clear as her gnarled hands clutched him, for he was still within her. He could not have let her use him against Straka; he could not risk being discovered.

Once again, she had done him the greatest service. He was not only away from the odious man, but he would soon be with the child. That glorious child with the delicious energy, powerful magick smoldering within her, unnoticed and untapped. The girl would embrace him, eager for the power he could give her.

His freedom was near.

PART II

THE RED TWINS

CHAPTER 26

"We got a package from Granny." Chloe called out as she came through the door. "And it's heavy."

"Oooo." Avery emerged from the kitchen, which took only two steps in their tiny apartment, rubbing her hands together. "I hope it's those cookies again. In a really *big* tin."

Chloe grunted, balancing the round box on an arm while trying to pull the key from the deadbolt at the same time. She pushed the door closed with her backside, eyeballing Avery with the chiding expression she reserved for her sister. "Your stomach."

Avery shrugged and took the package.

Chloe sniffed, wrinkling her nose. "Burn the popcorn again?"

"Meh."

"I keep telling you not to use the 'Popcorn' button on the microwave. It's always too long."

"Blah, blah, blah."

Avery hefted the package, eyes brightening. She shook it with no regard for any fragile contents it might hold. Avery frowned at not hearing the telltale rattle of the cookies her grandmother got her hooked on over two months ago. 'Crack cookies,' Avery called them; she could eat an entire tin in one sitting. And she had.

"I don't hear cookies." Avery pouted, then sniffed the box. Her upper lip twitched. "Damn, it stinks."

"I know. I carried it up four flights. It might've been in a cargo bay with a bunch of rotting fruit." Chloe waved a hand in front of her nose. "You know it's bad when you can smell it over burnt popcorn."

Avery put the round box on the kitchen table and tried to rip off the top without success, wishing she would stop chewing her nails down to the skin. Chloe brandished a steak knife at her with a condescending eyebrow lift. Avery smirked but took the knife anyway. She sawed through the many layers of masking tape around the edge.

"You're going to cut yourself."

Avery wasn't listening. The strange sensation in her gut gave her pause. Was that excitement or… fear? She couldn't tell. Maybe a mixture of both. Why? The old hatbox probably held a molding fruitcake. They both hated fruitcake.

She dropped the knife on the table and slid her hands to the sides of the box. Was it warm? Her forehead creased as she cocked her head to the side.

"What?" Chloe sat in a chair and stared up into Avery's face. "I've never liked that look." She squinted. *"What?"*

Avery snorted, but her eyes were locked on the box. For a split second, she had no desire to open it. She'd rather chuck it out the window.

Chloe leaned back in the chair, eyebrows rising at her sister. "You're *scared* of it?" She rubbed her palms on her thighs.

Avery rarely shielded her thoughts and emotions from her sister; it was just too much work. Their deep connection was helpful most of the time; neither of them had to say much about what they were feeling. But other times, like now, it was annoying.

"Whatever," Avery said, flipping the lid off in a grand,

sweeping gesture. She didn't watch it sail across the room or notice when it collided with the canisters on the counter; her eyes were fixed on the bit of gray peeking out from beneath wads of newspapers. Chloe leaned over to peer into the box.

Avery sucked in a breath, her spine snapping to attention. She didn't need to see any more to know what it was.

The book of blood and skin.

Chloe turned slowly to her twin, eyes and mouth widening in unison. *What did you say?*

Avery scooped up the wadded papers, careful not to touch what lay beneath, and tossed them to the floor. She stared at the gray book, its binding ugly with deep grooves and puckers, scrunching her face at the smell. Her fingertips dug into the sides of the box. She'd never seen it before. All those years ago, locked in her grandmother's cabinet. It said her name—just that one time. She'd felt its strange warmth on her palm *through* the cabinet door, but she'd never *seen* it. Goose bumps rose on her arms as she exhaled.

Chloe shivered. Her gaze left her sister's face to glance at the book, but a bright bit of yellow on the floor caught her eye. "Oh! There's a note."

She retrieved the rumpled sheet of legal paper from within the pile of discarded paper. Chloe nudged Avery with an elbow, waving the note between her eyes and the book. Avery twitched, jarred from her trance, and snatched it from Chloe's hands.

My dear granddaughters,

I cannot tell you how much it pains me to bring you into this, but I don't feel I have another option. I would ask you to destroy this book, but it cannot be destroyed. You must hide it away until I'm able to see you again.

All my love forever,

Your grandmother

"Okaaay," Avery said, turning the paper over, looking for more. "Way to be cryptic, Gram."

Chloe took the note and read it twice more. "Granny's handwriting was always so neat, so precise, but this is a mess. She was obviously stressed when she wrote it. Or maybe the arthritis in her hand has gotten worse?"

"I guess she's coming back to Boston?" Avery asked, peering over Chloe's shoulder to read it again. "Bring us into what? And what does she mean 'this book can't be destroyed'? And—"

"Shush!" Chloe let her eyes leave the paper only long enough to glare at Avery. "'*Until I'm* able *to see you...'* What a strange way to phrase that. Maybe she's in the hospital?"

Avery gave an exaggerated shrug and made a face. "Am I allowed to speak now?"

"No. I'm calling." Chloe pulled her messenger bag from its spot on the lower rack of their overcrowded baker's rack. Freeing her cell phone from its pocket, she tapped on the image of her grandmother's laughing face, with Chloe and Avery each kissing a cheek, in her Favorites list. She tapped the speaker button, placing the phone on the table.

The other end rang until voicemail picked up and Chloe hit disconnect.

"No point in leaving a message," she said with a groan. "She doesn't know how to check it although I've showed her, like, a thousand times."

"Old people," Avery harrumphed, and they grinned at each other.

"Well, wait. What time is it in Prague? She might be asleep."

Avery stiffened as Chloe rubbed her forearms. "But you don't believe that, do you?"

Chloe's alarm became hers; the hairs on the nape of her neck prickled.

After several calls during what would've been Magda's late morning, Chloe shared the contents of the box and her gnawing unease with Vivian. The three of them tried for two days to reach Magda without success.

When Chloe finally located the apartment manager, the old man hadn't known a single word of English. Chloe tried simply repeating Magda's name, but the manager's words only increased in volume and rapidity. She chided herself for not having had Magda teach her more Czech than the names of her favorite dishes.

It didn't take much for Chloe to convince Avery they needed to actually go to Prague to check on their grandmother. Vivian wanted to go, but with the recent reorganization of critical care departments at the hospital, she was managing fifteen nurses now, half of whom didn't want to be managed by her. There was no way she could leave anytime soon.

She mollified herself by paying for the girls' airfare, which was considerable without a longer advance purchase. Vivian used the rest of her credit card limit to pay for the tickets, but she didn't tell the girls that. There was a pit in her stomach. Her daughters had never been more than a few miles away from her, and as a family, they'd never traveled farther than a hundred miles from Boston. Now, they were going to Prague! A twinge of jealousy worked its way into the ball of worry, and she tutted herself for being petty.

What also worried her was Magda's cryptic note. Only Vivian knew about Magda's magickal workings and the elixir sustaining her for so long. *Had she run out of time? Was she able to keep her promise? Is she gone now?* A lump lodged itself in her throat.

Vivian had never wanted to know more than the scant bits Magda told her. The images of Magda's hands flaming up with green fire and Curt's body burning away flashed across her vision, and she recalled the moment when Magda leapt onto Curt's back. Experiencing that horrible evening had been enough. Ignorance was bliss, she'd told herself and never pressed Magda for more.

But now, it tormented her. And like the girls, Vivian had no idea what this book was. She remembered Magda flipping through a book as Curt lay dead on the floor, but she had been too dazed to pay any attention to it. Was it the same book?

Upon inspection, Vivian refused to pick it up. She was sure she'd never be able to wash that stink off her hands. Vivian watched from across the coffee table as the girls examined the thick pages, pointing at the scratch-mark writing, with Chloe trying to make sense of it. Even with her love for books, Chloe wasn't keen on touching it either. Avery did most of the flipping, providing snarky and colorful commentary with each of Chloe's suppositions.

And Chloe hadn't protested when Avery took a barbecue lighter to the corner of one page. The trio stared with widening eyes as the little flame parted around the corner, not touching the vellum or affecting it in any way.

Accepting the unspoken challenge from the book, Avery took it to the kitchen and clicked on the largest burner on the gas range. She held it over the hissing blue flames, with Vivian and Chloe huddled close behind her. The flames danced around the ugly thing as if an unseen force field protected it.

When they returned to the living room, no one spoke. The girls resumed their spot on the sofa, sitting with their shoulders pressed together, Chloe's long hair draped over her left shoulder to keep it out of the way. One of Avery's eyebrows peaked, and Chloe nodded. Vivian had seen this behavior many times but never commented on it. They were identical twins, after all, and although there wasn't any scientific data proving twins could communicate telepathically, she had no doubt her daughters could. That made her proud, knowing her daughters were different in an extraordinary way.

It was Chloe who finally spoke aloud. She picked up where they'd left off earlier, scrutinizing the angry-looking marks and slashes. The knot in Vivian's belly swelled. To the eye of a nurse,

Vivian was certain that "ink" was blood, but she wasn't going to say that out loud.

With what little she knew about Magda's secret life, Vivian prayed she'd not gotten herself into something… dark. *Oh, Magda. Please be okay.*

Vivian drove the girls to the airport the next day. The most affordable fare was in the late evening. Avery bounced in the seat beside her as Chloe's nose stayed buried in an English–Czech dictionary.

Terminal A at Boston Logan was blessedly unpopulated at that time of night. Vivian helped Avery haul the bags from the trunk of her Fiat 500 while Chloe stood on the curb, still staring at her book, repeating phrases in Czech and scribbling notes in the margins.

"Why didn't you get the e-book? You know you can make notes and highlight stuff," Avery said in a patronizing tone with an expression to match.

"Yes, I know that. I'm surprised you do, though," Chloe snarled at her. "This was three dollars at the used bookstore. That's why." She poked herself in the chest. "College student."

"Now, you need to call me. A lot." Vivian grabbed both girls and pulled them to her. "I want a play-by-play, you hear me?" She tried to keep the humor in her voice, but the last few words caught in her throat.

"Yes, Mother," the girls said in unison. Vivian laughed and waved them off. They walked backward several paces, blowing kisses to her and waving with both hands.

Vivian waited until they rounded the corner to let her face fall. *Be safe, my girls. Oh my god, be safe.*

CHAPTER 27

THE FLIGHT WAS LONG, WITH THE LONG LAYOVER IN Dublin making the trip nearly unbearable for Avery. The concern she squirreled away began to work its way out, making her legs twitchy. Her knee bounced constantly when she sat, and they had been sitting a lot. Avery hardly realized she was doing it until Chloe placed a hand on her leg. Avery shrugged and proceeded to crack her knuckles. Chloe let out an exasperated groan.

"Hey," Avery said. "You have your thing, and I have mine." She jutted her chin at the book in Chloe's hands. "And if I have to listen to you mumble any more sentences from that damn book, I'm going to beat you to death with it."

Without a glance, Chloe moved to the farthest row of seats at their gate.

The *other* book, the behemoth filling her backpack, banged against her back with each step. Her T-shirt clung to her moist skin, and she took the pack off at every opportunity to cool her skin. *What is up with this stupid thing? Ugh, I hate books.* Her cavalier attitude helped push the unease away, but only a little.

Crowds of people flowed through Václav Havel Airport, and Chloe huddled behind her sister, letting her carve a path. Avery plowed forward, following Chloe's directions as she read off the signs to get through passport control and out of the bustling place.

They veered toward the first taxi booking stand to order a taxi. The lady behind the counter greeted them in English spiced with a thick accent Avery found sexy. By the time they walked into the bright sunlight, a taxi was waiting for them.

Open book in hand, Chloe squared her shoulders and bent down to stare the driver in the eyes.

"Dobrý den," Chloe tried, her tongue tripping over itself. *"Mluvíte anglicky?"* She cleared her throat and repeated the words with more confidence.

The driver grimaced but barked a laugh. *"Ne."*

Ready with her notes, Chloe proceeded. Avery watched the older man's amused face as she sounded out each word carefully. His brown caterpillar eyebrows rose and fell with every other word, reminding Avery of two contenders sizing each other up.

He has to know at least some *English*, she thought to herself. *He works at an airport! He's just screwing with her.* Avery had to admire him; she'd probably do the same thing to young, naïve-looking tourists. She pulled in her lips to hide the smile.

The driver guffawed when Chloe finished, giving her a thumbs-up with both stocky hands.

"Ano! Ano!" He gestured at them both to get into the back seat.

"High five." Avery lifted her palm in the air. Chloe smacked it hard with a wide smile. "I'm impressed."

Chloe balked. "Wait. Did you just compliment me? That's going on my calendar."

"Good job!" The driver's eyes gleamed at Chloe in the rearview mirror as he pulled away from the curb. "But your accent is terrible. Did you know?"

Chloe's mouth fell open, and the chuckle Avery had been stifling burst from her mouth.

"You speak English!"

"Of course, of course." He laughed again. "Practice makes perfect, yes?"

Chloe fell back against the seat, and Avery snorted at her sister's face. His undeniable logic was being digested in Chloe's brain, and it didn't appear to taste very good.

"Man after my own heart."

Chloe glared at her. "You're a terrible sister."

Avery pushed her against the door with her shoulder, snorting more laughter.

The driver introduced himself as Stanislav but said they could call him Stan since he liked them. They looked like "good girls." The phrase made Avery's face pucker.

Chloe quickly forgave Stan and scooted up, listening intently to his well-rehearsed history lesson as the drive took them past a blur of greenery and apartment buildings. Avery didn't share Chloe's enthusiasm. She shifted the backpack; a corner of the book was digging into her calf.

Avery Parsons.

She snatched her hand away. Hot prickles stung her skin. It was the same throaty voice that had said her name when she was twelve. She glanced at Chloe; she mustn't have heard. Chloe was fully engaged with Stan, arms hanging over the seat, listening to his dissertation about some enormous castle complex they must see before leaving Prague. Avery pulled in a breath through her nostrils to calm herself.

Avery turned her gaze to the passing traffic, fists clenched and jaw locked. But the blur of people and buildings in the narrowing streets couldn't hold her attention. She tried not the think of the book or of what her grandmother had hidden from her. This book had to be some serious magick. It *spoke*. It knew her name!

But Avery wanted nothing to do with magick. Not since she'd hurt Hartley. She flinched as the unwanted image of Hartley lying comatose on a hospital bed broke through her guard. He could have died from what she'd done to him, and Avery still had no idea what that was. Working with the birds at the zoo had been different, cathartic even. It calmed her in a way kicking a heavy bag didn't. Besides, she wasn't using magick, just her natural rapport with all things feathered.

She huffed in her throat, curiosity pestering her. It wasn't every day she was called out by a book. Not to mention an indestructible one. Avery closed her eyes, pictured the wrinkled, smelly thing in her mind, ensuring her sister didn't hear.

What? She put as much animosity into that one word as she could. Avery gritted her teeth, waiting for the book to respond. But no response came. After several minutes, she allowed her back to relax into the soft seat.

"What brings you to my beautiful city?" Stan's cheerful voice interrupted Avery's solitude.

Chloe frowned at the question, and his caterpillars came together.

"We came to check on our grandmother," she said, her enthusiasm deflating as she spoke those words.

"She is sick? In hospital?" Stan tilted his head, eyes darting from Chloe to Avery.

"Well, that's the thing. We don't know. She's not been answering her phone for days." Chloe had been doing a great job at keeping her worry buried beneath learning the Czech language and getting absorbed in Stan's lecture, but now reality forced its way to the surface. Avery put a hand on her sister's back.

Stan's face went through several emotions, and he settled on a grandfatherly it's-going-to-be-just-fine face. "Don't worry, young Chloe. If she is anything like you, she is busy taking all the tours around the city."

Chloe gave him a thin smile. He grew quiet, and Chloe settled back in the seat. Avery took her sister's hand. Chloe's mind noted the tower sentinels marking the Legion Bridge and watched the Vltava River whizz under them without interest.

She's all right. Avery gave her hand a squeeze.

No. No, she's not.

The hostel was nestled within a row of other four- and five-story buildings. Each one had a unique façade—adorned with different stone, paint, and window ledges—but they were smashed together as if they had been one long building once. The girls piled out, Avery stretching and yawning as she looked around.

Chloe retrieved their bags from the trunk while Avery bent down to Stan's window to pay him. Her eyes bulged when Stan told her the fare.

"Holy crap, Stan! Seriously?"

He shrugged, his expression a little apologetic. "I don't make the prices, young Avery."

Still staring at him with big eyes, she presented her credit card.

Stan waved as he drove off, wishing them well, and Chloe waved back. "What a nice man."

"We are taking the bus from now on." Avery grabbed her twin's arm to get her to stop ogling at their surroundings. "Come on. Let's get checked in and drop this crap off before we head to Gram's apartment."

Chloe nodded, reluctant to turn away from the stunning mixture of Gothic and neo-Renaissance architecture. *I wish we had more time here.*

Time is money, Avery replied. *Money neither Mom or us have.*

"You really want to lug that heavy thing around some more?"

Chloe asked as Avery hefted the pack onto her back after dumping the rest of its contents on their double bed. Avery blinked at her several times, then shrugged.

A short bus ride and, thankfully, only a bit of walking through cramped streets brought them to their grandmother's apartment building. It was a story shorter than those smashed against it, made ugly by years of graffiti poorly covered and tagged over again. The main security door had a crack the length of the glass that had been "repaired" with layers of tape now curling and peeling from age. The stench of stale beer and cigarettes wafted toward them on the slight breeze from the dive bar across the street. Chloe grimaced at the idea of her grandmother living here. It looked nothing like the modern apartment buildings they'd seen on the walk there. Maybe her grandmother was tight on funds.

The button to her grandmother's apartment cracked when Chloe pushed it and remained stuck in the depressed position. It made no sound, and the door lock didn't click open. She pushed several of the other yellowed, plastic buttons. No buzzing, no ringing. Nothing.

"I don't think they work," Avery said, resting her chin on her sister's shoulder.

"Ya think?" Chloe sighed. "How are we going to get in?"

Avery yanked the door handle, and it clicked open easily. "Real secure."

Bounding up the narrow staircase, Avery was the first at her grandmother's door. She slapped both palms on it repeatedly. "Gram!"

Chloe leaned into the doorjamb and sniffed, praying she wouldn't smell a decaying corpse.

Heavy footsteps came to the door, then stopped. The girls sought one another's hands as the door opened.

"Who the hell are you?" Avery stepped in front of Chloe, jutting out her chin.

Filling the height of the doorway was a man in his midthirties, dressed in a vintage-looking black suit that fit him well. His jet-black hair was slicked back from his high forehead, his Van Dyke neatly trimmed, framing tight lips. The bold darkness of his suit and hair made his smooth complexion appear almost ghostly white. The man's lean face was stone as he glared at the unwelcome visitors.

Avery blanched, then stiffened. Chloe caught her eyes when they darted to her, and she tilted her head in question. Avery's jaw locked as she brought her hands up to grip the straps of her pack at the shoulders.

The man's expression softened, his full lips melting into a handsome smile. He flashed perfect white teeth at Avery, whose defiant glare refused to be disarmed by such a smile.

Nervous laughter spewed from Chloe, and she used her shoulder to push Avery behind her.

"Sorry. What my sister means to say is"—she looked down at the neat list of notes nestled in her book—"*dobrý den, hledáme naši—*"

"Stop." He raised a hand, shaking his head with eyes closed. "Please." When he opened them, their dark sparkle made Chloe's heart flutter. "I speak English." The combination of his baritone and heavy accent made for the sexiest voice Chloe had ever heard.

"Oh, god. Thank god!" She laughed again, powerless to stop herself. "Good." She nodded to him but couldn't keep eye contact. "We are looking for our grandmother, Magda Hlavacova. Is she home?"

"Who?" The corners of his mouth lowered, a groove formed between his perfect black brows. He shook his head slowly, as if he were thinking. "I don't know that person. I have only lived here a few days."

The girls exchanged confused glances, and Chloe checked the address on her phone again.

"But I do know the person who lived here before me passed away."

The twins gaped at him.

"If that was your grandmother, you have my deepest sympathies." He put a hand to his heart and dipped his head. He backed away, closing the door.

Chloe stared at the door but didn't see it. The man's words raced around in her head until each one crashed into one another, no longer making a sentence she could comprehend.

"No." Avery grabbed her sister's wrist and yanked her around. "Nuh-uh. We are finding the manager." Chloe nodded, and they ran down the stairs.

Avery's fist on the manager's door made it quake in its frame. The resident flung it open, unveiled anger on his lined and dogged face. His watery eyes were clouded with age, but they still managed a nasty glare.

"Co chcete?" he shouted and turned his attention to his bruised door. His words were too fast for Chloe to understand, but their meaning was clear.

"Prosím, prosím," Chloe begged, raising her hands, palms out. *"Hledáme naši babičku, Magdu Hlaváčovou."* Her brain couldn't remember any more words. It was too hard to think and hold it together at the same time. "Our grandmother, Magda Hlavacova, does she live here? In this building?" She gulped air to keep from sobbing.

"Jděte pryč!" He jerked his hand up at them.

"Dědo, nech toho!" A teenaged girl ran up the stairs, backpack bouncing as she took the stairs in twos. She came up beside them, putting herself between them and the old man. "Please forgive him."

She turned and placed her hands on his chest, a rapid fire of words flying from her lips. Something Chloe could only assume was an expletive shot from his lips in Avery's direction, and he jerked his arm at them once more, turning his back as he did so.

The girl closed the door quietly with an apology in her eyes.

"He is not well, my grandfather." She seemed to search for the right words but tapped her temple instead.

Chloe nodded and took in another deep breath. Avery took her hand. "Do you know Magda Hlavacova?"

The girl dropped her eyes to the floor and licked her lips. Chloe's heart sank, and she leaned against Avery, who locked her knees to keep them both upright.

"I am sorry." The girl looked up, biting her lip. "She went in her sleep, grandfather said, a week ago."

Chloe covered her face. *It's not true. It can't be.* Avery's body was rock-hard beside her.

"But we called your grandfather!" The sharpness of Avery's voice made Chloe jump, dropping her hands. "Several times! Why didn't anyone tell us?"

The girl shook her head. "I'm sorry, I don't know."

Avery pushed Chloe aside. "Your fucking grandfa—"

"Avery, don't," she said, grabbing her shoulders, "that won't help." Avery shook under Chloe's hands, her body heat rolling off her, mingling with her own. Chloe was dizzy and tightened her hold on Avery just to keep herself up.

"Please." Chloe inhaled sharply. "Please tell us what happened. Where's her body? Where are all of her things?"

The girl seemed dazed by Chloe's questions. Her eyelids fluttered, most of the expression leaving her face.

"She was late on the rent. He used his key when she didn't answer." Her voice was flat, and she seemed to look beyond Chloe. "She was in bed, she looked asleep. Grandfather called the authorities, and they took her body away." She finally blinked and took a breath. "We didn't have any phone numbers of family, so all of her things were donated to the church."

"What!" Avery jerked free of Chloe. "Are you fucking kidding me? A person dies and you don't notify anyone, and you just give all her stuff away?"

Chloe tried to intervene but she couldn't speak, she couldn't think.

"I am sorry," the girl said again, without the same feeling as before. "But she was old, yes? Old people die."

"Wrong thing to say, bitch." Avery reached for her, but Chloe grabbed her arms, tears streaming down her face. She pulled Avery, stilling spewing expletives and threats, down the steps.

CHAPTER 28

JOSEPH STRAKA STOOD IN THE MIDDLE OF THE apartment, his mind locked on to the teenaged girl downstairs, the one speaking to the redheads that had come looking for Magda. His lips moved, telling the girl what to say. His words flowed from her mouth; controlling the simple-minded was so easy.

The short-haired tomboy, though, might prove challenging. No matter. They would accept the story as everyone else had even if he had to tap into their minds to make it so. He could do that right now, save the bother of working through the young girl, but he enjoyed watching their anguish. The old man's addled brain had been the easiest to manipulate. No one questioned his words, no one bothered about the old woman after they'd heard she died. She was ancient, after all.

Josef released the girl when the crying sister forced the fiery one out the lobby door. He had examined the twins' energy, checking for anything useful, as they stood cow-eyed before him. He'd sensed a flicker of oddity around the tomboy. Her energy shifted slightly as he'd appraised her. In retrospect, it was nothing. Most likely her pathetic attempt to protect herself and her sister. Their paltry magick was nothing to him. Low intellect, foolish, not even true kin of Magda. That was a shame. He could have used their blood to recall the old woman's spirit to this plane. He growled at the thought of her.

In a fit of anger, he had blasted Magda's body with demon-fire. It was quick, more than she deserved for such a grievous betrayal, but his temper won out. Plus, he had no time for something more elaborate. He must find his book! He'd torn through the apartment looking for it or anything leading to its whereabouts. He'd roamed the city for a trace of its power. *Nothing.* Magda's pretend granddaughters knew nothing either.

Days and nights he had spent bent over sheets of paper, scribbling what he could recall. But there was a great deal, and much of the book's contents changed with his need. He remembered many of the simpler spells and incantations, but the one thing he must have, the ritual to rend the Shade, was long and complicated. The snippets he recalled were pointless without the whole of it. Disgusted, he'd shoved the stack of papers to the floor, momentarily considering sending them up in flames. But no, he might have use for the bits he could remember.

He had already acquired five of the thirteen men needed. Finding his enemies was no challenge. The stench of their fathers' and grandfathers' betrayal was easy to follow. He held them, enchanted into a stasis, in a makeshift cell in the seldom-used storage room under the old apartment building; a spell on the hallway and door kept anyone from going in that direction.

Josef stared at the litter of papers. He must reach out to his sovereign.

He hung his head. Which was worse, losing the book or her inevitable disappointment in him? *Twice* a failure now. His cheeks flamed. Josef pushed his shame aside with a deep exhale and closed his eyes, releasing his hold on this reality. He let his spirit drift, picturing his demon master.

Muraal. The sound of her name reverberated around him, rippling out into the Void. *I require your guidance.*

There was no response. Had he lost the ability to speak to her, to hear her? Without the book, was pain needed again? It was born from her realm, so perhaps it was the key to their connection.

He'd not known the origins of the carcass that emerged from within him when he'd begun the pain ritual to create it. The gaping wounds on his back, his reward for hours of flagellation, tore open wider at Muraal's command, and he'd borne tremendous pain. The agony of a blood crossing from the Voll into the mortal world. Muraal had told him of her sacrifice, of letting one of her children die to come through and impart her magick to him.

Josef had been driven by a voice—a deep, thick voice not Muraal's, and he'd fashioned pages from the entrails and the cover from the thick skin. The voice whispered the words into Josef's mind, and he scrawled them on the pages with the creature's blood.

Josef took a corkscrew from the kitchen and held his palm out. He never feared the pain, never. It had always brought him what he desired, and he relished it.

Before the corkscrew broke the tender skin of his palm, a pinprick touched the edge of his psyche. She was coming. Her presence filling his mind sent waves of euphoria through his limbs, across his skin, and trapped the unnecessary breath in his lungs. Josef grasped the countertop with both hands to remain standing.

Find the book. Each word a dagger in his brain.

Then she was gone. The heat left him in a rush; the anger in her voice echoed throughout his body, buckling his knees.

I will. He clenched his fists, pushing himself up.

"I will." His tight voice cut through the silence of the apartment.

She would speak no more to him, he was sure of that. He had let his arrogance get the better of him yet again. Last time, he lost his life; this time, he lost something much more precious.

CHAPTER 29

The girls staggered out the lobby door, Chloe still pulling Avery along. They clung to each other once outside, ignoring the quizzical glances from passersby.

Avery helped Chloe to the nearest bench and shooed away a mewling black-and-white cat coming toward them. Her sister's unconscious habit of attracting cats when she was upset or stressed had always annoyed Avery, who'd never come to like them even a little bit.

Another cat came down the sidewalk in a full sprint. Avery scowled at them. *Go away!* Chloe put a hand on her sister's arm. They didn't listen to Avery; cats never did. Both paced a few feet away, eyeing the sobbing Chloe.

Avery held Chloe tightly, so tight she feared hurting her, but Chloe held on as her shattered soul spilled out.

She let go of Avery suddenly and bent over, hands on knees. She gulped air as the sobs racked her chest. Avery rubbed her back but had no words of comfort to give, her tears staying locked up.

The hand not on Chloe's back was in a ball pushing against the metal grating of the bench. A knuckle popped. Her sister's emotions mixed with her own bordered on overwhelming, and this bit of discomfort Avery forced on herself provided the focal point needed to keep from breaking down.

The book hadn't spoken again, thank god, but remained warm against her already sweaty back. Avery found its warmth and weight oddly comforting. But what it had said when the man opened the door—

Granny died alone. All alone.

Avery shook her head and lifted her eyes past the tall buildings across the street, bedecked with scaffolding and busy workmen, at the pristine blue sky, blinking away tears. A few pigeons perched atop the roof peaks, silent and staring, but nowhere near the number that used to gather when she was younger.

It shouldn't have been like that. She should have been home with us. Chloe quaked under Avery's palm.

Tomorrow, I'm coming back to that son-of-a-bitch manager, mental or not, and get every detail out of him.

She bent down and laid her forehead atop her sister's head. "Let's get back to the room." Avery kept her voice soft. "We need to call Mom."

Chloe nodded, wiping her face with both hands. Avery made sure Chloe was steady before getting up. She walked into the street to look for a taxi.

Avery felt Chloe's heart lift a little as she ran her hands over the silky fur of the two cats who came and rubbed themselves against her calves. She stopped and allowed herself to experience Chloe's calming ritual.

The tortoiseshell cat was very pregnant; Chloe cupped a hand to her belly, wishing the babies a happy and healthy life. She thanked both cats for their comfort, and they mewed in reply but seemed reluctant to leave.

Avery let out a long breath. It helped her a tiny bit, but she'd never admit that to Chloe.

"But you said we didn't have the money for another taxi ride," Chloe said, straightening and pulling her messenger bag strap tight across her chest.

Avery returned to the bench and took her sister's hand. They started toward the nearest main street where she assumed taxis were likely to be.

"We'll eat ramen for dinner."

Chloe bent over in the folding chair in their modest room, staring at her phone clenched in both hands. The small image of her mother on the screen was blurry, and she blinked several times to clear her vision. A tear splashed onto the screen, and she wiped it off with a thumb, tracing circles around her mother's beautiful face.

Except for Avery's ever-changing hairstyle, they all looked so much alike. Red hair straight as a board, their skin covered in freckles like a star-filled sky, and soft hazel eyes. The three of them had been mistaken for sisters once. Vivian had surfed that happy high for days. The edges of Chloe's mouth quirked up at the memory.

Chloe couldn't bring herself to push 'Call.' How was she going to tell her the woman who'd been the closest thing to a mother she ever had was dead? Her mother was going to ask all kinds of questions Chloe had no answers to.

Steam from the shower billowed out through the open bathroom door, filling the room. It was tiny, about the size of the room she and Avery had shared growing up, but it was modern and comfortable for a hostel. And everything was white. Clean white walls, sheer white curtains, white linens, a tiny white laminate table with a white plastic domed lamp and a single white chair. For a brief moment, Chloe felt like she was in an Ikea display.

Avery had been in there a long time. She was crying; Chloe sensed it. As much as Avery considered herself invincible, she was often the more vulnerable of the two sisters. Chloe always knew and always saw it, as clear as day, especially when Avery pinched her lips or made fists or held her chin too high. The classic signs of Avery bottling it up. And, of course, she felt it. Chloe didn't want extra emotion right now, but blocking Avery out was *hard.* She sighed and put the phone to her forehead. Sometimes being a twin sucked.

Without another thought, Chloe tapped 'Call.' Vivian answered before she'd even gotten the phone to her ear.

"Chloe! Oh my god, why haven't you called me sooner? Is everything okay? What's wrong?" Vivian's words came out in a rush, and Chloe's resolve crumbled. Sobs came again, stealing the air from her lungs, and took over her body. Her mother's voice rose in volume, but she couldn't comprehend the words flying at her.

Avery took the phone from Chloe's vise grip. "Mom!" She had to repeat it several times for Vivian to quiet down. Avery had a towel wrapped around her, the points of her pixie locks dripping water down her forehead. She didn't sit.

"Mom, listen!" Avery barked, making Chloe flinch. She leaned back in the hard plastic chair, pulling her knees to her chest as the shuddering calmed. Forehead on knees, she listened to Avery recount the last two hours.

Even though the phone wasn't on speaker, her mother's outcry was clear. Chloe covered her face. *Mom is all alone hearing this.* Fresh tears fell at knowing her mother was so far away with no one to comfort her. She was dating someone, finally, but she was keeping him a secret. Maybe he could be there for her.

Avery's sentences were cut off many times, and she waited patiently, repeating herself again and again to cut through her mother's cries and flurry of questions. She spoke with no emotion in her voice. A few times her words stuck in her throat, but she powered on, appearing unfazed by the emotion being poured out on the other end of the line. *Avery the robot,* Chloe thought.

It seemed like forever they talked. Chloe just wanted to sleep. She wanted to sleep for a week and wake up to find that it had been just a super crappy dream. No. They only had a few more days here, and they had to find out more about Granny: where her body was buried, more about what happened. She hoped Avery hadn't offended the manager's granddaughter too much with the profanity and threats of bodily harm. They would need her to communicate with and soothe the grandfather.

Chloe's eyes fluttered open. The room was dark. Confused, she sat up, the stiff blanket falling from her shoulders. She must have fallen asleep. How'd she gotten in bed? There was a small lump beside her, snoring softly. Avery was in a fetal position with the covers pulled tight over her head.

She wiped her crusty eyes gently, picking off the larger bits from her eyelashes. Her head and sinuses throbbed from the relentless crying. *Shower.* How long had it been since she last showered? Or ate? Her stomach protested the mere idea of food.

Chloe showered and dressed quietly, creeping like a mouse around the small room. She checked the time on her phone: nine thirty. She needed to get out and walk, get some fresh air into her lungs. The quick research she'd done on hotels included neighborhood safety at night, and this one had gotten good ratings. She stuffed a thin sweater in her messenger bag and stole out the door.

Her body felt so heavy; it was hard to pick up one foot and make it go in front of the other. Chloe paused on the stoop of the hostel and took a deep breath. The night air was surprisingly fresh for being in the middle of a great city and tinged with the scents of the restaurant a few doors up. Even the tantalizing smell of roast chicken did nothing for her stomach. Chloe was comforted by the close buildings and narrow lanes crammed with small cars; it was well-lit and clean, which added to her calm.

Turning her face to the night sky, she took another deep,

shaky breath. "Okay, feet. Move." If memory served from her research, this direction held a little market. Hot green tea, really strong, sounded amazing right now.

Too many people walked the sidewalk with her, and she drew in her elbows. Old couples, young couples, couples with kids in strollers. Everyone happy—laughing, kissing, holding hands. Her heart grew heavier as she watched them. Tourists, she guessed, turning her mind to analyze them, with their cell phones going up every few minutes to take a picture of something old or a selfie in front of something cool. She didn't consider herself a tourist although she'd like to be. *Maybe I'll come back one day.* She'd love to see where her grandmother had grown up; maybe the orphanage was still around, even though Granny had nothing good to say about it.

In truth, right now, Chloe wanted to go home. She wanted nothing more at this moment than to have her mother's arms around her, feel her hand smoothing the back of her hair as her mom whispered comforting words in Chloe's ear. After they found out what happened to Granny's body, she'd see about flying home early. The two full days remaining of their trip felt unreasonably long right now.

With eyes cast down, she inspected the pattern of the small, gray bricks making up the sidewalk, wondering how old the stones were. She stopped at a corner to get her bearings. *Very touristy.* Which was fine. That meant they'd speak at least some English at the market, and she wouldn't have to get out her dictionary. Her brain simply wasn't up to the challenge. She located the sign of the market, swaying in the gentle breeze, not far ahead. *Please have green tea.*

She strolled past brightly lit stores, lively with business at this time of night. Chloe slowed her pace by a resale shop with a narrow floor-to-ceiling window front, crammed with all kinds of household items artfully arranged to grab the eye. Fancy pocket knives splayed open to show their freshly sharpened blades, a vintage gold Rolex Chloe instantly wanted, polished copper tea kettles beautifully beaten by time, garish cocktail rings of the sort old ladies just loved. Except her Granny. Granny didn't care for flashy things. Chloe swallowed the lump in her throat.

Her feet carried her through the open door, and she was immediately greeted by a plump, balding gentleman at the back. She raised her hand, giving him what smile she could. Thankfully, he was busy with another customer and wouldn't seek her out anytime soon, she hoped.

She wandered around the close, uneven aisles, sometimes having to turn sideways to get through. It smelled like an old library mixed with a hint of moldy tobacco. Each shelf and table was crammed with so many things, in no apparent order, that her darting eyes could barely take everything in. Chloe kept her hands clasped firmly behind her. *You know you. If you pick it up, you're gonna buy it.* She tightened her fingers together.

A glint of yellow caught her eye. She picked her way around stacks of boxes and old chairs to a dust-covered table in the far back corner. She moved aside a broken cuckoo clock and gasped at the treasure behind it. A large, yellow crystal ball beckoned, pulling loose her clasped fingers. Chloe lost her resolve and closed her hands around its bulk, lifting it with the greatest care. The sphere was free of dust, unlike everything else around it, and *warm.*

It was exquisite. While it had a substantial fracture partially through it, it appeared solid. It wasn't made of clear glass but looked to Chloe like some type of quartz, yellowed with age or maybe it had always been that color. The crack splintered in a linear pattern, giving it layers of dimension when lit from behind. She held it up to a lamp stationed behind her, turning it this way and that, peering deeper within.

Inside the facets, her grandmother's face flashed, and she nearly dropped the heavy sphere.

What the—? The largest straight-line fracture within the crystal wavered for only a millisecond, and Magda's face flashed again. *Did that just happen* in *the crystal ball or just in my head?*

Chloe squinted, turning the crystal again, bending closer to the light. She gave it a quick shake, as if it were a snow globe, then tutted herself.

"Líbí se Vám?" The shopkeeper startled her with his sudden appearance at her elbow, and she snapped up straight, gripping the ball tighter so she wouldn't drop it. "You like that, yes?"

"It's beautiful." Chloe returned his smile. She found that she clutched the ball to her chest, as if he'd come to take it from her.

"As is the young lady who holds it." Below a deeply lined forehead, his eyes twinkled at her. "For you, I make good deal."

Here comes the sales pitch.

When he told her the cost in US dollars, his pained expression suggesting she was stealing it from him at that price, she choked.

Frowning down at the sphere in her hands, she couldn't make herself put it back. She'd never wanted to buy something so much in her life. Did it look that obvious? She was hooked, and any shrewd shop owner could see that. Chloe had never played poker.

She was also terrible at haggling and too embarrassed to insult him with a lower price. Her mind flew through the budget spreadsheet she meticulously maintained. There wasn't enough there, but damn it, this crystal ball belonged to her.

"Do you take Visa?"

CHAPTER 30

Chloe sat quietly in the dark room with her new treasure in her hands. She knew only a little about crystal balls and their purpose. The shopkeeper said it was yellow quartz, but he didn't know where it came from; his wife had found it recently on one of her many shopping journeys. Chloe hadn't read much on them when they first got into magick as kids. *It's a shame.* She hefted the beautiful, imperfect stone in her hands. *This is something I could really get into.* There was a world of information in books and on the internet awaiting her when she got home.

A snort came from the lump still within the covers, and it shot upward.

"Grammy!" Avery threw the blanket off and stood beside the bed, slightly crouched in some sort of fighting stance. Chloe's throat constricted at the oncoming rush of Avery's unchecked grief. She placed the sphere on the side table, nestling it in her sweater, and went to her sister.

She hugged Avery, gently at first, then tightened her arms when Avery clutched her, pushing her face into Chloe's shoulder. Avery's chest quaked as she took deep breaths, but no tears accompanied them. The girls stayed locked for several minutes, swaying gently from side to side. Then Avery nodded against

Chloe's neck and pushed her sister away gently, nodding again when their eyes met. Avery tried to speak, but the words stuck, so she coughed instead and stepped back.

"God, I need some coffee," Avery grumbled with a dry throat. "There's no room service here, is there?" Avery rubbed her fingers vigorously across her cropped hair and fell into the folding chair.

"Careful!" Chloe jumped, catching the crystal ball before Avery's elbow made contact with it. One more good smack and it might break in half.

"Oh, god. What did you buy?" Avery leaned forward, squinting in the darkness at the glassy object clutched to Chloe's stomach. Chloe sat across from her on the bed, presenting the sphere as she would a sacred artifact. Avery sighed and flicked on the lamp. The sudden brightness made them both wince.

"Okay. *Wow.*" Avery reached for the sphere. "That's cool." She took it carefully, her hands splayed wide on either side to ensure a good grip. "I've never seen a crystal ball so big." Avery leaned into the light, inspecting as she turned it round. "It'd be really impressive if it wasn't busted. I hope you got a discount."

Chloe bit her upper lip, hands out in front of her, anticipating a slip at any moment.

The deep fissure grabbed Avery's attention, and she peered closer. The lamplight danced along its edges, reflecting deep shades of gold with the slightest movement, twinkling and glinting.

"I saw Granny in it," Chloe said sheepishly. "Well, I think I did anyway. It was probably just in my head."

Avery opened her mouth, undoubtedly to throw a jibe at Chloe. Instead, Avery moved to sit beside her sister and leaned sideways, pressing her shoulder against Chloe and touching heads. A tear traveled down Chloe's freckled cheek, and Avery pressed a little harder.

"What are we going to do?" Chloe's voice cracked as she

spoke. There was a great deal to do before they could leave, but her mind was blank.

Avery shrugged with a long sigh.

She ran her palm across the polished surface once more, entranced by the pronounced crack. Her palm found a jagged break in its surface too late; it nicked her, and she snatched her hand away.

"Ouch." Avery looked at her palm, frowning.

Movement out of the corner of her eye brought her attention back to the sphere. A tiny drop of blood traveled inward from the invisible snag. She glanced at Chloe, whose jaw hung open, eyes threatening to pop out. *Good, I'm not seeing things then.*

Both sisters gaped as the trickle of blood worked its way into the depths of the fissure. Upon reaching the center, it bloomed outward. Light red ribbons mingled with liquid gold, rippling and flowing smoothly within the confines of the sphere. Having reached the boundary, the swirling cloud drew back in on itself to the center. It blinked out, and in its place was the face of their grandmother.

The twins shrieked in unison, with Chloe scrambling back on the bed to the wall, Avery snapping to attention, nearly dropping the crystal.

"Gram?" Avery held the ball at arms' length, as far as she could stretch, head cocked to the side.

Magda smiled. Her dark eyes shimmered within the sphere, gazing at each sister. Her face was a little distorted as she hovered within the facets, bobbing as if in water, but unchanged from the last time they'd seen her.

Chloe discovered she was crying when she covered her face with her hands. She pushed her palms against her eyes. *Am I really seeing this?*

Um, yeah. I see her too. If we've lost our minds, at least we are together on it.

Chloe placed a pillow on the side table and gestured for

Avery to set the sphere on it. Avery obeyed, arms still outstretched, elbows locked.

They sat on the bed, shoulder to shoulder, staring at the impossible image of their grandmother's head floating within the cracked crystal ball.

"Granny," Chloe said, barely above a whisper. "Is that really you?"

"Yes, my Chloe." Her voice was clear, but her words echoed slightly.

"Wha—? How—? Are you really dead?" Avery blinked rapidly at the sphere.

Magda's smile faltered. "I am, *beruško*."

Avery looked at Chloe for a little help, but she was as dumbfounded as Avery.

"Okay, Gram, you are going to have to explain this."

The wrinkles around her grandmother's mouth deepened as her smile turned into a small chuckle.

A flash of annoyance rose in Avery. "This is not funny."

Chloe put a hand on Avery's knee. "In your letter… '*Until I am* able *to see you again…*'"

Magda's expression turned solemn. "I wouldn't have brought you into this if I thought there was any other way." She closed her eyes, shaking her head. When she reopened them, they were full of sadness.

"What '*this*'? *What* is going on?"

Chloe squeezed Avery's knee.

"I'm sorry, Gram." Avery gulped, sniffing back tears.

"Don't apologize, my Avery. I know this is terrible for you. For both of you. I will tell you all that has happened."

The girls settled back, Chloe pulling her knees to her chest.

"When I was about your age, I was married to a man I did not love. Then I met a man who was everything I'd ever wanted." She looked away. "He was so handsome, so kind. With piercing midnight blue eyes, a voice like velvet, and a smile that made my heart stop. I was a fool. I didn't know the kind of man he was until it was too late."

The man in Granny's apartment?

Impossible.

Magda took a deep breath, which struck Avery as odd since she was dead and her head was floating in a glass ball.

Shut up and focus, Chloe chided.

"On the night he was murdered, he asked something of me, and I promised I would do it. If I had only known..."

They listened with widening eyes to their grandmother's tale of naïveté, lust, and demons. Magda's words were slow and careful, but full of the emotion of a woman racked by guilt and regret—and loss. She told them of Josef Straka, a man of dark magick who tried to bring a great demon and its horde into this world. About his death and the night she brought him back.

Avery's jaw came unhinged. "Demons, Gram, seriously?"

"Brought him back?" Chloe's voice quivered. *It was him!*

"Yes." Her eyes flickered to both girls. "The book I sent you is full of dark magick—evil and twisted—and I used it to bring him back to life," Magda said, the regret plain. "And with it, he can tear into the barrier between our worlds, letting the demons free."

Heat flared from Avery. *The book of blood and skin.*

"Yes," Magda said, staring at Avery. "The book that spoke your name when you were a girl—the book you felt through the cabinet door. The one I told you was nothing." Magda waited for Avery's reproach but received nothing but a dazed expression. "I tell you now that I have lied to you both. I never wanted you anywhere near dark magick, so that is why I steered you toward something much safer, more innocent. And you did love animals so."

Avery glared at her grandmother, folding her arms across her chest. Chloe leaned forward.

"Go on, Granny, please." She gave Avery a side-eye, and her arms relaxed a bit.

Magda continued, telling them of a spell she started in 1937 but was unable to complete because of the war. Decades had passed, and she was forced to come back because the life-extending potion had run out. Both girls found their voices then; questions flew at Magda. She held up a hand. They quieted and sat back.

"I completed the spell a short time ago, and Josef Straka once again walks in the land of the living. It was only then that I discovered the depths of his evil, what his purpose truly was. I have no magick in me—I cannot stop him. That is why I sent you the book. While I have read it a thousand times, I know it will not work for me. I tried to use it against him, and it did nothing. I took a gamble that it would for you, *berušky*, since there is magick in your blood. It spoke to Avery, so I hoped—" Tears filled her eyes, and she turned away.

The girls sat in silence, holding each other's hands as their grandmother fought back her tears.

"Granny…" Chloe balked, then swallowed. "How did you die, Granny? Did he… did he k…" She couldn't bring herself to say the word.

"He did not kill me, my Chloe. I had to escape him and keep what I'd done secret. There was no other way." She could no longer hold their tear-filled eyes. "I had to take my life."

A whimper caught in Chloe's throat. Avery pushed herself from the bed, disappearing into the part of the room where the lamplight did not reach.

"You killed yourself." The words sounded like broken glass. What desperation her grandmother must have felt! The sheer hopelessness and fear that made her feel she had to die to escape! Chloe squeezed her eyes closed, trying not to picture the state her grandmother had been in or what that man had done to her.

"How?" Avery's sharp voice came from the dark corner of the room.

Magda shook her head. "That is not important." Her head turned in the direction of Avery's voice. "Avery, please."

It was several minutes before Avery obeyed. When she returned, her wet eyelashes glinted in the light. She snatched a tissue from the box on the floor and blew her nose loudly.

"I know the answer, but I need to hear it." Chloe swallowed. "It's that man in your apartment, isn't it?"

"That man is Josef Straka," she said flatly.

Avery growled, "I'm going to kill him."

Magda's expression hardened. She stared directly at Avery, capturing her gaze. "That is *exactly* what you must do."

CHAPTER 31

AVERY LAY IN THE DOUBLE BED, MIND SWIMMING, EYES fixed onto a poorly repaired crack in the white ceiling. It had been nearly one o'clock when Magda insisted they get some sleep and refused to say any more. She vanished from the crystal ball, with "go to bed" echoing in her wake. But Avery wasn't going to sleep anytime soon. Chloe tossed from one side to the other, each movement quaking the mattress, with an occasional grunt of frustration. Avery kept her thoughts inward.

This is unreal. Demons, a resurrected psycho, my grandmother's head floating in a crystal ball—where is the rest of her?—and we have to kill said psycho—again—because Gram brought him back to life. And she had to kill herself to get away from him.

A fresh wave of grief choked her remaining thoughts. *Oh, Grammy.*

Avery pulled the covers to her chin. *Not to mention a book is talking to me.*

The book. So it wasn't just a magickal book, but an *evil* magickal book. *Great.* She snorted under her breath. *No wonder it wants to talk to me.*

Avery's sarcasm wasn't working; the chills still came. She turned onto her side and pulled the blanket over her head.

What the book had said to her as she stared up at tall-dark-

and-creepy made sense now. *"Do not tell him of me."* Its sudden words had made her almost jump out of her skin. Chloe had looked at her questioningly, but only for a second.

That guy is going to want this book, and I guess the book knows that.

I do.

Avery went rigid. Instinctively, her thoughts shot toward her sister, who hadn't moved in the last few minutes. It didn't seem the book's voice touched Chloe's mind.

She fought the urge to tell it to fuck off.

Hiding from him, are ya?

It was maddening when it didn't respond after several minutes. *Look, book. You keep trying to talk to me. So, talk, dammit, or shut up and go away.*

Something akin to a smirk touched her mind. Was that from the book? Did books smirk?

You will soon learn to read me. Do not be afraid, Avery Parsons, for I will help you.

How will you help me? Help me do what? Avery waited impatiently for its answer, but nothing came. *Jerk.*

Chloe had no idea what time it was when she woke, but it seemed like she'd only just fallen asleep. Her body refused to move even though her bladder was insistent. Her bladder finally won, and she rolled out of bed.

Light peeked through the thin blinds of the only window in the room. Chloe pulled on the rumpled clothes she'd taken off only a few hours ago and plodded downstairs to the market she'd aimed for last night. She returned to the hostel's kitchen with a box of green tea bags, several fresh, fluffy pastries, and *gasp*, instant coffee. Avery might throw the jar at her, but beggars couldn't be choosers. The coffeepot in the kitchen was out of service.

Chloe made her sister a cup of coffee in the microwave, crinkling her nose at the unsavory tang. She'd never liked coffee in the first place, and the instant stuff smelled terrible.

Avery took the steaming mug with only a grunt and sipped it in silence, much to Chloe's surprise. They both resumed their places around the crystal ball as if it were a television and waited.

"How's the coffee?" Chloe asked, inhaling the aroma from her cup of green tea. *Heaven.*

"Pretty terrible," she said, taking another sip, "but I'd drink rancid motor oil at this point." She looked at cloudy dark liquid in her mug. "Which I think I am, actually."

Growing impatient, Avery knocked on the crystal ball. "Gram! Wakey, wakey."

Within seconds, the center turned to swirling gold and white mist, then cleared to reveal the face of their grandmother.

"Where have you been?" Chloe asked.

"I wanted you to rest." Magda eyed both of them. "You two have not slept enough."

Avery snorted. "Can you blame us?"

"We should call Mom." Chloe's words hung in the air.

After a heated debate last night about what exactly to tell Vivian, they had decided she should know everything. Well, almost everything. They'd agreed that telling Vivian Magda had committed suicide was not something she needed to hear. Vivian had been beside herself with grief at learning of Magda's death; her return, at least in some way, would be a great relief. They hoped.

"This is not going to go well at all," Avery murmured, then downed the rest of her coffee.

Chloe used an app she'd downloaded on her phone to make a free video call to Vivian. She answered before the first ring had ended.

"Chloe! What's wrong? Did you find out more about Magda? What happened?" Their mother's face was pale, her eyes red, lids puffy, from either crying or lack of sleep, or both.

Avery took the phone when Chloe choked. "Mom. Hi. So, um, we have news." But Avery didn't continue, her mouth stopping at half open, the words apparently stuck or nonexistent. She pushed out a breath and turned the phone to face the crystal ball.

Vivian screamed.

Chloe snatched the phone from her. She wanted to throttle Avery, who leaned away, mouthing a pained "I'm sorry" repeatedly. Chloe looked at the ceiling in her Mom's apartment, the sounds of gasping sobs clear.

It look Magda's voice to bring Vivian back to the phone.

Vivian raged at them for playing such a cruel trick, and it took a lot of talking to get her to believe this was no trick. Then she cried more, which made the girls cry as well. Anger returned after that; Vivian furious with Magda for getting into dark magick, getting herself killed, and then bringing her young, innocent daughters into it. Luckily, she hadn't asked how Magda died.

Magda let her yell, offering no defense of her actions, her face working to remain unaffected by Vivian's words.

She demanded her daughters come home immediately. Let this Josef Straka do whatever the hell he wanted; she didn't believe a single word of that demon business, no matter Magda's story. Chloe begged and Avery argued, while Magda stayed silent. Vivian needed to vent before rational thought returned. Although, under these circumstances, that might take a while.

In the end, Vivian relented and made Magda promise to keep her girls safe. She would join them as soon as she could. All three told her to stay home, and she finally agreed with an angry flail of her arms. The call didn't end well. But with so much emotion and four headstrong women at odds, it couldn't have ended any other way. Chloe would give her a few hours to calm down, then call her back, without Avery or Magda.

Avery chewed her thumbnail, resting her back against the wall on the bed, staring into space. Chloe smacked her arm lightly as she paced by; Avery's habit was really annoying, and she was trying to think. Avery grunted but dropped her hand.

"All right. We have less than two days left. We don't have the money to stay any longer. So, we need to find a spell or ritual in this book that will get rid of this Josef guy. *But* we don't know how to read it, so I'm guessing you're going to read it to us." Chloe recited the facts as if they were a shopping list, then looked at her grandmother, whose frown deepened. "Did I miss anything?"

"A great deal," Magda said. Her eyes moved to the book lying beside her on the table, and she sighed. "Let's do this one at a time." She motioned for Chloe to sit.

"As for staying longer, don't worry. I have a good bit of money saved, and you are welcome to it. There is just one thing. It is in my apartment."

"Of course it is," Avery mumbled, pushing herself from the bed.

"Avery, sit." Magda's stern voice surprised them both. Avery sat. She waited for Avery's face to lose its impudence. "Josef is away at night, always. That is when he does his rituals and things. You will be safe going there. Wait until sunset to leave."

And let's add breaking and entering to this list of craziness, Avery thought at Chloe.

"No, I have a key hidden." Magda's gaze fixed on Avery.

Mouths dropped open. "You can hear us, Granny?"

"Since when?" Avery's voice rose an octave.

"Yes, but only since I have been… like this."

The girls shared a look, making Magda grin. "Don't worry. I'll try not to listen."

At dusk, the girls made ready to leave, with Avery hefting the book into her pack. She'd thought nothing of it; it seemed like just another item to be taken along.

"Do not take that." Magda's tone was fierce. "He will know it has been there. He can feel it."

"But when we went to your apartment before, it was in my backpack. He didn't act like he sensed it at all." Avery hadn't told them what the book said to her—or that it had started speaking at all.

The groove between her grandmother's brows deepened, still clearly visible within the moving facets of the stone. "Even so. It is safer to leave it."

Avery waited a moment for the book to protest, then shook her head at herself. She left the book beside the crystal ball.

The spare key to the apartment was still where Magda said, atop the window frame at the end of the hall. Even though they had seen the man leave twenty minutes ago, head high, strutting down the street, Avery's palms itched with trepidation. Chloe was right against her shoulder; she was always her sister's shield. Chloe's stringy arms would be useless in a fight, not that she expected to run into any trouble, and Avery was certain she could best a tall, skinny guy like Josef Straka, alive or not. *Well, unless he has some zombie ninja skills or something.* But Chloe could probably talk him into submission.

The apartment was dark. The faint smell of something charred hit Avery's nose, as if he'd burnt a steak on the stovetop several days ago. *Dead guys eat?*

"Pew," Chloe whispered. "That's worse than your burnt popcorn."

The room erupted with light, and Chloe gasped. Avery stood by the floor lamp. The place was a disaster. Someone had gutted the single armchair, masses of foam and stuffing scattered around it; the end table lay on its side, its drawer several feet away; and a tattered rug was crumpled in a corner. The living room and kitchen were one room. The refrigerator was away from the wall, the oven door was open, the whole appliance askew. The contents of the kitchen cabinets were strewn all over the floor.

After the girls took in their surroundings, Avery caught Chloe's glare.

"What?"

"Turn that off!" Chloe hissed.

"Why? Gram said he'd be gone all night."

But Chloe's face screwed up with insistence, and Avery switched off the lamp.

They used the flashlight apps on their cell phones to work their way to Magda's bedroom. The apartment was easy to navigate; it only had three rooms.

"I wonder what he was looking for," Chloe whispered, standing in the doorway to her grandmother's bedroom, which was in a similar state of disarray. He'd flung the twin mattress and box spring to the other side of the room, and every drawer in the short dresser was beside it, turned upside down.

"Why are you whispering?" Avery made her voice too loud on purpose, earning her a dramatic shush. Chloe was so easy to annoy. *I bet he was looking for the book*, she thought, careful to keep it from her twin.

"Gram's money, maybe?"

"Why would a ghost need money?" Chloe still whispered. She turned her flashlight to her sister in time to witness the shrug. Then Avery's nostrils flared and her body stiffened, eyes fixed on something behind Chloe.

"What?" she said, turning.

Chloe added her flashlight's beam to Avery's. On the floor by the window was a long pile of gray powder… ashes?

"Oh, Jesus," Avery said.

Chloe stepped forward to inspect the oddly shaped mound. *Ashes? How did he burn something right here without catching the place on fire? And that's a weird pattern, almost like a person—* Chloe yelped, dropping the phone to cover her mouth. It narrowly missed the gray mass.

"Is that—?"

"I am going to kill him," Avery spit through clenched teeth.

She came to stand beside Chloe but was too angry to unclench her fists. Josef Straka had set fire to their grandmother's body. How it hadn't torched the whole apartment she had no idea, but it was probably some dark magick crap. The girls stood together, staring at what remained of their grandmother. Chloe swayed; Avery stepped closer so her sister to lean against her.

Chloe swallowed. "Do we do something?"

"Like what? Vacuum up her ashes and take them with us in the canister?" Avery regretted her words immediately, seeing the hurt on Chloe's face. With an apologetic twitch of her mouth, she took Chloe's hand and gave it a squeeze. "Gram's with us, in the ball."

"Right," Chloe said, standing straighter. "Let's find the money and get out of here."

The money was easy to find; it was strewn all around the bathroom. Wads of US and Czech currency littered the floor, and a small gold ingot lay in the shower basin. The stash Magda had hidden behind the toilet tank was no longer a secret, and it was apparent Josef Straka hadn't been looking for money.

"Damn, Gram!" Avery said, taking her backpack off and kneeling. "I wonder where she got all this loot. And the *gold!*"

Neither of them had ever seen a gold ingot. Chloe picked it up and held it under the light of her phone. There was no insignia or stamp; it must have been melted down at some point and made smaller.

On hands and knees, the girls scampered around the bathroom floor, bumping each other often, gathering up the bounty like children under a smashed piñata.

Chloe sat back on her heels. "I wonder what he's going to think when he gets back and finds all the money gone."

Magda's mind raced with worry as she waited for the girls to return.

How had Josef not sensed the book? Does Avery have some magick shielding it from him? It was hard to know what magick Avery had or didn't have; she suppressed so much. If she was shielding it, she might not even know.

Magda hadn't yet asked Avery if the book had spoken to her again; there was too much going on. Hopefully, Avery would have told her, but then again, Avery did like her avoidance. Magda sighed. It was difficult to linger here in the quiet nothing, but at least she didn't feel the passing of time.

Magda had left out a great deal from her tale: of the souls she had trapped for Josef, of how exactly he was able to rise again, the details of the spell altogether. She would have to tell them soon enough, but not now. The looks they gave her already were too much to bear.

She dreaded what she had to tell her granddaughters next.

CHAPTER 32

"Granny! Where did you get all this money?" Chloe blurted once the lock on their door was secured.

"You said *some* money. This isn't some." Avery unzipped her pack and dumped its contents onto the bed, shaking it vigorously to get every bill and coin out. "And the gold!"

"That is what remains of what I brought with me when I left Czechoslovakia." Magda gestured with her chin at the gold ingot in Avery's hand. "I had six bars that size, hidden in pockets I'd sewn into my coat."

"But where did you get gold?" Avery turned it around in her hand, feeling the weight of the small bar, mesmerized by the glimmer it captured from the lamp. "And why the crappy apartment if you had all this money?"

Magda was quiet long enough for Avery to turn her attention back to her, right eyebrow quirked.

"The apartment was the only one I could find in a hurry within walking distance of Vyšehrad Cemetery… where Josef was buried."

"Aaand?"

"The gold was part of what Josef had instructed me to take from his house."

Avery dropped the ingot on the bed.

"Granny!" Chloe came up behind her sister. "He'll be looking for this!"

"He has no need of money as he is now. It is rightfully mine, in any case. All he cares about, all he needs, is the book."

All heads turned to the gray tome resting beside the crystal ball.

"Come." Magda's voice was grave. "It is time you learned how to read it."

"You're not going to read it to us?" Chloe asked.

Magda shook her head. "If I could spare you this, *berušky*, I would. But as I've said, there is no magick in me. I am certain, I feel this in my gut, that you will have more success with it than I."

"But Granny, if you aren't magickal, how can you be here?" Chloe gestured at the sphere. "In a crystal ball?"

"You don't need magick to be a ghost. You only need a restless spirit."

"Good to know." Avery plopped onto the bed. Leaving the book on the side table, she flipped the cover open, her head cocked, expecting some cryptic comment from it. Her bravado covered her unease. It knew she was going to learn to read it. This evil magickal book was also psychic, apparently.

Chloe moved to sit by her sister, peering at the marks on the page. *There's no way anyone can make sentences out of this mess.* Avery hmm'd an agreement.

"There is a way," Magda said with a wince. "A terrible way."

"Granny?"

"In order to read the book"—Magda swallowed—"you must take a life." Two jaws dropped. "And you must enjoy it."

Stunned silence hung between them. Avery was the first to sober. "Oh, come on!"

Avery was half up from the bed when Chloe grabbed her arm, pulling her back down. "Granny, please. We have to *kill* someone? That's ridiculous."

The old woman is right.

Avery's spine cracked as she bolted upright.

You must take a life, and you must enjoy it.

She stared at the book, nostrils flared, breath trapped in her lungs.

A hawk screeched; the flash of a boy covering his bloody face as he ran filled her vision. The memory of how glad she was at his suffering was as sharp as the day it happened. Then the Hartley boy sprawled on gray linoleum, blood pouring from his nose, a teacher trying to staunch the flow with a wad of paper towels. How Avery felt staring down at him in the hospital haunted her dreams although she'd never told a soul, not even Chloe. Part of her had wanted to let him languish, let him die; he was an awful person who didn't deserve to live. It shamed her to admit she wavered; she'd only been fourteen! If her grandmother hadn't called to her, urging her forgiveness, she wasn't certain what would have happened.

And now this book *wanted* her to kill.

"Avery, what is it?" Magda said.

Avery. Chloe's cold hand was on her shoulder. *You're scaring me.*

Avery swallowed hard and dug her fingertips into her legs. "It's been speaking to me," she said through tight lips. She ignored their gasps. "Since we got here."

She relaxed her fingers and rubbed the sweat from her palms on her lap. Her eyes darted to Magda and Chloe, then returned to the book.

"When we first got to your apartment and met... *him*, it told me not to mention it to him. Then later, it told me it could help me after I learned to read it. And just now"—she sucked in a breath—"it said you were right."

Magda's face hardened.

"What else have you not told me?" The edge to her grandmother's voice made Avery flush with shame.

"Nothing, Gram." She cleared her throat. "Nothing. I swear."

Magda turned to Chloe. "And you heard nothing?"

Chloe shook her head vigorously.

Avery's back slumped. "Why did it pick me?"

Because you have darkness inside you. Magda closed her eyes.

Avery shuddered. *That's why.*

Magda's eyes snapped open at hearing Avery's response in her head. They stared at each other, Avery's ears hot with shame. *I'm sorry, my Avery. I hadn't meant for you to hear that.*

Avery sagged. *You're not wrong, though.*

Her grandmother had always known that about her, hadn't she? She'd tried to help her curb it, to learn how to control it; Avery only ever wanted to ignore it. *But how does the book know?*

Chloe rubbed her sister's arm, oblivious to their exchange.

They sat in silence, every second picking at Chloe's skin until she was ready to scream. She rose and walked to the bathroom, which was only a few paces in the room, then to the window, and back again. They let her pace, saying nothing, knowing Chloe's mind was working on the problem at hand.

But there were so many problems. Chloe had no idea why a book would reach out to Avery. Maybe because Avery's magick was stronger than hers? She didn't know how that could be. Avery never used her power; Chloe used hers every day. *But for good,* she thought to herself. And from everything she'd learned so far, the book was the opposite of good.

"Okay, so, back to this taking-a-life business." Chloe turned, one hand on hip, one finger pointed at Magda. "What *specifically* does it say, Granny? I mean, does it say a *human* life must be taken?"

Avery blinked several times, as if coming out of a trance. Her face brightened somewhat. "Right! Could I, like, smash a bug and we're good? I hate bugs."

Magda seemed stunned by the suggestion. "I don't know, honestly."

Avery hopped up and began searching the room. "There's got to be a bug here somewhere."

The windowsill yielded only dried husks of long-dead bugs and, after a few minutes, they gave up.

"Outside," Chloe said, grabbing the room key. They were out the door before Magda could say anything.

The cobblestone alley behind the hostel was bright with golden light from the lamps fixed to the buildings lining each side. Avery peered in the shadows behind trashcans while Chloe pushed discarded boxes around with her foot.

"A-ha!" Avery moved a rusted and dented trash bin aside, deranged glee on her face.

"Die, cockroach, die!" She stomped on the scampering bug and then another appearing from beneath the can. Two more met the fate of their kin. She hopped around in the shadows, cackling as light crunching sounds came from under foot.

Chloe stood agog at her sister.

Avery looked up. "What?"

Chloe scoffed, smacking her sister playfully on the arm. "Come on."

It hadn't worked. Avery stared at the words for nearly ten minutes, and they remained unreadable slashes. She exhaled an expletive and sat back. "What now?"

Magda was quiet. Chloe didn't press her. The idea of killing a person was just too horrible to bear. *How could she do this to us? There must be another way!* Chloe clamped her trembling hands together.

"Ask the book." Magda's face twisted in turmoil as she spoke. Chloe's mouth fell open.

Avery hesitated, then squared her shoulders. She turned her body to the book and grasped the mattress on either side of her legs.

Chloe reached out purposefully with her mind to catch the

communication between her sister and the book, but she heard nothing. She could read some of the conversation on Avery's face; she glared at the wall as if she could burn a hole through it, gritting her teeth.

When Avery's jaw locked, they both knew the book had spoken.

"Tell me," Magda said.

Avery licked her dry lips. "The life you take must have a soul."

"No!" The color drained from Chloe's face.

I can't let you do that. Avery took Chloe's hands. *I won't. I'll do it.*

Chloe squeezed her eyes closed. Magda opened her mouth, but Chloe's eyes snapped open and her sudden words cut her off.

"Now, let's just wait a minute. Why don't we work our way up the food chain? It's apparent bugs don't have souls. What's a step up from that? What about a fish? Or a snake?" Chloe was grasping at straws, but anything was better than the reality lurking ahead of them.

"Not a snake," Avery said, then her stomach offered a suggestion. "Lobster! What about a lobster? I *love* lobster."

Magda nodded grimly. "It's worth a try."

The girls went to the front desk to ask for a cooktop and pot. The prim, fifty-something woman behind the counter, her hair in a bun so tight it pulled her eyebrows up, stared down her nose at them.

"There is no cooking in rooms." Her words were clipped and quite clear behind her nasal-laced accent.

Avery pulled something from her pocket and leaned forward, resting both elbows on the high counter. Her right hand flicked out, thumping a bound wad of US currency in front of the sour woman. "How about now?"

Chloe couldn't see her sister's face, but her voice dripped with arrogance.

The woman scoffed, arms folding over her chest. "The apartments two blocks down caters to spoiled Americans." She fixed her eyes on Avery. "You go there in morning." Her meaning was clear.

Chloe sensed the heat rising in her sister and grabbed Avery by the wrist, yanking her back before the expletives started. Chloe nodded to the woman and thanked her, backing away.

The woman shifted her beady glare to Chloe. "You go there in morning, yes?"

"Yes, we'll go there in the morning." Chloe's head bobbed as she pulled Avery around her and pushed her up the stairs.

"You roll over too easily." Avery threw Chloe a side-glare, stomping up each stair.

Chloe bolted in front of Avery, blocking her path. "She's kicking us out because you tried to bribe her." She let out an exasperated 'ugh' and started back up the stairs. "She probably thought we were going to cook up some meth or something. I'd kick us out too."

"Oh, yeah. We really look like a couple of meth heads."

CHAPTER 33

The creamy white stone façade reflected the bright morning sun, making Chloe shield her eyes as she peered up at the opulent, four-story building. The keystone of the massive arched doorway featured the laughing face of a bearded old man staring down at her. With its crown of leaves, the carving reminded her of the green man. His laugh seemed to turn into a frown as she passed under him. *The shadows playing tricks,* Chloe thought.

The small portico smelled of wood polish; the heavy, double wood doors gleamed in the sunshine. *How much is this going to cost?* Her palms sweated as she followed Avery into the lobby.

The grand space made Chloe feel underdressed and grubby in her plain khaki shorts and her favorite 'Adopt, Don't Shop' pink T-shirt. Marble columns dotted the vast room; a circular lawn of red carpet in the center swirled with a gold filigree pattern. A crystal chandelier hung at the apex of the ceiling above a circle of gold chairs and couches. Classical music played softly from somewhere. She couldn't identify the lovely scent filling her nostrils, but it was certainly coming from the copious amount of fresh flowers filling the vases situated on every available flat surface. She hugged her messenger bag to her and hurried after Avery. The loud clicking her rolling bag made across the marble floor, echoing off the high, slightly concave ceiling, was cringe-worthy.

Avery's smile broadened, eyes glittering, as she took in all the pristine marble and shiny brass. "Now, this is more like it," she murmured, head bobbing.

"Oh my god, we can't afford this," Chloe whispered in her sister's ear. Avery tsked, waving a hand.

Avery marched toward the tall reception desk made from the same marble as the columns and floor. Behind it stood a fresh-faced young man, with flawlessly coiffed blond hair and a model-perfect chin dimple. His face lit up at seeing them.

Martin, as his gilded name badge read, vibrated with so much hospitality Avery groaned aloud, earning her a hard poke in her back from Chloe. Undaunted, Martin continued his welcoming spiel, flashing a perfect-teeth smile at Avery and keeping eye contact. Too much eye contact.

"You're barking up the wrong tree, buddy," Avery said, grabbing her sister by the shoulders and pushing her forward.

Chloe's cheeks burned, and her ears turned scarlet. Hoping the sputtering noise she made sounded like laughter, she wandered away as Avery finished the transaction with Martin. Chloe could hear him chattering nonstop as he checked them in, extolling the grandness of the view their room had and all the amazing things they could see, places they should definitely visit while they were in Prague. He would be happy to arrange special tours for them. Avery let the very thin yet fit young man ramble, smiling and nodding as required.

I wonder how much hair gel it takes to keep that cowlick in check?

Chloe didn't look; she was heading toward the elevator, carrying her rolling bag.

Avery's smirk as she joined her sister in the elevator earned her daggers.

"You're a terrible sister. Have I told you that yet today?"

"Nope." Avery guffawed. "Not yet."

The short-term apartment was fully furnished, and with finer things than Chloe had ever had, all of which came with a matching price tag.

"We really need to watch our spending," she said, eyeing the expensive-looking abstract artwork on the white walls, the white leather furniture, the modern, round glass dining table. Offsetting the white decor was a glossy black credenza and large flat-screen television mounted above it. The far wall was a bank of windows, making Chloe mouth a 'wow.'

An uneven sea of white buildings with red-tiled roofs lay before her. Capturing her gaze in the distance was the Church of St. Nicholas; Martin had mentioned its patinaed spires and massive dome. If she stretched a little to the left, she could see the whole span of the Charles Bridge. Chloe groaned. *So much to see, but we can't.* Maybe after this was over, they could make time.

"Pfft," Avery grunted. "There's plenty of money. And it's not like Gram's going to be spending it."

"I can hear you, you know," came a muffled but clearly annoyed voice from Chloe's messenger bag. Avery grimaced and sought refuge in another room.

"Sorry, Granny." Chloe pulled the heavy crystal from her bag and looked around the living room for a good place to set her. A large, shiny metal candleholder sat atop the glass-and-brass coffee table. It was a bundle of black twists, flecked with gold leaf. Welded on the top was a shallow dish holding a white, three-wick pillar. Chloe replaced the way-too-flowery-smelling candle with her grandmother. *Perfect.*

After unpacking, the girls set out to find a fish market, or a store selling live lobsters.

Martin beamed when the elevator doors opened, and he extended his arms in greeting. Avery shrank away from his high-pitched welcome and beelined for the circle of gaudy gold furniture.

His attentions were aimed at Chloe this time, and she

blushed and giggled, much to her added embarrassment. She managed to ask him where they could find live lobsters. Apparently, it was a very unusual request, and he begged for a few minutes while he searched the internet. Chloe wandered away again, thankful to escape her shame.

Success was proclaimed with a triumphant "Ha!" and he waved the girls over. There was a large supermarket in Praha 9 selling lobsters from a tank, but they would need to take the metro. He offered to escort them personally on his lunch break if they could wait another hour.

Chloe declined his generous offer and backed away, waving and smiling like a fool. Avery had no trouble remarking on her abysmal flirting skills as they pushed through the lobby doors.

The morning was bright; a few wispy clouds streaked the summer sky. The green trees and chirping birds lifted Chloe's spirits, and the walk along the bustling street to the metro station took her mind from their errand, or, rather, what they would have to do next if it didn't work. She prayed lobsters had souls, then laughed at herself for praying for something that sounded so ridiculous.

Martin's directions had been perfect. As they surveyed the enormous tank of live lobsters at the back wall in the supermarket, each with their claws banded shut, Chloe felt sorry for them. Although not a true vegetarian, she ate nothing she deemed 'cute,' like lamb or calves or bunnies. She'd never had lobster before, not because she thought they were cute but because they resembled a cockroach too much for her liking. Avery, on the other hand, seemed to enjoy everything Chloe disliked, which she probably did on purpose just to annoy her.

Avery salivated at the tank. Her eager eyes darted around the aquarium, the lobsters pushing and scrambling over one another, striking out with useless pincers. She gestured to one appearing particularly feisty.

"That one!" Avery pointed, following the fleeing lobster

around the glass with her finger. "He looks like he's got a big, fat, juicy soul."

The woman standing behind the tank blinked several times at Avery, then donned thick rubber gloves coming up to her elbows. Chloe left her to watch the capture of her prize. Now that they had a full kitchen, they needed groceries.

Chloe completed the sale without the need for her dictionary, mumbling a few words in Czech, her heart heavy with what was next while her mind repeated how ridiculous this was.

Avery examined the largest pot in their well-stocked kitchen. "Larry will just have to fit in this. I don't see anything bigger."

"How can you name something, then kill it?" Chloe asked, filling the pot with water.

"Easy. Watch." Avery rubbed her palms together. "Oh, dammit. You forgot butter."

Chloe relocated Magda to the counter overlooking the kitchen. Avery felt her grandmother's gaze follow her, but Magda remained quiet; the worry etched on her face needed no words.

Avery placed the lobster in the pot atop the electric burner set on high and held it in with the lid. *Do I need to watch it die?* she asked absently, not aiming the question toward the book or Chloe. Her bravado was fading. *This is stupid. It's not going to work.*

Chloe sat at the counter beside Magda, watching Avery hover over the pot. With a hand firmly on the lid, the lobster clanking against it for its freedom, Avery motioned to her twin.

"Get over here. You're the book lover, not me."

Chloe shook her head. "This is all you, sister."

Avery tsked, turning back to the pot. In a weird way, Avery wanted to be the only one to read the book. It had spoken just to her, hadn't it? That meant something. *Ha, look at me! Wanting to read a book. Add that to the list of firsts on this trip.*

Chloe covered her ears when screams pealed from the pot.

"It's not really screaming." Avery scoffed. "That's just the sound of air escaping its shell." Chloe didn't uncover her ears.

The sounds were soon replaced by the rattle of shell against metal, the lobster being jostled around in the boiling water. Avery's mouth watered though she still lamented the lack of butter.

After she was sure the thing was dead, she turned off the burner and turned to Magda, a questioning look on her face.

"Do I need to eat it first?"

Magda appeared to shrug. "I don't know, my Avery. Try to read the book first."

The twins settled onto the stools at the counter. Avery rubbed her palms on her shorts, clearing her throat. She pulled the thick book toward her.

"Here goes nothing," she murmured, flipping the cover open.

The rust-colored scratch marks appeared the same as they had before, creepy and unreadable. She glanced at Magda, who motioned for her to keep looking. Chloe pressed into her shoulder, peering at the page also, stealing glances at her sister's face.

The minutes crawled by with no change.

Tears welled in Chloe's eyes, and the hint of hope on Magda's face vanished.

"Oh, Granny." Chloe put her face in her hands. "We just can't take somebody's life!"

"We won't have to," Avery breathed. The chills passing over her skin left goose bumps in their wake. She followed the scratchings on the page with her fingers as they transformed, or rather as they became words she could recognize although written with few letters. The warmth she'd always felt from the book was replaced by tiny sparks of energy snapping into her fingertips without pain. Her grandmother spoke, but her attention was locked on to the markings that had been gibberish seconds ago.

Something else churned deep beneath the awe. Avery hadn't meant to give it more than a second of consideration, her mind transfixed by what was happening before her eyes and on her skin. But tremendous satisfaction pulled the corners of her lips wide. Her spirits soared. At last!

What? Avery shook her head, blinking to refocus. She turned the thick pages slowly, mesmerized once again by the formation of words, for now they *were* words to her.

Words cascaded into sentences, sentences into passages. Her pulse hammered in her ears as their meaning became clear. Dread eclipsed awe.

"Oh my god." Avery tore her eyes away and stared at her grandmother, whose face was twisted with regret. "This book—" Her throat dried, and she swallowed to speak again. "This thing is very wrong."

Magda squeezed her eyes closed and turned away.

"What…" Chloe gulped. "What does it say?"

Avery turned her head slowly to her twin, blinking to focus. Chloe gasped.

She disregarded the look on Chloe's face and returned her attention to the book. Her lips parted, but she didn't speak. Avery flattened her hand on the page and closed her eyes to the tantalizing sensations traveling into her.

Yes, the book hissed in delight. *Yes, Avery Parsons. With me, you will have all the power you desire.*

Avery caught her breath. She never thought the book's voice had sounded muffled or far away before. But now, it was clearer, more intimate, as if the person speaking was sitting closer than her sister.

She opened her eyes and followed a line in the book with her finger. *"Suka yeh—"*

"No!" Magda's face loomed large in the crystal ball. "You must not speak them aloud until you need them."

Magda's tone snapped Avery from the book's grip. She wobbled on the stool, feeling dazed and very warm. Chloe pulled the book away slowly. Avery's eyes followed. Chloe closed it and pushed it to the end of the counter.

He was jubilant.

The girl held such power within her, buried deep and ignored. Much more than he had experienced before her mind was fully open to him. And better still, she had learned combat. Not that he would need such skills, but it made her body stronger. He could sustain her for much longer, far beyond the typical lifespan of fragile humans.

Her desire for easy power, to lash out at those who crossed her, had not diminished. She would be easily molded for his purpose. Of that, he had no doubt.

Now that she could read him, it was only a matter of time.

CHAPTER 34

Josef Straka had no need for sleep. He paced in the apartment, hands clasped tightly behind his back, while his mind raced round the twin redheaded granddaughters of Magda Hlavacova.

When he'd entered the apartment after the morning sun had fully crested, he knew someone had been there. He focused his mind to look back, to trace the energy lingering in the rooms. The sisters' anxiety tickled his skin, and he smiled, reveling in their worry. Especially the long-haired one. Josef delighted in her tears over the old woman's ashes and laughed aloud at the echo of the fiery one's threat.

Josef cared nothing for the money, but now he wondered. If Magda had told them about the money, she could have also told them about the book. It still grated at him that he could not *see* what she'd done. He cursed her again for burning out her eyes.

He lashed out at the floor lamp, the only thing remaining upright and unbroken, and it crashed to the floor, the bulb popping dark when it shattered. Josef preferred the room dark anyway. The brightness forcing its way through the worn shades was almost too much. He found he now detested the light of day. But he needed to find the sisters; he needed to follow their trail in the wretched sunlight.

Josef plodded along the sidewalk, his head high with shoulders tight, hands behind his back. People in his path were thrust away before they made contact. Shocked at the sudden push, they whirled and saw nothing, staring in confusion at the tall man in the black suit striding past. A trio of young men, covered in tattoos with shaved heads and piercings in their faces, took offense to the shove that could only have come from the *hajzl* walking with determination past them. The biggest of the trio called out and reached for the man's shoulder. Without a backward glance nor a break in his stride, Josef sent flames into the young man's hand that quickly engulfed his entire body.

He paid no attention to the screams and shouts, nor to those running. These pathetic humans were nothing, and they would soon be only puppets of the horde and he their master. His thoughts turned to Muraal, and he reddened. His shame refused to leave him.

After two blocks, the girls' trail vanished, as if it had never been there. No faint traces lay in the wind or clung to the walls of buildings. Nothing. Josef frowned. Even if they'd gotten into a taxi, he'd still see their trail. He turned in all directions, scowling.

And then he heard it.

Two words uttered from the book, an incomplete phrase started with awkwardness and abruptly cut short.

His hope surged, his mind searching for the direction they'd come from. Josef barreled forward. He stopped in the middle of an intersection only to have a car screech to a halt, clipping his leg. It did not move him; he did not feel it, and the driver jumped from his car with shouts and curses. Josef narrowed his eyes as the man grabbed his face in agony, his skin melting underneath his hands.

Gone.

Josef's roar echoed off the buildings around him, making people shrink away. He stomped back in the direction of the apartment.

Someone is reading my book. My *book! How is that possible? I am its master!*

Then a sneer took his mouth. Only a few more words needed to be spoken.

CHAPTER 35

THE GIRLS SAT IN SILENCE AT THE DINING TABLE. AVERY ATE the lobster without much interest, and Chloe pushed the ramen noodles around in her bowl. She didn't have to eat ramen now that they had extra money, but she liked it. Her eyes tracked her sister's movements, waiting for a sign she was ready to talk. Magda had faded not long after the book was closed, saying she needed to think.

The moment those two strange-sounding words left Avery's lips, Chloe no longer sensed anything from her sister.

Can you hear me? she thought at Avery for the tenth time. Chloe reached out again, searching for any shred of thought or feeling from Avery. But there was nothing—no annoyance, no anger, no heat, no sarcasm, no laughter. Dead air from a radio station. They had learned to put up barriers between themselves on occasion, but it was more like a sheer curtain than a wall, a sign to the other sister that she wanted some privacy. Chloe didn't feel the invisible partition. It was as if Avery wasn't there at all.

It was… unsettling, to be alone with herself, to not have the comforting, albeit sometimes annoying, presence that had been with her all her life. She felt hollow, like an empty well.

A lump rose in her throat. What was causing this? Chloe's unease grew with each passing minute.

"Want to talk about it?" Chloe whispered.

"Talk about what?" Avery said at full volume, not meeting her eyes. She chewed on a plump piece from the tail like a robot.

Chloe longed to ask if Avery still sensed her but kept silent, enforcing her silence by shoveling a forkful of unwanted noodles into her mouth. The tension grew heavy as the minutes crawled.

Avery pushed back in her chair and stood. "I need some air." She left without her phone or backpack, or even a backward glance.

The piercing chirp of her cell phone made Chloe jump. Vivian's smiling image glimmered on the screen.

"Oh, god." Chloe gulped.

Avery felt odd. Her mind spun with the horrible things she'd read and the memory of a voice that sounded way too pleased with itself, and way too close.

She shoved her hands in the front pockets of her cargo shorts as she roamed, eyes cast down. Her stomach churned; either the lobster sought revenge or the ugliness of the book's intent gurgled bile in her belly.

Why did that nasty thing choose her? Avery admitted to a darker side, but what was in that book went far beyond dark. *When Grammy called it evil and twisted, she wasn't kidding.*` The few pages she'd read were filled with horrific ways to hurt people and use their agony to fuel whatever awful spell you were intending. She shivered despite the late afternoon sun on her back.

The book said it would give her all the power she wanted. *I don't want power, do I? Hell no.* She had all the power she needed in Punch-o and Lefty. Avery snorted a laugh. She hadn't referred to her fists by those names since she was a teenager. And her roundhouse kick had taken down guys almost three times her weight.

Besides, magick has brought me nothing but problems. Magick brought a dead guy back to life. Magick made Gram kill herself. Magick will let demons into our world.

"Fuck magick," Avery grumbled. Even as she said the words, she knew the truth. Magick was the only thing that would stop him. The thought of having to read more of the book brought a wave of nausea. She sat down on the nearest bench and leaned over, taking deep breaths to ease the urge to vomit. *What have I gotten myself into? What has Gram gotten me into?*

Avery reached out to her sister for comfort, but it was quiet. Avery looked for the clothes-hanger-on-the-doorknob sign telling her to stay out, but it wasn't there. Nothing was there. She sat up. *Chloe?* She searched the corners of her mind for the ever-present traces of her sister. Chloe was gone.

Chloe! She waited a few seconds for the expected shout of 'go away' in reply.

Avery pushed off from the bench, running back toward the apartment, yelling at people who were too slow to move aside.

Had Josef found them? Chloe couldn't defend herself against a man like him!

Stop, Avery Parsons.

She skidded to a halt, using a signpost to keep herself from tumbling forward.

The unearthly voice was a harsh whisper in her ear. She wheeled around, hunting for its source. *Go away!* Avery imagined her barrier, the same one she used on Chloe, but it wouldn't come.

You will listen.

Its words echoed painfully within the confines of her skull. Avery clutched her head with both hands. People on the sidewalk stared in disgust at the young woman who was clearly going through addiction withdrawals.

Do not fight me.

She cried out, pushing her fists into her temples, and staggered into an alleyway. Back pressed to the rough wall, she railed against the pain.

I don't want you in my head! Get out, get out! You're hurting me!

I am not the cause of your pain. Do not fight, and the pain will end. Each word was a penknife stabbing into her brain.

I don't want you or your goddamn book, or whatever this is! Go away!

Through the pain, Avery distinctly felt what she believed was a sneer.

It is far too late for that.

Avery hunched over, sour acid releasing itself onto the pavement, chunks of lobster tail with it.

"Chloe." She wiped her mouth with the hem of her T-shirt. "She better be okay."

Nothing has happened to your twin.

Hands on knees, she gulped air. Why could she no longer feel Chloe? That seemed too intimate a question to ask *it*, and she wanted it gone.

She relaxed her back against the warm brick wall, glaring at nothing in the middle distance. *What do you want?*

I wish only to help you. Josef Straka will come for you.

Avery's skin jumped.

Be calm. Its voice sent ripples across her skin. *I can help you.*

How? And why? Aren't you supposed to be his *book? Didn't he write you?*

He may have penned me, but the book is of my blood and my flesh. I choose who wields me.

Revulsion rolled in her twisted gut. It *was* skin she'd held in her hands! Blood she'd traced with her fingers! She gulped more air, rubbing her palms vigorously on her shorts, trying to rid herself of the lingering feeling of its hard skin on her fingers.

"How can you help me? And you never answered the 'why.'"

Read my pages, learn the knowledge within them. All will become clear.

His presence faded, and she knew he wouldn't speak anymore. *He? It, dammit*, she growled at herself. *It.*

Avery pushed off from the wall and stepped back into reality.

Avery's not-so-gentle kick rattled the apartment door. It flew open, revealing a startled Chloe. Avery greeted her sister with a big smile and presented her hands; each held a large, golden-brown triangle sprinkled with sugar on a paper square.

"I found a crepe stand. A. Crepe. Stand!" She placed them on the dining table.

"Oh!" Chloe licked her lips. "*Palačinky*. Yum!"

Avery rolled her eyes.

"I only got two. They took forever to make." She pulled the chair close to the table and rubbed her palms together. "We should go back later."

Chloe sat beside her and immediately dug in. An 'mmm' escaped her lips. "This is heaven. The marmalade filling is still a little warm."

After swallowing the first mouthful, Chloe cleared her throat. "So, Mom called."

"Oh, crap." Avery lowered the bit of crepe at her mouth. "I forgot about Mom."

"How could you forget Mom?"

Avery frowned. "What did you tell her?"

"Oh, god. I had to lie." Chloe sagged in the chair. "Yeah, I know, I suck at it. Don't give me that look. I told her Granny had a code key for deciphering the book."

"Good one."

"She asked what was in the book, and I said it just seemed like potions for stuff to give people rashes or make them lose their hair."

Avery's skepticism rose high on her forehead.

"She bought it, though. I think."

Avery scoffed and tossed a bit into her mouth, flinging chocolate onto her chin.

Chloe pushed sugar granules around on the paper with a finger. She took a deep breath, then huffed it out. "I can't feel you anymore."

Avery's chewing stopped. She swallowed; it now tasted like ash. She put out her hand and Chloe took it, squeezing hard. They met each other's eyes.

"Why do you suppose that is?" Chloe asked, searching her sister's taut face.

"I don't know," she said too quickly, shrugging out of reflex.

"It's because of the book, isn't it? Something in it, something you read?"

Avery pulled her hand away and leaned her elbows on the table, putting her face in her hands. "I don't know," she repeated.

She was lying. The book now occupied the part of her being where her sister had always been. Her breath quaked in her chest, and she sat back, eyes glossy with tears and fixed on Chloe. *It's inside me, Chloe, I can feel it.* Her sister's face didn't respond; Chloe truly no longer sensed her.

Chloe wrapped her arms around her sister. Avery's quivering shoulders and matching breaths revealed what her sister could no longer feel. Chloe tightened her arms around Avery.

"Look." Chloe gently pushed her away to lock eyes. "Let's get on with this Josef business, get it over with, and then we can chuck the book in the river and go home. Okay?"

Avery nodded, her face hardening as she wiped away a single, fat tear.

Chloe picked up the last morsel of her treat, motioning to Avery to finish as well. Avery regarded the half-eaten crepe with its warm chocolate-hazelnut spread smeared over the paper, no longer wanting it. She finished it anyway, keeping her face free of expression.

They retired to the sofa with the book. Avery's palms were clammy as she held the ugly, smelly thing, knowing now it was human skin. *What kind of horrible person makes a book out of a person's skin*? She shuddered, placing the book down quickly on the glass coffee table. *That explains the stink.*

The crystal ball was still nestled in its metal throne. Magda's image swirled to clarity in the depths of the yellow sphere; the lines texturing her face appeared deeper. The three exchanged glances, and all eyes turned to the elephant in the room.

Magda's voice was solemn. "It is my belief that everything evil can be made good, and everything good can be made evil." Her gaze moved from the book to Avery. "It is your *intent* that makes the difference."

"Oh, Gram." Avery sighed, sinking into the back of the sofa.

"Well, that's very… optimistic." Chloe gave her grandmother a consoling smile.

"So, that's what we're doing here? The 'power of positive thinking'?" Avery didn't conceal her sarcasm.

Chloe picked at the seam of her shorts. "You don't have anything, um, more concrete, do you? Like firsthand experience or anything?"

Magda turned away, letting out a deep sigh. "When I used the book, it was out of necessity. It *is* evil, as you saw, Avery, but good can be achieved with it as well. Its spells protected me, saved my life, extended my life, and… kept harm from coming to others." She winced. "I tried to shield you from dark magick, steering you toward animals and lighthearted, simple spells. But now, I have done the unthinkable. I have dragged you into the heart of evil, and I cannot undo it." Magda faded.

"Granny, wait!"

Chloe reached for the ball but drew her hands away when Magda returned, her anguish etched on her face.

"I cannot imagine what words it whispers to you, my Avery"—her voice caught—"but you must be strong."

"Of course, Grammy, of course." She wanted so much to

hug her grandmother. "I'm not afraid." The words escaped her lips without permission. She *was* afraid.

Magda's eyes turned hard. "You will tell me everything it says to you, yes?"

"Yes! Of course, Gram." Avery never had a problem lying in the past, not even to her grandmother, but the words stung as they rolled out. Why didn't she want to be honest with her?

Magda's stare lingered; Avery was certain she was expected to confess.

"Granny," Chloe said, scooting to the edge of the sofa. "What do we need to do to stop him? We don't want him letting in this demon horde, obviously…" She made a face and held up a hand. "This all sounds ridiculous. I'm sorry, but this is difficult to wrap my brain around. The only reason I sort of believe this is because your *head* is floating in a crystal ball right in front of me. And Avery is hearing voices, supposedly from this book here, and—"

"Just one voice." Heat rose in Avery's cheeks. "And there is no 'suppose.' You don't believe me?"

"I do, but—"

Avery stood, grabbing the book with both hands. "This book is made of a person's flesh, the words are written in his blood!" Anger coursed through her. How dare Chloe doubt her! "And I think he's a little pissed about that. Straka may have written this book, but *he* chooses who gets to use him." *And he's chosen me.*

Chloe leaned away, eyes wide and speechless. Magda shrank within the sphere. Avery loomed above her with a savage expression.

What did I just say? Avery blinked. *He's* chosen *me?*

The heat flowing into Avery's arms slowly withdrew to its source. She dropped the book onto the sofa, confusion distorting her face. "I—"

Magda pulled in her lips, and the two deep lines between her brow joined. "You said you would tell me everything it said to you."

Fire sparked again in Avery. "Get off my case! This is all your fault anyway. Because of you, that psycho is back! Because of you, I have a stalker creeping around in my head." A knuckle popped as her fists clenched. "How could you have sent this to me? You know what I'm capable of!"

Magda's face fell; her image fluttered within the crystal.

"What?" Chloe gaped at Avery. "What are you talking about?" She turned to Magda. "What don't I know?"

Neither answered. Avery glared at the book. *Whatever it is you want, I won't do it.*

Chloe stood and put a hand on Avery's shoulder. Her chest deflated under Chloe's gentle squeeze, and Avery sat. Chloe pulled the book onto her lap. Avery's head snapped in her direction. Her gut reaction was to snatch it away, but she stopped herself. She exhaled, releasing the anger she held with it, and the room shifted. Avery took her spinning head in both hands.

For the briefest moment, a low rumble of amusement rolled in the back of her mind.

Chloe put the book aside and pulled her sister into her arms. "It's okay," she murmured against Avery's hair, rubbing her back. "It's okay."

Avery nodded against her sister's neck, and withdrew.

"I'm so sorry, Grammy. I don't know what came over…"

The yellow quartz sphere was empty.

CHAPTER 36

THE MEMORY OF HER SISTER'S EYES PLAGUED CHLOE'S dreams. Was that frightening change required to read the scratch mark writing? Was it the effect of some spell she'd been reading? Or was it evidence of the book's influence on her?

Avery's light hazel eyes had gone almost black, the pupils nearly lost within the growing shadow. Only after Chloe closed the book and pushed it aside had Avery's eyes returned to normal.

Maybe I should tell Granny. There's obviously something in Avery's past bad enough to hide from me. She might need to know this.

The worries and secrets surrounding them picked at her until she gave up on sleep. Avery's tossing and kicking hadn't helped. Chloe left their apartment as the sun rose and returned with more sweet crepes.

She waited until Avery stuffed herself and downed a cup of coffee before asking her what she meant about their grandmother knowing what she was capable of. Avery answered with silence, as Chloe expected. She sipped her coffee and stared at the bank of windows. *Maybe it's better if I don't know.*

Golden mist bloomed within the crystal and resolved into their grandmother. Chloe wished she could hug her. Avery's words had cut her deeply, and the pain lingered on her face. But playing the blame game was pointless; nothing could change the path she'd put them on. They had to push forward. Chloe reached for the book.

It was difficult for Avery to keep Magda's gaze. "I'm so sorry, Gram. Really."

"It is not for you to apologize, *beruško*. You could never be as upset with me as I am with myself. What I have done to you, my Avery, what I have exposed you both to, is unforgivable." Her eyes glossed over. "And I am afraid it will get much worse."

Chloe took Avery's hand.

Magda turned to Chloe. "You asked me what is needed to stop him. The answer lies in there." She gestured to the book with her chin. "Although which spell will work, I don't know. He has one hundred souls tethered to him, providing him with eternal power. There is no spell in the book to rescind what was done. But the book is strange." Her voice deepened, eyes entranced. "The words *move*. They may read one way at one moment, then be completely different the next. Not always, though. I never figured out how or why."

Avery tried to hide her shiver by repositioning her legs on the sofa.

"Avery, remember what I said? That everything evil can be made good? You should read the passages with the intent to send Josef Straka back into the afterlife. With your connection to the book, the words might change to our benefit." Magda studied her granddaughter's face, which remained unreadable. But Avery nodded, pulling the volume from Chloe's lap, and slowly opened it to the first page.

"This is where it gets worse, and I am very sorry." Magda released a shaky breath. Chloe's hand tightened around Avery's clammy palm. "The words… they will… hurt you. When I spoke the vile words, they cut my throat. Then after—" She turned away.

"Cut my throat?" Avery stared openly at Magda.

Chloe leaned in. "After what, Granny?"

"After the words are spoken, they will punish you." She squeezed her eyes closed, tears glittering in her lashes. "When the dark magick flows through your veins, it is the most wondrous feeling. It is like nothing else. But after the power leaves, pain comes."

Avery lowered her eyes to the book in her lap. Chloe studied her sister's face for any sign the book was speaking to her. Avery pulled her hand from Chloe's and massaged the back of her neck, stretching her chin around until her neck cracked.

Magda frowned. "Why do you two no longer speak?"

The sudden change in topic brought Avery's attention back. She stiffened.

"The book has cut her off from me," Chloe blurted. "Since she learned to read it." Chloe glared at the slash marks on the page, covered by Avery's slow-moving palm.

Chloe looked up at her sister. "You're scaring me," she said, nodding at Avery's hand.

Avery snatched her hand away. "What?"

Chloe's lips flattened.

"Look, this whole situation is messed up." Avery scrunched her face under two pairs of probing eyes. "You need to cut me some slack, okay? Or, here"—she tossed the thick book to Chloe, who scooted away—"you read it."

Chloe loved books, but not *this* book. She was secretly happy it hadn't chosen her—if 'chosen' was the right word. She raised her palms in surrender.

"All right, then." Avery huffed, taking it back. "What do I need to do, Gram?"

Magda's hard gaze traveled between the twins, her frown deepening, then she gave a small shake of her head. "Find something in the book, something simple, and try the words so when the time comes to really use them, you'll know what to expect."

"Get used to the throat-cutting and pain, you mean?"

Magda winced. Chloe scooted closer and pressed her

shoulder against Avery's. They shared a glance, an apology without words.

Chloe watched Avery's fingers follow the groupings of marks. *How on earth could they be considered a written language?* 'On earth' being the question. Her desire for knowledge pinged jealously for a moment. She'd love to know what the words meant, where they came from, who wrote them. But fear nixed that; if evil magick and demons were involved, she'd happily stay ignorant.

Page after page, Avery's eyes and fingers skimmed the text. Her mouth went dry and her skin crawled at what the book conveyed. The ritual to tear open something called the Shade was long and gruesome, and she couldn't make herself read all of it. Some sentences took longer to understand; they lacked the basic sentence structure she was used to and at times seemed just a collection of words put together with no apparent meaning. She mentally inserted a preposition here and there to make sense of the phrases.

Avery's heart sank with each turn of the page, pulling her into a black abyss of dark magick. *Does everything involve blood and killing?*

She wanted no part of it, and yet she found the magick impressive—nothing she'd ever read about when she'd studied. The ability to control other people's minds, her favorite one so far, except for the bit about having to hold a human brain in your hand. The capability to walk through walls involved slathering oneself in the melted fat of— *Nope.* She could fly if she was willing to take out and eat a male eagle's heart. *Who would do that?!*

Avery groaned, begging her stomach to calm. *This Straka guy was a sick mo-fo, that's no lie.* She shook out her hands and rubbed her sweaty palms on her thighs. Avery turned another page, and movement grabbed her eyes. She squinted and peered closer.

A cluster of red marks within a short passage shifted. They faded out almost entirely, then reappeared as different collection of marks.

She sucked in a breath. "Are you seeing this?"

"No, what?" Chloe bent forward. "What am I looking for?"

The words darkened as they reinked into the thick page. Her lips formed the words without speaking them, the movements of her mouth awkward.

The presence in her mind twitched with anticipation.

There is great magick at your fingertips. Do not be afraid.

The voice billowed around Avery's brain like a slow wind, making her light-headed.

Speak them aloud. Learn their true meaning. Feel their true power.

Yes, yes. I want to learn them, she replied dreamily, a smile on her lips.

Be warned. Once the words are spoken, I can no longer shield you from him.

Avery blinked several times. *What? Shield me?* She sobered with an angry snort, annoyed she'd let him play her, and forced the dizzying sensation away.

It is of no matter. You are strong. With me, you will be invincible. Faint sparks traveled into Avery's fingers. *Speak the words.*

Avery cleared her throat, aware of her grandmother's scrutiny.

"Here goes nothing." Avery turned toward the gaudy white-and-gold frosted vase on the entry table.

"Ix rezahl suka yr."

The vase exploded. Glass bits burst apart and rained down as snowy glitter. Both girls sprang to their feet, Avery's arms raised in triumph. The book tumbled to the floor.

"Yes!" Avery pumped her fist in the air. "I just made that

ugly vase explode! A few wicked-sounding words and *boom*! No studying, no rhyming chants. I think I'm gonna like—"

A pulse of energy reverberated around the room, quaking the walls and windows. Avery dropped her arms; the hairs on the back of her neck rose.

Chloe gasped and grabbed her chest. "Wha—"

A crack of thunder sounded like a gunshot. Three shrieks pealed in unison.

Josef Straka stood before them, surrounded by wisps of black vapor quickly drawing into him, solidifying his form. His teeth were bared, framed by the sharp lines of his black mustache and beard; his dark brows nearly touched. His fists crackled with sparks of lightning.

Chloe squealed and leapt from the sofa, diving behind the safety of the armrest. Fear locked Avery in place, but she stole a glance to the book at her feet. Blocked by the coffee table, Straka couldn't see it.

Josef's tall, lean frame in the same black suit filled the entryway. Heat radiated from him; Avery felt it on her bare arms. The sharp tang of ozone stung her nose.

"How *dare* you!" His roar resonated off the walls. Chloe whimpered.

Movement attracted his attention; the crystal ball swirled with liquid gold and mist. The face of Magda Hlavacova glowered up at him.

Josef's eyes bulged. *"You,"* he hissed, his fists shaking at his sides. Magda returned the hate in his glare.

His jaw worked as if to speak, but his lips pinched white. Josef tore his eyes from the old woman in the sphere to the short-haired girl challenging him. He appraised her, lip curling, then he scanned the room.

Josef's eyes flashed green fire when they returned to Avery. "Where is it?"

Avery pushed aside the terror paralyzing her muscles. She

knelt, eyes locked on their intruder, and picked up the gray tome, wrapping it protectively in her arms.

His mouth fell open for the briefest second. Josef flexed his hands, a resurgence of lightning crackling around his fingers. "*That* belongs to me."

A sneer tugged at Avery's upper lip. "Not anymore."

The heat of the book against her breast filled her; the knot in the back of her mind unraveled, feeding her confidence, strength; a jumble of words aligned themselves in her mind.

Avery stared at Josef Straka as a victor would at her fallen contender.

His lips drew back from his teeth. Josef narrowed his vision on the book, lifting his right hand. It jerked in Avery's arms as if someone was pulling at it. She steeled her muscles, tightening her arms around it.

Don't worry, I got you.

Josef growled, taking a step forward, lips parting to speak.

Avery's hand shot out. *"Ix h'het suka!"*

Josef staggered back with an enraged roar, eyes wide with disbelief, and the same crack of lightning that brought him ripped him away.

CHAPTER 37

Josef flashed back to the apartment, his roar echoing in his wake. He'd not chosen to leave; the girl repelled him with words only his book could have shown her.

Impossible! He bellowed again, shaking the old plaster walls around him.

He'd been unaware his book lay only a few feet from him. *What magick does this girl possess that she can shield my book from me?*

Flames arose from his fists, and his whole body shook with rage. *And that gypsy bitch!* Magda had sent them the book and told them how to read it! How had he not seen this? Not felt the lingering traces of the book on the girl when he first encountered her?

He let the flames crawl up his arms to engulf his entire body. The demonfire glowed with greens and deep oranges, whips of blacks dancing at its edges. Josef closed his eyes and let the fire burn away his anger.

The flames died away, drawing inward to the center of his chest. His mind was clear now.

"Muraal, we must speak."

The Void carried his words, but no response came. His temper flared. She could not ignore him. He had given his life for her! He was the one who suffered for the book's creation. She would answer him.

He pushed his mind into the Void and through it, past the emptiness and silence, into the Voll.

His master perched atop her throne of smooth black rock, wings cocooned around her. Her silent presence, even in apparent hibernation, brought a shiver to his spine. He steadied himself.

"Muraal, you will speak to me." Josef's voice echoed in the vast darkness, growing louder with each ripple.

The form upon the stone broke apart; wings lashed out, cutting the stillness like razors. With her powerful legs, she vaulted into the air in a high arc, landing before Josef; the ground beneath her taloned feet crumbled under her bulk. Her wings drew back, and flames engulfed her eyes. A massive arm flew out and slammed into his chest, sending him flying backward.

"You dare to command me?" Gravel rolled deep in her voice.

Stars filled Josef's vision as he scrambled backward on the rocky ground. What stood before him now was not the Muraal he knew, the feminine creature that stirred his passion.

The monster grew larger before him, its seductive female curves giving way to thick ripples of stony muscle over churning liquid fire. The tapered eyes rounded to gaping pools of black oil, the full lips tearing into a line of jagged, rock-like teeth. Its fists were like boulders clenched; the sound of stone against stone made the ground underneath Josef quake.

My true form, imbecile.

He threw himself forward, facedown with arms outstretched.

"Forgive me, my la— my lord, please! I was distraught!" He sniveled before it, its heat burning into him. The demon loomed over Josef, and he mumbled more apologies as fast as his lips could move.

Its ragged breath slowed; its fists unclenched. It stepped back from Josef.

"Why have you come to me so?"

Each word pummeled Josef's body, each word a club to his brain. He held his screams in his chest. He gasped for air he did not need and pushed himself up to all fours, keeping his head bowed.

"The book has been used by another."

Muraal's low growl sounded like rolling thunder.

He braced himself, fearing another blow at any moment.

"Josef Straka, you disappoint me." The rumbling words changed in tone, as did the body speaking them. He dared to raise his eyes enough to glimpse the taloned feet before him, becoming once more the supple yet strong legs of the Muraal he knew. His eyes traveled upward, following the changing body until he met the fire-tipped almond eyes that had mesmerized him since boyhood.

Her long fingers, tipped with talons, rested on her full hips. He kept his eyes from lingering between them. He rose slowly, tottering on frightened legs.

"Please forgive me," he said, his eyes cast down.

"Do you leave me another choice?" Her voice was low, her anger plain. Muraal stepped around him, the tip of one talon tracing the line of his shoulders. "I gave you all that you needed, yet you stand before me in disgrace."

Heat filled his ears. "Please forgive me," he repeated, sounding like a coward, his words betraying him.

"As you have already said." The edge in her voice made his legs weak.

"I—" Josef forced his thoughts to calm. *I am her chosen one; she needs me.*

Her talons sank into his shoulder. Hot pain sent him to his knees. "That is correct, my arrogant one."

His eyes popped open, and she smiled as she retracted her talons. The smile did not steady him.

"And you have failed me greatly."

Muraal faced him once more. She opened her wings wide,

revealing vast darkness within them. Cries of her children rose from their depths, and Josef went cold.

"I am patient, Josef Straka. I have been here for an eternity. I can wait for another. If one such as you has come along, there will be another in time as well."

Her threat hung in the air, and her smile curled grotesquely wide on her face.

He held up his hands. "No, please, my lor… lady. I will not fail you again. But the book—"

"I sacrificed one of my children for that book. For you!" Muraal snapped and he flinched, bending low at the waist.

"Then why can another use it?" Josef said before thinking. Muraal raised a clawed fist and he fell forward, arms covering his head. She dropped her hand with an angry hiss.

"I do not know why." Her wings flashed in annoyance. "Show me." Her hand closed around Josef's face. Images flooded his vision as Muraal raided his memories. She snorted in disgust and pushed him away.

"Who is that child?"

"The granddaughter of the woman I entrusted to resurrect me. There is little magick in her, yet she used the book against me." The words tasted foul on his tongue.

"There must be more in her. Is your arrogance blinding you *again*?"

Muraal narrowed her eyes to the distant Shade, the black wall of her prison, other worlds slightly visible through its fluttering depths. The fire beneath her skin undulated.

"Something is not right here, Josef Straka. Get her and the book. Discover the truth."

"But how?"

"I grow tired of your impotence," she growled, and he raised his palms to her again in submission. Muraal's hand reached out and encompassed his face once more, her talons digging into the back of his skull. He braced himself; if she killed him now, it was no more than he deserved.

"You know that I cannot affect the ways of Man." She brought her lips to his ear. "But I can *touch* them," she breathed. His body warmed with the power she sent into him. "You will be my conduit, Josef Straka, and I will help you get your book back."

CHAPTER 38

See what I offer you, Avery Parsons?

The surge of power when Avery spoke the strange words was far more intense than any adrenaline rush she'd ever had.

Heat blazed through her body, bringing with it a confidence she'd never known. As the torrent of energy raced in her blood, Straka's movements slowed. His lurch backward and the look on his face as his eyes and mouth widened in slow motion were nearly comical. Then sharp light filled her vision. It sank its spears into the tall man, yanking him away.

It was unlike any magick she'd experienced before, not even during her astral projection to Hartley's hospital room.

Avery wanted more.

The addictive feelings were fading now, much to Avery's disappointment, and she shivered from the sudden chill. She realized Chloe was shaking her.

"Avery!" Chloe shouted, jostling her sister's shoulders again. Her eyelids fluttered and pupils refocused, and she put a hand on one of Chloe's arms to steady herself.

"You can stop shaking me now."

Chloe stepped back. "What was that?" Her head swiveled back and forth from Avery to Magda. "What was all of *that*?" She flung her arm in the direction where their intruder had stood. When neither immediately answered, she collapsed into the sofa, planted elbows on knees, and let her face fall into her palms. "I think a little pee came out."

"Avery." Magda's voice was rough. "How did you know how to repel Josef?"

Avery opened her mouth to answer, then closed it. She'd not read anything like that yet in the book. She looked at the book still clutched to her chest. "I'm not sure."

Magda studied her granddaughter. "And how do you feel?"

"Cold," she said, and hugged the book tighter. It was very warm. She swallowed tentatively and felt nothing. "The words didn't hurt my throat, and I feel fine right now." *More than fine!* She bit back a smile. Even with the magick fading, she felt invincible, stronger than she'd ever felt in her life. Avery wanted to find the nearest gym and go a few rounds with a heavy bag or the biggest guy there.

Avery returned Magda's stare. "You felt pain afterward because there's no magick in your blood." Avery's jaw fell open at her words.

Magda's image flickered. "The book has told you this?"

"Yes… no. Well, sort of." Avery frowned, trying to find a way to explain. "I just knew, I guess." *I did?*

"I can't take this." Chloe reached for her bag and stalked out the door. She yanked the door closed too quickly, catching her bag on the inside handle. With an exasperated grunt, she wriggled the strap free and stomped down the hall. Avery moved to follow.

"Let her go." Magda put her withered hands over her face. "I had no idea Josef could sense the book that way."

Avery sat before the crystal ball, picking at a fold on the book's rough cover. *Ew. Stop that. That's somebody's skin!* She wished she'd stop forgetting that little detail.

"All the time you had the book, Gram, it never spoke to you?"

Magda dropped her hands; a deep sigh left her nonexistent lungs. "Never."

"Lucky you."

"Has it told you what it wants of you?"

Avery shrugged and scooted back into the sofa. "Just that he —*it, dammit, it!*—wants to help me. With what it doesn't say. It doesn't fork over much information, but when it does, it's annoyingly cryptic." Avery rubbed her neck again. The energy had finally drained away, but *it* was there, far behind her eyes, sitting at the base of her skull like a stone.

And it's in my head, Grammy.

But her grandmother could no longer hear her either.

"You must be strong, my Avery." Magda paused, but Avery could not meet her eyes. "You know what the book is about. You know your weakness—do not let it tempt you. I beg you."

Avery gulped, still staring at the plush carpet. She fidgeted, feeling naked in front of her grandmother.

"Remember the hospital room, when you held that boy's fate in your hands—"

"That's not something I'll ever forget."

"Good." Magda's voice was grave. "You must always remember that you struggled with it and that you overcame that darkness."

The girl's head snapped up.

"I know what happened. I was there." Magda's expression held no judgement yet shame burned Avery's face.

"Whatever is inside that book has a purpose for you. And we both know it is not a good one." Magda reached out, seeming to forget she was cut off from the living world, and dropped her hand with a restrained sob. "I can help you, my Avery, just as I did then. But you have to *talk* to me."

Avery threw the book to the other end of the sofa. "Why did you send it to me?"

Magda winced. "I didn't know some *thing* lurked inside it. I am so sorry, *beruško*. But even if I had, there were no other options open to me."

Avery couldn't find words. She pulled her knees to her chest and let her forehead fall onto them.

"You are strong, my Avery, a fighter! Not just in body but in mind. The singular proof of that is you *forgave* that boy—you let go of your anger and hatred of him. I know how hard that was for you."

"Hardest thing I've ever done in my life," she said into her knees.

"And your sister doesn't know. As close as you two are mentally, you shielded that from her. More proof of your strength." Magda waited until Avery lifted her head, and she held the young woman's tear-filled eyes. "Its power is tantalizing, I know, and we must use it to stop Josef, but remember that you have own power, your own magick. Whatever it wants from you, you will not let it have it."

Avery nodded, releasing her knees. *That's right, I have my own power, dammit.* She squared her shoulders, swiping a wayward lock of hair from her eyebrow.

"I think I found the spell Straka needs. It's just… awful—animals' heads and throat cutting." Revulsion rocked Avery's stomach. "If I could, I'd rip out those pages and give it back to him."

She studied the confetti remnants of the glass vase littering the floor. "And you were right. The words did move."

Magda followed her gaze. "Remember it. That one may be useful."

Sudden pressure hit Avery's stomach like a punch. She instinctively reached for the book and fell atop it as the pressure shoved her down into the sofa. She tried to push herself up, but the smothering weight lay across her entire body. Every defensive move she knew to escape an attacker flew through her mind, but she couldn't move; the very air around her had become a crush of boulders.

Magda cried out, her face in pain. "Avery, run!" She vanished.

A swath of darkness whipped around the room. Sunshine through the bank of windows blinked out, as if the sun had been ripped from the sky. The heaviness moved with it, and Avery bolted to her feet, the book clutched to her chest.

Avery Parsons, you must—

The thick, opaque curtain snuffed out not only light but warmth. Piercing cold seized Avery; her exhaled gasps turned to frost.

The blackness came at Avery. It yanked at the book in her arms. Such strength from the otherworldly force shocked her for a fraction of a second. It snatched the book free.

Avery lunged forward, grasping the book in midair, jerking it from the fingerlike tendrils of shadow.

The shadow recoiled with a muffled rumble. Something shoved her again, and pain flared behind her eyes. She shrieked and pushed back with her mind, clutching the book for reassurance although it, too, was cold.

The wisps of black advanced once more, its tendrils menacing. Its desperation to possess the thing she protected was clear.

Avery cried out again but not from pain; determination locked her on to her target. Picturing the blackness as physical attacker, she struck out once more with her mind, with her *magick*, a solid force that drove the thing toward the far wall.

It convulsed with a muted roar, succumbing to the power that heaved it backward. It drew in its lashing tendrils, seeming to make itself more solid.

Avery readied herself for another attack, a snarl on her lips.

"Come on, bitch. I can do this all day."

With an outward pulse, the swath of moving darkness flashed away, its rage echoing in its wake.

Using the mind and body of Josef Straka, Muraal eased a tiny sliver of herself into the human plane. No more could she do, the Shade prevented that, but it would be enough.

The old woman's spirit had been dispatched with the faintest thought. Her hold on the mortal world was tenuous, being the thread of love for her granddaughters and the desire to make right her many wrongs. The defiant girl with the book was too strong for Muraal's limited reach. There was more magick in her than it appeared. How had Straka not seen this?

The book lay silent in the girl's arms. Muraal's attempt to draw it out unsuccessful. It had not answered her summons; she'd felt it shrink away from her presence, using the girl to protect it.

Muraal bellowed fire and ash, flinging Straka's body into a column of boulders. The sounds of breaking bones and cries of agony should have cheered her, but did not.

Selecting her first child as the sacrifice for the book's creation had been a mistake.

Yet Muraal sneered, enjoying the memory of its demise. A blood crossing was the only way to leave the Voll; its writhing white carcass wrenched apart as it traveled through the Shade into Straka's physical body, where it was spat out. A fitting end for the man it used to be.

She knew now that it had betrayed her. But to what end? What was its goal? It couldn't possibly regain its life, or its memories, in that world. However, it now had a portion of Muraal's power. Its essence should have faded into oblivion when its task was complete, when it finished relaying her magick to Straka in the form of the book. Obviously, it had not. Somehow, it had tricked her.

Muraal no longer possessed the magick she had imparted to it. Without it, she would remain trapped in the Voll forever.

"Traitor!" Muraal whirled her body sideways, sending a massive wing into an outcrop of stones. They exploded with a deafening crash that reverberated around the confines of her dark prison. She would deal with that child once she was free. If it imagined it suffered before within her, Muraal would show it new levels of agony.

Her threat to Straka had been hollow, but he need not know that. Even if another did come along a century from now, it would not matter. The power needed to rend the Shade lay within that book; she had given her child that, and more. Straka *must* get the book back!

Muraal retrieved Straka's limp body and reconnected to the human plane.

The shred of Muraal's energy followed the trail of the twin. The gentle, naïve mind of Chloe Parsons lay open before her like an invitation.

What a delight this would be; she had not played with humans before. They were so fragile, so easily manipulated. She eagerly awaited the day when she could cross into this world fully. What fun she would have!

Muraal wafted behind the girl, tasting her anguish, the latent fear clinging tight to her skin. She tapped the girl's mind, sending a spike of panic through her. She whirled around with bulging eyes, her face ashen.

She fed the girl a flash of Straka towering over her, reaching out with gnarled claws as fingers. The girl shrieked and attempted to increase her pace but succeeded only in stumbling. Muraal laughed aloud; this one's delightful terror made her even more appealing.

Muraal propelled the girl forward, sending jabs of unseen touches to her hot, glistening flesh.

She grasped the distraught girl in midstride, sinking her talons into her psyche.

CHAPTER 39

Avery shook where she stood, adrenaline-fueled blood pounding in her ears. It took several deep breaths to slow her thumping heart.

She bit her bottom lip, forcing herself to focus on what just happened. That thing was not Josef Straka coming back in a different form. It was darker, larger, more… evil. She had no idea what it was, but she knew exactly what it wanted.

Her grip eased on the book. It was warm again. "You were no help."

But I didn't need its help. I did that. Me! Gram was right—

"Ah!" Avery dropped the book to clutch her head as the presence keened sharply. Then it vanished.

A rush of fear and panic sent Avery to the floor. Chloe's piercing cry shot through her skull.

"Chloe!" She scrambled to her feet and ran from the apartment.

She bounded down the stairs by twos and threes. She hurled herself over the last stairwell, landing with a huff onto the ground floor just behind the reception desk. Martin jumped with a girlish yelp.

"Martin! Which way did Chloe go?"

He sputtered for a moment, looking for English words in a rush.

"She said for a walk. I told her of the *ostrov*, island, park not far. To the left from here, then straight a few blocks. You cannot miss it."

Avery bolted for the door, and Martin ran from behind the desk, his loafers smacking loudly on the marble floor. "What is wrong? Should I call police?"

"No," she called as she barreled through the lobby doors. *No police can help with this.*

She ran, shouting her sister's name with every breath, reaching out with her mind for any sign of her. The book's presence was gone, the hollow space filled once again by her twin. How she missed that! But this feeling was different now, not calm, reassuring, steady, as it used to be. It was pulsing fear and struggling, reminding Avery of someone drowning.

Chloe hadn't made it far. A lump was folded over in the wide stoop of an empty storefront, head on knees, a curtain of long, glossy red hair fallen forward. Three stray cats sat around her, eerily quiet, staring at her with the ends of their tails flicking rapidly.

"Chloe!"

The cats hissed and darted away but remained close. Avery gripped her sister's shoulders, and Chloe's head rolled back, mouth slack. Her eyes were open, lids stretched back further than humanly possible; inky pools replaced hazel. The black swirled out, snapping its wisps across the whites like a spider stretching its many legs. Avery stifled a scream and hauled her sister's dead weight into her arms.

An elderly couple reached out to assist, saying rapid words in Czech that Avery didn't understand. She waved them off, not caring if she was rude, saying her sister had just had too much to drink.

Martin was still standing in the lobby. He rushed to hold the doors open.

"Is Chloe okay?" He clasped his hands before his heart. "I call *doktor*?" His big eyes begged for Avery's attention.

"No, Martin. Thanks." She pounded her floor's button on the elevator panel with a fist. "Low blood sugar, that's all. She just needs some OJ." She pulled Chloe into the tiny elevator, wishing the doors would close faster.

"Gram!" Avery was breathless coming through the apartment door. She struggled with Chloe's weight now. Avery dropped her unceremoniously onto the sofa and fell to her knees before the crystal ball. "Grammy!"

Magda's face materialized slowly within the aether. She appeared pained, her skin taut, lips a thin line. Avery grasped the sphere and stood above Chloe.

"What's wrong with her?" Avery gulped air to steady herself.

A small cry escaped Magda's lips. "Put me closer."

Magda peered into Chloe's misshapen eyes, seeing dark magick crawling within the innocence of her granddaughter. Chloe's body twitched, as if tiny charges of electricity were traveling through her or she was fighting whatever was happening to her. "There is an evil spirit in her."

The blood drained from Avery's flushed cheeks. "Do you think it's that thing that came after me?"

"I don't know, maybe. Avery, you must do an egg cleansing. You must draw out the spirit and trap it."

Her grandmother must be joking, but her face was hard, almost angry.

"A what?"

Magda gritted her teeth. "Set me down. I will tell you what to do." Avery put her back in the metal cradle then stood before her, feeling more helpless than she ever had in her life.

"Chloe bought eggs, yes? I'm sure they are not black or from a black chicken, but we must make do."

Avery's mouth fell open, not comprehending the words spilling out of her grandmother.

"Avery, focus!"

Magda's sharp tone jolted her, and she pushed out a breath.

"You have power, my Avery, you *know* you do. It will be enough, I believe, to pull whatever is inside your sister out. Now, do as I say."

"Okay." Avery nodded, flexing her hands and then shaking them out. "Go."

Following her grandmother's instructions, she ran to the kitchen and retrieved an egg from the refrigerator. She broke open a bulb of garlic and rested the egg within its fat cloves, then peeled a layer of skin from an onion and covered the egg with it. *Stop thinking how stupid this is and just do it.* She removed four steak knives from the drawer and put a pot of water on the stove to boil.

"Now, make room for your sister on the floor. You'll need to draw a pentacle around her."

"A what?"

Magda's anxiety took over the volume of her voice. "Do you remember nothing of what you learned?"

"No, Gram, I don't!" Avery said, slamming the knives onto the kitchen counter. "All that stuff was stupid, and so is this." She threw her hands up in the air, tears springing to her eyes. "And I can't think at all right now! Except how this is my fault."

Magda's face softened. "Oh, *beruško.* This is not your fault."

"Yes, it is! It's Straka. He wants this damn book, and I didn't give it to him." She turned her face to the ceiling. "Come and get it! Take it! I want my sister back!" She covered her face and fell to her knees, sobs taking control.

"Avery, listen to me. If there is fault to be placed, it is on me alone. But this is not the time. Get up, move this furniture, and put your sister on the floor."

"None of this makes any sense," Avery said into her hands. "Eggs, garlic, onion, knives. Seriously?" She dropped her hands and looked at her grandmother, defeat clear on her face. "I wish you could just wriggle your nose or wave a wand and fix this."

"You did always want the easy way, my Avery. But in this, as with most magick, there is none. Stop doubting what is in you. Remember the hospital. Your magick saved him. I guided you then, I will guide you now. Trust yourself."

Hadn't she also pushed away that mass of shadows that came at her earlier? Avery sniffed and got to her feet, resigned to do her grandmother's bidding. *I can do this.*

Pushing the coffee and dining tables to the bank of windows, she lifted Chloe from the sofa. She was burning up. Her clothes stuck to her skin, her breathing rattled wet in her lungs. Avery suppressed another rush of contempt for herself and gently laid Chloe onto the carpet.

"Is there white chalk or enough salt to make the pentacle?"

Avery went through the desk and dresser drawers looking for chalk. Not finding any, she returned from the kitchen with a salt shaker only fit for a doll house. "Yeah, um, no." She set it aside. "What about shaving cream? It's white, if that's what we are going for."

"Well, if that is all we have, then that will suffice."

At her grandmother's direction, she started above Chloe's head, squeezing a thin line of shaving cream at an angle beside her body. Details from her childhood lessons were slowing coming back to her. The pentacle was a star with a circle around it, but she couldn't remember what the points signified. She stopped.

"We don't have enough shaving cream for this," Avery muttered to herself. "Oh!" She jumped up and headed to the kitchen, returning with an aerosol can of whipped cream.

Magda forced a smile. "Necessity is the mother of invention."

When she finished the encompassing circle, Avery stood. "That looks terrible." And it did. The straight lines were anything but, full of lumps and squiggles, and the circle was a messed-up oval around a disproportionate star—within it, a now-still Chloe.

Avery turned to Magda with questioning eyes.

"Are there any gaps in the lines?"

Avery examined her handiwork. "Nope."

"Then it will do. Get the knives now."

Avery placed a steak knife above Chloe's head, stabbing its point into the beige carpet. *We're not getting our security deposit back now for sure.* She placed one at her feet and the remaining two by her hands, each jabbed deep into the plush carpet.

"So, what's the point in this, Gram?" Avery said, giving the knives a dubious eye.

"Get the egg and I will tell you."

She returned with the egg, still resting in its onion and garlic nest, and stared at Magda with expectation.

"You will draw the evil spirit out. The knives you have pinned to the ground bind the evil from going anywhere else. It has no choice but to enter the egg. Once that's happened, you will drop the egg into the boiling water. Normally, we put the egg in a burning fire, but…" Magda shrugged.

Avery opened her mouth to let the string of sarcasm loose but clamped it shut. "All righty then."

Magda frowned. "Avery, listen to my words. You *must* believe this will work. You must *will* it to work. Your intent in this spell is key. There is everyday magick in the items you hold, they are your tools, but it is your magick that will bring them together to contain the spirit and draw it out. It is critical you focus on that. You must picture the spirit within your sister. You must picture it drawn out of her and into the vessel, the egg, where it will be trapped. Do you understand?"

She exhaled a deep breath through her nose. "I do, Gram."

Avery stepped into the circle, careful not to disturb the squiggly lines. She knelt, studying her sister's tortured face.

"I'm getting you back," she whispered, freeing strands of hair stuck to Chloe's splotched cheeks.

Starting on her forehead, Avery rolled the egg gently clockwise. Across the crown of her head, down around one ear, across her face, then to the other ear.

Avery pictured the dark shadow that had attacked her. She assumed it was now in Chloe since it had no success with her. She closed her eyes and envisioned the thrashing tendrils intertwined within Chloe's veins. She imagined them being pulled up, the black wisps drawing away from the red flow, out of her sister and into the egg she gently pressed to Chloe's skin. Avery's heart thumped almost painfully, and she fought to keep her breath calm, to keep the hand holding the egg from shaking. She could so easily screw this up, maybe even hurt Chloe without meaning to. *Don't think like that!*

Her stress must have been written on her face. Her grandmother's soft voice broke into her thoughts.

"You can do this, my Avery. Focus, don't let your mind wander. Do not doubt yourself."

Avery returned to the image of the moving shadows within her sister. Her mind took hold of one thin stand and pulled.

Faint wavelets of energy tingled the palm of the hand holding the egg.

"The egg must not leave the body," Magda whispered. Avery nodded, slowly rolling the egg around Chloe's neck, moving down to her chest.

Chloe bucked. Startled, Avery nearly crushed the egg on her sister's collarbone. She froze. Chloe grunted, her legs kicking out.

"Avery, continue!"

Still in a clockwise motion, she rolled it over Chloe's breasts and midsection, coming around the side to travel up to her left arm. The pleasant tingling, stronger now, moved up Avery's arm into her torso, blossoming hope. She'd forgotten this feeling!

Avery had felt it only once before, when she and Magda sat on Magda's bed. The energy, her magick, began as a tiny seed deep within her; she remembered being amazed by the feeling, distracted, and she'd lost it. With her grandmother's gentle prodding, the magick returned and expanded, lifting from her torso and rising, carrying her spirit to the hospital.

It was unlike the power of the book, nor what she'd felt when the hawk came or when she'd stood over Hartley.

The sensation wasn't harsh or jarring, but light and cool. It made her feel happy, like she could take on whatever came at her. Not with anger or fists, but with love and kindness. Those things had strength also.

This must be what good *magick feels like.*

In her mind's eye, she pictured the egg pulling at the shadow's spidery fingers.

I can do this!

Avery tried to ignore her sister's twitching body.

She slid the egg back up to Chloe's shoulder, then across to the other arm. Avery's magick, feeling her own magick actually *work*, made her tremble. She tightened her fingers around the egg. Closing her eyes, she refocused on the thick, black threads drawing free from Chloe's blood, the egg absorbing them like a greedy sponge.

Chloe's chest convulsed, and a piercing scream burst through her pinched lips. The egg quaked violently as she gripped it harder so it didn't slip free, praying she didn't crush it.

Sound gurgled in Chloe's throat. A low growl parted her lips. The deep, unearthly sounds shook her torso, bringing her spine to an arch, then she slumped back to the floor. A spark shot from the egg into Avery's palm, and she yelped, dropping the egg onto Chloe's chest.

It quivered between her sister's breasts. Veins of deep green and dark gray began to crawl along the pristine white shell of the egg until it was solid black.

"Avery! Put it in the water!"

As she reached for the egg, it burst in unison with a burst of laughter from Chloe's lips.

Spongy black gobbets smelling like rotten flesh peppered Avery's shirt, arms, and face and covered Chloe's upper body. Avery held back the lurch in her stomach. *Don't puke, don't puke.* She wiped her mouth with the back of her hand.

The smoking black gelatinous globs began to move. Avery recoiled as the stinking mess absorbed into Chloe's skin. The bits on Avery, Magda's crystal ball, the floor, the walls, rose into the air and shot back onto Chloe's body, where they disappeared beneath her skin.

Slow laughter rolled in Chloe's throat. But it wasn't her laughter. A wide smile grew, revealing slimy, blackened teeth.

"The book for your sister." Sprays of black spittle accompanied each hissed word.

Avery slapped both hands over her mouth to keep from screaming.

"Avery, get the book! It must help you!" Magda's voice reflected Avery's terror.

Her magick was gone now, no trace of hope left in her. It took a moment for Avery to register her grandmother's words and pull her eyes away from the grotesque image of her sister.

Avery jumped on tiptoes out of the circle. She grabbed the book and settled herself cross-legged beside Chloe.

Book, you have to help me. She hugged it to her chest, then placed it in her lap. She combed through the pages, growing more anxious every second the book did not respond. Chloe had stilled, the grotesque smile frozen on her face and her now solid-black eyes locked on Avery.

There is great danger, Avery Parsons. One who should not know of you does, and it holds your twin's essence. It spoke slowly, the tone of its voice grave, making the tiny hairs on Avery's arms stand on end.

What is it?

Muraal. The creature Josef Straka wishes to allow into this world.

Avery's jaw unhinged.

"Tell me," Magda demanded.

She shook her head, the book's words echoing inside. "He said that the monster Straka wants to bring here has got Chloe, her 'essence,' whatever that is." *Can this get any more fucked up?*

You must take this seriously, Avery Parsons. There is more than just your twin in peril.

I don't care about whatever else is going on. Tell me how to save her. NOW.

The voice was quiet for several minutes. Anxiety turned to irritation, and Avery's palms itched to throw the damn thing across the room.

Look to the book.

She scrutinized the pages, scanning each line and flipping to the next. Avery was halfway through it when hope sparked anew. A collection of markings faded and morphed, twisted and pulsed, then shimmered to a stop.

"Yes." Avery exhaled. Her grandmother said something, but she ignored it. She repeated the sibilant words in her mind, trying to figure out each one's strange pronunciation. She gasped at the end of the passage and gnashed her teeth.

"I'm *not* doing that."

The old woman's puerile magick did not work against Muraal. I will give you all the power you will need. But if you wish your twin to wither to nothing under the creature's slow torment, then by all means...

Chloe's body twitched once more, a whimper escaping her blackened lips. Avery slammed the book down beside her and raced to the kitchen. She rifled through the drawers, looking for the smallest knife.

Returning to the circle, she laid the book gently onto her sister's midsection. Ignoring Chloe's disturbing face and taking her slack hand, she recited the first passage. The rough words slipped easily from her lips, and the energy of those words raced through her veins, filling her with pulsing heat.

Avery muttered an apology and gritted her teeth as she slid the sharp paring knife across the soft palm of her sister's left hand. Bright blood sprang through the cut and pooled quickly. Her grandmother shouted something, but Avery couldn't stop to argue. She turned Chloe's palm over and placed it atop the open book.

She repeated the next passage twice. Chloe thrashed, and Avery used both hands to hold her sister's hand onto the page.

Chloe's body bucked, back arching to a painful degree. A shriek came from her lips, but the voice was not hers.

Muraal! Avery thought at the blackness of Chloe's eyes. *Fuck you, you bitch. Get out of my sister!*

Avery hissed the last phrase with more venom as she pressed her sister's hand down flat. The spattered blood soaked into the page, the text darkened, and the book itself quaked. Chloe bucked violently once more, then her taut body relaxed, a long sigh leaving her lungs.

The force of Muraal's failure thrust Josef back into the mortal world. He lay on the floor of the apartment, his mind burning. He writhed in pain as Muraal's influence faded from him.

You had better hurry, Josef Straka, lest you lose mastery over the book. The voice of the true Muraal, full of gravel and promises of great pain, sent spears of agony through his body. *Lest you become one of my children forever.*

CHAPTER 40

The nauseating stench of burnt rotten meat assaulted Chloe's nose, then invaded her stomach. She rolled to her side and vomited. Avery brushed her sister's hair out of the way.

As she sat up, Avery placed a cool, damp washcloth on Chloe's forehead and she took it, pressing her whole face into the refreshing cloth. Then, strong arms clamped around her, forcing a little air from her lungs.

"You're choking me," Chloe said, trying to free herself from Avery's crushing embrace.

"Oh my god, are you okay?" Avery pushed back to look at her but didn't let go. "What did that son of a bitch do to you?"

Chloe leaned sideways, putting her forehead on her sister's shoulder. Avery stroked Chloe's back, running her fingers gently through the long tangles of hair as she did. She was quiet for a long time. Magda hovered in the crystal sphere, worry deepening the lines in her face.

Chloe surveyed the living room, seeing the smeared white cream all over her and Avery, and knives jabbed into the carpet. "What did you do?"

"Never mind that." Avery helped her sister up and eased her onto the sofa. "Oh, wait!" She grabbed Chloe's hand and turned it over. A hiss escaped her lips. The palm Avery had drawn the small blade across was smooth, albeit clammy; there was no open wound, no scar, no mark of any kind.

"What?" Chloe looked at her sister, then at her palm. Avery and Magda exchanged glances, with Chloe ogling each. *"What?"*

"Nothing," Avery said, dropping her hand. "Water?"

Chloe sighed, too tired to play Avery's game. She nodded, resting her head against the back cushion.

After downing the whole glass, she wiped her face once more, then bundled the washcloth in her clenched hands.

"Chloe." Magda kept her voice soft. "Did it hurt you?"

"No. It didn't really hurt, but it was very… unpleasant." She tried a light chuckle but failed. "The thing was huge—a monster, Granny. Shaped like a woman but looked as if she was made of moving lava that's starting to cool, if that makes any sense. Horns curled around her head, massive wings with a spike at the top. She—*it*, really, it's not a woman—just stared at me, grinding its jaw, like it was straining to keep hold of me. I was on the ground. I felt rocks jabbing me but I couldn't move, and it was so cold, and really dark."

Chloe took a deep breath, letting it out slowly through her nose, pushing away the lingering fear. She was safe now, thanks to whatever Avery had done. Chloe wasn't sure she wanted to know, especially with that ugly book sitting open right beside her.

She rubbed her sweaty palms on her legs. *I'm safe now*, she repeated. *I'm fine.*

Chloe rolled her head to meet her sister's anxious gaze. "It was in my head. It felt like it was squeezing my brain. And I saw things in its mind too. It has been trapped in there for a very long time."

Avery scooted closer and rubbed a hand up and down Chloe's arm.

When she didn't continue, Avery increased the massaging pressure of her fingers. "Where's 'there'?"

"Um…" Chloe searched the horrid memories for a name. "The *Voll*, I think." She leaned forward, giving her sister an 'I'm okay' expression. She put her palms to her face, then raked her fingers through her hair, combing it over to fall down the front of one shoulder. "Its name is Muraal. It's been imprisoned there forever—it doesn't even remember how long." She hugged herself, vividly recalling the creature's seething anger and frustration, its desperate desire for freedom. "Can I get some hot tea, please?"

Avery was off the sofa before Chloe finished her request.

"It wants out of there in the worst way. That's why it picked Josef. He's very powerful. He can open the barrier between here and the Voll. The Shade? Yeah, the Shade—that's the barrier. Well, not 'open' really. Ugh." She groaned and squeezed her head with both hands. The nightmarish images, the barrage of information, the angst of the creature, bumped against one another in her brain. "So much…" *How am I ever going to sleep again*?

"Take your time, my Chloe." Her grandmother's soft words were like her warm hugs had been. "Breathe."

Chloe took the steaming mug Avery presented. She took several sips with her eyes closed, then leaned back.

"All he needs to do is damage the Shade enough for Muraal to do the rest. The book is the key. It has the ritual he needs to perform." Chloe turned to meet her sister's gaze. "He can't get that book back, Avery. No matter what."

"He won't." Avery stared at the gnarled gray book resting on the floor amid smears of shaving and whipped cream. She raised a hand to the base of her skull, then dropped it, giving a little shiver.

"If he does, that thing will come through with all her little… demon children." Chloe paled. "They are horrible. Nasty white skin over grotesque, hunched skeletons. Big head, no nose, no eyes or ears." Her whole body shuddered. "They want us, Avery. Humans. They want to *be* us." Her eyes bulged. "To live *inside* a human so they can experience everything we do."

Avery's chin rose. "We won't let that happen." She took her sister's hand and squeezed. "We won't."

Only a little grandmotherly prodding convinced Chloe she needed to rest. Avery lay beside her, to protect her, and quickly fell asleep as well. Magda watched over them, never taking her eyes away as night turned into day.

Magda mulled over the incantation the book had Avery recite, and the blood it required. The words had been innocuous enough, proclaiming the presence unwelcome and that it must return from where it came, yet the last phrase Avery said had been so low, between clenched teeth, that Magda hadn't caught the words. When she'd questioned Avery about it, Avery couldn't remember. It was all a jumble in her mind now.

Not a hint of a mark remained on Chloe's palm, and no blood had spilled from the pages.

Guilt and shame twisted a knife in Magda's heart. She wondered if she'd ever had a heart; if she had, she wouldn't have done this to her granddaughters. Instead, she gave it to a man who turned out to be one of the devil's own. And more devils with him.

The twins woke in the late afternoon. Chloe showered while Avery made her some green tea. She sipped her tea in silence on the sofa as she stared beyond the crystal ball into the middle distance. Avery picked at a fold on the book's cover. Magda grimaced.

"Granny"—Chloe scooted to the edge of the sofa—"tell me everything about the spell that brought him back."

Avery turned her attention to her grandmother. Magda had known this time would come, yet a pained sigh slipped from her lips.

"Let me first tell you that I was young, and very foolish. But that is no excuse, I know."

It was difficult to watch her granddaughters react as her past deeds poured out of her. The gasps, the looks of revulsion, resentment, judgment. Magda had convinced herself long ago that selecting only those men who were villains in life was justified. They did not deserve a peaceful afterlife. But the binding of the mother and her child washed Magda's previous good intentions away.

As she told the tale, she found she had no more tears. She told them much more than Chloe asked for—everything she'd left out before—the words refusing to stop.

She recounted how she'd fallen for a handsome, caring doctor—a welcome escape from a brutal husband, whom she'd killed without qualm in order to read the book. How she'd begun to fulfill the promise she willingly made despite her instincts screaming against her deeds. How she'd come to look upon the book as an ally rather than a foe. How, as an old woman, the memories of her previous life had returned on the cusp of a heart attack, and of how she was unable to fight the compulsion to return to Prague, to fulfill her promise. And finally, of how Josef revealed his true nature and sent her into the Voll, and how she ensured her soul's freedom from him.

Magda was able to stem the tide of words before confessing what she'd done to their father and what the book was truly made from. Chloe had been to the Voll; she might soon put two and two together, just as Magda had.

At the end, the twins sat silent, neither able to look at Magda.

Chloe's heart plummeted. The woman who had always been her true grandmother although they shared no blood—the sweet, loving, giving woman who'd helped raise and guide her—now seemed like a complete stranger. The person Magda described wasn't the person she knew. Chloe could forgive much of what Magda had done, but the souls of the poor mother and little girl! What manner of suffering were they going through?

"I can't believe how much you lied to us." Avery's hard voice matched her eyes. "And all for an evil dick. You took the easy way out, and now you want us to clean up your mess."

"Avery!" Chloe dropped her hands. "That's not fair."

"But she is right." Magda's gaunt face looked ancient. "I did exactly that, didn't I?" She turned away and faded.

"Was that really necessary?" Chloe glared at Avery. "I feel betrayed too, but come on. You heard what she's been through. Josef used her. He put a spell on her. She put *flames* to her eyes, Avery, think about that!" Chloe took a deep breath. "She's suffered enough."

"Doesn't your back hurt from all the rolling over you do?" Avery let out a derisive snort and stood. "This is bullshit, Chloe, and you know it. Look at what's happened and why. You were mindfucked by a *demon from another world!*"

Chloe leaned away from her sister.

"That woman lied to us! Our whole lives! Nice little Grammy—here, play with these little animals, read these baby books on magick. Do you know how much more powerful we'd be if she'd been honest with us about our magick?"

Chloe's jaw dropped.

"I don't know why I said that."

Chloe could see the anger draining away from Avery's face, taking the flush of her cheeks with it. *I wish I knew what was going on inside you.* Some of it was written on her body—the clenched jaw, the tendons straining in her neck, the fists. She was struggling, fighting something. Not her anger at their grandmother. This was something else. *'How much more powerful we'd be…'*

Avery slumped back into the sofa, staring at the wall opposite them.

While Chloe had honed her spark of magick with animals, Avery had given up on hers. She didn't want to work at it; it was too hard. She took the easy route with everything, and usually excelled. Avery used her magick on the birds when she interned at the zoo, whether she realized it or not. She'd probably be a full zookeeper by now if their rules hadn't changed. As a teacher and trainer at the gym, she had an outlet for her stress, which had kept her pretty steady. But now, this wicked book was showing her—or giving her, maybe—magick she didn't need to work for, ugly words that made extraordinary things happen. Power she hadn't *earned.*

Chloe would dispose of the book somehow when this was all over. With its influence gone, she could get her sister back. But right now, Chloe would leave this outburst alone. The cap had exploded off of Avery's bottled anger, and it would reseal itself, as it always did.

She lifted a hand to smooth a few spiky locks of Avery's hair back in place.

"What's this?" Chloe fingered the hair above Avery's left ear. She plucked out a strand, peering closely at it.

"Ouch!" Avery smacked at Chloe's arm. "What did you do that for?"

"Look." She presented the strand. "It's a *black* hair. You've got a couple of them."

Avery frowned, taking the short hair, squinting at it. In the bathroom, she flicked on the fluorescent bulbs framing the mirror. With a quick series of zaps, they snapped to glaring brightness.

"Huh," she said, rotating her head for the best view of the offending hairs. Several black strands lay scattered within Avery's bright red crop, dull in appearance, lacking the sheen and softness of her normal hair. "What's up with that?" She raked her fingertips over her scalp, mussing the top with aggravation, and began yanking out the coarse hairs.

"Don't pull them out." Chloe appeared behind her. "What's the saying? 'Pull one out and three grow in its place.'"

"Isn't that for gray hairs, though? Besides, this isn't a good look for me. Remember when I went black a few years ago?"

Chloe wrinkled her nose at the memory. The stark color had made Avery look angry all the time, and ten years older.

Avery huffed, smoothing the sides of her hair back down. "I'm hungry. Let's find some food."

She grabbed Chloe's arm when she turned from the doorway and pressed her lips to Chloe's ear. "Don't tell Gram."

Chloe lifted a brow, then nodded.

They packed up their treasures, Chloe cradling the empty crystal ball in her messenger bag with a pang of guilt and Avery stuffing the heavy book in her backpack. Chloe opened her mouth to protest, but closed it. There was no telling what could come at them next. They might need it.

She blanched. *I can't believe we need that terrible thing. What have we gotten ourselves into?*

Chloe tried once again to get her mother on the phone, but it went straight to voicemail. She hung up with a concerned 'hmm.'

"I guess she's working another shift. That's the third time I've called today."

Avery waved away her concern. "You know she's got more work than one person can handle. If she's not at work right now, she's probably asleep."

Chloe was a little disappointed Martin wasn't at the desk. He was cute, and seemed to like her, but he was probably that way to all the guests. A pretty young woman stood in his place, speaking rapidly in Czech and laughing with a couple who were obviously going out for the evening.

The man was dressed in a tailored tuxedo, and the woman wore a glittering silver gown with pinned-up hair. Chloe caught Avery admiring the backside of the lady in the gown. She dipped her head to the girl behind the reception desk with a roguish smile on her lips that made the young woman blush.

Chloe snorted and pulled at her sister's elbow. "Come on."

They took a slight detour as Avery followed her nose to a street vendor selling *halušky*. Without even knowing what was in it, Avery ordered two bowls, her mouth watering from the rich smells of ham and dumplings. She convinced Chloe, whose protests against ham had fallen on deaf ears, to get one also. Bags in hand, they headed for the *ostrov* Martin had told Chloe about.

Nighttime had little effect on the number of people ambling through the streets. Strings of lights and streetlamps cheered the veil of evening, warm golden glows from shops and restaurants lined their walk, and laughter tinkled all around them. Avery eyed a pub as they passed, seeing its long polished wood bar sporting at least ten taps, each with a colorful or ornate pull. She smacked her lips.

"An ice-cold beer sounds so good right now. A few beers would make this all better." Avery stopped, ogling a young man downing a full glass. "And a few extra would make me forget," she muttered under her breath. Chloe took her hand, tugging her along.

"But, but… Prague is supposed to be the beer capital of the world, you know. Stan-the-taxi-man said so!"

They walked down Národní toward Legion Bridge. The long strip of parkland lay in the middle of the Vltava River, which cut Prague nearly in two. Throngs of young people climbed the stone steps leading to the island park from the bridge. Chloe peered over as they waited their turn to go down, not wanting to push themselves through the crowd. A small concert had just let out. She sighed. She didn't want to be around so many people right now. Avery squeezed her hand. But as the mass on the steps dwindled, few remained in the park.

The girls took the wide dirt path leading away from the restaurant overlooking the river, away from the raucous laughter billowing from the bar on the upper deck. They passed only a few people, much to Chloe's delight. She blushed at the young couple locked in a passionate embrace, the girl sitting on the man's lap.

They found an empty bench at the north end under a large tree, facing the Charles Bridge.

The island park was a tonic to Chloe's nerves. Its trees were thick with leaves, birds tweeted and chirped, the grass was lush, and she took off her shoes to indulge her feet, the earthy carpet cool and slightly damp. She closed her eyes, drinking in the crisp aromas of nature. The faint ripples of water lapping on the short, sandy beach helped soothe Chloe's mind.

"This is really nice," Avery said, falling onto the bench and stretching her legs out. Chloe joined her, setting her messenger bag gently on the ground and pulling it open, positioning the sphere so they could see Magda better in the sparkling lights reflecting from the city across the water. Her grandmother hung back in the shadows of the crystal.

"Did you ever come here, Granny?" Chloe's voice was conversational, thinking it best to just forget what had happened… and what was said.

Magda came in to focus and swiveled to take in her surroundings. Her expression softened. "Oh, yes. *Střelecký ostrov.* It was always a lovely place. It is good to see it so well maintained. Josef and I—"

Shame sent her back to the depths of the sphere.

Avery tried calling her mother again. It rang once, then went to voicemail. Avery huffed with annoyance, shoving her phone back into her shorts pocket.

They ate their dinner in silence, with Chloe pushing the chunks of salty ham from the dumplings and bits of cabbage.

"I can't believe you don't like ham. What's wrong with you?" Avery leaned over to scoop up the discarded meat.

Chloe gave her sister a fake snarl, then let out a long sigh, resting the half-empty bowl of food in her lap. Avery leaned her head on Chloe's shoulder. Chloe put her cheek atop her sister's head.

"It'll all work out," Avery said. "Soon, you'll be back to boring lectures and cleaning up dog poop. You'll see."

Chloe grunted a laugh. She missed those boring lectures, the comforting routine of classes and exams, the litter of kittens or puppies that seemed to come in every week this time of year to the shelter. She couldn't wait to go back to that. But would anything be the same after this? The terrifying image of that monster seemed to invade her calm every time she blinked. Its wicked smile, eyes full of fire. Chloe shivered and pushed the memory away.

Avery straightened. "You okay?"

Chloe hmm'd an assent, shoving a spoonful of *halušky* in her mouth.

CHAPTER 41

After Avery finished the remnants in Chloe's bowl, they sat back, shoulder to shoulder. Avery stared at the slow-moving black water, chewing her thumbnail. Chloe gazed out at the Charles Bridge, marveling at how its lights made it shine like gold in the dark, the arches looking like links in an elaborate necklace.

"Can you believe all this?" Avery said, punctuating the absurdity of their situation with a snort.

"Nope," Chloe answered without looking at her.

"When this is over, you should ask Martin out for a beer."

Chloe straightened. "What?" She gaped at her sister as if she was a crazy person. "You know I hate beer!"

They both laughed. Chloe would never have the courage to do something like that, and Avery knew it. Besides, there was no point. They weren't staying after this. Well, perhaps a little sight-seeing before they left. *Maybe I could ask Martin to be our tour guide.* Chloe blushed.

Chloe had begun to mentally list all the places she wanted to visit, when a sleek white cat came from under the bench and rubbed itself against her legs with a low mew. She emitted a lengthy 'aww' and stroked the cat's back. Avery folded her arms across her chest.

"When that thing had you, you were back in my head," Avery said quietly. "But after... Well, I guess the book's evicted you again." She tried to smile and took Chloe's hand. "Want to talk about it? It sucks not knowing what you're feeling."

"I just want to go home." She leaned against the back of the bench. The cat made another pass around her legs, then disappeared beneath the bench, presumably going back to where it had come from.

Avery grunted an assent then stood. "It's close to midnight. Let's get back to the apartment. I don't know about you, but I'm ready for some more sleep."

They walked in silence to the stone steps. Avery glanced back at the lively restaurant, its upper deck crammed with people.

"When this is over, you can get as plastered as you want," Chloe said.

"Don't think I'm not gonna." Both girls laughed.

Lined with tall streetlamps, Legion Bridge was well lit, which made Chloe feel safer. Their cheery glow reflected on the wide brick sidewalk, damp with humidity. A few couples walked, others leaned over the side, admiring and pointing at the splendid night view of Prague. Chloe admired them—no one seemed to have a care in the world. And she was certain none of them were on a mission to stop a dead guy from letting a demon take over the world.

The twins walked hand in hand, taking comfort in the physical connection since their mental one no longer existed.

Behind them, car tires screeched, followed by the sound of a sharp hiss. The girls cringed and turned around. An old car continued on, the driver either unaware or not caring they'd just struck a cat. No one else on the bridge appeared to notice.

Chloe quickly looked away, but it was too late. The image of a white cat lying in the street with its hind legs flattened was burned into her vision. Was that the same cat she'd petted only a few minutes ago? *No, no, no.* She shoved her bag at Avery, grabbing the sweater from beneath the empty crystal ball, and ran. Avery shouted after her to be careful.

Why isn't anyone else helping? She fell to her knees beside the yowling feline. "Oh my god, you poor thing!" The injured cat tried to flee, pulling its useless back legs behind it, trailing blood. "No, sweetie, no. Please. Don't be scared. I'm going to help you."

Chloe slowed her breathing, willing herself to be calm so she could radiate comfort to the suffering animal. She edged closer, paying no attention to the vehicles speeding past her, and held her hands above the cat's hind quarters. Chloe couldn't heal his injuries, but her magick would ease his pain and soothe his frightened mind. Animals understood much more than people gave them credit for and were much more receptive to energies than humans.

From her heart, a coolness flowed. Magick lifted the tiny hairs on her arms as it traveled to her hands. Her fingertips twitched slightly as her magick streamed into the broken limbs of the white cat. In the right light, she could see it. Never under the harsh fluorescent bulbs of the vet clinic or the shelter, but there in the halo of a streetlamp, trickles of faint white light poured from her fingertips.

Chloe had honed her healing magick over the years, with hopes that one day she could actually repair injuries, or at least help them along significantly. She used her magick as often as needed and had become adept at concealing what she was doing from others. Knowing she could help the "lesser" creatures was the only thing that kept her from breaking down at each tragic case coming in the door or giving up on her dream of being a veterinarian. People could be so cruel and stupid, and this incident was something Chloe saw much too often.

The cat stopped and turned his anguished face up to his rescuer.

"That's right, sweetie, it's okay. Let me help you." Chloe smiled at his glassy, bright green eyes. The cat panted, trembling as he looked at her without fear. Thankfully, the traffic had died down. In fact, there wasn't a single car or motorcycle in sight. *Good.*

With her thin sweater, she covered his back end, whispering loving words while still emitting soothing energy. She leaned forward with gentle hands and lifted him into her arms. The cat surrendered to her embrace.

Chloe stood, checking the traffic before she started across the road. The bridge was empty. *It figures people would run off rather than stop and help.* Only her sister remained, standing stiff, clutching Chloe's bag, wearing an expression of amazement at what she'd witnessed her sister do.

The mewling cat grew quiet and Chloe stopped, praying he hadn't died in her arms. The cat met her gaze. For a split second, his green eyes blazed.

Streetlights burst around them, and the bundle at her chest quaked. She yelped and cowered down, covering her head with her free arm to protect it from the raining glass. The cat lurched violently in her arms, desperate to get away from the frightening sounds of exploding bulbs. Chloe tightened her grip, murmuring words of comfort.

The cat seemed to grow larger and heavier. He leapt from her arm with an angry hiss, and she reached out to catch him before the broken creature hit the ground.

As if the wind had taken him, the cat flew out from the sweater, whipping behind Chloe. A burst of green light made her cry out and stumble backward, shielding her eyes. Something grabbed her upper arm and yanked her around. Burning cold wind seized her torso.

Avery screamed.

"This was too easy," Josef Straka purred into Chloe's ear, his long fingers like ice embedded into her slender neck. He chuckled and inhaled her scent. "You revealed so many weaknesses to Muraal. I had trouble deciding which one to exploit."

Fear stole her breath, paralyzing her limbs as her mind struggled to comprehend what was happening.

"You motherfucker! Let her go!" Avery ran at them but skidded to a stop when the hand around her sister's neck burst into green-black flames. Spears of pain jolted through her neck. Not heat, but agonizing cold radiated down her shoulders and chest. The flames flickered with a sickly green color, dancing under Chloe's chin as if they were a fistful of snakes.

Panic snapped her back to herself. Chloe tried to jerk away, but his hand tightened, pressing her back to his chest. His torso was a solid brick wall, his cold chilling down to her core.

Chloe dug her short fingernails into his wrist, but his flesh was stone. The biting chill creeping into her body brought memories of the Voll, the helplessness that suffocated her, trapped in Muraal's world. She couldn't go back there. Would he take her back there? Chloe kicked her feet forward and thrust back against him, hoping to knock him off center. He only chuckled in her ear.

Oh my god, Avery! Please help me! Chloe's frantic eyes sought her sister.

It'll be okay, Avery thought at her sister, pushing hard on the words, begging them to break through. *I won't let him hurt you.* Chloe's bulging eyes told Avery she hadn't heard.

Avery took another step as anguish for her sister twisted in her gut. Josef gripped Chloe by her upper arm, positioning her as a shield between them. The bridge was dark; the broken bits of glass crunched under Avery's sneakers. But Josef and her sister were clearly visible in the undulating halo of green light seizing Chloe's throat.

Where are cops when you need them? Not that cops would do much, but I'd love to see his ass get tased.

"Give me the book," Josef said calmly, giving Avery his ready smile.

The presence stirred at the back of Avery's psyche yet remained silent.

"Fuck you. Give me my sister."

His chin jutted out, smile grinding down into a sneer. "You need to have more respect, little girl."

Avery grunted. "Whatever. You're nothing but a resurrected dead guy with a hard-on for a demon."

Josef growled, his hand tightening around Chloe's neck. A shriek erupted from her pinched lips, tearing her mouth open wide, her knees buckling.

Avery lunged, and he jerked back, yanking her sister with him.

"Uh, uh, uh." He jeered at her.

"If you hurt her again, I will kill you." Avery glowered. The heat building in her belly flooded into her torso and down her arms. She straightened and squared her shoulders. "Scratch that. I'm going to kill you regardless, so…"

Avery cocked her head with a curl of her upper lip. She clenched her fists and called to the book.

Stay your hand, Avery Parsons. Its calm voice infuriated her. *This is not the proper time.*

The anger on Josef's face melted, much to Avery's surprise, his eyes hooded. He turned his attention to the whimpering young woman in his arms, struggling pitifully. He ran his nose along her ear, as a lover might, and moved his hand across her midsection.

"Do you think me a kind man, Miss Parsons?" Josef brought his eyes back to gaze upon Avery's face, then moved them slowly down her body, making Avery cringe. She had a sudden urge to cover herself as if she were naked.

"Give me the book, or your sister becomes my *mistress*." He said the last word as if it were a morsel of delicious food in his mouth. Avery's revulsion immediately returned to hatred.

Book! You will help me. NOW.

No.

"Fuck!" She threw her hands in the air. Avery wanted to rush him and beat him to death with her own hands.

"Or maybe I should take you." His eyebrow rose with consideration. "I do love a fighter. Your grandmother wasn't very much of one, you know."

Avery charged.

Josef vanished in a crack of black vapor, taking her sister with him.

"No!" She skipped to a stop. "No! You bring her back!"

"Give me the book." Josef Straka's disembodied voice echoed around her. She whirled, waiting for the coward to show himself.

"All right! Fine!" She stomped over to her discarded backpack, ignoring the book's itch in her mind.

A snap of thunder brought Josef Straka before her, still clutching Chloe to his chest, her tear-filled eyes imploring her sister for help. Avery pulled the book from the pack, throwing the pack back to the ground.

The silhouette of someone jogging toward them appeared at the far end of the bridge. She opened her mouth to call out, but the person vanished in a violent swirl of green mist. The stench of burnt flesh wafted past her, stinging her nostrils. Avery turned her eyes to Straka, who only smiled. She wanted to rip that smug look off his face. Had he killed all those people on the bridge?

You cannot give me to him, Avery Parsons.

"The hell I can't."

Josef's expression hardened. "The book… speaks to you?"

She ignored him.

You would sacrifice every human in this world? You would let them become puppets of Muraal's mindless children? All for a single person?

"But…" Her fingers twitched as she held the book to her chest. Her sister! Avery couldn't let him have her, no matter what!

At her hesitation, Josef squeezed a shriek of pain from Chloe.

Avery's muscles froze as she propelled the book from her chest, meaning to throw it at Josef's feet. The presence swelled within her; familiar words bombarded her mind.

She fought against them, her lips working hard to remain closed. Waves of hot energy took control of her muscles. Her arms drew the book to her even as her brain screamed against the motion.

Avery's mouth opened without her permission. The strained muscles in her jaw began to cramp, being forced open from the inside. Josef straightened, suspicion narrowing his hard eyes. He squared the girl's body in front of him, insulating him from whatever her twin was planning.

With a painful pop of her jaw, Avery's lips burst open. *"Ix h'het suka!"*

Josef Straka staggered back with a shout, his face twisted with rage, but his grip on Chloe held fast. Power surged through Avery's body, filling her veins. She repeated the words in a voice not hers, helpless to make them stop.

In a burst of lightning, the man and her sister were gone.

Suddenly released, she collapsed onto the pavement. Tiny shards of glass bit into her bare knees. She screamed into the night, hot tears streaming down her face as she called her sister's name again and again.

"What did you do?" she said, now able to throw the book to the ground. Avery slammed both fists onto it, beating it with each shattered breath. *"What did you do?"*

CHAPTER 42

Be still, Avery Parsons. There is hope.

With a shriek, she flung the book down the deserted bridge. It landed on the slick road with a heavy thud. She gathered her sister's things with blurred vision and shoved them into her backpack. Magda wasn't in her crystal.

You cannot save her without my power.

Avery spun around, expletives on the tip of her tongue.

"You took over my body!" She stomped over to the book and kicked its spine. It skidded across the slick pavement, flipping on a rail groove and tumbling to a stop. "You *used* me to send Straka away. He has my sister, you son of a bitch!" Avery chased after it, meaning to kick it again.

This isn't helping, Chloe would say if she were there. With an exasperated groan, she snatched it up.

"You will get my sister back or I *swear* I'll find a way to rip you apart." Something akin to smugness emanated from the presence. Her fingers dug into the sides of the hard skin, their pressure sending tiny sparks of power into her hands. Ignoring the enticing sensation, she thought for a moment of the river on both sides of her and pictured arcing the book into the drink like a basketball. But no, she couldn't do that. Not yet anyway.

It's right—she grimaced—*I can't get her back without it.*

A car horn blasted behind her, making her jump and run to the sidewalk. She threw the driver the finger as he rolled past. Traffic once again traversed the bridge; people were walking toward her from the left, and a cyclist was coming from the right. She gawked in both directions, amazed by whatever magick Straka had used.

"How can I find her?" she asked through clenched teeth, refusing to say *we*.

Look to the book.

"You've said that before," she grumbled, tempted once again to chuck it into the black water. "And you will *not* take control of me again. Do you hear me?"

I did only what was necessary. Josef Straka cannot be allowed to rend the Shade.

"I don't give a shit about him or whatever his fucking plans are. I want my sister back. And if I have to give you to him in exchange, I will." Avery glared at the book, the anger in her heart traveling down her arms to squeeze it as hard as she could, hoping to bring it pain.

The book didn't react to her words or her exertion. It was quiet, which she found just as annoying as when it spoke.

"Avery! Chloe!" The muffled shouts came from within Chloe's messenger bag.

"Grammy!" She dropped the book and knelt, rifling through the bag for the crystal ball. Magda hovered within, her face worried. "Grammy!" Avery gripped the cold quartz. "That son of a bitch took Chloe!"

Magda covered her face, stifling an agonized cry.

"He wants the book in exchange." Avery spat the words out. "And I'll give it to him, Gram. I will." She bit her lip before telling Magda that she'd tried, and it had stopped her.

Magda dropped her hands. "You cannot." Her face grew hard then, and she narrowed her eyes at Avery. "Use your magick, Avery. Call the birds. Find her."

"What? I don't know how to do that!"

"You do! Deep down. Did you not use that magick every day at the zoo? When you calmed the frightened birds, eased their pain after injury?" Magda raised her shoulders. "Did you not call the hawk to save your sister?"

"I..." Avery gulped and looked away.

"Use your power now. What birds are here? Call to them, tell them what you want. Get them to fly to find Chloe."

The conviction etched in her grandmother's features was almost enough to push Avery's doubts aside. Could she do that? What other choices did she have? She gathered their things and ran down the steps back into the park.

It was eerily quiet. No one meandered on the path; the couple they witnessed earlier making out on a bench had gone. Or had Josef killed them, dispatched them like that person on the bridge? She hadn't seen anyone come up the stairs, but she hadn't been paying attention. Even the birds were silent. The only sounds were the soft crunch of compacted dirt under her feet and the lazy flow of the water around the island.

Avery walked briskly to the north end once more, opening her energy to feel the birds hidden in the trees. At least, she assumed that's what she was doing based off what her grandmother had taught them long ago, the stuff Avery had scoffed at: being quiet, listening, breathing. She inhaled deeply through her nose. With each exhale, she cast out the negative emotions gripping her. It took many breaths, making Avery light-headed by the time she reached the sandy shore.

She laid her pack against a tree, positioning the crystal ball so Magda could see her. Avery closed her eyes and listened. She tuned out the light traffic droning behind her on the Charles Bridge, the voices from the streets carried to her by the breeze, the rumbling of a small boat through the water.

A rush flitted across her skin. The light electric sensation didn't come from the book, but from the swelling in her chest. She *had* used her magick often, but she had never truly understood what she was doing. She'd speak to the birds in their mind, and she could feel their stress and pain, but nothing like what Chloe had done with the cat. Avery changed her own energy to whatever soothed or placated them, and then it just happened. Maybe she could do that now?

Avery nodded to herself. *Here goes nothing.*

She walked to the nearest copse. The lights within the park had been shattered as well when Straka appeared, but she didn't need light to sense the many pairs of eyes following her. She focused on the Ural owl perched in one of the largest trees, surveying her with his small black eyes set inside a large, round head. He ruffled his striking feathers, a mass of light gray streaked with dark brown, as he regarded her.

I need your help.

The owl's mind was open and calm, as owls usually were. He had seen what transpired. He'd been watching them since they entered the park. She was unusual for a human, and he wanted to watch her; all the birds watched her.

Can you follow him? Can you find where he took my sister? Her eyes welled with tears and she let them fall, her induced calm overtaken by the memory of her sister's face twisted in pain.

The owl sensed her anxiety; her energy flowed into him, but he did not shy away. He considered her with narrowed eyes, then turned his face away. He would not help. The matters of humans meant nothing to him. And there was great evil in that man, who was no longer a man. He must find his next meal.

Please! She shouted, and his body lurched. He screeched at her, flapping his wings, and screeched once more.

I'm so sorry. I didn't mean to yell. Please, please help me. I don't know what else to do. She covered her face and slumped over with fresh sobs.

The owl spotted movement in the distance and launched himself silently from the branch.

Frustration burst from her chest. *I need help!* Her thoughts echoed across the canopy. A cacophony of squawks and cries answered, with each bird flying up and away from the strange human. The sounds of rustling branches and chaotic flapping wings filled her ears. Avery was immediately sorry, but the harm was already done.

It was several minutes before she could speak again. "No go, Gram. Seems I can't do anything right."

Magda didn't answer, and Avery couldn't bear to look at her.

"We'll find another way," Magda said, her voice somber, devoid of the judgment Avery expected.

"The book, you mean." She turned her red eyes to her grandmother, who nodded grimly.

Cradling Magda in Chloe's bag, she gathered their things and headed back to the apartment.

He reveled in the taste of her anguish. Her fire, so easily fueled, would serve him well. She would not yet admit how she liked the power in her hands, how it felt coursing through her body, but he knew the pleasure she suppressed.

He would continue to remind her, to give her samples of what she desired deep down, what she refused to acknowledge. The kernel of darkness she held locked away lay open before him, ready for action and purpose. He was keenly aware of her mind; the shadowy recesses held so much potential. She would soon crave his power, he was certain.

Her threats to give him to Straka were hollow. She would not give him up. His was the only power she could use. Her innate magick was scattered, unfocused. Her failure tonight was proof of that. The girl wanted the path of least resistance. She could use his magick without study or trials. So much power was at her fingertips, and he would show her how easy it was to harness.

As her anger grew toward the man who stole her twin, the more her eager mind welcomed the words from his pages. Her openness increased with each angry breath. She would know all of him, and soon. He basked in his growing triumph. His freedom was finally—

"Mom! Oh my god!" Sorrow stole the rest of her words, turning into labored gasps to contain the sobs in her chest.

"Avery! Where are you? Why haven't you been answering? I'm been calling and calling—" The line went dead, and Avery shouted into the phone.

It was simple to keep Vivian Parsons from her daughters. Those electronic devices were barely any effort to manipulate. He was unable to affect the old woman, but that did not matter. She was not aware of him. She had relied on the book throughout her life also, and she was turning the girl to him as well.

He relished the girl's panic, the flood of emotions the sound of her mother's voice had induced. He should have allowed this sooner. Her agony was exquisite. The racing of her blood, the pounding of her strong heart, the heat rushing across her skin. Yes, she was perfect. Her untapped power would be his freedom.

He let the girl wallow for another moment, then prodded her to get up; she'd slumped against a brick wall. He fed her images of Straka and of what he might do to her sister. Her response was exhilarating. Within half a breath, she was running.

CHAPTER 43

Vivian ran past baggage claim, head swiveling to catch signs for any sort of ground transportation. She was immensely grateful there were signs in English. She'd stuffed only the essentials in her hobo bag and withdrew the maximum amount of cash her bank would allow in one day.

The girls still weren't answering her calls and texts. It had been nearly two days. Granted, she'd been traveling for nearly twenty hours, in an airplane for most of them, but she should have at least a few voicemails. She questioned whether her phone was still working even though she'd bought the international plan from her carrier before she left. With clammy hands and panic rising in her gut, she called their customer service department. They assured her the plan was in effect, which made her heart beat faster.

The white row of taxis greeted her, as did the surprisingly cool air of the evening from a recent rain. It would have been refreshing if she'd given a thought to it. Vivian jumped into the first taxi in the line and gave him the address to the girls' hostel. She sat in the back seat in silence, both hands gripping her phone.

Intermittent patches of light and dark scenery blurred past as Vivian stared, unfocused, at the window. Her eyes tracked the droplets of water streaking horizontally along it, slowing or increasing in speed as the car drove on. She had no interest in knowing what exciting history or amazing architecture she was in the midst of. Vivian just wanted to find her daughters *safe*.

"I am sorry," said the short, middle-aged man behind the desk in surprisingly good English. "They check out a couple days ago." His forehead puckered, his thick brows joining as he frowned in response to Vivian's reaction.

Her shoulders trembled. "Did they say where they were going? Did you see them leave?"

The man shook his head, the lines around his mouth deepening. "I am sorry, no."

Vivian managed a nod and walked on unsteady legs to one of the two chairs in the small lobby. *Why would they check out? Are they on their way home? Should I call the police*? She debated asking the man where the nearest police station was, but no, she shook her head at her reflection in the dark window. *Now is not the time to overreact. If they aren't at Magda's apartment, then I'll overreact.*

She tried Chloe's phone again with no answer and followed it with another text in all capitalized letters. Tears sprang to her eyes as she gazed at the contact image of her innocent Chloe, cuddling a pair of tabby kittens from the shelter.

"Oh, my sweet girl." She touched the screen. "Why aren't you answering?" Through blurred vision, she pressed 'Call' under Avery's laughing hazel eyes, shadowed from the bright sun by a baseball cap.

Vivian leapt from the chair when the ringing stopped. "Avery?"

"Mom! Oh my god!" Avery's voice sounded panicked.

"Avery! *Where are you?* Why haven't you been answering? I've been calling and calling— Avery? *Avery!"* She shook her phone. "No!"

She implored the man at the front desk to try her daughter's number with his landline. Maybe, just maybe, it was a problem with her cell phone. He looked uncertain, as if he wasn't allowed to call outside numbers, but her tears and quivering chin persuaded him. He tried both of the numbers, but each line rang and rang, never going to voicemail. Vivian wanted to scream.

With pinched lips and phone clutched in her hand so tight her knuckles were white, she marched out into the dark night, arm raised for a cab.

Vivian raced up the narrow stairs of Magda's apartment building. She paid no attention to the person coming down and bolted to the side to get out of their way. An arm shot out, blocking her path. She lost her footing with the sudden stop and clamped on to the handrail to keep from tumbling backward.

"Hey!" Craning her neck, she saw a tall man in a black suit standing two steps above her. She was momentarily taken aback by his handsome face and dark, piercing eyes. She recovered herself and gave the man the stern look she saved for unruly patients.

"Excuse you." She indicated with her hand that his offending arm still blocked the way. The man stared, eyes widening as they probed her face.

Vivian flew from stern to angry and pushed at his arm. "Let me by!"

A sneer crawled across the man's lips, making Vivian's skin prickle.

"How lucky I am today." His voice was deep and smooth. "Hello, Vivian Parsons."

CHAPTER 44

"Why are some of these pages blank?" Avery sat cross-legged on the sofa, inside the circle of bright light from the end table lamp, insulating her from the darkness of the living room. Avery had spent the last half hour flipping through the book's blood and gore with little reaction, feeling more numb now than anything else, and discovered random pages were blank. Had they always been blank? She shook her head; she had no time to worry about that now.

The book didn't answer. It had been quiet since she threatened to give it over to Straka. *Good.*

Avery continued through the pages, coming to a stop when she reached the spell her grandmother used to raise Straka. She read over its lengthy prose, her mind wandering. What would she do to save Chloe? Magda had killed her husband to read the book; she'd enjoyed watching his eyes go dark. She'd trapped one hundred people's souls to raise her lover. One hundred! Deeds Avery never in a million years would have thought her little Grammy capable of.

Could she take a life? Would she kill for her sister?

"Yes." Avery answered without hesitation. *In a fucking heartbeat.*

She briefly imagined beating that creepy smile off Straka's

face. Avery shuddered at the memory of his hand moving across Chloe's stomach, his lips moving against her ear. She'd enjoy watching him die. A huff left her lips. How alike she and Magda were. Avery glanced at the empty sphere still nestled in her backpack on the dining table. Sitting at the edge of the darkness, it looked washed of its golden hues. She wanted to apologize again to her grandmother, feeling more akin to her now than ever before.

Avery set those thoughts aside and read through the long spell again. Her fingers drifted across the words, her mind working to make sense of them. *What would Chloe do?* Avery tried to think like her sister. *Break it down*, she imagined Chloe would say. *What parts sound particularly important?* The chest of coins, the engravings on the coins, grave dirt, white gauze strips, souls. The common factor throughout the elements of the spell were the coins. Copper *stotin*, Gram had said.

She did a quick internet search on her phone. There wasn't much information to be had. The copper five stotin hadn't seen circulation, but she could pick one up for about five thousand Euros. Her eyes bulged, and she set the phone facedown.

"Gram? How important is that particular coin? The stotin."

Magda slowly resolved, her face drawn. Avery wondered how a ghost could look so tired.

"I don't know exactly. Josef had already collected the coins needed. I only followed the steps of the spell. As you can see, there is no explanation for anything, merely instruction. I learned from later study that copper is used to direct energy, among other things, so I believe that is why it's used in the spell. To direct the spirit's energy to Josef. And the coin itself—many cultures put coins on the eyes of their dead as payment to the ferryman. Or to simply keep their eyes closed."

Avery scrunched her face. "The ferryman?"

"To pay for their passage to the underworld. It's Greek mythology." Magda shrugged. "To me, for this spell, I think it *blinds* them from their journey. They cannot see where to go.

Added to that, their energy is tethered to Josef, so they are trapped."

They cannot see where to go. Avery mulled over Magda's words.

She rubbed her tired eyes and tousled the choppy hair atop her head with both hands, letting a yawn loose. The spikes of adrenaline and fear, the rush at hearing her mother's voice and the frustration when they were cut off, and the emotional crash afterward had taken their toll. *Oh, and can't forget the jet lag.* Avery stood, shook out her arms and legs, then performed several kicks, jabs, and spins to get some energy flowing again.

The living room was a complete mess. She hadn't paid attention to it until now. The white creams were dried and crusty, smeared so much there was no telling what the design had been. The knives were still embedded in the carpet, and the furniture sat where Avery had shoved it; a few of the dining table chairs lay on their sides. Not to mention the lingering stench of rotten meat—faint, but noticeable. *It's a good thing we're not in a hotel. They'd totally kick us out after maid service saw this.* She groaned at knowing she'd have to clean it up. Thankfully, Chloe's vomit hadn't been chunky.

Digging through Chloe's bag, she pulled out two pennies from her coin purse. She jiggled them in her hand as an idea formed. They were the closest thing to copper they had, although pennies didn't have much copper in them anymore. She slid them into the front pocket of her shorts.

Avery had no way of finding Chloe, but she didn't need to. Straka would find her.

"Are you ready to face him, my Avery?" Magda's grim face matched her voice.

"Yep."

"Look at me."

She picked up the sphere and held it before her face. Her grandmother appeared a husk of what she had been in life. What would happen to her when this was over?

"You're probably tired of hearing me say this, but you *must* be strong, *beruško.*" Magda peered deep into Avery's determined eyes. "And I don't mean just against Josef."

Avery swallowed.

"You can defeat him, I know this. And you can defeat *it.*"

"You'll be with me, right?"

"As much as I am able, my Avery." Love trembled in her grandmother's eyes, the longing to hold her granddaughter just once more plain.

Avery blinked away the tears springing up to sting her eyes. "Listen, Grammy, about what I said before, about you taking the easy way out and stuff… Can you please forget I ever said those terrible things?"

"Already forgotten, *beruško.*" Magda held up a hand to the smooth quartz. "I love you with all my heart."

Avery cleared her throat. "I love you, too, Grammy."

"Now," Magda said, straightening her shoulders, "let's go get your sister."

Avery set her jaw with a sharp nod.

She wrapped the sphere in a T-shirt and placed it in her backpack, setting the book in with it. She hauled the heavy pack onto her back, pulling the shoulder straps tight.

With a deep breath, she narrowed her vision to the clock on the wall.

"Ix rezahl suka yr."

The clock exploded. The words came so easily, spilling from her mouth with no effort, the surge of magick lifting her spirits. *I got this.* The corner of her mouth curved up.

Josef Straka snapped into the living room with a crack of thunder and black vapor. *That's a pretty impressive entrance*, Avery admitted. *I wonder if I'll be able to do that.*

Avery crinkled her nose at the tang of ozone and silently thanked him for his predictability. She stood before him, holding her palms up in surrender.

With fists pulsing, he scanned the room.

"Come on." She jutted her chin out. "Let's get this over with."

His upper lip curled. She steeled herself as he reached for her.

There's truly no other way, Magda lamented. He'd taken her sweet Chloe! She held a gasp in her throat, a useless holdover from her living body. She'd done more harm to her granddaughters than she could have imagined in her worst nightmares.

It had only been about Josef. Send the girls the book, they could defeat him with its magick. Magda would guide them. But it had become much, much more. The book contained an *intelligence*.

She had held it in her hands for decades, known every word of its horrendous magick, willingly called to its power many times, and known nothing of what lurked within. It was fashioned from the skin and blood of one of those twisted little demons. How it had gotten here from the Voll she couldn't guess, but what presence was inside it? It couldn't be the mental remnants of the creature; they were nothing but mindless savages driven by uncontrollable cravings. The book was cunning… and patient.

Had Josef known? Could he have put it there? No, he said he wrote it—only that. But he might have lied. Josef had lied about everything else.

And this presence lay dormant, or slumbered, until Magda had given it to the one person it had ever called out to. A person with a seed of darkness inside her. If Magda had known, she would have… what? Had she had any other options as she'd lain on the floor of her bedroom, ancient, powerless, dying?

Magda pictured the tiny black hairs peppering Avery's temples; she hadn't let on she'd seen them. The book wasn't only speaking to her, its magick was *changing* her. What did it want!?

She screamed into the abyss, yet the sheer size of the limbo she drifted in swallowed up any sound she could make. Here she would remain, clinging to the tiny opening in the Veil until her granddaughters no longer needed her.

Yet she felt so useless. How much more power did a restless spirit have? Her regret and sorrow and shame allowed her to peek through the Veil, to reconnect with those she'd put in harm's way. But the power of restlessness was finite; Magda could linger only until her business was finished. What else could she possibly do to achieve that end?

CHAPTER 45

Vivian struggled against the invisible grip of Josef Straka. "Chloe! Avery! Wake up!" Vivian's voice strained from shouting, unsure if they could hear her through the roar of the whirlwind clutching her.

Her daughters lay within the grisly circle of dead and dying men. Neither had moved since she'd come to, finding herself hovering a foot or so above the tall grass outside the circle, her arms pressed to her body by icy fingers of wind. Her eyes darted around the wide, manicured clearing. They were in some sort of park, Vivian was sure of that. A narrow paved path curved around the glade, flanked by tall, straight trees. She prayed for someone to jog or stroll by—better yet, a night watchman patrolling the park. It was pointless to hope. If this were a park in Boston, she sure wouldn't be out walking around in it at the dead of night.

Vivian glared at the man who had taken her, now dressed in a flowing, black robe. Her screams when he sliced each man's throat had gone unnoticed. Their pitiful struggles were useless against whatever force locked them in place. In the light of the many torches surrounding them, their clothing glistened black, soaked in blood. The slightly curved blade of the long dagger appeared to be painted a glossy deep red; the man's hand gripping its hilt looked as if he wore a wet, crimson glove.

Just beyond the circle swelled a dark curtain, growing wide and reaching outward, in slow pulsing waves. A tiny slit marred its smooth surface. Within it loomed a gigantic creature although Vivian could only make out its silhouette. The horns on its head curved upward and out, flanked by massive wings that twitched and flexed. Its eyes were swirling pools of liquid fire trained on the man below it, following each long swipe of his dagger.

I can't be seeing this!

There was movement swarming around its thick legs. She couldn't tell what it was, but it couldn't be good.

This is real! Vivian thought for the hundredth time. Everything Magda and the girls had told her was real. Even though she was seeing this, it was still too much to believe. But there was no mistaking what was happening.

She knew well the smell of blood. She knew how much blood the body held, and the pallor of the skin when it had drained away. The tall man's face held no concern for his heinous deeds. He repeated the same phrase in a strange language Vivian had never heard before as he moved to each man. The ones still alive twitched helplessly, frightened eyes following the blade as best they could with their faces toward the sky. The man closest to her was just a boy, maybe nineteen at the most. Tears streamed from his eyes.

No, wait. I have *heard words like that before. When Curt came to the apartment that first time, and again when Magda created that green fire to burn his body away. Oh, Magda! What have you gotten us into? Where are you?*

Vivian pulled her eyes from the horrific scene, narrowing her vision. Only her girls mattered.

A familiar voice cut through the fog choking Chloe's mind. It called her name and her sister's, near the edge of hysteria, over and over. Chloe tried to get up, but her arms and legs were so heavy. No, not heavy. Bound.

She pressed her face to the moist ground, head pounding, throat dry. The short grass was cool and refreshing; the earthy scent filled her nostrils, helping clear her mind. There was another scent carried by the breeze, making her stomach pitch. *Blood.* She recoiled, bringing her knees to her chest. The last thing Chloe remembered was Straka's roar in her ear and his long fingers biting into her neck as the image of Avery's distorted face was eclipsed by blackness.

Oh, Avery, I hope you're coming for me. And that Punch-o and Lefty are up to this.

Chloe's attempt at humor died away as her ears keyed on the deep voice droning behind her—wicked words similar to those Avery uttered from the book, accompanied by whimpering and strained grunting. Dread crept over her; she didn't want to open her eyes.

Chloe wriggled and discovered her hands were behind her back and that something lay against her.

The familiar voice was growing clearer, more urgent, desperate.

Mom? There was no way her mother was here. She was in Boston. But that voice! *No way.*

Chloe blinked and lifted her head, shaking it gently to clear the nagging fog. The pressure against her back moved and emitted a groan. *Avery*! She twisted her shoulders just enough to see Avery's form in the darkness, on her side, silhouetted by flickering light. *No, no, no.*

"Avery!" She prodded with her feet, tied at the ankles, but Avery was silent.

Chloe braved a look around when her name was called again. She gasped at the nightmarish scene and cowered against her sister, trying to make herself smaller.

A wide circle of men surrounded them, bodies standing frozen in place. Each one's arms were cast out to the sides, heads craned upward, revealing red gore where their throats should be, the whole of their blood soaked down their clothing. She tried to scream, but a familiar image hovering outside the circle caught her eye.

"Mom!"

Josef Straka laughed and flicked his hand at the woman. She fell to the ground but recovered immediately, bolting toward the twins.

Vivian didn't hesitate to push between two of the dead men, ducking under their stiff arms. She threw herself down, wrapping her bound daughter in her arms. Vivian pulled Chloe to her knees, and Chloe stared at her mother in disbelief, finally collapsing against her chest, sobbing. Vivian bent to shake Avery, and Chloe gripped her arms.

"*Mom!* What are you doing here? How did you get here?"

"After you told me what happened, I got on the next flight." She pushed Chloe back to shake her shoulders. "*You didn't tell me you'd left the hostel!* I went there, and you'd checked out. Neither of you were answering my calls or texts! Well, Avery answered once, but we got cut off. I almost went to the police. I was going to if you weren't at Magda's apartment." Her eyes darted to the man who now stared at them, beaming with arrogance at the trio, and gathered her daughter tighter in her arms.

"We didn't—" Chloe's voice left her, and she swallowed to get it back. "We didn't get any calls or texts, Mom, honestly." She cowered in the shadow of the tall man.

A moan drew their attention. Avery's eyes fluttered and then squinted, confused by the woman holding her cheeks and showering her forehead with kisses.

Panic shot through Avery when she realized she was tied up. She thrashed in someone's arms, not listening to the voices telling her to calm down. Vivian pulled the frantic girl's head to her lap and stroked her short hair, murmuring soothing words in her ear.

"*Mom?* Oh my god!" Avery managed between heaving breaths. Vivian answered the same questions Chloe had asked as she helped Avery to her knees.

Avery gaped around her, shocked at what they were in the middle of. "Oh, crap. This is the ritual to rip the Shade."

The book hovered beside Josef Straka, waist high. His smile faded as he looked between the redhead and the book. His lip curled.

"The book is mine once again, young Avery." It still grated him that it was used by another. Worse still, it *spoke* to her. It had never spoken to him.

When he'd retrieved the book, he probed deep within it, searching for whatever entity or consciousness that could *speak*. The book revealed everything that it had ever been used for. He saw nothing more. It was impossible the creature Muraal sent through the Voll had survived. Even if some small part of it had, her "children" were mindless beasts, with no thoughts of their own save for the unquenchable yearning for light and heat. The creature had been the vessel of Muraal's magick, its body given to create the physical book. When its purpose had been fulfilled, the disembodied voice faded, the carcass remaining as the thick tome.

Josef studied the fiery redhead with his clinical eye. Perhaps she was simply delusional. She was certainly unstable; it could be her imaginings, her mind unable to cope with the brutal power the book offered. Schizophrenic, perhaps? He briefly wondered who the girl had killed. Even with all her bluster, she was no killer. Perhaps that act had pushed her mind over the edge.

Josef reconsidered his promise to hand her over to Muraal.

He might keep the young woman for himself. Her fire aroused his passion; it would be great pleasure to break her.

His thoughts returned to Magda, and he scowled. *She should see this.* He lifted his free hand. From the discarded bag outside his circle shot the yellow quartz sphere straight into his palm. He peered into it, teeth bared. The wizened visage of his old lover glared back at him.

"Isn't it wonderful," he said, lifting his dark eyes to the trio, fingers gripping the ball, "that you all are together again." He hefted the orb, his sneer deepening. "You should thank me." He laughed deep in his throat and tossed the sphere at the cowering women. Vivian lunged to catch it.

"I'm glad you are here to witness this, my *love*." Josef centered his gaze on Magda, giving her his smooth, ready smile, the smile she'd fallen in love with. "Without you, I would not be here." He bowed at the waist, dipping his head.

The old woman glowered, and his smile melted into a jeer as he studied her current state of being. Useless encased in the crystal ball. Could he draw her out and shackle her spirit? He would certainly try after Muraal was freed.

A deep rumble from the recesses of his psyche jolted him. *Muraal.* He turned his attention back to the remaining four men, chiding himself for getting distracted. There would be no mistakes this time; his power was much stronger than when he was human. These men could not escape.

He raised his face to look upon the shimmering black mantle hovering in the sky just above the shortest man. The thin Shade allowed a glimpse of his master on the other side. Her face was stone, her fiery eyes locked on her Chosen One, taloned fists clenched at her side.

Avery prodded the book once Josef's back was turned.

Do not let him know we speak. Its words were clipped as if it pained it to speak to her.

Avery turned her face to her mother and sister. Vivian held Magda at her belly.

I cannot be yours while he walks this plane.

She grimaced. *What makes you think I want you? I just want this over. I want the four of us out of here. How do we kill him?*

He has no life to take.

You're not being very helpful!

She felt a distinct flare of irritation from it.

You must take his power from him.

And just exactly how do I do that?

I cannot tell you. Not now.

A burst of frustration left her lips.

"What is it, Avery?" Her mother whispered. Avery raised a single finger, asking for patience.

He will know, Avery Parsons. He will know that I exist. Only when the time is right can we act.

We. She sighed, closing her eyes. *We're finally 'we.'*

Vivian's face still held questions.

"Let this play out, Mom. We have a plan." *You better have a plan, book.*

"We?" Chloe asked. Avery jerked her chin in the book's direction.

Chloe studied her sister's face. Avery held her gaze as Chloe's shoulders sank, and watched the flames of the torchlight reflect in the gloss of tears forming. Chloe looked away.

"What?" Avery leaned in. Chloe muttered, "Nothing," then noticed her mother trying to loosen the rope around her wrists. Magda sat on the ground, keeping an eye on Straka.

Vivian dug her short nails into the tight knots, whispering an apology if she was hurting Chloe. The main knot was just about loose when Magda shouted.

A violent updraft sent Vivian flying.

CHAPTER 46

Avery followed her mother's flight through the air with a defiant shout. Vivian landed hard on her back outside the circle, knocking the air from her lungs.

"We can't have that, now." Straka's mocking tone echoed throughout the circle. Avery whipped her head around. The book floated at his side. He sneered at the scowling young woman as he flourished his free hand in their direction.

A burst of icy wind engulfed the twins. The girls gasped and braced themselves to keep from being knocked to the ground. The wind carried Straka's laughter as it whirled around them. He turned back to the man in front of him.

Vivian fought to regain her breath as she tried and failed to push herself up on her elbows. An invisible weight seemed to sit on her midsection. Vivian grunted and thrashed, pushing with her legs against the ground, trying to get out from under it. It pushed down harder, and she fell onto her back, gasping to retain the air the pressure forced from her lungs.

Avery strained against the ropes holding her limbs. She twisted and pulled her wrists, the rope biting into her skin.

The black mantle before them was thinning; the gash was growing longer and deeper with each throat Straka slashed. Only one man remained, elderly and frail. Straka stepped before him, raising the dagger in the air, blood oozing down his arm, and lifted his jubilant face to the monster behind the rippling curtain.

Avery yanked repeatedly to get a hand free; although the bindings were slick with her blood, they wouldn't loosen. She closed her eyes and pictured the rope around her wrists. She took a deep breath, focusing intently on the rope and *only* the rope, and whispered, *"Rezahl."*

She yelped at the snap of burning against her raw skin as the rope fell away. She shook her wrists free and reached into her front pocket.

"Chloe!"

Her twin tore her attention from their struggling mother. Avery locked eyes with Chloe and inched forward on her knees, extending her right hand. Chloe worked her right hand free, tearing her skin against the rope, mumbling appreciation for her mother's hurried efforts. She grasped Avery's right hand. In it were two pennies. She stared at the coins and gave her sister questioning eyes.

Avery clasped her sister's hand once more, ensuring the pennies held firm between their palms. She dug her knees into the ground, holding her place against the thundering gale around them.

Now, Avery Parsons—the book's words were urgent, tinged with anticipation—*open your mind, let me flow into you freely. Do not fight me any longer.*

She gritted her teeth. *Do it.*

The surge of magick was massive, a dam holding back an ocean breaking open, and Avery bit back an outcry at its onslaught.

Thousands of words assailed her brain as vibrant sparks of hard light, feeding her power. She felt as if pure fire coursed through her veins, yet without the pain of burning—it was glorious! Her bones felt like iron, her muscles steel.

She raised her face to the whirlwind around them, her

triumphant smile unnaturally wide, drinking in the heady sensations of sheer invincibility and strength and... *freedom.*

Avery lowered her eyes to her sister and reached out with her mind. *Chloe.*

Chloe cringed, not only from the voice of her sister once more in her head but from the sight of her. Shadows of the torchlight distorted by the winds skittered around her face, making her cheeks appear sunken, her eyes bulbous in their sockets. Green flames flickered within as they narrowed with determination.

Say this with me. It was not only Avery's voice that spoke; there was another within it, deep and confident. The rupture in the mantle was growing wider. Avery's hand squeezed hers, bringing her attention back. *Ready?*

Chloe raised her chin. *Let's do this.*

Magda tore her eyes from her granddaughters, knowing they were doing something to thwart Josef. *I must help them!*

He lowered his blade to the old man. Magda pulled in the gossamer trails of her spirit, praying she could do what she intended. She gathered the whole of herself into the crystal and imagined the fissure a conduit and herself vapor.

Please, please, please. She pushed, slipping into the fracture, and propelled herself from the crystal ball.

Magda's spirit flew at Josef. She couldn't touch him, couldn't snatch his hand away from the old man, but she could distract him.

Unbridled anger erupted from her hollow chest. The piercing, unearthly shriek took him by surprise, cutting into his ears. He dropped the blade to cover them. Josef turned to face whatever propelled itself toward him. She blasted through his upper body, and he staggered back.

Her wispy, translucent form reeled around, attempting to

obscure his vision, releasing in her screams the pent-up shame, rage, and pain she had over everything she'd done, everything she allowed to happen. Josef flailed, swatting and cursing at the white vapor with both arms.

Muraal's furious cries at him shook the very air; spittle as fire flew from her mouth. Her enormous fists slammed against the Shade, sending violent ripples across its surface.

With a curse and a blaze of green from his left hand, he cast Magda from him, sending her flying from the circle.

Josef recovered the dagger and raised it to the man's whiskered neck, swiping it across as he bellowed the last of the words needed to rend the Shade. A thin line of red blossomed as the old man's skin separated.

Magda came at him again, whipping around his head once more. He jumped back, his face twisted with rage, his cut unfinished.

He brought the blade up, emblazoning it with demonfire to rid him once and for all of the wretched woman.

Searing pain shot through Magda as the fiery green blade raked her torso. Emerald flames hissed and spit as they ate away her sheer form. Magda took her eyes to her granddaughters.

A column of shimmering winds encircled Avery and Chloe, both locked on each other in whatever magick they worked against Josef. She prayed her paltry efforts had given them enough time.

Only Vivian could see her. She called to Magda, tears streaming as she clawed at some invisible power holding her down. *Oh, my daughter.*

"I'm sorry," Magda mouthed as the flames devoured the last of her. *I'm so, so sorry.*

Energy burst into Chloe, projected from her sister. The wicked slash marks from the book rushed into her mind, forming frightening words, bringing with them the knowledge of a type of magick she wanted no part of. The foul words traveled to her mouth; they tasted like acid, but she did not hesitate.

"Ryks'zu dex yi u'aan," the twins chanted in unison. *"Sukar aan Der'zu rezahl. Kih zyadu sukar zeda!"*

With a howl, Josef spun around, searching for the source of the impossible words. The sisters faced each other, on their knees with hands clasped, and repeated the phrases again.

Josef staggered backward at the violent wrench on his power, the dagger falling from his grip. Muraal clawed viciously at the tear in the Shade as Josef clutched his chest, pain twisting within.

Rising from the ground, in jagged ribbons of silver white aether, the one hundred chained spirits drew forth.

Each spirit had a ring of red flame around their neck, extending into a whipping snake firmly embedded in Josef's chest. The fiery light from so many souls was nearly blinding. A strip of gauze covered their eyes, holding a coin over each, but they saw him, they *knew* him, and raged at the injustice of what he'd done to them.

The embittered cries of spirits filled the air, voicing what it meant to be kept from their natural journey. To be imprisoned in an empty void, lingering in the nothingness, alone and confused. Sightless.

Josef cried out and bolted, breaking through the circle of dead men.

A new circle formed, one of torment and vengeance. The army of spirits hovered in the air around Josef, their tethers taut, preventing him from running further.

The last drop of blood trickled from the old man's throat.

The force on Vivian's body weakened, and she jumped up. Another eruption from the monster quaked the ground, sending her to her knees. She pulled her eyes from the preternatural gale slowing around her daughters and the ghosts encircling the terrified Straka.

Massive black talons broke through the wound in the quivering barrier. Vivian shrank away from the monstrous nightmare only a few feet from her: its jagged mouth dripping lava, two holes above it blazing orbs. The creature roared as it widened the breach. High-pitched peals of ripping echoed around her. Vivian struggled to regain her feet as the ground shook.

The opening tore lengthwise, revealing the full height of the creature. She stared at the impossible thing, paralyzed with fear. Its matte-black skin resembled cracked rocks with fire moving below the surface. Vivian could feel heat on her face. It pulled its massive wings in, its horns coiled upward, narrowing around its head to allow it to pass through. It brought its clawed foot down on the bottom of the tear to wrench it outward. With a triumph roar, the great demon stepped a taloned foot through into this world.

The ear-splitting sound snapped Vivian back to life. She hurled herself at the creature, slamming her body against hot stone. Vivian pushed against its chest, the skin of her palms sizzling. She cried out. Not from pain but determination. She pushed again with more force, leveraging her foothold in the tear itself.

"Ryks'zu dex yi u'aan!"

Chloe held her sister's burning stare, her body locked in the embrace of tumultuous magick. Spirits loomed around Josef Straka; he was barely visible through their ethereal bodies. But her attention was on Avery—runnels of black moved through her short hair, replacing the brilliant red.

The spirits shrieked in unison, releasing their rage against their imprisonment in howls carried by the wind, filling her ears with their anguish.

"Sukar aan Der'zu rezahl! Kih zyadu sukar zeda!"

The lashes broke free from Straka's chest, his shouts drowned out by the snapping sound of a hundred tethers.

They set upon the man who had stolen their afterlife, who had sentenced them to an eternal vacuum.

He cried out for Muraal as they tore into him, shredding skin from muscles, muscles from bones. His pitiful squalls faded to gurgles, those quickly replaced by the cracking sounds of bone. They wafted back and let him fall to the ground.

A blast of emerald light exploded from the body of Josef Straka. It passed through the spirits, disbursing their huddled mass with cries of shock. The pulse released the circle of dead men from their invisible bonds, each collapsing to the ground with a sickening thud.

The yellow quartz crystal ball split in two with a loud crack.

The shock wave at Vivian's back added the force she needed to drive the monster back into its world.

Startled by the brilliant flash, Muraal tumbled backward, its maw stretched wide in an enraged roar. Vivian tripped forward with it, catching herself on the fluttering edge of the rupture before she fell completely into the cold, black world.

Her brain registered the agony throbbing in her burnt palms, but she ignored it. She lunged backward, pushing off the bottom edge of the tear with her feet and landed on the grass. Fear stole the air from her lungs as a long-taloned claw reached for her.

Vivian scrambled backward on the soft ground, kicking her legs to get them free. A thick talon hooked one of Vivian's boots in mid kick, and yanked her into the Voll.

"Mom!" Chloe screamed.

The death of Josef Straka flashed away the energy holding open the gaping wound in the Shade. It sealed up in a violent swoosh, with Vivian behind it.

The force of the Shade sealing shut snuffed the flames from the torches. The sisters released their clasped hands, letting the pennies fall to the ground.

The crowd of spirits still hovered around the broken body of their dead master, their sheer, silvery-white forms undulating as if the wind still blew. It was eerily quiet as each lifted their hands to their faces and pulled the gauze from their eyes, the strip of cloth disappearing in their fingers.

The coins fell away from their hollow dark pits, landing on the grass with soft thuds. Sighs of relief reverberated within the assembly. The spirits began to fade one by one.

One spirit lingered. A young woman, wringing her hands, searched the throng, wafting up and around and through souls rejoicing in their freedom.

A little girl pushed her way in and out of the wisps of white vapor disappearing around her toward something she desperately wanted to reach.

"Zofie!" the woman called out and sped forward, arms outstretched. The girl jumped into her arms.

"Matka!" The child clung to the young woman, and they swirled around in a burst of laughter.

Mother and daughter faded together, threads of silver intermingling, disappearing into the moonless night.

CHAPTER 47

AVERY GOT TO HER FEET. SHE WOBBLED WITH A BREATHY 'whoa' and returned to her knees. She put a hand on either side of her head, as if it were spinning and the world was not. The images around her shifted, coming in and out of sharpness in the dark surrounding them. Her hair felt different, coarse and hard. *Probably just dried sweat.* Avery sat back on her heels as the dizziness passed.

"Mom," Chloe whispered, staring up at where the monster had seethed from the other side of the Shade.

She squinted at Chloe to get her sister into focus. Chloe stood, frozen.

"Where's Mom?" Avery's throat throbbed, and she swallowed. Her eyes registered grief from her sister, but her mind and body were easing down from a tremendous high. The glorious sensations were not fading as they had before. The magick wasn't leaving her; it was receding deep within, readying itself for her to call upon it again.

Avery wanted to smile, to bask in the feelings of this moment, to cry out, "I did it!" but a part of her was certain she shouldn't do any of that. As the triumph of having Straka's body torn apart wore away, realization of some great loss settled in. But she didn't know what.

"She—" Chloe bent over, hands on knees, gulping breaths.

Avery shook her head, making fists then releasing them, and stood. The magick was quieting, and Avery could see Chloe clearly now.

Chloe pulled herself upright. "Mom—she shoved that monster back into the Voll. She tripped, tried to get away. She almost was! But it grabbed her. She's in there… with it."

"No." Avery whirled, searching for her mother. She stopped in the direction holding traces of burnt flesh in the air and closed her eyes. The struggle between her mother and Muraal came to life. Her mother had been behind her; Avery hadn't seen what happened.

But her new powers replayed the scene in raw clarity. Her fearless mother, hands pressed against the searing rock-like flesh of the demon, the muscles in her arms straining as she pushed, face determined, not afraid. The pulse shoving her forward, the outrage on Muraal's face as it tumbled backward, long talons curling around her mother's scuffed boot. The piercing scream as she disappeared into the blackness.

She glared at the emptiness in the starless sky where the rupture in the Shade had been, where her mother had been taken.

"Mom's not dead," Avery said, her voice flat. She brought her gaze to meet Chloe's. "I know she's not." *How do I know that?* Was it the book? *The book!* Avery wheeled around, eyes locking on the object beside her. She knelt, laying her palm atop the book. It was cold.

"Avery!" Chloe yanked Avery up by her elbow. "Forget the damn book! What do you mean, she's not dead?" Chloe's tears trailed down her red cheeks. Avery's lack of agony, lack of any sadness in her expression made Chloe's nails dig into Avery's skin. Chloe shook her. "Come on!"

Avery brought her hands to her face, inhaling deeply to help gather her thoughts, and raked her fingers through hair that desperately needed to be washed.

"She's trapped, not dead. The Voll is a prison..." Avery couldn't explain anymore; she was dizzy again, pain throbbing behind her eyes. Her body suddenly felt too heavy for her bones to hold up.

"How do we get her out!?" Chloe screamed, shaking Avery again.

Anger flared and Avery shoved her sister. She hadn't meant to push that hard, but Chloe fell on her backside. Hurt and surprise replaced the anguish on Chloe's face.

"I'm sorry," Avery muttered. She'd never laid a hand on her sister in anger before. Avery closed her eyes, widening her stance to remain upright, and clenched her fists, willing the anger to go away. She pushed it out, the way her grandmother had told her. *Breathe. Relax. Be still. Breathe.* Her chest lightened, and some of the weight lifted from her shoulders.

What is the matter with me? It wasn't only her hair that felt odd; *she* felt odd but couldn't pinpoint exactly what it was. She didn't sense the book anymore—well, not like it was. Before, it had been a jagged stone at the base of her skull, but now, Avery wasn't sure what she felt.

Avery opened her eyes to Chloe's heartbroken face.

"What? I said I was sorry."

"How-can-we-get-her-out?" Chloe spit each word through clenched teeth. "I've been in there. You have no idea what it's like." A gasp choked her breath. Chloe scrambled to her feet. "Promise me we'll get her out!"

Chloe's words slapped at Avery, each word sobering her a bit more. *Mom.* She exhaled a ragged breath.

Avery stepped to her distraught sister and took her hands. "I don't know how, but I *promise*. We'll find a way."

Chloe collapsed into Avery's arms. Avery held her, ignoring the momentary annoyance at her sister's sniveling. *What the hell is wrong with me?* Avery frowned. She hugged Chloe close, wondering why she wasn't as grief-stricken as she should be. *Muraal won't kill her. It can't.* She blinked. *How do I know that?*

After a few breaths, Avery gently pushed her sister away. "We have to go. It'll be morning soon." She glanced to the east where the night was beginning to soften.

Chloe nodded, wiping her cheeks. She surveyed the scene around them, her eyes fully adjusted to the darkness. The carnage, the reality of what Straka's ritual had consisted of, was clear. She put a hand on her stomach. "My god."

The twins were silent. Avery cast her eye at the figures on the ground without much feeling.

"Oh! Where's Granny?" They searched with their cell phone flashlights. Chloe caught a glimpse of the sphere under the crooked leg of a dead man. Chloe refused to touch him. Avery snorted, throwing aside the man's leg.

"No." Chloe knelt beside the two halves of the dulled quartz, its color the barest hint of the golden yellow it had been. "Is she gone?" Tears glossed her eyes. "For good?" Avery didn't answer. Chloe wrapped the pieces in her sweater and placed them in her messenger bag.

"Why do you want to keep those?" Avery's tone was tinged with annoyance.

"Many reasons," Chloe said, not looking at her sister. She pulled out her phone. "We have to call the police."

"What?" Avery said. "We can't."

"Our fingerprints and DNA are everywhere, Avery. We don't have a choice." She sighed heavily, releasing the tightness in her shoulders. "Besides, we've done nothing wrong."

"And just *what* do we say, hmm? That our grandmother brought a guy back from the dead who killed these men so he could open a portal to Hell and let a demon in?" Avery's fingers dug into her hips.

"These men are someone's husband! Someone's father! Someone's son! We can't just leave them here, we *have* to tell the police. Their families have to know!" Chloe stared at her sister's hardened face in the bright glow of the cell phone light and took a step back, lips parting. "Oh, Avery." She covered her mouth.

Avery's hair and eyebrows were matte black, their red sheen and luster gone. Her formerly hazel eyes were nearly black, and it seemed as if she'd lost a great deal of weight. Her cheekbones jutted out, temples sunken, and the hollows at her collarbones held shadows. The cords of muscle in her neck moved when she swallowed.

"What's happened to you?"

Avery's eyes darted to the book on the ground then back to her sister. Chloe bent down and flipped through the book, mouth falling open. All of its pages were blank.

"It doesn't matter," Avery said, pulling Chloe up by the wrist. "These men don't matter. We need to go." Chloe yanked her wrist free.

"How can you say that?" Chloe's voice went up several octaves. "Their families need to know what happened to them!"

Avery glared at her twin and flexed her fingers, knuckles popping. She examined the gore around them.

Men of all ages lay sprawled across the manicured grass, wet from their blood. Some were dressed in business suits, others in jeans and T-shirts, a few in uniforms, each face twisted in terror, muscle and sinew gaping where their throats had been. The bloodless skin seemed to glow in the predawn gloom.

And, lastly, the dismembered carcass of Josef Straka. Her lip curled. *You deserved that. I'm glad you suffered.*

The pungent stench of death hung in the still air.

She nodded to herself. Avery lifted her hands at her sides. *"Ezus."*

Brilliant green flames burst from her fingertips. Chloe cried out and stumbled back.

Demonfire. Avery raised her hands before her, turning them this way and that. *Fire of Vengeance. It has no heat and will do what you tell it, consume what you tell it and nothing more.* She sneered at the hungry flames. *The magick I could do with a single word!* Soothing coolness snaked up her arms. It felt right, natural… and so easy. *It should have always been this way. It will always be this way now.*

She paced the circle, passing her hands over each dead man, setting them ablaze with green and black flames. Avery ignored Chloe's shouts. She had to do this; there was no other way. This little adventure couldn't be explained away, so it had to go away.

Chloe darted past her and snatched the book from the path of swiftly moving fire.

More sibilant words flowed from Avery's lips, like the lyrics of a song she knew by heart, encouraging the fire to rage outward. It crawled across the ground at the behest of its master, spitting and crackling, consuming all matter despite the dampness. Burning flesh and cloth replaced the stench of blood and death. Chloe retched behind her.

When the demonfire died away, nothing but a large swath of scorched earth remained.

Avery turned to her sister with a look of triumph. A hard slap across her face sent her sideways. Chloe stepped to Avery, staring deep into her twin's changed eyes, hand poised to strike again.

"Come back to me, Avery! Right. Now."

Dazed by the slap and something else buzzing in her head, Avery staggered back. Chloe brought her hand across her sister's face again.

"Get out of my sister!"

The hot welt of a full palm throbbed on Avery's cheek. She fell to the ground, scrambling away from her oncoming twin. Chloe fell to her knees and raised her hand again. Avery lifted her arms to shield her face.

"Stop, Chloe! Stop!"

Chloe grabbed Avery's wrists, trying to pull her arms away from her face. "Show me your eyes."

Avery could have easily thrown her off, but she couldn't think straight; her brain felt as if it were swelling beyond the confines of her skull.

"You can't let it win, Avery. You have to fight!"

Avery thrust her arms out with enough force to send Chloe backward. Avery scampered up on all fours, crawling away from her sister.

A deep, angry voice screamed in her head, demanding her attention. Avery pushed at her temples with her palms, her own scream overtaking the one in her mind. She fell to her side, still clutching her head. Chloe pulled Avery to her, wrapping her arms tight around her twitching sister. Avery muttered hissing words as she trembled, arguing with herself, her voice changing slightly with each retort. Chloe held on.

"You won't let someone else take control of you. You aren't weak. You've never been weak. Fight it, Avery. Fight." She whispered more words of encouragement in her twin's ear, tightening her embrace as Avery grappled against losing who she was, and who she could be.

Several minutes passed with Chloe rocking her sister, recounting aloud memories of childhood fun and games, of their mother and grandmother. One by one, Chloe's words broke through the miasma threatening to suffocate her. Avery clung to those words, the love behind each in her sister's soft voice, and hauled herself up with them.

Avery's body finally relaxed, and her hands dropped from her head.

Chloe released her only enough to look upon Avery's face. Though her hair remained unchanged, her eyes were the soft hazel they had always been, her cheeks were full once more, her skin no longer stretched over her skeleton.

"I'm… I'm sorry," Avery managed, pushing herself up as Chloe's arms fell away, to rest on her rear. "I—" She put a hand to her forehead.

Chloe helped her sister up and held on until she was steady. She stepped back, studying Avery's black hair, mussed and spiked with sweat and dirt, and the deep grooves between her once delicate brows. Avery's teeth chattered, and she felt cold to her core.

"Whatever was in that book… it's inside you."

"I know."

CHAPTER 48

Neither girl's phone had coverage, and Vivian's phone was dead. With no idea which way to go, the twins followed the paved path north, hoping the well-kept lane would eventually lead them to a populated area. The path paced along a narrow creek, running happily, gurgling and tinkling, blissfully unaware of the atrocities that happened only a dozen yards from it.

"Oh, wait!" Avery jogged back to the blackened patch, inspecting the ground, moving the ash around with her shoes. She hung her head. "Dammit."

"What?"

"Those coins. The ones on the ghosts' eyes. They're worth, like, five grand *each.* Well, maybe only a couple hundred with all the scratches, but still!"

With everything that's just happened, she's concerned with getting more *money.* Chloe kept her thoughts from her face. She needed to give Avery the benefit of the doubt right now. Who knew what was going on in her mind and body. Avery had won the battle a few minutes ago, but Chloe knew it wasn't over. Not by a long shot. Avery's appearance was proof of that, and her haunted eyes held something within them Chloe couldn't truly see but she *felt.*

When Avery had watched her slide the gray book into her bag alongside the pieces of the sphere, Chloe was certain something *else* tracked her movements also, and that something didn't appear happy with what she was doing.

Chloe hooked an arm through her sister's. They continued in silence, Chloe thankful for the growing light. The gray of predawn melting into soft blues and pinks gave her a measure of security, as did the rhythmic sounds of the soles of their tennis shoes slapping the pavement.

Then her heart skipped a beat. *Mom.*

The vision of her mother driving the demon back into the darkness was burned in her memory. Mixed in with her anguish was pride. What strength! What fearlessness! Chloe didn't think she could've done that.

It brought to mind a crumpled snapshot of her mother, her fingers bent into claws, raised at a disgusting, frightening man in her grandmother's doorway, a man who'd had her by the neck only a moment before. Her mother was brave and strong; she'd hold her own in the Voll, Chloe reassured herself. *But for how long?*

Chloe's breath stopped as she once again relived her brief time in the Voll. She knew the desperate fear her mother must be experiencing in the icy blackness, with that monster towering above her, all its little demon 'children' dancing around its feet, gnashing their tiny, sharp teeth at her. Chloe shuddered. She'd been there only in spirit, but her mother was there in full body. *We'll find a way to get you back, Mom. I swear.* She hugged Avery's arm.

The forest flanking both sides of the path was coming alive, following the rise of the sun. The crickets quieted, their serenade replaced by other insects Chloe couldn't identify. A trio of squirrels chased each other in the treetops to their left, and birds chirped in morning conversation. A branch snapped behind her, and she jumped. The fear from the past few hours still clung to her skin.

"Oh, would you relax." Avery's eyes flitted to the sky.

"You know it's not over, Avery." She braved a glance behind her. "The stuff we've seen! There's no telling who or *what* is out there."

"*I'm* out there," Avery said with her chin high, wiggling her fingers at Chloe, reminding her of the magick she could wield with a single word. "We'll be fine."

Chloe bobbed her head, conceding Avery's point. Although what her sister could now do with the essence of the book inside her terrified Chloe. *But enough of that thinking. One problem at a time.* Getting back to their apartment safely was first on her list.

As if the universe had been reading her mind, a tall box of an apartment building appeared over the trees ahead of them. They broke out into a run.

Within an hour, they were ensconced in their apartment. They'd been in Kunratice Forest, come to find out, and luck deposited them not far from a metro station.

Chloe removed the pieces of the crystal ball from her bag and placed them back onto the candle stand; the dish of the stand curved just enough to hold the pair together somewhat. She rubbed the side of one half.

"It's cold," Chloe said, mournfully. "Maybe we can hot glue it back together. If it's solid, maybe Granny can come back."

Avery went into their bedroom without responding and pushed the door closed with her shoulder. She'd lost all concern for Magda. She'd served her purpose and was finally gone.

"What the f—?" Avery stopped dead. *Served her purpose!?* She glared at herself in the dresser mirror. Then she saw.

"Oh my god," she breathed, approaching her reflection. Even when Avery had dyed her hair black years ago, it still had gloss and looked healthy. This color was pure coal. No longer sleek and soft, the dry, coarse hairs felt like they would break easily when she passed her fingers through them, but they didn't. She rubbed her ugly, matching eyebrows and scowled. With her fingertips, she pulled her forehead skin taut, hoping to make the two grooves between her brows disappear. It wasn't lasting. Avery peered into the mirror, scrutinizing the color of her irises. They looked normal enough although she didn't recall having so many flecks of darker colors peppering the hazel.

"What have you done to me?" she murmured. *And what more do you have planned?*

Avery locked her elbows as she pressed her fists into the dresser. She leaned close to the mirror, staring hard into the pupils of her reflection.

"You won't win."

She waited several heartbeats, not blinking, not looking away, for a sense of a smirk or comment, or the slightest sign it was in there. Nothing. She straightened.

Maybe I've already won.

Avery stripped off her filthy clothes. As she pulled her T-shirt over her head, a faint whiff of blood made her queasy. She closed her eyes, banishing the vivid memory of blood and gore. Those men needed to remain faceless to her; Avery couldn't take back what she'd done.

But she hadn't done anything wrong! There was no way they'd have been able to talk themselves out of jail time for that horrific scene. It would have been all over the internet, and the television news here and in the States. It would've haunted them for the rest of their lives. Ruined them! She had no choice.

The hot shower soothed the tight muscles in her neck and shoulders. She stood underneath the pulsing water, picturing her troubles washing down the drain with the water. *No such luck.* Avery sucked down the sob. *Mom.* She covered her face with her hands. *How do I get you back?*

Her mother wasn't dead. The creature Muraal was incapable of killing her, of killing period. She was certain about that, and it gave her a small degree of comfort. Avery had no idea how she came about those certainties. A lot of things swirled around in her brain she couldn't grasp yet, like whispers at the edge of hearing, or images just a little too far away to see clearly.

Avery hoped she would soon have clarity on all of this, or at least enough to get her mother back. The incredible power the book contained was the only way to rescue her. And now, *she* had that power.

He had only ever felt the cold, seen nothing but the black, and known nothing but the relentless cruelty of a monster.

But now, at long last, he was freed from his many prisons: the Voll, Muraal, Straka, the book. If there were any before that, he could not remember them.

He could smell the world around him, taste the air on his tongue, feel the delicious warmth of the water on his skin. Well, not his *skin, but near enough. He did not consider the girl a prison; she was his vessel. He, without form, needed shape; he, without life, needed a host. And she was pliable, easily made to do his will. Her body and her magick would sustain him in this mortal world for lifetimes; Muraal's magick would feed her desire for easy power and gain him whatever he wished.*

When her body wore out, another would be ready. He had already ensured that; only one more step remained.

For now, he would lie quiet and revel in his new body, in his new world, indulging in all he had coveted for eons. He had time; he need not rush.

He sneered at the hubris of the girl. He would let her believe whatever she liked.

For now.

DON'T BUY ME A COFFEE

Please Leave A Review Instead

I am thrilled you spent time with me by reading *Copper Pennies*, and I really hope you enjoyed it. As an independent author, I rely on your positive support. Could you take moment and leave a review on **Amazon, Goodreads, B&N,** and/or **wherever you purchased it**? Just a few words would be wonderful! You don't have to be Tolstoy. You can if you want, though.

Get Book Updates. No Rambling.

I don't blog very much, so don't worry about getting bombarded with emails that you couldn't care less about. But I will keep you up to date on my writing progress and any news that I think is awesome.

Sign up for book updates at
http://www.carriedmiller.com

ACKNOWLEDGMENTS

Although an author starts out sequestered in her silo, chained to her desk with a judgmental cat staring down from her cat condo and a German Shepherd asleep behind the wheels of her chair, she invariably must reach out passed the internet to *actual people* for their help and expertise.

It was a long and difficult road to get *Copper Pennies* to you, and I have so many people to thank for helping me.

Let me start with Sonya Lano, a resident of Prague. She was invaluable when it came to verifying the Czech language and the descriptions of the city. While Google Earth™ and Google Street View™ are amazing resources, nothing beats having boots on the ground. I can't thank her enough!

I don't think *Copper Pennies* would have the depth of story it does without the input and support from my editor, Kristen Tate, of The Blue Garret. Thanks a thousand, lady.

Priestess Emerald Fire Rose a.k.a. Cynthia Stevens of the Coven Raven Oak, thank you once again for sharing the deep magickal knowledge you carry within you.

Many thanks to Mary Jane Bennett for lending her nursing expertise, and to my girlfriends with children—a subject I know frighteningly little about—who got peppered with questions.

Beta readers are essential and I want to thank those that gave me their time and great feedback: Ceridwen Long, Paula Guenther, Hollie Mansfield, Morgan Hazelwood, Judy Fort, Esther Rabbit, Annmarie Meyer, Roxi Moser, Precious Castellanos, and Rebecka Sheehan.

The more eyes, the better, and proofreader Kelly Cozy of Bookside Manner was just what this novel needed.

My critique partner for a time, Rae Harding, needs a high-five too for reminding me of my bad habits.

At lastly, to my better half, Neal, who deserves a shout-out also not only for his support but for his practical assistance. I needed to know what being choked felt like so I could write about it better, and he was happy to oblige. (Boy, people are going to think we're really weird now.)

ALSO BY CARRIE D. MILLER

Does the elusive white raven, who has shadowed Aven through each of her lives, hold the secret to her release–or is it the cause?

ABOUT THE AUTHOR

Carrie D. Miller was born in Hutchinson, Kansas, on October 31. She credits her vivid imagination, as well as her sugar addiction, to being a Halloween baby.

In a former life, she was an executive in the software industry for many years. Her career in the technology world included software product management, website design, training, and technical writing just to name a few. Although Carrie's written a great deal over the decades which has been read by thousands of people, software documentation allows for about as much creativity as pouring cement. At the age of 45, she decided to chuck it all to become an author which had been a life-long dream.

When her nose is not in a book or in front of a monitor, she can be found inventing cocktails, hanging out in the pool, or in the kitchen making something yummy and unhealthy.

Sign up for book updates at
http://www.carriedmiller.com

Follow Carrie

Manufactured by Amazon.ca
Bolton, ON